For

A.F.C.O.

&

For
The paddock faithful, unfaithful
and would-be faithful if they could
just get their hands on a pass.

'Dupont F1. My name, my team, my way.'
Vincent Dupont

'God is probably the only person Vincent Dupont considers his equal.'
Kate Ellison

WORLD CHAMPIONSHIP ENTRY LIST

No.	DRIVER	TEAM
1	Riccardo SANTOS (BRA)	MARTINI MAGNA RACING
2	Jake SWEENEY (USA)	MARTINI MAGNA RACING
3	Fernando ALONSO (ESP)	SCUDERIA FERRARI
4	Felipe MASSA (BRA)	SCUDERIA FERRARI
5	Enrico COSTA (ITA)	DUPONT LAMBORGHINI F1
6	Marcel MÜLLER (DEU)	DUPONT LAMBORGHINI F1
7	Jenson BUTTON (GBR)	MCLAREN MERCEDES
8	Sergio PEREZ (MEX)	MCLAREN MERCEDES
9	Sebastian VETTEL (DEU)	RED BULL RACING
10	Mark WEBBER (AUS)	RED BULL RACING
11	Lewis HAMILTON (GBR)	MERCEDES GRAND PRIX
12	Nico ROSBERG (DEU)	MERCEDES GRAND PRIX
13	Pastor MALDONADO (VEN)	WILLIAMS F1 TEAM
14	Valtteri BOTTAS (FIN)	WILLIAMS F1 TEAM
15	Kimi RAIKKONEN (FIN)	LOTUS F1 TEAM
16	Romain GROSJEAN (FRA)	LOTUS F1 TEAM
17	Paul DI RESTA (GBR)	FORCE INDIA F1 TEAM
18	Adrian SUTIL (DEU)	FORCE INDIA F1 TEAM
19	Daniel RICCIARDO (AUS)	SCUDERIA TORO ROSSO
20	Jean-Eric VERGNE (FRA)	SCUDERIA TORO ROSSO

WORLD CHAMPIONSHIP CALENDAR

DATE	GRAND PRIX
28.03	AUSTRALIA
10.04	MALAYSIA
25.04	BAHRAIN
09.05	SPAIN
23.05	MONACO
06.06	TURKEY
27.06	BRITAIN
18.07	GERMANY
25.07	HUNGARY
22.08	EUROPE
29.08	BELGIUM
12.09	ITALY
03.10	JAPAN
17.10	BRAZIL

CHAPTER 1

The B4063, Oxfordshire
Friday, 1.37 p.m.

A smell of burning rubber snapped me out of my thoughts as I accelerated up the steep country lane. I fumbled under the unfolded map, artfully balanced between the gear stick and the passenger headrest, and released the handbrake.

Hello, I'm Kate, nice to meet you.

Too informal.

Good morning, Kate Ellison, thank you for seeing me.

Too humble.

I cursed the Interview Tips website that chirped on about 'radiating modest confidence'. Was I confident I'd cruise the interview for a press officer in Formula One, one of the biggest televised sports events in the world? Of course I bloody wasn't, and the only thing I was radiating was sweat and epinephrine. A small part of me wished I didn't have the interview, because once it was over, everything would be downhill and disappointment. Rather than having the opportunity and losing it, I was starting to wish I didn't have it at all.

The right-hand turn shown on the map by a tiny white line was nowhere to be seen. As I neared the brow of the hill, I hoped for a view across the land and a glimpse of the elusive factory, but the hedgerow thickened into a tangle of opaque bramble. The yellow petrol tank 'Reserve' light flickered on.

In five years as a celebrity publicist, I have gained extensive hands-on experience.

Well, I've made *Big Brother* contestants sound intelligent, made a post-partum forty-something breakfast TV presenter look like a top model in *Marie Claire*, and saved the UK's favourite weatherman both his job and a life of rodent-related ridicule.

Although I have no direct experience in Formula One, I follow the industry closely.

Or rather, obsessively. I haven't missed a Grand Prix since I was thirteen, and autosport.com is my homepage.

I'm glad you asked me about the impact of the new powertrain regulations …

Aaaagh, no bloody idea. Should I get my coat?

The road! THE ROAD! I dropped the map, pulling the steering wheel down hard on the right.

I skidded and bunny-hopped into a stall inches from tyres that dwarfed my car. The hammering of my heart in my ears began to dull, replaced by shouting. I opened the door, peered out and saw, way up above, an angry, muddy arm gesticulating from a red tractor cab.

'Oi, ever heard of the *Highway Code*? Get on the right side of the road!'

I had buckets of excess adrenaline aching to be vented. As I stabbed at the temperamental seat belt release, I caught sight of my watch. Twelve minutes until the interview and totally lost ... now was not the time to take on an angry farmer with monster- truck tyres.

'Sorry, but I'm ...' I left the seat belt in place and peeled the map off the windscreen, where it had flown with the force of the braking.

'Yeah, yeah, everyone's a bloody racing driver.'

'Hardly – I'm in a Fiesta.'

'Reverse!' the farmer yelled. 'You're scaring the animals.'

I craned my neck around the hulking machine to see sheep wandering in all directions.

This was really not how I envisaged my drive to a team in one of the most high-tech and glamorous industries in the world.

I turned the key in the ignition, fumbled the gear stick into reverse, and surrendered to the surreal rural tableau confronting me. In spite of the bitterly cold air that had filled the car, a fine film of sweat covered my body. I sat rigidly forward in the seat with my elbows high, in an attempt to prevent blouse-on-skin contact. I glanced thankfully at the jacket swinging on the coat hanger on the back seat.

I acknowledged a second mud-encrusted farmer following up the back of the herd, who shooed the stragglers past, then I turned again into the narrow lane. Still no sign of intelligent life, irate tractor driver included, let alone a state-of-the-art factory housing six hundred highly skilled workers.

*I wanted this job so much it was crippling my ability to speak or think. I was a good, no, a **great**, press officer, and I'd work harder than anyone else because this was the only job I'd ever really wanted.*

But how could I say this without sounding trite, desperate or psychotic?

This was why I had given up a law degree to take a junior position at Smith, Bickle & Price PR – in spite of relentless maternal emotional and financial blackmail. I wasn't going the same route as my dad, who after thirty years as a solicitor in a family firm in Dorset underestimated the national chain that swept into town, picking off his clients one by one until his firm limped to a slow but definitive demise.

I did not want a solid career, as Mum so proudly described the law industry and pretty much any job that involved an ill-fitting suit and a gold nameplate on the door. I did not want habit or routine. The verbs 'fade', 'fizzle' or 'wither' were not going to be used to sum up my career.

Smith, Bickle & Price taught me that public relations was my thing, but after five years I needed a bigger challenge. I'd had enough of office 'news' made up of pregnancy rumours, new boyfriends and tattoos. I wanted real news, major happenings, worldwide significance. I needed to work for an opinion leader, a trendsetter. Someone courted by national or, even better, international media. Someone who mattered.

I needed to work in Formula One. More importantly, I needed to work for Vincent Dupont.

I checked the clock on the dashboard. Ten minutes.

My phoned beeped. Three text messages received. I clicked on the first, from 'Danny': housemate, best friend and personal cheerleader.

I wanna team cap signed by Vincent! D xx

I pulled over on a wide bend to let an oncoming Volvo estate pass, drained the last warm dregs from the Coke can, and clicked on the second text, from 'Janey McGuiness DLFr':

Gd luck 2day. I'm in meetings all day but will try 2 pop in & say hi. PS. don't b a fan.

Janey was the Dupont Lamborghini hospitality manager. I'd only met her once and knew Danny had practically strong-armed her into getting me an interview, but it turned out she'd been quite the school bully, and she owed him more than one favour.

The third message was from 'Dad'.

mother & i wish u all bert. fingers cropped

He at least was very excited about my interview. It was his passion for F1 that had got me interested in the first place.

'It's the James Bond of sport, Kitkat,' he'd say. 'The best drivers, fastest cars, most exotic locations, biggest budgets.'

But for all the superlatives, I always felt Formula One lacked a human side. A role model who lived up to these values. The drivers were hidden behind faceless helmets. In interviews, they spoke in platitudes. The team bosses, while clever, weren't dynamic or inspirational. Then, two years ago, Vincent Dupont burst on to the scene. Striking, stylish, successful, and king of the soundbite. He personified F1, or rather all that made F1 more than just a bunch of car races. He was impeccably dressed and had his own branded private jet and mega-yacht, and even flew his own helicopter. The media loved him: opinionated, amusing, and always approachable. He had pulled off the impossible by winning the world championship in his first year running the team. Christ, he'd even cracked the States. *Time* magazine put him on the cover and called him Mr Formula One.

And he would be my boss.

As I rounded another left-hand bend, I caught sight of a sign barely visible among the foliage. It was the Dupont Lamborghini F1 team logo, with an arrow indicating a lane to my right.

Halle-flipping-lujah!

I pulled sharply into the lane. It widened and sloped down to a small grey building next to a black security gate. From the gate on one side and the security building on the other a neat but hostile black fence spread out in both directions. To the left, a metre-square plaque sported the team logo carved out of expensive-looking granite, stylish but surprisingly discreet. Above it a line of tall flagpoles, annoyingly not visible before, displayed a row of billowing team flags.

I pulled up in front of the security guard who was standing to attention outside his booth. His erect posture and buffed shoes screamed 'ex-army'. His solid frame looked uncomfortably squeezed into his corporate black suit and tie. He was ready and alert. I hoped he wouldn't shoot.

Dupont Lamborghini TechQ
Lower Bledcote
Friday, 1.55 p.m.

Clutching the Dupont Lamborghini-logoed plastic name badge and suppressing a grin, I accelerated slowly past the gate into the inner sanctum. Immediately on the left, next to a helipad, a nervous-looking guy in a black rain jacket and headphones shouted into a walkie-talkie. I took two deep yoga breaths.

The slate-grey factory was set in a vale surrounded by a perfectly manicured lawn. Inside the grounds, nature was well and truly tamed. There wasn't a stray leaf or weed, and the grass looked like it had been ironed. The façade of the main building was dark mirrored glass; even in the weak winter sunlight, the reflection gave an almost other-worldly glow. It looked more like a modern art museum than a factory. Past the main building a small path took me into a previously invisible sunken car park.

I pulled into the first free bay marked 'Visitor', and checked my watch. Five minutes. Just enough time to make myself presentable. I'd left the house in such a hurry and knew after two stressful hours in the car any make-up I'd applied would have found refuge in the creases around my eyes or along the neck of my shirt. I reached for my handbag, which had emptied its contents over the floor of the passenger seat after the tractor debacle.

In my peripheral vision something moved. I looked up: there was nothing but a security camera on the entrance pillar, pointing in my general direction. I hesitated, concealer stick poised under my right eye, before dropping it back into the handbag. I pulled my hair into a ponytail and put on some lipgloss. I was applying to be a press officer, after all, not a grid girl. I stuffed the contents back into my handbag, pulled the jacket off the hanger, took a deep breath and headed towards the main door.

The path to the entrance was interminably long. It ran parallel to the glass-fronted factory and I couldn't escape the feeling of being on display. This made me think about how I was walking, and suddenly just putting one foot in front of the other demanded unaccustomed concentration.

What would the people be like who actually worked for a championship-winning F1 team? My mind drifted to the fantasy of a super-race of the über-talented. I killed that confidence-building train of thought.

As I approached, the glass double-front doors slid open noiselessly to reveal the Dupont Lamborghini Formula One car, seemingly floating at eye level. Each of the main components was suspended independently just a few centimetres from the next, like an aerial jigsaw ready to be put together. As I got closer I could just see tiny transparent threads leading up to the double-storeyed ceiling.

'Can I help you?' came a voice from somewhere.

'Oh yes.' I turned suddenly, nearly catching my eyebrow on the corner of the aerial car's front wing.

'That happens often,' the voice laughed.

Searching for a face for the voice, my eye was drawn to a glass shelf proudly displaying the F1 constructors' and drivers' world championship trophies. Underneath sat a petite redhead behind the rather oversized reception desk.

'I'm here to see Patricia in human resources. I'm Kate Ellison.'

'Yes, she's on her way, please take a seat.'

'This is rather unusual, but we're going to have to sit down in Vincent's office as we're currently renovating the west wing, and that's the only free office right now.'

I followed Patricia along a white corridor behind reception and up a wide spiral staircase.

Oh my God, I'm going to Vincent Dupont's office.
My heart started to race again.
Don't be a fan.

At the top of the stairs, my shoes sank into a thick-pile ivory carpet. A tired-looking girl in an elegant black dress nodded without smiling at Patricia as we walked past into an imposing room that looked like a luxury hotel suite.

'OK, here we are,' Patricia said with a nervous giggle. 'Take a seat.' She pointed to a chair at the end of a long meeting table. She sat to my left with her back to the long glass wall that looked on to the lawn and the heliport.

'So we're looking for a press officer for the team. It's an important role working for Helen Miller, our media manager, but ultimately reporting in to Vincent Dupont.' She spoke in a loud whisper, which became almost silent as she mouthed Vincent's name. 'Media relations are a top priority for Vincent and the team, of course. He's very …' – she swallowed audibly, and then mouthed – 'hands-on.'

I had never imagined 'hands-on' could sound so terrifying.

'How long have you been in your current position?'

'I've been working at Smith, Bickle & Price for five years.' I spoke quietly in response to her whispered tone. 'I look after media relations for the talent. I'm responsible for daytime TV presenters and new reality TV stars.' I cringed inwardly as I said 'stars'. 'Working on their profile in the media, building it at key points, lying low when necessary.' I smiled but Patricia kept looking over her shoulder towards the heliport, where the man with the headset was pacing and staring at the sky and back at his watch. She looked at me, raising her eyebrows to indicate I should carry on.

'Er … so that means I deal with all media requests, deciding which features are right to do when, prepping the talent for interviews, working with photographers to get the right image across.'

My interviewer's eyes were dancing between my CV lying in front of her, the door, and something over my shoulder. A phone on the console behind me rang, and she jumped up as if tasered to answer it. Relieved by the interruption, I scanned the room.

There were two paintings on the wall. The one next to the meeting table appeared to be a Jackson Pollock. Behind Vincent Dupont's desk I recognised, incongruously, da Vinci's *Last Supper*. The layout was the same, with Jesus in the middle, but the apostles were different. There was Julius Caesar, Napoleon in his bicorn hat, Alexander the Great, I assumed from the plumed helmet, and Einstein, Shakespeare and Mozart as the Judas, Peter and John triumvirate.

I squinted to make out the figures on Christ's right: the distinctive beard of Abraham Lincoln, the wide-brimmed hat of General Custer, and the only black man in the painting had to be Martin Luther King. There were three figures I couldn't identify: maybe the one with the long beard was da Vinci himself. The superficial details were all there, but something was wrong …

'Sorry, Kate.' Patricia sat down, blocking my view and snapping me out of my thoughts. 'I didn't mean to interrupt; please continue.'

Continue what? I can't remember what I was talking about. My mind's a blank, and my mouth is so dry. Rehash some jargon.

'We work to a strategic plan,' I waffled, 'to co-ordinate career trajectory with media exposure.' My mind filled with the young pop star turned TV presenter I was working with who'd just received acres of coverage for unstrategically collapsing in her own vomit outside it-club Mahiki.

Patricia ran her finger down my short CV. I tried to anticipate her thoughts; nerves made my voice accelerate.

'While I don't have direct Formula One experience, I am used to media demands and requirements, working to tight deadlines, accommodating important people's needs.'

Calm down, don't be desperate.

'Hmm,' she said. Finally seeming to focus, she leant forward on the table. 'Vincent demands one hundred per cent commitment and does not tolerate mistakes.'

'Ok, then.' I answered with an inappropriate laugh, correcting it into a cough and an earnest, if unoriginal, 'I am one hundred per cent committed.'

There was a muted whir of helicopter propellers. Patricia shot a glance over her shoulder at the door, where the surly assistant had now appeared.

'Pat,' was all she said.

'Yes, OK,' Patricia replied, leaping to her feet. 'You need to meet Helen: please follow me.'

As I followed her out of the door I turned to the painting again.

That was it! That was what was strange about the men in the painting ... they all had Vincent Dupont's face. It was Vincent Dupont as all the great men of history!

I stood in the stark white corridor, trying not to fidget. I hadn't seen much of the factory, or –what did they call it – the TechQ, but it took minimalism to the extreme. There weren't any apparent surfaces, and I couldn't even make out where the doors started and finished. Patricia had disappeared into the wall somehow, having instructed me to wait while she checked Helen's availability. I was left adrift in the soulless chamber that connected reception to the stairwell in Vincent's office. He would have to walk this way.

The noise of the helicopter's propellers seemed to peak. It must have landed.

It wasn't a wide corridor. There was nothing to sit on, or hide behind. No magazines or pictures on the wall to pretend I was looking at. There was nothing to help me blend in or look busy, so that I could try and convey even a basic level of intelligence. Nothing to do but stand and shift from foot to foot.

My adrenal glands were on the verge of meltdown, having been pumping at maximum capacity all day. Patricia's palpable terror of Vincent's arrival hadn't helped calm my nerves. I had expected admiration from his staff, not outright fear.

The propellers began to slow. He'd be out of the heli and en route to the entrance ... by foot or car? Was it a question of minutes or seconds?

My arms hung limply by my sides. Should I greet him and confidently hold out my hand to shake his? I shifted my handbag from right to left shoulder to free up my hand. Or should I say nothing, and try to avoid eye contact? After all, he had no idea who I was, I was just loitering in his way.

If he spoke to me first, I should reply with something intelligent. *Oh, God.* At this point, I'd settle for not looking like a security risk.

'... well, wash the gravel ... of course, all of it. My driveway is white, never grey!'

The door at the end of the corridor swung open and Vincent Dupont strode through, face impassive, posture erect, snapping his mobile shut. I recognised the famous tan and jet- black hair smoothed down like a forties film star's. Considering he'd just got off a helicopter, it was amazing that there wasn't a hair out of place.

I resisted the overwhelming urge to stare, and in a weak attempt to look busy I clutched my newly purchased fake Hermès Birkin and tried to lock the buckle. It was tricky enough to keep me occupied for a few split seconds as the footsteps advanced with a tortuously slow tap ... tap ... tap.

When I couldn't hold off any longer, I glanced up and was caught in the intense glare of his narrow green eyes.

'Oh, hello,' I said on impact, in a strange sing-song voice that I'd never used before. My right hand shot out into his path. 'I'm Kate Ellison.'

His stare shifted to my extended hand, which consequently wilted, along with any remnants of professional resolve.

He gracefully swerved around my limp hand. Tap ... tap. I stared at the departing grey cashmere overcoat until it disappeared up the stairs. The tap tap of his shoes became muffled as he reached the carpet. A faint waft of expensive cologne was all that remained.

'Oh, I'm so sorry to have left you out here so long.' Patricia appeared behind me and I felt a wave of loathing towards her for subjecting me to that humiliation.

'Helen was in the middle of a live radio interview and I couldn't interrupt ... well, you know how it is,' she said, with a shrug and an annoying little laugh. Now the model of speed and efficiency, she ushered me through the door into a large office where the movement and noise were in stark contrast to the austere corridor I had just left.

'In case you meet Vincent, by the way, he doesn't shake hands.'

We walked between slate-grey desks set in blocks of four. The twenty or so people in the office were quite subtle about giving me a once-over glance as I walked by. I scanned the room for Janey, but no sign.

It was a pretty average office scene, although surprisingly neat. As I crossed the room, trying to keep up with Patricia's strange speed-shuffle, I noticed that no desk resembled mine at the agency, where only an A4-size workspace remained between the piles of papers, magazines and newspaper cuttings. The partitions were also markedly free of boy-band calendars, lewd newspaper cartoons or family photos. Definitely a more mature bunch than my agency colleagues.

On the far wall, where we were headed at breakneck speed, were three glass offices. I recognised Helen straight away. She often appeared at the back of racing driver photos or TV interviews. She was leaning back on her chair laughing into the phone; as she saw us approach she smiled and waved us in.

'Listen, Gordon, I've got important people to see now, and can't waste any more time listening to you wittering on.' She broke into a loud, throaty laugh. 'When there's some real news, you and four hundred other accredited media will be the first to know.' She laughed again as she hung up.

'Hello, hello, you must be Kate. Great to meet you, please take a seat.' She gestured to two black leather armchairs in the corner of the office. 'Thanks, Pat, I'll call you in a bit.'

She put her black thick-rimmed glasses on the desk and walked across to take the seat next to me, placing her mobile, BlackBerry and office handset on the coffee table. She wore a neat grey skirt and navy blouse which suited her curvy figure. She looked early forties.

'You must have had a hard time finding the place. We really are in the arse-end of nowhere, aren't we?'

'Er … yes, I have to say I didn't expect you to be based somewhere so remote.'

She leaned in towards me, looking serious. 'It's all part of a strategy to keep us working all the time, as there's bugger-all else to do.' And there was that great infectious laugh again.

I liked Helen immediately. She made me feel so comfortable I finally felt I could relax.

'That was Gordon Barry on the phone.'

Of course, Gordon Barry, the Telegraph's *legendary F1 journalist.*

'He claims Vincent has blown the team budget and hasn't got the focus to win.'

'That doesn't seem like a concern for someone who commutes to work in a heli,' I gushed. 'And those two trophies in reception pretty much disprove the will-to-win question.'

She smiled and glanced down at my CV, which Patricia had left on the coffee table, then pushed it away.

'So, why Formula One, Kate?'

You really have to ask? my inner fan yelled.

'Well, I think sportsmen and key figures in sport are among the world's most influential these days. They are more recognisable than many heads of state. I think Vincent Dupont is one of the most inspirational and admirable figures out there right now; he's cultivated an exceptional image, and has a lot of media power.' I heard the outpouring of too many words as my rambleometer belatedly kicked into action. 'And, well, for a press officer it doesn't get any better really, does it?'

Helen raised her eyebrows with a bemused smile. 'No, Kate, it doesn't.' She chuckled. 'The thing is, in Formula One image is everything. The "illusion of success" is what keeps sponsors paying the team the hundreds of millions we need to go racing every year, even when track results are mediocre. His image is what makes Vincent fascinating to the media. He perfectly embodies Formula One – glamorous, stylish, successful. He's worked very hard to create it, and it's our job to keep the dream alive. Our four-hundred-million-dollar budget depends on it. Media coverage means money, and money means the power to win. It's the Formula One Holy Trinity.'

As she was talking her mobile, in silent mode, lit up with three or four messages, and her BlackBerry let out a few intermittent pings.

'Our number one priority is to protect Vincent and the team's reputation and image at all times. They must look perfect, always. There are over four hundred accredited F1 media, not to mention the unlimited number of international journalists, whose job is to find the cracks, and believe me, they're good at it, and it's our job to make sure there are never any to find. Vincent's Achilles heel is the prank-loving Harry Bircher, the Martini Magna team boss who makes it his life's work to publicly ridicule him. And throw in a highly strung and vocal star driver, and, well …'

The phone handset she'd laid on the coffee table emitted a repetitive monotone ring. Helen glanced at the name and gave me an apologetic look as she picked up.

'Yes, yes, OK.' She hung up. 'OK, Kate, I have to go, so here's the thing. It's important you don't have any romantic ideals of this job as glamorous, jet-set, befriending drivers, parties, et cetera. This isn't a job for an F1 fan. The press officer's role will without doubt be more demanding, menial, relentless and physically exhausting than you can imagine …'

A few months later I would recall Helen's speech word for word, but as I sat there like a nodding dog on speed, the broken record of *please like me, please give me the job* playing in my head, her words just sailed over me.

'… but if you survive long enough to get your business cards printed, you'll learn from the best, and in terms of PR proficiency, Vincent is the best.'

'I'd hope to emulate your career, Helen. Fifteen years in Formula One, that's an amazing record.'

As she was talking Helen had managed to check her text messages and scroll through her BlackBerry emails, and she was now checking her computer screen. She looked up and chuckled, and her whole body joined in.

'One season at a time, eh?'

With a tap of the return key she closed the laptop, ran her hands through her hair – a nervous action I'd noticed her do a few times while we'd been talking – picked up a notebook and pen, and walked to the door of her office.

'Apparently there are some official working hours but they're pretty irrelevant: you need to stay until the job is done; media deadlines are never convenient hours, and we're working across many time zones. Oh, and you'll need to travel to all the races. Are you still interested?'

'Absolutely,' I said, finding myself giving a cringeworthy thumbs-up.

Great Rainforest Fun Run
Battersea Park
Sunday, 9.45 a.m.

'So how far are we supposed to run, Em?' I leant on Danny's shoulder to stretch my thigh muscles. The solid cloud of my breath was slow to disperse.

'Well, guys,' – Em thumbed through the sheets on her clipboard, pausing to pull the earflaps down on her

Nepalese woolly hat – 'every lap you complete saves an acre of rainforest; the average is five. It'd be really great if you could manage that.' She gave a supportive beam.

'I thought you said it was just about taking part?' Danny said, handing Em his mobile. 'Can you hang on to this, and if Paolo calls, tell him one o'clock at the Pig and Whistle.'

'Yeah, take mine too, please.' I pulled out the Nokia from my tracksuit pocket. 'How many laps is Freddie doing?' I waved at Em's rugby-playing boyfriend, who was squatting down in a much more professional warm-up routine.

'About ten, I think.'

'We can do ten, can't we, D.?'

'Ten! No, we can't. Christ, look at me, I'm in D&G, it's next year's sample, hot off the production line.' He stroked the skin-tight gold leggings. 'I'm not sweating in these. Why did you have to say "average", Em? You knew that would fire Kate up.'

'Deforestation is a crime.' Em gave a 'fight the power' sign and a guilty grin before heading off to a pop-up wall covered with black and white photos of indigenous people.

'It's supposed to be a bloody fun run,' Danny grumbled through a yawn.

'Come on, think of the trees.' I nudged him gently in the ribs.

'Trees my arse, on the bus you said it was for Indian orphans.'

'Just think of it like modern-day confession. A few laps equals a clear conscience that we've done our bit to save the world.'

'Or the trees, or the orphans ...'

'Exactly, now let's get nearer the front.'

I pulled Danny by the arm as we snaked through the crowd of a few hundred towards the hemp-rope start line. As always in London events, it was a totally mixed crowd; a few serious-looking athletes, more serious-looking tree lovers in natural-fibred running outfits and matted festering hair, a group of women in their fifties all tied together in a rope line, a few who were indefinable as runners or passers-by, a woman dressed as the Pearly Queen of London, and a man attired as a giant bee.

Em had two ambitions in life, to marry well and to save the world. Well, to cure poverty, fight Aids, stop pollution, protect endangered species ... et cetera. Danny and I were the opposite of politically active: PP, Em called it – 'politically pathetic'. But Em was my oldest friend and the three of us were flat- and best-mates. As we pursued our increasingly diverse career paths, outside of work hours we were inseparable. We had formed an unconditional support network, which meant Danny and I baked organic free-trade muffins, edited guilt-inducing leaflets, and even embarked on the odd sporting endeavour; Danny and Em turned up at calendar and perfume launches for me, full of loud gushing praise and excited autograph requests; and Em and I always offered to model for Danny's work-in-progress fashion website, but found ourselves editing text instead.

A gun sounded and the crowd of do-gooders surged forward. Danny and I broke into an awkward jog, trying to find space among the many advancing feet.

'Eurgh, it's freezing ... we've run fifty metres, and already half these people stink of BO.' Danny screwed up his nose and pushed me diagonally towards the grass verge. 'I've got to get out of this crowd.'

A group of teenage girls smoking on a bench, who had been eyeing the runners with derision, broke into pouts and giggles as we passed in front of them. Since Danny and I had met six years ago in Fresher's Week at Manchester uni, this had happened a lot. It was usually followed by looks of surprise or outright envy in my direction. Danny was gorgeous, universally and indisputably good-looking, like a younger, cheekier George Clooney. He was loved by women, the young, middle-aged and pensioners alike. And he only had eyes for Paolo.

We ran half on the gravel path, half on the frozen grass that crunched underfoot. I liked to think I was a regular jogger, but I probably only managed a run every couple of weeks. Once I got past the initial horror of the first five minutes, I found it was one of the best ways to clear my head. I needed that today. All weekend I'd been churning over and torturing myself with Friday's interview. There was nothing worse than missed opportunities. Well, actually there was – messed-up opportunities. Nerves had made me sound like a crazed Vincent fan. They wouldn't even give me a signed autograph card, let alone a job.

We passed the trestle table lined with rows of plastic cups full of water to start our second lap. The crowd of runners was now widely spread. My breath was too shallow and my stomach too nauseous to drink anything. I was beginning to regret the ten-lap declaration.

'Did you get a chance to check the text on the site?' Danny downed his water and chucked the cup onto the grass. It was swiftly swept up into a recycling bag by a thin girl with multi-coloured braids.

'I'll do it after the pub this afternoon, but it was already fine last time I checked. More than fine, it's great. I really think you're ready to launch it.'

'I still have some technical kinks to iron out. It needs more time.'

Freddie thundered past in his navy rugby shirt, thick public-school hair a-flowing. 'Great job, you two.'

We waved back.

'As long as you aren't stalling. I mean,' – I paused to take two big breaths as my lungs fought against the double challenge of jogging and talking – 'you know better than me in the whole web-environment, but if you've got a great concept you have to move before someone else does it.'

'Sure, but if it's not ready someone will just do it better, quicker.'

I tried to look at him, but he was a stride ahead of me.

'Who could do an interactive personal shopping site better than a personal shopper for Harvey Nichols who's a web genius?'

'Anyway,' Danny continued, 'I think I have a good chance of a pay rise with the new boss, which would give me a bit more of a cushion in my slush fund, and in the meantime I'm getting real consumer feedback on top brands.' He turned with a cheeky grin. 'Plus I get to keep my staff discount.' He twirled in his latest discounted purchase.

'You always said that job was temporary while you built up the site. You said you could only ever be your own boss ...'

'Ka-ate.' He started jogging backwards with the smile he used to break my serious rants. 'Can we leave the *carpe diem* speech for now – we're not all made like you.'

Halfway into the fourth lap my legs doubled their weight and my head felt so light I thought I might faint. Danny was holding a steady rhythm but hadn't attempted to chat for more than a lap.

'That's it. I'm finished.' I bent double, panting as the blood flooded and burned my cheeks.

'Thank God! I've started sweating vodka. I knew those shots last night were a bad idea. Come on, let's walk to finish the lap.' He levered me up and linked arms, supporting me under the shoulder. We hobbled on; now that I'd surrendered there was no energy left to walk straight.

At the end of the path a good hundred metres away, Em was standing on the trestle table, waving her arms at us and pointing to my phone.

We squinted, trying to lip-read.

'I think she's saying Patricia ...' Danny said, as I shot like a catapult from the crook of his arm, running with huge gazelle steps and a single focus.

CHAPTER 2

Dupont Lamborghini TechQ
Wednesday, 3.10 p.m.

'He said what?'

Vincent's stare was blowtorch intense. For the five minutes I'd been sitting in his office perched on the edge of the low leather chair, airing my clammy hands, he hadn't looked at me or even acknowledged my presence. The meeting was directed at Helen and a point on the grass outside the window that kept drawing his attention. If only that was still the case.

I felt light-headed as the blood drained from my brain. Why was I incapable of thinking before speaking? Why couldn't I have just sat and listened, as Helen had suggested? Out of the corner of my eye, I saw Helen rub her hairline as she closed her eyes in a long blink. There was my confirmation. Three days into the job, in my very first meeting with Vincent, I had made my first major mistake.

My nervous fingers flitted over the BlackBerry keypad.

'Well, er ...' – I cleared my throat – 'Yes, he said, erm, "Team bosses these days are nothing more than empty corporate suits."' I repeated the words in a monotone to try and dampen their now-so-apparent incendiary nature. '"The visionaries are gone. I want to re-inject some of the Formula One magic."'

'The loo seat king said that?' He stared out at the lawn, his voice a tone higher than before. His fist was raised by his ear, clenched in a white-knuckle grasp of a small plastic bottle.

'Harry Bircher did, yes, Vincent,' I answered unnecessarily, repositioning my bottom on the chair edge.

Helen laid her glasses on Vincent's desk and shrugged. 'It's archetypal Harry, provocative and inflammatory.' She made a sweeping movement with her hand in an attempt to extinguish the small fire I had ignited. 'Right, so as I said, that was it for the coverage today.' She closed the final page of the bound file on Vincent's otherwise paper-free desk.

He sat motionless and erect in his perfectly tailored white shirt and black suit, just the minute rise and fall of the lapels revealing the life beneath.

'Empty corporate suits ...' He swivelled slowly on his heavy black-leather chair and stared out over the grass lawn. He released his grasp on the bottle, removed the small lid, and sprayed both palms and fingers liberally, holding his hands erect to air-dry. Each movement was precise and unhurried. A faint medicinal smell filled the air.

'Now I'd like to just recap the main points for the new car launch, as it's in two weeks' time.' Helen was attempting to move the meeting forward.

Helen had suggested I sit in on Vincent's daily media update, where she summarised the coverage in a bite-size one-minute synopsis, tailored to our boss's concentration window. As she was winding up, Gordon Barry's article announcing the Martini Magna launch beeped its arrival on my BlackBerry. My schoolgirl need to impress, to get myself noticed by having a piece of worthy news, took over. I blurted out its arrival almost simultaneously, paraphrasing on the hoof details of the aircraft carrier location and performance by Beyoncé.

Vincent rolled off the chair to a standing position; Helen flinched almost imperceptibly. He started tapping the pockets of his jacket and trousers.

'Natalie!'

The sullen PA appeared at lightning speed at the door with a silver tray bearing a packet of Marlboro cigarettes, a silver lighter and a cut-glass ashtray.

Vincent grunted. 'Get Laurel and Hardy in here.'

After two minutes of watching Vincent pace and smoke, Gideon Black, the rumpled, overweight technical director and a skinny, bald man with frameless glasses, who had to be star designer Etienne Clément, walked in. The nicknames were pretty fitting.

'Forget presenting the new car here at the TechQ, we're launching in Paris.' Vincent sat down, tilting the chair back and blowing a thin stream of smoke towards the ceiling. 'We're a French team, so we'll launch in the heart of our homeland. The car build must be brought forward one or two days so we can get it out there, since I'm not changing the date.'

The technical director exhaled audibly. 'Vincent ...' His voice was gentle but firm. 'You said ... you insisted our sole objective was to win. You've already cut the budget in half, you can't ... it would be detrimental to the car build to condense the time frame.'

Next to me, the designer strummed his fingers repetitively on the file he was holding. He started shaking his head like a stir-crazy zoo elephant.

'Vincent,' – Helen's tone was soothing, as if she was talking someone making a suicide threat off the window ledge – 'we discussed focusing this year on the racing, as we don't want to give fuel to media reports that you prefer fame to results. Plus we want to kill the stories that the budget is being wasted.'

'The media decides neither my agenda nor my budget plan. Anyone who seriously questions my will to win should change their career to reporting on badminton.' He smiled to no one in particular. I smiled in support.

'Of course it's all about victory.' He held his cigarette like a dart and jabbed it in the air, before striding towards the window. 'What they can't see is that Formula One is so much more than just racing. It is brilliance and aspiration. Boundaries surpassed. The unachievable achieved. Dupont Lamborghini F1 is so much more than making two cars drive fast on a track.' He paused. With his back to us it was unclear if he had finished. None of the meeting participants moved. Vincent turned, raising his hand as if to silence the masses. 'For the hundreds of millions of F1 fans worldwide, we are the closest they'll get to a religious experience.'

The silence was stifling. I stared at a point on Vincent's immaculate desk, intent on avoiding everyone's eyeline.

Next to me the designer spoke quietly, as if to himself: 'But it's me, and not God, who designs world championship-winning cars.'

Vincent glared at Gideon.

'Get it done.'

Etienne stomped out gesticulating, followed by Gideon.

Vincent turned to Helen. 'The launch has to be fabulous, 'Elen. Raise the bar. Get me that Sarkozy.'

He pulled a file of paperwork out from a drawer.

'Natalie, coffee.'

Helen looked at me, nodding in the direction of the door. The meeting was over.

'Any meeting involving Harry Bircher's name is going to end badly, or very expensively,' Janey said as she dragged me by the arm into the marketing kitchen, the only place we were allowed to eat and drink. 'Vincent's raison d'être is to be richer and more famous than Harry, and to trounce him on-track.'

'I really messed up, didn't I?'

'You drove a wedge between Vincent and the technical department, laid him bare to media criticism for his lack of focus.' She ripped open a packet of expresso capsules. 'And for a team who may have major budget worries, you drove the budget for the car presentation up from a hundred thousand dollars to about ten million. And all this on your third day.' She pushed the capsule into the machine and it whirred into action. 'Quite some faux pas.'

'The technical guys must hate me. Shit, will Helen fire me?'

'No. Well, not yet anyway. Helen needs someone to last in this job. It's Vincent you've got to worry about. Your best option is to keep as far off his radar as possible. Survival and sanity rate here is pretty much proportional to the amount of time spent with him. You either get fired, or you end up like Natalie!'

I flopped forward on to the bar, leaning my chin on my hands. I felt like I was ice-skating in flip-flops.

'But look, you're lucky you've got Helen to hide behind: she'll cover your back, and she knows how to handle Vincent.' Janey pushed a cup of expresso under my nose. 'She's pretty much the best boss you could hope for.'

The door flew open and in strode a skinny man with an oversize voice. He dropped some keys on the bar top: a silver Sunseeker Superhawk logo skidded towards my plastic coffee cup.

'You've got to grab the ball and run with it. Pin them down to some facetime.' He opened the fridge and took out a bottle of Evian, pulling the sport lid open with his teeth.

Janey rolled her eyes.

The door swung again and a ruddy face with high-waisted chinos ambled in.

'You're spot on, Mikester.' He looked from Janey to me. 'Oh, I say, hello there ladies. Tuffy.' He thrust a bear-like paw at me, which I duly shook.

'Kate, hi.'

The other man seemed only then to register that the room wasn't empty.

'Mike.' Clamp-like handshake, released only when I yelped.

Janey huffed. 'Mike is client service manager, which means he looks after sponsors. Tuffy is … er … he looks after VIP guests. Kate is the new press officer. Intros over, now can we get on?'

They left with a shrug (Mike) and a wave (Tuffy).

I helped myself to a bottle of water. 'This is my dream job, I just want to get it right.'

'OK.' Janey swallowed her coffee in one, flicked her hair back, and leant her elbows on the bar surface. She was distracted for a second by her reflection in the chrome kettle and pulled an odd pout. 'Well, for a start you need to drop that "dream job" crap and get realistic. You're in, you've got the uniform and the pass, now what's your strategy?'

'Well, I've been hoping to sit down with Helen …' Her pout was off-putting.

'No. I mean look, me, I'm like Switzerland. I don't take sides, I don't invest time in making allies, I'm neutral. I'm not interested in getting into Vincent's inner circle, too close for comfort. No, I do my job so I'm watertight, cover my back and exploit the perks. And it works: I'm the longest-standing member of marketing, as I had three pre-Dupont years at Chapman Racing, survived Vincent's buy-out, and I'm still here two years later.'

'But I can't manage his press if I don't know what he wants.'

'He wants to win, full stop. And not just the world championship, but in every aspect of team business.'

'Ok, but ...'

'And your job is to make sure he always looks like he does.'

And with a flick of her black mane, Janey spun on her kitten heels and pushed through the door back into our office.

TF1 Studios, Paris
Tuesday, 7.10 a.m.

With under a minute to go to the Sky News interview slot, I practically thrust an ambling Enrico through the studio's double doors. Vincent and Marcel were having their microphones fitted, seated in front of a wall of Dupont Lamborghini sponsor logos. Vincent looked in horror at his dishevelled champion.

'Helen!'

'Here I am. Expresso, Enrico.' Helen pulled the driver's coat off with one hand and shoved a small plastic cup under his nose with the other. Throwing the coat on a chair, she stuck a cap over his bed hair and steered him towards the chair next to Vincent, straightening the collar of his team shirt as she folded him into his seat.

I watched in awe.

'OK, ready in three, two, one ...' The producer counted them in.

The camera rolled and Vincent was transformed in front of my eyes. Rigidity gave way to suppleness as he swung an arm behind Enrico and slipped into an almost imperceptible slouch. He used a lot of eye contact with the interviewer, pausing after each question to consider his answer, and smiling or looking contemplative whatever the context required. He looked immaculate in a dark grey tailored suit with elegantly Dupont Lamborghini-logoed pocket and aqua tie, not 'turquoise' as I had mistakenly called it. Perfect corporate colours. Perfect corporate image. The camera was drawn to Vincent, sitting between a scowling Enrico Costa and his inanely grinning new team-mate Marcel Müller. He knew it and he loved it.

Two weeks had passed in a blur of eighteen-hour day, six-day weeks. Changing the location for the launch and staging a production to rival the opening of the London Olympics was a colossal task.

The launch was a presentation of the new car with its new livery (paint job and stickers) and the driver line-up, and a declaration of the team's goals for the season: to win, unsurprisingly, and why this year was *the* year. There was a dearth of F1 news pre-season, and so it was a chance to make a big noise before on-track performance determined the coverage. While the tendency among the teams had drifted towards low-key, low-budget presentations, Harry Bircher had thrown down the gauntlet and now it was an ego face-off, like a pre-fight boxing press conference, just without Don King. Two seasons ago, Vincent had triumphed in round one; Harry countered last season, stealing Vincent's world championship crown. Round three would be the ultimate showdown.

The six subsequent interviews – BBC, CNN, Sky Germany and Italia, TF1 and Bloomberg – had been set up by Helen to run in succession, with two-minute breaks. It was the news programmes that provided the really big viewing figures that sponsors craved. This was why we had to crowbar Vincent and the drivers out of bed, hours before the launch would start, to hit the breakfast news in Europe and catch as many international news programmes as possible. An added bonus was that when the sponsors woke up in their Parisian hotel rooms and turned on the TV, the Dupont Lamborghini F1 team and their logo would shine back at them. And they could enjoy their breakfast in the comforting knowledge that their millions were well spent.

As the camera finally switched off, by the time the interviewer turned to thank him, Vincent had already taken off his shirt mic and was grilling Helen on the time plan.

I took my phone out of my bag to change it from silent mode. Four missed calls, three messages received. I checked the call list and when Charles, the Hotel Le Bristol's manager, came up three times I hit 'call sender' immediately.

'Madame Ell-ee-sonn, we 'ave some confusion 'ere.' Charles managed, as only the French can, to speak with a mixture of politeness and utter disdain, which always made me feel I had to apologise. 'Your chauffeur arrived 'alf an hour ago with Monsieur et Madame Kato; they 'ave checked into suite 803.'

'I'm sorry … I mean that's great, Charles, thank you.'

'*Mais pas du tout, Madame.*' *Oh, here it comes.* 'Now I have a Monsieur Kato at reception, guest of Monsieur Dupont, wanting to check in to ees suite.'

'But I don't understand.'

'*Moi non plus, Madame,*' he exclaimed with evil triumph. 'Zere are two M. Katos and only one suite. Ah suggest you make some calls and find out who exactly is in mah suite.'

One nil to Charles in the power play.

Number one in bold red type on my 'Launch: to do' list was ensuring a perfect arrival for Vincent's priority guest, Mr Shinsei Kato. His full name and the fact that he had a wife was the extent of my knowledge of Mr Kato, except that Vincent had called seven meetings about his travel logistics, and their welcome gift had been hand-carried on to the Gulfstream. *Ergo*, they were extremely important.

Dior had custom-made a perfume for Mrs K., and I had had to get a replica set of the new-season driver overalls made up to his exact measurements, with 'Shinsei Kato' embroidered on the belt. Helen had made Alpinestars sign a confidentiality contract to make sure the production stayed totally secret and didn't result in a press feature on our 'new driver' line-up!

I pulled a wad of papers out of my bag and thumbed through until I found the contact list. I had pencilled Mr Kato's details on to the bottom as Vincent had been specific about keeping his presence unofficial. I tried to remember what the time difference was to Tokyo as I punched in his secretary's office number. From the UK it was about eight hours forward or back – I couldn't work it out as my brain was buzzing with too many questions on how such a problem could have arisen. I'd checked he'd boarded the plane, made the driver arrive forty-five minutes early, and even had a name sign in Japanese made up for the driver. A low ring that sounded a long way away sounded in my earpiece. A female voice answered in Japanese.

'*Yuko-san.*' I was proud to have mastered the use of the Japanese polite form, '*-san*'. 'This is Kate from Dupont Lamborghini F1. I'm afraid we seem to have some confusion.' I was deliberately vague and paused, hoping she would fill in the blanks.

'Awwwwww Kate-san,' said the quiet voice in an indecipherable tone.

Long pause.

'Problem Mrs Kato, very sorry, very sorry.'

'I see *Yuko-san*,' although I didn't, but she was apologising, which could be good. 'Erm, yes Mrs Kato. Is everything ok?'

'Ahhhh, not good Kate-san, but doctor say soon better.'

Things started to fall into place in my overloaded brain. If Mrs Kato was sick then she wasn't here, so the right Mr Kato was in reception (still not great news) and the wrong one was in the suite. At least we knew who to evict.

'I am very sorry to hear that *Yuko-san*, please give her our best wishes.' I wound up quickly. Charles had a mess to clear up.

I looked up to find the studio empty. Everyone had gone bar a sound technician who was on the floor detangling a mess of cables. Grabbing my bag and coat I ran down the stairs two at a time and out of the front door, just as the doors closed on the two Mercs parked in front.

Damnit. I sprinted as well as I could in new heels. As the car pulled out from the pavement, I lunged and slammed my hand on the rear window.

'*Cédric, Attends!*'

Cédric duly braked and with the momentum I smacked into the wing mirror, ricocheting back into the rear passenger window. Ignoring my bruised shoulder and pride, I rushed round to the front passenger door and climbed in. Vincent and Enrico were chatting in the back.

It was a fifty-fifty chance. Why couldn't it be the car with Helen and Marcel?

'I'm sorry about that,' I muttered to the passengers, who didn't let up in their comparison of Rolex Daytonas.

I dialled Charles at the hotel. Depending on the traffic, which thankfully was a bit heavier now, we'd be back in fifteen to twenty minutes, and if Mr Kato was still waiting in reception I'd do better to perform a swift hara-kiri than have Vincent find his ultra-VIP guest roomless.

'Charles, it's Kate, err Madame Ellison.' I spoke in a hushed whisper. 'The right one's in reception, the wrong one in the bedroom.' I hoped he would understand my cryptic message.

'*Mais, quel histoire! Jamais ...*'

I didn't have time for his recriminations. 'Please regulate the situation. We'll be arriving in about ten minutes. Oh, and Charles, please check the gifts are still in the room.' I hung up and prayed for a traffic jam.

'Keht?' I snapped out of my thoughts and turned back to Vincent. 'Get Marcus a 'aircut.'

Shit, who?

'I'm sorry, Marcus?'

'And tell 'im to stop grinning like a monkey, 'e looks like an idiot.'

'Ah yes, Marcel, of course.'

'My guests 'ave arrived?'

'Umm yes, they, er, he's at the hotel.' I tried to hold eye contact. 'His wife's unwell and won't be joining him.'

'And the Philharmonic?'

'Yes. There was some snow in Vienna so their flight was delayed, but they're now all on-site, setting up with Paul.'

'Tell 'Elen, I want to change my speech.'

'Ok, I'll have her bring the latest draft to your suite for your revision.' *Christ, it was already version twenty-seven.*

'What's next?' he said

I shuffled through my papers. 'You have an informal breakfast with Mr Kato. Then coffee with Signor Bertelli from Lamborghini.'

'I know where he's from: he owns forty per cent of my team.'

'Of course you do. At twelve Helen will then take you all directly to the VIP partner lunch in the private room at the Louvre.' My lips decided now was the time to struggle with consonants. 'The photo shoot is on-site at five p.m. and then the guests will arrive for the launch from five-thirty p.m. for kick-off at six p.m.' I inhaled deeply, having relayed the schedule without a breath.

Vincent looked out of the window, having lost interest around midday.

Cédric pulled up in front of the hotel. A crowd of fans had amassed since we had left this morning. They were crowded round the first car, but when Marcel and

Helen got out they backed off, disappointed. A professional fan with a wad of photographs still asked Marcel to sign, but on seeing the second Mercedes draw up they left Marcel, pen in the air, to surge with his colleagues to the edge of the pavement. The hotel doorman and two newly appointed security colleagues pushed through the horde. The doorman opened the car door while the other two men pushed the fans back, to form an aisle to the hotel entrance.

'En-ri-co, Vin-cent,' chanted the French band.

Enrico got out first and marched with his head down towards the door, signing one poster with a squiggle without looking or slowing his stride and then dropping the pen on the pavement.

Vincent took his time proceeding through the crowd, signing autographs, stopping for split seconds for photos, but always at a distance from grabbing hands and hug-searching arms. He Viraguarded his hands, squirting the disinfectant spray discreetly as he disappeared into the revolving door. The security men enjoyed their new role and were zealous in holding back the unthreatening crowds.

My eyes shot round reception but there was no sign of a Japanese businessman. The ritual disembowelment could wait. As Vincent and Enrico disappeared into the lift, Charles slithered sycophantically out past them, with a tight smile and head bowed. As the doors closed he swung round to catch my eye and with a flick of his head indicated I should follow him.

'You do know zat Kato is one of ze most common surname in Japan, do you not?' Charles employed his most superior tone.

I mentally slapped his pointy patronising face while I waited silently for an update.

'Monsieur Kato is in his suite,' he said with a sigh.

'Charles, you are the best. And the gifts?'

'Ze perfume is untouched. Ze other will take a lee-tle longer, Madame.'

I frowned.

He leaned in. 'Monsieur Kato *numéro deux* was, 'ow should I say, *wearing* ze gift, Madame,' he said with a raised eyebrow. 'Madame Kato was taking some souvenir photos. Laundry are cleaning ze overalls now, but I could 'ardly confiscate ze camera.'

I visualised the scene and stored it to relate to Danny once today was over.

'You did great, thank you, Charles.'

Helen met me at the front door with bags of media packs and two helmet boxes.

'How are you bearing up?'

'OK thanks, I can't believe it's only mid-morning.'

'It's a long day, pace yourself,' she said, handing me the mountain of driver trappings. 'I'll look after getting Vincent and co to the lunch; can you monitor the pyramid set-up? The Louvre director is getting edgy.'

'On my way. Oh, and we need to get Marcel a haircut.'

'I thought as much, I've booked him in the hotel salon. This is JB, our team photographer and one of the best snappers in the paddock … midfield.' She sidestepped his elbow jab. 'He's coming in the car with you to set up the shoot.'

I looked over the mound of suit bags to a short, grubby man with a cheeky smile.

'Well hellooo, baby,' he grinned. 'Worry no longer, your sexual salvation has arrived.'

I was getting used to the faux sexual banter that went hand in hand with most conversations.

'Nice to meet you JP; shall we go?'

'JB, it's a B, babe. Just think BJ back to front.'

Trying to block out that revolting allusion, I staggered back to Cédric under a pile of suit bags and helmet boxes. JB followed with an inordinate quantity of camera bags and equipment.

'There's the test driver,' squealed a young female fan, who was eighteen at most.

I turned to see JB acknowledge her with a wave and a wink.

'What was that all about?' I said, once we were settled in the back seat and Cédric had pulled away from the kerb.

'Yeh, I met 'er in the bar last night.' He grinned with mock innocence. 'She wanted to shag a driver, and who am I to wreck a young girl's dreams?'

I rooted around in my bag for my phone, partly to check I hadn't missed anything and mainly to avoid chatting to JB. I needed a few minutes of peace.

Cour Napoléon
4.50 p.m.

'Easy does it, easy does it!' Paul, the event producer, shouted through a megaphone to Dave, chief truckie and his two colleagues, who were hoisting the brand new Dupont Lamborghini chassis up the front face of the pyramid. Two were hauling it up by ropes from the back while Dave steadied the nose. Six Louvre supervisors stood menacingly behind Paul. The tension was palpable.

'Mate, you don't need to remind us to be careful,' Dave said through gritted teeth as he lay flat on the pyramid face, legs astride, holding the nose steady by the front track-rods. 'Etienne will sauté my balls if anything happens to this car. Your breakfast was older than some of these parts.'

I was freezing and my feet ached. I had been standing in as Vincent for forty-five long minutes while JB set up the 'perfect launch photo'. He alternated between barking orders and recounting gratuitous, unpleasantly specific details of the legally questionable liaison between test driver and schoolgirl.

'Two centimetres to the left … it was lucky cos I'd picked up a case of galloping knob rot from the twins in Sao Paolo last season but it had just cleared up, so it's like it was meant to be … stand up straight, for God's sake … a little bit Catholic, but I tell ya, under that school uniform, she was a feisty little mademoiselle … put your arms on their shoulders, Kate … I think she must be a dancer: she was really supple, like she could …'

'JB, shut up!'

Paul's assistant stood in as a decidedly more jovial Enrico and the Louvre events girl stood in for Marcel. We had tried several different combinations and now were a good twenty metres in front of the car, for a long low shot with the threesome in the foreground and the car and pyramid rising directly behind. JB assured me it would make for a powerful image.

'Stop moving, Kate!'

'Wait, I've got a text message.' I wriggled my phone out of my trouser pocket and pressed 'show'. 'Oh, God! Helen's on her way with Vincent and the drivers. ETA five minutes.'

I stepped over JB, who was taping a cross on the pavement below my feet, and ran over, waving my arms at Paul.

He took one look at me.

'Shiiiit,' he boomed, still superglued to his megaphone.

'They're en route,' I said, trying to catch my breath as I surveyed the surrounding carnage. Paul had attached an intricate system of invisible ropes and wires to hold the car in place but Dave was still supporting the chassis from the front, looking flushed and sweaty. There were boxes and cables everywhere.

'Five minutes, everybody!' shrieked Paul. 'Everybody with free hands clear all rubbish into the truck. Electricians, tape down all wiring. All vehicles need to move to the area designated in the Tuileries. Mr Bocelli's team, laser technicians, catering staff please wait under the pyramid. My team, keep securing the car until I say stop. Let's go, people! Except you, Dave, don't you bloody move.'

The hundred or so people who had been milling around all day suddenly shot into action. Incredibly, by the time the black Mercedes pulled up at the kerb four minutes later it looked presentable – well, all bar spreadeagled Dave.

Vincent got out of the car first, and stood for a second observing the scene. A hundred people stared at him and held their breath. He scowled at Dave and walked to Paul, who was orchestrating the removal of a giant screen that had shielded the racing car from the view of those in passing vehicles. I hovered behind while Helen remained with the drivers, shivering despite team-branded ski jackets covering their overalls. Enrico complained loudly on his mobile while Marcel clutched his briefing sheet and grinned.

'Ah, hello, Vincent, how are you?' Paul radiated a superficial calm.

'Well?'

Paul jumped into a theatrical and exhaustive description of the set and the mechanics of the car reveal, culminating with a wave of his hand above his head in a triumphant flourish.

Vincent grunted, staring at the pyramid, his expression unreadable.

'The Louvre should be aqua.'

'I beg your pardon?' Paul's shoulders dropped a good few inches.

'At the reveal,' – Vincent pointed impatiently at the museum – 'the Louvre should be lit up in aqua.'

'All of it?' said Paul, his voice catching in his throat.

Helen appeared next to Vincent and pointed to her watch. He turned and strode off towards JB as Paul picked up his megaphone and yelled: 'Laser team!'

The media started arriving at 5.30 p.m. The three charter flights had landed between 4.15 and 4.45 at Le Bourget, from where they were bussed in.

The TV crews and photographers headed straight for the tiered platform in the centre of the seating area, each marking their territory with a tripod. The print media, on the other hand, headed straight for the trays of champagne and beautifully presented canapés held by elegant, and uniformly handsome, waiters in Lanvin suits.

I had had a lull of energy before the photo shoot. The pace had slowed and my body revolted with heavy exhaustion and head-spinning hunger. I'd eaten two croissants at 6.30 a.m. and nothing but a bag of peanuts since. But once Vincent and the drivers arrived, adrenaline reclaimed control. It was becoming my drug of choice.

My jaw now ached from smiling at the guests. I had introduced myself to several dozen journalists, most of whose names I immediately forgot, answered countless questions on interview possibilities, sidestepped requests for one-on-one interviews (those who were getting them knew in advance), and practically tackled a Spanish cameraman who had slipped past the barriers and tried to get under the silk sheet covering the pyramid.

At 6.30 p.m. Paul made an announcement for the guests to take their seats. I found a place to stand next to the production booth, where I was close to the pyramid entrance. I was really pleased Helen had told me to stay front-of-house while she supervised behind the scenes: I didn't want to miss a thing.

At sunset, the temperature had dropped to five degrees Celsius. The four hundred guests stood in front of the seats, set in two diagonal lines to complement the pyramid's form, clapping their hands or rubbing their arms to keep warm. Small clouds of breath were visible in the cold air created by the low buzz of polite chatter. A cordon had been placed along the road behind which the public had lined up. I looked back to a sea of faces. Some home-made banners hung over the cordon: *Enrico, sei il nostro campione per sempre. Vincent je t'aime.*

The guests were still shuffling into their seats when Paul's voice boomed again, this time in surprisingly good French: *'Madames et Messieurs, Monsieur et Madame le Président de France.'*

I looked up to see Tuffy bouncing in just behind Nicolas and Carla Sarkozy, who smiled in acknowledgement of the applause of the crowd. As they walked towards their seats in the centre of the front row the photographers burst into action, a battery of flashes lighting the evening sky. As if on cue, Vincent stepped out from the side of the silk sheet and walked towards Sarkozy, with a wide smile and arms spread. They man-hugged and backslapped as the flashes exploded.

My eye was caught by Mike, a few rows back, who had strong-armed Signor Bertelli away from his conversation to witness this affirmation of success, power and fame.

'You know that'll be the shot that gets used, and it doesn't have the car in the background.'

I turned to the hushed voice and shook the extended hand of a man with smiley eyes, salt-and-pepper hair and a rumpled tweed blazer.

'I'm Gordon Barry; you must be Kate.'

'Yes, I'm so pleased to meet you.'

'He's pretty PR-perfect, your boss.'

I smiled and nodded as we watched the spontaneous launch prelude play out.

'I can learn a lot from him.'

'Me too,' replied Gordon, a mischievous twinkle in his eye. 'An image that perfect suggests truths intended to be hidden.'

On stage the two separated and Monsieur and Madame Le Président turned to take their seats. Vincent headed back to the pyramid, beaming. The raft of security personnel moved to the edges.

'*Monsieur et Madame Le Président*, ladies and gentlemen, would you please welcome Mr Andrea Bocelli.'

The audience stopped clapping and rubbing as from the side of the silk sheet the renowned tenor appeared in a black dinner jacket and white bow tie, hand in hand with two tiny ballerinas in beautiful translucent silver-winged outfits. He took his place in front of the microphone to the left of centre stage, touching it briefly with his hand to confirm the position. He nodded and smiled at the burst of applause. The ballerinas took their places at opposing edges of the stage. The silk pyramid glowed from inside, its surface rippling in the breeze.

Invisible to the audience, the Vienna Philharmonic struck up the first notes of Puccini's celebrated aria. The sound electrified the frosty Cour Napoléon. Andrea Bocelli launched into the first words: 'Nessun dorma …'

The audience responded with a spontaneous ovation. The ballerinas ran up barely visible wires to the apex of the pyramid, where two other ballerinas appeared from behind. Elegant and nature-defying acrobatics followed, as they appeared to fly like ethereal fairies.

For the first time that day all the noise that had filled my head – the to-do lists, time plan minutiae, endless names and job titles – was gone, replaced by the sound of this wonderful voice. I felt my eyes well up with exhaustion and emotion. I looked around at the Louvre, the stellar front row, the pack of international media.

It didn't get any better than this. It had been the longest, most stressful and extravagantly funded day of my life, with a hundred potential pitfalls, and I had loved every minute. This time last month I had been smearing cover-up on the *Big Brother* winner's lovebite-scarred cleavage. I wasn't quite sure how I had pulled it off, but I was working with people at the top of their game. Vincent Dupont was exacting and scary but he had an almost preternatural understanding of media and presentation. Gordon Barry was right: he was PR- perfect.

The *Vincero* 'I will win' crescendo filled the Louvre courtyard, the sheet flew up, and the ballerinas seemed to disappear into the night sky. I held my breath, expecting to see Dave splayed on the glass face. Instead the brand-new Dupont Lamborghini chassis was balanced perfectly on the controversial landmark. Vincent was right: the Louvre completed the image, illuminated in blue. The crowd roared their approval. Vincent, Enrico and Marcel lapped up the applause as they stepped out on to the stage like best friends.

Vincent's speech was entertaining, succinct and absolutely nothing like the version that had been prepared and amended twenty-eight times. He then jumped youthfully off the stage to shake Sarkozy's hand, backslap him once more, and kiss Mrs S. before they were led away to their waiting limo.

On Paul's cue the guests got up, the sponsors heading for the dinner below the pyramid, and the print and TV media staying above ground for the interviews. I honed in on Enrico, whose interviews I was to manage, squeezing past a couple of the British journos I'd met earlier, a staffer from *Motoring Weekly* and a freelancer for the *Express*. I tried to catch their eye to smile.

'Well, how much do you think that little spectacle set Vince back, then?' the freelancer said smugly to his colleague. 'Did you see the face on Gideon Black? Not too chuffed to see his budget frittered away.'

'Should have just burnt the money; at least we'd have been warm,' laughed the other, waving at the waiter for a top-up.

I pushed on through the crowd.

'Dad, it's me. Did you and Mum watch the news?'

'Jean! It's Kate. I said it would be – grab the other handset. Hey, Kitkat, of course we did. We even recorded it – well, we think we did. Did you press record *and* play, Jean?'

'Yes, I'm pretty sure I did. Hello, darling. This is all very exciting. We watched Sky News, and I brought in the little portable from the kitchen and we watched TF1 too.'

'And? What did you think?'

'Quite extraordinary, my, my. Who was that man who kept hugging the president? I don't know if that went down well. But what an elegant man!'

'That's Vincent Dupont, Mum. He's my boss.'

'I say. Well, perhaps some of his style will rub off on you. I'm sure he wouldn't approve of you dressing like a scruff.'

'Mum, for crying out ...'

'It was a cracking show, Kitkat. You can be very proud.'

'Thanks, Dad. I'm still on a high. I don't know if I'm going to be able to sleep. I can't quite believe I was a part of it all.'

'What part of it were you, exactly?' Mum said. 'Dad said you did the interviews ...'

'Jean, I told you ...'

'I just want to be sure, so I can tell my red hatters. This PR business didn't exist in my day.'

'It's ok, I helped organise the event and the interviews with Helen, my boss. I don't actually do the interviews; the journalists do them with the drivers and Vincent.'

'Oh, right.'

There was a pause. It was always hard work having a three-way conversation.

'Well, you enjoy the moment, sweetheart, but I have to say you do sound tired. I hope they aren't working you too hard?'

'Of course they are, Dad, but I love it. Vincent's amazing; he understands better than anyone I've met the power of image. It's a lot to take in, but I can honestly say it's the best job ever.'

'Well, good for you then. We're very happy to hear that, aren't we, Jean?'

'Yes, and we'd be even more so if you popped by to see us – the Paris-Deauville connection is pretty fast these days.'

'I can't Mum, we fly back tomorrow and there's a ton of work to prepare for the first race. I promise I'll come as soon as I can.'

'Now hang up please, Graham, I've got something to ask my daughter.' Mum's trying-to-be-normal voice was anything but. 'Now, don't forget your Dad's birthday next month; call me about it when you get home. I've got a great plan!'

'Will do.'

I barely found the energy to hang up before my eyes closed and my head sank into the plump feather pillow.

CHAPTER 3

BA7310 London–Melbourne,
somewhere over the Indian Ocean
Thursday, 4.30 a.m. Australian Eastern Time, GMT +10

'Thank God you're awake.' Janey's perky face appeared in the small corner of space where I'd gingerly lifted my eye mask. 'I am sooo bored. You're a crap travel partner, really, you've been asleep since we took off.'

I pressed the button in the seat arm, whirring up gently to a semi-vertical position, and pushed the eye mask up to my forehead as my brain slowly cranked itself into action through the fuzz of sleep.

'Sorry, I was knackered, and it's such a novelty to fly business.'

'You don't say,' she smirked, looking down at my blue travel socks. 'You should order some breakfast; they've got great croissants.' Her beautifully presented tray table smelt very good. I realised I was starving.

'Everyone's on this flight. The marketing guys from McLaren, Lotus and Red Bull wanted to meet our new press officer, so I had to introduce them to comatose you.'

'You didn't!' I whipped off the eye mask and shot my seat up to vertical.

'I'm kidding.' she slurped her pink frothy smoothie, enjoying my horror. 'But you did start to dribble at one point.'

I rooted around under my footrest for the in-flight wash bag and an emergency hair and breath remedy.

'I was hoping to get first view of the new meat this season, first pickings and all that, but so far it looks same old, same old.' She started on her second croissant.

I waved at the flight attendant to get the breakfast tray. 'But I thought inter-industry relationships were forbidden?'

'Oh my God, you actually read the staff guidelines?' Janey said, louder than necessary.

'Of course I did.' I dry-brushed my teeth with one hand and pulled the tray out of the armrest with the other. The attendant unfurled a stiff, white table cloth and decorated it with small white plates of croissants, muesli, fruit and a frothy pink smoothie.

'It's only a matter of time before you get swept up in F1's testosterone tsunami – don't fight it, just surf the wave. Where else would us girls get such disproportionate pulling odds?'

I wanted to counter that her very vocal wave-riding with various industry personnel was the reason I, her sofa-sleeping housemate, had needed such a long unbroken sleep. Even without the sacking threat, her grunts and howls would drive anyone to celibacy.

I had to stifle a jaw-drop when we walked into the Crown Towers lobby, all outsize chandeliers, Las Vegas staircases and the glitzy like. I had picked up on the requisite blasé approach to all things five-star, but it took quite some effort.

The power-shower experience was a total body workout. It pummelled my jet-lagged brain into life, then back into a vegetative pulp before I finally surrendered, wrapping myself in the huge fluffy dressing gown and funny flat slippers. I pretended to contemplate the oxygen face spray and selection of herbal boosters in the minibar until I saw the price list, then leapt child-like on to the multi-pillowed bed.

My body was leaden but my head was over-revved, jittery with nerves and excitement about my first Grand Prix weekend. In a few hours I would actually walk into the Formula One paddock, I would really be let in, it was my new office! I channel-surfed but somewhere between Fox News and Nickelodeon, my eyeline was drawn to Vincent's Louis Vuitton suitcase, standing to attention by the door. I threw on some jeans and a t-shirt to start on my to-do list.

I 'carried not rolled' the Damier Keepall as per Natalie's instruction, just as I had carried on rather than checked in said luggage for all twenty-eight hours of my journey door-to-door. I took the lift back to reception, to be escorted up in the private lift to the über-VIP lobby reserved for guests of the hotel's villas. There was a slick handover to Vincent's butler, Dwayne, who eyed my wet hair and unironed t-shirt with professionally-tempered suspicion, before taking the suitcase and *wheeling* it down the thick carpeted hallway to one of the two 'presidential suites'.

'This is all for him!' I blurted out as the heavy double doors swung open to reveal a sitting room the size of my London flat.

'Yes, ma'am. At Crown we are proud that our suites exceed any premium guest accommodation in the world.' And they could be proud of his PR indoctrination.

I stepped into the enormous semi-circular room whose floor-to-ceiling windows gave a postcard view across Melbourne to the sea. It was all stylish neutral tones, with sufficient gold touches to say 'luxury', 'opulence' and 'yes, Kate, you've been outed as a five-star fraud'.

'Through here we have the office.' Dwayne indicated an elegant maple desk with leather surface. 'And on the other side of the sitting room is the dining room. Now, should we unpack in the dressing room?' His voice seemed to lose some of its positive energy.

'Right, yes, good idea.' I knelt down to unzip the suitcase. 'Vincent, er, Mr Dupont is very specific about how he likes his room prepared.' I pulled the list of instructions out of my pocket that Vincent's untrusting PA had both emailed and provided as a colour printout.

Dwayne produced an identical list from his pocket.

'Mr Dupont has been our guest for the past two years. We are very honoured to host him again.'

'Team clothing.' I handed over the pile of shirts. It was much bigger than my uniform pile, as Vincent had three shirts per day allocated because of the high temperatures. He would be in Melbourne for three days, so that was nine shirts and six pairs of trousers.

'Please see they are pressed and hung on wooden hangers in the closet.'

'Sure thing, ma'am.' He laid them carefully over the back of a velvet armchair.

'Now the shoes.' I carefully handed over the three shoe bags one at a time for buffing. Dwayne played along with the charade, taking each bag with due care. 'Do you think you can have everything ready for Vincent's arrival early afternoon?' As instructed in bold red type, I lied about Vincent's arrival time by half a day to ensure no risk of human error or delay.

'Without question, ma'am.'

And please stop with the 'ma'am'!

Next I brought out the pillow, duvet, sheets and towels, vacuum-packed in nifty plastic bags. The butler handled them as gently and reverently as if they were Fabergé eggs.

'That's the bag finished.' I continued my monologue of stating the obvious as Dwayne looked on patiently. The most embarrassing part was yet to come. I took out the bumper pack of Viraguard antiseptic wipes and, with a self-conscious smile at Dwayne who was doing a good job of rising above it, I set off around the vast suite in search of telephone handsets and remote controls. I found and wiped five of the former and three of the latter, and finished with the taps, toilet flush and door handles.

I left the pack of wipes and five pocket Viraguard sprays on the desk with the weekend schedule and contact list laid out neatly next to the Mont Blanc pen. Finally I took out the three packs of Marlboro Reds, and three silver lighters. I left one set on the desk, one on the coffee table and one in the bedroom. I ran my fingers down Natalie's commandments, which ended with the bold, red, italicised words 'Success is in the detail'. I scanned the room one last time. All done. Vincent could now safely enter his $AUS8,000-a-night suite without the risk of microbes, creases or nicotine withdrawal.

The phone in the room was ringing as I closed the heavy double doors.

'Hi, Natalie, yes, all done …' Dwayne's voice was silenced by the thick mahogany.

I perched nervously on the round sofa in the opulent lobby of the Crown Towers hotel, feeling self-conscious and a bit of an impostor in my starchy team uniform. To my left a group of Ferrari personnel stood chatting in their red trousers and short-sleeved shirts, and two guys from Lotus were studying a map with the concierge. It was 10 a.m. Australian time, and I'd already been up for hours.

I checked my phone for text messages.

Hey glamour puss, sorry 2 hassle but any news on yr room. do I need 2 find a new tenant? hope not. em xx

Glamour Puss, yeah right, my hands still reeked of antiseptic from cleaning Vincent's loo.

I synchronised your home PC so u can come home for few hours without panicking that u missed sth. In return I demand gossip! danny

I started to type a reply to Em, when the lift opened and Helen and Janey walked out together. I clicked 'Save to Drafts'.

'Hey Kate, let's go,' said Helen, waving to the Ferrari group. 'Have you got your pass and your laptop?'

'Yes, they're in here,' I replied, tapping my computer bag.

'Put the pass round your neck,' Janey snapped humourlessly. 'And guard it with your life. Don't lose it, and for God's sake don't ever lend it to anyone.'

'Er, OK, sorry.' I rooted through my bag, pulling out the green cigarette-packet-sized plastic tag and looping the lanyard over my head.

The valet pulled up in our hired Toyota Tarago and we piled in, with Helen in the driving seat.

'Hey Janey, you're being quite intense,' said Helen, engaging first gear and pulling away from the kerb.

'*Never* underestimate the value of that pass.' Janey twisted back from the front seat to jab her finger at me. 'More than half of my job involves keeping track of guest passes, eking them out to partners and telling Fortune 500 CEOs' wives that there's no pass for them in the contract. I am the pass witch. And that flattering title means I will not spend half a day in the FOM office begging for a replacement cos you left it hanging on the bathroom mirror.' She turned forward, pulling down the sun visor and flipping open the mirror. 'So if you forget it or lose it, you stay in the hotel all day and see how understanding Vincent is.'

'Jeez, Janey, I got the message.' I clutched the lanyard to show I understood, turning the pass over and flinching at the unflattering black and white photo on the back.

'Your pass is green so you can't go in the pit lane or grid, unless you want it confiscated. Helen has the access-all-areas red pass.'

Helen navigated confidently through the wide Melbourne streets. Coming from the grey British winter it was like dreamland: sunny skies, the wide Yarra river, and pavement cafés. The town had really embraced the F1 onslaught, with chequered flags billowing from lamp posts and rainbow-coloured displays lining the street.

'It's your first race weekend so all the journos will want to meet you. They'll take the opportunity to ask for something, but remember all interviews have been pre-agreed and pre-planned. We don't do impulsive.'

Helen turned into Albert Park. An initial wall of circuit personnel in bush hats, their faces smeared with thick white sunscreen, checked the pass stuck to our windscreen and waved us through.

Fans in various teams' merchandise mingled about. I spotted a group in Dupont Lamborghini shirts and felt a burst of pride. Large posters saying "If you drink and drive you're a bloody idiot" hung from railings and display boards at regular intervals.

'Remember,' Helen said, 'after the track sessions, whether we finish first or last, Dupont Lamborghini does not make mistakes and none of our partners is ever to blame. There are no problems, only solutions.' Her eyes were fixed on the asphalt road. 'When Vincent or the drivers get hot-headed they absolutely must not speak to the media. Every criticism of the car will be linked to a multi-million-dollar sponsor who does not pay to hear that their engine, tyres or brakes are crap.'

We pulled up at a third security control. This time the security guards were in logoed blue shirts and jeans. They checked the car pass and looked inside the car to check our passes as well. They directed us into a car park marked 'paddock personnel'. We parked and climbed out.

Under a large metal structure boldly displaying the Australian Grand Prix logo, less officious security staff stood at a set of aluminium turnstiles. I copied Janey and Helen, lifting my pass to the sensor panel on the left. It emitted a two-tone beep, my unattractive photo flashed back at me on a screen above, and the turnstile rotated forward. That was it. I was in the paddock. The hallowed sanctum of Formula One, the most popular sport in the world, that I'd just learned wasn't easy to access even with a fifty–million-dollar sponsorship deal. I clenched my jaw, forcing my features into blasé mode. Excitement was bubbling up and it was all I could do not to yelp and kneel down to kiss the earth, Pope-like.

Don't be a fan. Easier said than done.

'Kate, are you busy?' Helen said as I came back from distributing USB sticks of photos to all the journalists in the media centre.

I shook my head as I took a big swig from the water bottle. The 80°F heat made me light-headed.

'I have to take Vincent to the FIA press conference. It would be good for you to come and see how it works. He's been called with Harry Bircher, Button and Alonso. Harry will no doubt try to wind him up.'

Vincent had arrived late last night and the team atmosphere had immediately stiffened. I had felt it in our car in the morning as we all sat, the engine running, outside the Crown Towers for thirty minutes until he strode through the glass doors and sat in the front seat next to Helen, the car filling with the smell of his cologne.

'Good morning', on our part, was greeted by silence that reigned for the first five minutes of the journey. Then he shot off rapid-fire questions at Helen: What day had Enrico arrived? *Tuesday.* How were the new uniforms working out? (The Lanvin-designed uniforms were elegant, but totally impractical for the mechanics. Helen's answer was diplomatic). Was Gideon confident for free practice? *Reasonably, although was he ever?* What was the weather forecast for qualifying and the race? *Dry and hot.*

What media programme did he have today? *Medium heavy. Helen went on to give details.*

Helen explained that attendance at the FIA press conferences was mandatory and being late incurred a fine. She said, 'Only the threat of losing money would ensure a bunch of self-absorbed egotists arrived on time.' Helen knew that it took three minutes to walk from our hospitality to the media centre, so we had left with four minutes to spare, to allow for a couple of greetings en route and to ensure Vincent's wait couldn't be more than 30 seconds.

Vincent took his place behind Jenson Button. Alonso walked in and sat on Button's right. I was caught off-guard and my inner groupie surged to the fore. I dug my nails into my thigh to stop myself giggling like a teenager. Just a few months ago I would have trampled over small children to get a photo with Alonso.

The drivers looked bored and Vincent sat ramrod-straight, staring at a space over the heads of the seated media. Everyone waited for Harry Bircher.

A mountainous figure filled the doorway,

'Sorry lads, but fat men can't run in this heat,' boomed an Essex twang, as Harry Bircher hauled his heavy frame towards the stage. An unnaturally buxom brunette in a tight skirt and heels followed him in and joined the line of PRs who stood up against the wall. I elbowed Helen gently in the ribs.

'Lisa, his press officer,' she whispered.

'Vince, mate.' Harry slapped him forcefully on the back. Vincent steeled himself, smiling tightly. 'I've missed ya. Awright boys?' he raised his hand to Button and Alonso, as he plonked himself on the chair next to

Vincent, wiping his brow with one hand and taking a sip of water from the provided glass with the other.

'Right, Bob, my man. Fire away.'

Bob Costanduros, the press conference host, who was sitting in front of the two hundred or so media people seated or squashed shoulder to shoulder along the back wall, nodded.

'So, first question to Harry and Vincent. You've both been vying for top of the time sheets in pre-season testing. Is this how you expect the season to play out?'

Vincent displayed his perfect dentistry as he and his nemesis exchanged gestures of 'After you ... no, I insist'.

'That, Bob, is the question. We know where we are, and I'm proud of how hard the team have worked to prepare the car for this season. But none of us will know for sure until we hit the track in qualifying tomorrow. I hope my friend Harry and I can offer the fans a tight fight for the championship.'

The Q and A proceeded as per Helen's briefing notes. The meaty questions were apparently saved by journalists for one-on-one interviews.

After about four questions each, Bob opened it up to the floor. A few hands went up and Bob called on a man with bushy grey hair in the front row.

'Oh, shit,' said Helen behind her hand; 'a real muckraker.'

'Derek Capshaw, *Daily News*.' He introduced himself with a lopsided smile. 'Vincent, over the winter you've invested in an extremely expensive factory refurbishment, you've refitted the interior of your yacht, and the team have turned up in Melbourne in designer uniforms.' He delivered the last point with a smirk. 'This season is a very important one for the team. Do you think the key to success is looking good?' He pulled his saggy features into a mock-innocent expression.

Vincent's smile widened but his eyes remained emotionless and locked on the shabby journo.

'Absolutely, Darren. But I see you don't agree.'

The packed room erupted in titters. The journalist, dressed head-to-toe in washed-out grey, attempted a second strike, raising his voice above the noise.

'It's Derek, actually, and do you not think your budget would be better spent on car development?'

'Dupont Lamborghini has one of the most significant budgets for car development. We've also completed our state-of-the-art CFD centre and we've built the supercomputer.' Vincent looked up with a broad grin. 'And I can assure you, that last item is one ugly piece of equipment.'

Hearty guffaws from the media people drowned out Derek Capshaw's attempt to get a precise budget figure. Bob wrapped up the press conference by thanking the participants. Vincent flung his arm around Jenson and they chatted intently as they left the room, followed by Harry and Alonso.

'Make sure Derek Capshaw doesn't get any one-on-ones with Vincent in the near future,' Helen whispered as we headed back towards the paddock.

'Hey, girls.' Lisa jogged up next to us. *With that chest she'd do better to walk.* Out of the corner of my eye I caught JB salivating as he focussed his 600mm lens.

'You know, there are more questions about the antagonism between those two than there ever are about performance,' she said, cheeks flushed from exertion. 'Sad, isn't it?'

'If we can get the focus back on the on-track activity then I, for one, am all for it,' replied Helen, and she waved as we turned into our hospitality suite.

'The thing is,' Helen continued once we were safely ensconced in our office, 'Derek Capshaw is a slimeball, but his question reflects a growing opinion – that Vincent only understands the show, and not the racing.' She turned and squinted at her laptop screen before picking up her glasses. 'We need a strategy to knock this on the head.'

I nodded my head slowly, frantically searching for something of value to reply. A suggestion that would prove I was proficient, and not just a liability. I had aggravated the problem with the flashy launch, after all.

'I think we should shift the focus to Vincent as a successful businessman. OK, so he has less experience in racing than the other bosses, but he knows how to make a business work, and that's the modern face of Formula One. For him the show is just part of that equation.' I was impressed by my conviction, although couldn't be sure I wasn't paraphrasing the infamous *Time* magazine article. 'I received a request this week for a major interview for a new series on CNN called *Sport Heroes*. Each hour-long programme will be an in-depth focus on a prominent sports figure.' I rooted around in my bag for my interview request file, finally pulling out the clear plastic sheath. 'A thorough high-profile interview could be the solution, as it allows time to show his business achievements and successful history before F1. As he's so adept in front of the camera, he could handle such a long interview.'

Helen stopped typing and looked at me over her glasses.

'Hmm. We ask for minimal footage of the heli and the yacht, et cetera, and focus on the business. He was the youngest-ever board member at Fontenay Paris before F1, so he has a history of success.' She smiled. 'We'd have to prepare it very thoroughly, but it could be a good option. Well done, Kate. Follow it up.'

I wanted to hug her.

Dupont Lamborghini F1 Team

PRESS RELEASE

Australian Grand Prix
Albert Park, Melbourne
Saturday

Qualifying
Qualifying at Albert Park ended in frustration for the Dupont Lamborghini F1 Team as Enrico Costa and Marcel Müller missed the cut to Q3 by less than a tenth of a second. They will start the race tomorrow from the sixth and seventh rows of the grid respectively.

Enrico Costa – 11th
'All weekend I've struggled with the balance of the car. Even as the grip improved through the sessions, the car remained difficult to handle. It goes without saying I'm extremely disappointed with this qualifying position.'

Marcel Müller – 13th
'This is a new track for me. I like it but just couldn't make the most of it because of a lack of grip. The team worked really hard to try and improve it, but I was sliding a lot.'

Vincent Dupont, Team Principal
'The qualifying positions do not reflect the performance of the Dupont Lamborghini cars. We'll analyse the data to discover why we failed to optimise the car's potential.'

Media Contacts
Helen Miller – Helenmiller@dupontf1.com
Kate Ellison – Kateellison@dupontf1.com

www.dupontf1.com

I had sat next to Helen watching qualifying on the two small TV screens in our office. The only information advantage I had over the average fan was the team headset which covered my ears. Channel 4, scan mode, picked up dialogue on both cars. Stilted and static-laced questions and answers passed between race engineer and driver.

I scribbled down 'oversteer, roll bar, brake balance' with little idea of their meaning. I was geared up to learning phrases parrot-fashion until I could find a non-condescending colleague for definitions. There was no need to trumpet my ignorance.

Q1, the first part of the qualifying session, had claimed its first five victims. The final seconds of Q2 were preparing to boot out the next five. Dupont Lamborghini was a top team, an ex-world champion team, so it went without saying that our drivers should survive to Q3, the final ten. The intention was top four.

'P11 Enrico, position 11, I'm afraid.' His engineer's monotone voice sounded in my ear.

'SHIT. It's all shit!' He pronounced it more like 'sheet', but the meaning was clear.

Helen jumped up and shot out of the door. I grabbed my dictaphone and followed.

'We're on air, we're on air. Watch your tongue, Enrico,' his race engineer pleaded.

'MACCHINA DI MERDA!'

I walked in through the door at the back of the garage, past neat piles of tyres and banks of data screens transfixing a row of head-setted engineers, with a sense of urgency. Stepping through the space in the middle of the branded hoarding I found myself in the garage, the location I'd seen on TV so many times. I tried to focus on seeing Helen through the frenzy of mechanics and engineers, some in team kit, some in full overalls and helmets.

I was jostled one side and then the other as truckies hurried by from all directions carrying tyres. I tried to find a neutral place to stand. The number one mechanic for each car stood in the pit lane. Other cars thundered behind him, loud to the point of physical even with the headphones on.

Over the radio, I heard '30 seconds ... 20 seconds'. Then mechanics from either side rushed forward into the pit lane as the two white, silver and aqua cars appeared, turning in and then sharply to the left to stop diagonally in front of their respective garage bays. The mechanics swooped in on each car; two attached something to the front wheels, one took over the steering wheel, guiding the car back into the garage, and two helped the rearward momentum, rolling the tyres with one hand and holding the rear wing in the other.

I leapt to the side, realising I was standing precisely in one of the reversing vehicle's trajectory. A bunch of photographers and a Formula One Management cameraman appeared in front of Enrico's side of the garage. Everyone seemed to be anticipating something. Helen gesticulated to a truckie who closed the Tensa barriers sealing off the three metres in front of the garage. She then whispered something to Enrico's physio and Dave the Truckie, who both set off towards Enrico's car.

Before it had fully reversed over the garage threshold, Enrico had undone his seatbelts, thrown out his gloves and pulled himself up to standing. He was pulling aggressively at the tag under his helmet. The physio took up a protective position next to the standing driver as the car was rolled into its final position, offering his arm for support as Enrico stepped out. Rejecting the arm, Enrico stumbled slightly as he caught his foot in a curly cable.

Pulling off his helmet he thrust it at the physio, who was forced into a step back as Enrico stormed towards the front of the garage, shedding his balaclava as he went.

And then there was Dave.

He moved his solid frame between Enrico and the extended dictaphones. At twice the size of Enrico, furious or not, Dave was able to halt the little Italian by gently taking his arm and guiding him back into the garage. Gideon appeared on his other side, putting his arm around Enrico's shoulder, and the fuming driver was ushered behind the rear wall. This all happened in a matter of seconds as I stood uselessly in the middle of the garage.

I followed the exodus behind the hoarding. Enrico continued to vent in the centre of a circle of Dupont Lamborghini's finest technical brains.

'The car is fucking bullsh-eet. It's an undriveable piece of crap.'

Vincent, who seemed to fall into an uncharacteristic placatory role around Enrico, said: 'Gideon will sort it out, Enrico. Won't you?' It really wasn't a question.

Gideon and Etienne exchanged a silent look. 'With all due respect, it's not as simple as that,' Gideon replied.

In front of me, Etienne's leg pulsed at a speed suggesting an imminent explosion. 'The aeromapping is off because we had to rush the wind tunnel programme. I did warn you …'

The stony silence was broken by Gideon, who turned to peer at the screens over the engineers' shoulders, massaging his left temple with his fingers.

'We need to analyse the data.'

The group filed into the engineering office. As I scribbled 'aeromapping' in my notebook, I looked up to see Derek Capshaw loitering in the garage doorway, complete with satisfied smile.

Dupont Lamborghini F1 Team

PRESS RELEASE

Australian Grand Prix
Albert Park, Melbourne
Sunday

Race

The Dupont Lamborghini team claimed fifth and seventh place in the Australian Grand Prix, a race where only nine cars made it to the chequered flag.

Enrico Costa – 5th

'This was a chaotic race with the two safety cars and a high attrition rate. Driveability improved a bit in race trim, and we have reliability on our side, so I was able to score some points today. This is not where we expect to be though, and so we'll do some homework before Malaysia.'

Marcel Müller – 7th

'I'm really happy to bring home some points in my first F1 race. I was lucky to avoid the first corner incident; the key was staying out of trouble. It was very hot out there and the wind made the handling unpredictable at times; I played it safe, as it was important to bring the car home today.'

Vincent Dupont, Team Principal

'A solid race from both drivers. Melbourne can often turn into a game of dodgems, so our strategy was to avoid trouble and bring both cars home in the points. The performance level is, however, unacceptable and so there will be intensive analysis at the TechQ before the next race.'

Post-race, Helen and I were at our busiest. She oversaw the media interviews and I got on with the press release writing, approval and distribution. It was almost seven p.m. when Helen walked into the office. I was scanning the team website and Facebook page, checking they were updated.

'There was a problem with the server at the factory so the results went up a bit late, but they're all there now,' I said through a yawn as I scrolled down the news page.

Silence. I looked up to see Helen staring blankly at her laptop screen.

'Are you ok, Helen?'

'What?' She looked flushed. 'Um, I don't know. I've just been fired.'

'Christ! Why?'

'I'm seeing Chris, you know, the finance director. It's quite serious so I wanted to come clean. I mean, at my age I'm too old to sneak about for these things.' She shifted her trance-like gaze to the window. 'It's ironic really. I've been in this industry almost sixteen years. Talk about bad timing to get into a relationship.'

'But that's ridiculous. He can't fire you.' Helen didn't seem to hear me. 'I mean, you know everything and everyone. Who on earth can replace you?'

'You'll be ok. Vincent likes you.'

'What do you mean? He barely even knows who I am.'

'No, he does. He notices everything.' She snapped out of her trance and started to collect the papers on her desk.

'But what am I going to do?' Panic made me selfish. 'I'll never survive without you!'

'Look, if Vincent feels he can't trust you or you can't protect him, you're out. If someone turns up who's of more value to him, then you're out. He's obsessive about control, every detail must be perfect. So you have to be one step ahead, or ...'

'I'm out. Yeah, I get it.'

'And Kate, everyone in this industry has an agenda.'

'Except you!'

'Hmph ... and look where that got me.' She slipped her laptop into her bag and stood up.

'You're going right now? But ...'

'I'm sorry Kate, I can't help you any more. You'll be fine.' She squeezed my shoulder and gave me a half-smile before heading out of the door.

I slumped back in my chair.

Fuck!

CHAPTER 4

KLIA Highway en route to Sepang Circuit
Kuala Lumpur, Malaysia
Friday, 8.30 a.m. Malaysia Time GMT +8

'So, Vincent, I'll, er, just run through your media and PR schedule for today. OK?' I did my best to sound confident as I leaned through the space in between the front seats of the Mercedes. I'd read the list through in my head so many times, my voice no longer sounded like my own.

'At midday between the two practice sessions you have an informal lunch with the Italian media: *Gazzetta dello Sport*, *Corriere della Sera* and *La Repubblica*.' Vincent stared forward in the passenger seat as Jefri, his chauffeur for the weekend, drove along the wide palm tree-lined highway. Janey sat next to me counting and sorting the tangle of guest passes.

'I've prepared a suggestion for your "Ten Style Tips for the Travelling Man" for *L'Uomo Vogue*. They're on your desk at the track. If you could let me know if they're OK, as the deadline is today.' Written in their entirety by Danny. Thank God for fashion-savvy best friends. 'And

Gordon Barry has asked for a sit-down to discuss the team budget situation.'

Since Helen had left, I didn't know if Vincent had started the search for a replacement, but none had yet arrived. I was doing my best to tread water and stave off the panic of certain career death by drowning. I couldn't see how it would be possible to survive without Helen. With time I could probably do it, but from the little I had seen of this industry, tolerance and patience did not rate highly, and mistakes cost multiple millions. What was proving a far greater challenge than dealing with the media was mastering Vincent's idiosyncratic value system, as – contrary to public perception – he was the opposite of laid-back. He had fired the incredibly capable Helen for the minor indiscretion of having a personal life. I'd be lucky if I lasted the day, let alone the race weekend. And with a CV that included only two months in Formula One, I probably wouldn't even get my old crappy job back.

This car journey was the first time I was dealing with Vincent face to face, well actually face-to-back-of-head, as he'd only arrived at midnight. In order to prepare for his arrival I had run laps of the paddock in the hundred-degree Kuala Lumpur heat, sweating a lot and achieving little, probably because my brain had melted on to the sides of my skull. Fear, imperfect preparation and a general inability to think straight had afforded me only forty minutes' sleep all night.

Instead of combating the exhaustion, the large glass of overly-concentrated orange juice I had downed at breakfast made me quite nauseous.

Vincent lit up a Marlboro Red. The air-con propelled the smoke cloud my way.

'So I pencilled him in at 4.30 p.m. I think it's best to nip this one in the bud.'

'Why is Bircher getting all the press?'

'I'm sorry …?'

'His fat face is all over the cover of some paper in my room, while I have to waste my time talking to old has-beens about stuff that's none of their business.'

'That's the *New Straits Times* that's got the Harry interview, it's just a local paper.' I addressed the back of his perfectly coiffed head; sudden nerves made it impossible to identify what exactly had pissed him off. 'Gordon is very well respected; he has some concerns, and I just think if you had a chat …'

He spun round, glaring. 'He's well respected? I'm team principal of Dupont Lamborghini F1. I don't have chats.'

'Right, yes, of course. In fact I'm preparing a major interview with you for a new CNN series that will have substantial impact and reach.'

His posture softened as he turned to face the front.

'Well the idea, I mean … my strategy is to focus on fewer big interviews to ensure a more concentrated message.' It had definitely been more of an idea, and not yet a strategy. The image of a basket overflowing with eggs filled my mind.

Vincent grunted, which I took to be an expression of approval.

I settled back on my seat, swallowing gulps of slightly less smoky air. As we turned into the circuit grounds I lifted my new red pass, official confirmation of Helen's departure, up to the window for the security control. Jefri pulled right up to the paddock turnstiles. No extra steps for Vincent. And in ninety per cent humidity every step counted.

'Keht,' Vincent said as the car slowed to stop. 'Adriana is coming today. Pick 'er up. I don't want Enrico dealing with these distractions.'

'Right, will do.' I did my best to fake chirpy as I caught Janey's smirk out of the corner of my eye. He strode off towards the turnstiles and Janey and I grabbed our handbags and laptop bags and hurried after him.

'Supermodel-sitter,' Janey said under her breath.

'Shut up.' I jabbed her in the ribs with my elbow. 'I don't suppose you could help? I've got a seriously heavy job list today.'

Her look said 'No chance' and she strutted off, giving a flirty look to Riccardo Santos, who was greeting Vincent with the handshake-shoulder-slap combo.

'Excuse me, madam.'

I turned to see a small, middle-aged lady in a white outfit common to airport beauty counters. 'You are with Mr Vincent?'

'Yes, that's right.'

'I'm sorry to ask,' – she rifled intently in her handbag – 'but my son is a big fan of him. A really big fan.' She pulled out a dog-eared photo of a young boy with a crew cut and gaps in his teeth, holding a puppy. 'This is him, my Majid.'

'Ah, he's very cute.'

'Yes, he was in remission then. But it just came back, the leukemia; he's in hospital again …'

This job, Formula One, absorbed my every waking moment, actually, *every* moment as I often dreamed about it too. Everything happened fast, not just the driving but problems, decisions, articles, hirings and firings. It was a self-perpetuating spiral of importance and urgency. There was too much going on, and too much to lose if you stopped or looked outside. It was like running on a treadmill that kept gradually increasing its speed. Then, every so often, someone hit 'Emergency Stop'.

'Oh, God, that's awful. I'm so sorry.'

'But he'll still watch the race. There'll be no stopping him. He says to me, "Mummy, I have to watch Vincent beat them all; he always wins, you know."' She smiled as her eyes filled up. 'I'm sorry to ask, but do you think maybe Mr Vincent could sign something for him? It would mean so much.'

'Absolutely, he'd love to,' I said, taking her by the elbow, gratified that I actually could do something to help. I steered us both determinedly to where Vincent was chatting animatedly with Santos, pulling a marker pen out of my bag as I did so.

Vincent was in full flow. '… So the control tower says, "But Mr Dupont, the visibility is too poor to fly – all helicopters are grounded." And I said …'

'Vincent, excuse me.' I thrust the mother forward. She was tiny and looked terrified at finding herself in the middle of their conversation. 'Could you please sign for this lady's son, Majid. The poor boy is very sick with leukaemia.' I took the top off the pen and handed it to him, then reached into my bag for an autograph card.

The woman remained frozen in her original position with the child's photo displayed in both hands.

Still facing Santos, Vincent's eyes flicked coldly to me, before returning smiling to his driver buddy. 'When it comes to getting my autograph, everyone has leukaemia.' He broke into a hearty guffaw, which Santos echoed.

He signed across the boy's face without looking, clapped his hand on Santos's shoulder, and they both headed for the turnstiles. 'It's so bloody hot in this country, I'm surprised anyone can reproduce!' They both roared again and Santos headed off towards the Martini Magna motorhome.

The mother remained rooted to the spot, but her eyes were now on the photo in her hands, the thick black squiggle covering one eye and most of the boy's teeth.

'Keht!' Vincent held out his briefcase, which he no longer wished to carry.

I had to go. I thrust the unsigned autograph card into the mother's hand, placing her thumb on the top to ensure it was gripped, and squeezed her awkwardly on the forearm before taking off in pursuit.

What the hell just happened? It was unlike Vincent to misjudge a situation so completely. Was he seriously trying to be funny? Could it have been a language thing? Maybe it wouldn't have sounded so bad in French. Why did he always have a character lapse around drivers? But however desperately I scrabbled around, it was impossible to spin that one. I didn't turn around as I walked on towards the team hospitality area: I couldn't bring myself to see the woman's horrified face staring back.

I watched the first practice session from the screens by the telemetry consoles at the back of the garage. I was closer to the action and information if anything happened. I had identified a couple of team members to whom I could ask inane questions, who would reply without laughing out loud and with a swallowable amount of personal ridicule.

The mood became almost party-like at the end of the session, when the drivers emerged with small smiles and no swearing. It was only Friday, so it was controlled optimism, but the black cloud that hung over the car's performance in Melbourne seemed to have shifted down the paddock. According to Rob, Enrico's race engineer, we were the only ones who managed to 'optimise the soft tyre'.

'Well that's great, Rob. Well done you.'

'You have no idea what I mean, do you, Kate?'

I shook my head.

'In this heat the tyre tends to fall to pieces.' He spoke in a hushed voice while scribbling on his clipboard. 'But we found a way to stop that happening.'

'Cool. How?'

'You don't need to know that.'

I headed back across the paddock to our office, which was housed together with Vincent's and the catering area in a white plastic tent with glass doors.

'Excuse me. Permesso,...' I picked my way across the sprawled chairs of Enrico's extended family, who were the only people in the paddock sitting outside in the team 'garden': a strip of Astroturf behind a white picket fence peppered with aluminium tables and chairs.

My body recoiled at the intense blast of icy air as I pushed open the office door. Once acclimatised, I felt refreshed and sufficiently fortified to tackle the Adriana issue. But my positivity evaporated on finding a sweaty JB plonked with legs splayed in my chair, hairy belly exposed, fanning himself with my 'weekend schedule' file.

'I was just a gnat's fart away from certain fucking death out there today.'

'Shift over, JB.' I snatched my file and pulled at my chair until he rolled on to Janey's.

'Honestly, I think I found religion. We should take a moment to praise God I'm sitting here right now and not lying in a neurotoxic coma at turn eleven.'

'I've got work to do.' He was working up to a big story. It would probably be amusing, although only about ten per cent truth, but I was too busy to humour him.

'So, right, I thought for this session I'm gonna go creative.' He scanned the small office to drum up a bigger audience, but Mike was transfixed as usual by Sunseeker.com and had his headphones on. It was just me. 'I tramped out to turn eleven cos they've got all that long grass and I thought, "I'll shoot through the grass and get some real fucking nature. It'll be beautiful."'

I considered putting on my headphones but knew he'd just increase the volume.

'So I'm lying there, gut in the grass like David fuck-ing Attenborough, or was it Bellamy … Anyway, Marcel hits the apex, locks up so he's sliding and it's mega, really "Sports Photographer of the Year" kinda stuff.' He was re-enacting the scene, leaning his chest across my desk with his imaginary camera positioned right above my keyboard, making it very hard to type or ignore him. 'And then, I just get this, like, sixth sense, you know.'

I caved. 'Of what?'

'Danger, man, danger. I kid you not. I lower the camera and turn slowly to my left and there is a cobra, a fucking cobra, standing up about two feet away with that hood thing out, bloody well staring me down.'

'No way.'

'I swear to God, I nearly fucking pissed my pants.'

'What did you do?'

'It was amazing, I got like this primeval survival instinct, I turned the camera and flashed it then jumped up and legged the fuck outta there.' He sat back, exhausted by his performance, taking a big swig from Janey's water bottle.

I skim-read the new messages in my inbox: nothing really urgent. There was a message entitled 'Flat Hunt' from Danny. I didn't want more hassle about moving out so marked it with a red flag to remind me to look after the weekend. I checked the programme for the hundredth time to make sure I was still on track: first practice session over, drivers in debrief, posted 'Meet the Media' notice in media centre, Italian press confirmed for lunch. So far so good. I clicked onto the BA website to check arrival times for Adriana.

'So when's her ladyship arriving?'

'Mrs Dupont's coming? You know, I need to check how to greet a baroness.'

'No eejit, the beootiful Adriana Oliveira.'

I minimised the webpage. 'Oh, she's not due this weekend.' I must have received about fifteen emails from Enrico's manager, Natalie, Adriana's agent, her publicist and someone called Joe, instructing me with varying degrees of politeness to keep Adriana's attendance out of the media.

'Come on, Kitty Cat. The 'ole paddock knows she's coming. TV Globo 'ave been filming the practice of the welcome ceremony.'

'The what?'

'She demanded some sort of traditional Malaysian welcome. Wiv dancers, headdresses, the lot. Wouldn't get off the plane wivout it. It's some time late afternoon.'

'Great, thanks.' I shrugged wearily; so much for 'incognito'. 'I'll find out and let you know.'

'Thanks Babe.'

VIP arrivals lounge, Kuala Lumpur International Airport 8.45 p.m.

I paced up and down on the small square of red and gold carpet, cursing under my breath. I really didn't have time for this. I had to get Vincent a tailored DJ by six p.m. tomorrow, confirm the drivers' post-qualifying interviews, get a hundred autograph cards signed, proof- read Marcel's *F1 Racing* feature, and write a detailed account of Vincent's entire pre-F1 life for Tomasz Ligas, the fastidious Polish researcher for the CNN *Sport Heroes* interview. The list went on. My job was expanding by the second. Not only was I the press officer and stand-in media manager, but Vincent's travel PA and now supermodel suitcase-carrier.

A small man wearing a gold sarong over a pair of white trousers and a pointy black hat burst through the door carrying a small gong. He shouted something and the receptionist pointed out through a security door towards the back of the room. He disappeared, muttering to himself. A rhythmic muffled drum beat started up from behind the door.

A few minutes later, the security door was flung open and two suited men appeared, walking backwards semi-inclined in front of a strutting Adriana. She was all long tanned limbs, beautiful bouncy brown hair and huge Dior sunglasses. I could see where the 'super' in 'supermodel' came from. I had never seen such an incredible gene blend in anyone real before. She had just got off a long-haul flight but her tiny silk camisole and inordinately long skintight jeans weren't wrinkled. She strode confidently in killer-heeled Jimmy Choos and it was a wonder she didn't topple over under the weight of the huge Gucci tote balanced in the crook of her elbow. Behind her two airport staff struggled with a trolley bearing a mountain of Louis Vuitton luggage, and following up the rear of the carnival procession in a burst of pink and gold were the beautiful giggling dancers. And JB.

As the perfect anti-climax I jumped up, still in team kit, make-up long since sweated off and hair two days post-wash.

'Hello, Adriana, I'm Kate. Vincent sent me, er asked me, to pick you up on Enrico's behalf.'

She strode past and I slotted myself in behind her and ahead of the burgeoning Vuitton trolley.

Jefri had the car door open right outside the exit doors and Adriana slipped into the back seat. The baggage was loaded into the boot, with a final bag placed on the front passenger seat, so I had no choice but to climb into the back seat too. Adriana gazed out of the window, away from me, iPhone clamped to her ear. The welcome committee piled up on the pavement and cooed and waved as the limo pulled away. Adriana turned with a brief regal wave. I looked back to see JB linking arms with two of the dancers and whispering in one of their ears.

'Baby, it's me,' she purred in her velvety Brazilian accent. Even her damn voice was sexy. 'I've arrived. Why did you send someone instead of coming to pick me up?' She pulled an enormous make-up bag out of her tote.

Hmm … I tried to sit invisibly still. She wiped a lipgloss wand across her ample pout and, now placated, giggled into the handset.

Ninety seconds later we pulled up to the Pan Pacific hotel entrance. Naturally a supermodel couldn't take the walkway that joined the airport to the hotel. A car, driver and an hour of 'someone's' time was required. That was how she survived in Jimmy Choos.

The hotel manager, two doormen and four valets stood on the hotel kerb ready to pre-breathe Adriana's air, and whatever else was required. The door was opened. She unfurled her endless legs, slid gracefully out of the car and disappeared into the hotel before I had untangled myself from the seat belt. I reached reception in time to see her disappear into the VIP lift with the hotel manager.

Job satisfaction was overrated.

To: graham.ellison@sfr.fr
From: Kateellison@dupontf1.com
Subject: Belated birthday greetings

Hi Dad,

*Belated happy birthday! Sorry I didn't call but things in KL
have been flat out to say the least. Em told me you called the
London flat a few times. I haven't been back there so much
as the commute is too long, I've been sleeping on Janey's sofa
near the factory instead.*
*I thought of you today cos I got in the lift with the two
Ferrari drivers, forgive me for not asking them to sign some-
thing for you but I'm trying to be professional.*
Gotta go
Kitkat xx

*PS. Tell Mum I haven't had a chance to visit the Twin
Towers or the Bird Park yet.*

Dupont Lamborghini F1 Team

PRESS RELEASE

Malaysian Grand Prix
Sepang, Kuala Lumpur
Saturday

Qualifying
Enrico Costa claimed pole position for the second year running at the Sepang circuit today. Marcel qualified with a career-best third and will start the race from the second row of the grid.

Enrico Costa – 1st
'I'm really happy to get pole here. I've always liked this track and I managed to get a good rhythm straight off the bat. We worked hard in practice yesterday and it paid off.'

Marcel Müller – 3rd
'I struggled with understeer in the high-speed corners yesterday but made some changes after my first run and it really improved. It'll be a tough race in this heat but we're in a strong position. My goal is to bring home some more points for the team.'

Vincent Dupont, Team Principal
'A strong result for the team with both cars in a good position to score points tomorrow.'

Media contact
Kate Ellison – Kateellison@dupontf1.com

www.dupontf1.com

Everyone was really psyched with pole position, not least the two mechanics who had found themselves enveloped in a hug by a bouncy mini-skirted Adriana as Enrico's name shot to the top of the timing screen in the final seconds of the session. Aware that he was in close-up on the live feed, Vincent punched the air then made a show of slapping most of the engineers and a good few mechanics on the back.

We had bought some breathing space from the performance criticism. But we were fire-fighting: it was a short-term solution. I had strong-armed Dave into revealing the reason for our seemingly strong performance. The tyres had been 'cured', a sort of heat treatment to make them stronger. It was borderline legal. Not information for the press release.

Dupont Lamborghini hospitality area, Sepang International Circuit
Sunday
10.50 a.m.

Gordon's head was thrown back mid-wheeze. With no sound or movement from him, I was considering checking his pulse, when he rocked forward, slapping his hand on his thigh. I had just recounted how during breakfast Vincent had decided to open some fan mail and a pair of worn and torn knickers had fallen into his wheatgrass juice.

'Oh, Kate, that's a beauty.' He wiped a tear from his eye. 'Bottoms up!' He raised his mug of Tetley, chuckling.

'He usually *never* opens his mail.'

'That, my dear girl, is divine retribution for his treatment of Helen.'

'But Gordon, seriously ...'

'Off the record, I know, Kate. Of course.' He lifted his glasses and massaged the bridge of his nose. 'So anyway, will he see me?'

'Fraid not. Well, not this weekend, he's chocka.'

Gordon raised an eyebrow in a question. 'I need to know his plan,' he said, more to himself than to me. 'He's obsessed with winning and yet he's cut the technical budget by half ...'

How the hell did he know that? I looked on in silence. When Gordon switched to journo mode I had to minimise words and reactions, in theory to not give anything away, but as he usually knew more than me it was more to conceal my ignorance.

'Lamborghini paid a fortune for their forty per cent. Where did the money go?'

I peaked in professionalism with a shrug.

'He must have a plan to get a finance injection from somewhere. He always has a plan.'

He was right, of course, it was unlike Vincent not to have thought of everything. But I had nothing to answer and that didn't seem to surprise Gordon.

'Janey, do you know what Helen actually did on the grid?' I squinted, shielding my eyes from the blazing sun with my hand as we stood outside the back of the garage. Janey stared intently inside. 'Everyone always looks so busy there. I don't want to get in the way.'

I had survived the weekend so far, but this was race day and included a trip to the starting grid. The Holy Grail. Tiny Chinese acrobats were performing an elaborate aerial routine in my stomach. I prayed for a boring race, a procession with no big incidents, no controversy and a solid finish for both cars ... but not on the podium. A podium result demanded a whole new set of imperatives and consequent chances to mess up. Anyway, it was just one more day to survive on my own. Vincent would have definitely hired a Helen replacement by the next GP. I twirled the red pass in my fingers. Although I liked having the pass – the ultimate access-all-areas pass – as if I'd finally made the 'cool group' at school ...

'Janey, are you even listening to me?'

'What, yeah, of course.' Her eyes remained fixed into the back of the garage.

'So what do I do? Can't we talk in the office? It's so hot my shoes are melting into the tarmac.'

'Just a few more minutes. This, my keeno friend, is the highlight of my race weekend.'

Two semi-naked mechanics crossed the garage partition carrying overalls. I followed Janey's eyeline through a gap in the partition to a bunch of naked bodies.

'You're such an old perv, Janey McGuinness.'

'You get your kicks where you can, Sister Abstinence.' She smiled. 'With the choice of looking at fifty out-of-shape *but* naked mechanics or discussing computer parts and Ayrton Senna stats with my Paddock Club guests, these are precious moments.'

'I take your point, but 'barrel' and 'scraping' spring to mind.'

F1 had about a one-to-thirty women-to-men ratio, maybe even higher. Perfect stats for any warm-blooded female. But right now I was treading water in the career opportunity of my life. If I could stay afloat I'd learn from a slick, successful and gloriously high-profile boss, I'd deal with top-level international media on a daily basis, and I'd continue to enjoy this fantastic lifestyle experience as a red-pass member of one of the world's most exclusive clubs. A private, or even a pervy, life could wait.

'OK, so the grid.' Janey gave me a quick sideways look. The mechanics filed out, overalls tied round their waists, fulfilling their fantasy, in clothing only, of being drivers for a few minutes. With them in clear view she lost interest and turned towards the office. 'What did Helen do there? Absolutely no idea.'

Dupont Lamborghini garage
1.35 p.m.

I watched the surge down the pit lane of engineers, mechanics and other personnel in ten varieties of team-branded overalls. It was the one time in the race weekend when the teams emerged from their respective garages and intermingled, united only in concentration and exhaustion. Grid trolleys piled with tyre warmers, spare tyres, cooling fans and wheel guns were pulled past. Physios carried spare helmets, umbrellas and driver drink bottles. Everyone had a purpose.

Marcel's car pulled out of the garage for the drive to the grid. Enrico was having his seat belts done up behind me. I had decided to walk to the grid when Enrico left the garage, and then hover around between Vincent and Enrico to help with interviews if required. I masked my nerves and excitement by imitating the universal furrowed-brow look. I was on my way to becoming a professional faker. Danny and Em were recording the BBC coverage at home and had a bottle of bubbly prepped to open on the sofa, should they spot me. I hoped Dad was watching too.

My radio crackled into life. There was something garbled that sounded like 'Kate'. I took my chances.

'Kate here.'

Static. Had to be Vincent. I turned and broke into a jog, trying to guess where he might be. I burst into the hospitality area, which was full with *famiglia Costa*. Adriana stood with Vincent, looking stunning in a tiny white sundress. He looked up with a scowl.

'Keht, take Adriana to the grid.' He put on his headphones and strode out of the door. *Fan-bloody-tastic.*

'Hi, Adriana. Shall we go?'

Looking somewhere straight over my head, she held out her hand and her large white Dior bag. I found my hand extending in spite of myself.

No. No. Don't take the ...

It weighed a ton. Full, no doubt, of essential supplies for a ten-minute grid walk.

Adriana strode to the door and stopped. I leaned past and opened it for her, shocked at how easily I slipped into serf mode. She turned and broke into a huge smile for Enrico's parents.

'*Ciao, ciao.* See you in a minute, Beppi. I'll kiss Ricky for you, Maria.' His parents smiled. They didn't speak English.

The grid was more than intense. Hundreds of people jostled for space on a small square area of tarmac. Mechanics, engineers, journalists, photographers, camera crews, drivers, managers, press officers, physios, ultra-VIP guests, a Japanese boy band and the Ecclestone girls. Working, strategising, spying, networking or just looking beautiful. Into this mêlée the cars arrived at not insignificant speeds aided by whistle-blowing mechanics, enjoying their once-in-a-weekend chance to push any, yes any, of the aforementioned personnel out of the vehicle's path. The car was finally king.

Enrico rolled into the white-painted box and in swarmed mechanics, engineers and data analysts. The car was lifted on to the jacks, laptops and cooling fans plugged in, tyre blankets donned, the cockpit shielded with an umbrella and a drink bottle proffered. As close as they could manage, a second tier of camera crews, photographers and journalists hovered.

As I watched Adriana pose for a group of photographers, marvelling at her affected insouciance, a Martini Magna mechanic in the team's lurid pink and purple overalls came into focus, shouting in the background. Within a split second Santos's car nose was visible just feet away from Adriana's strappy heels. I grabbed at her arm, my fingers overlapping round the tiny bone, and pulled. She shot me a death-look before spotting the tyre a few centimetres from her ankle.

Leaving his helmet on the monocoque, Enrico climbed out of the car, put on his Oakley sunglasses, and went to lean on the guard-rail at the edge of the track. He kept his head down, sucking intently on the drink-bottle straw as his physio shadowed him with the umbrella. TVs crews hovered in his orbit, with reporters with microphones extended at the ready, and cameramen jockeying for a stable position, cameras perched on their shoulders. Enrico caught no one's eye.

Vincent used the moment when Adriana was surrounded by photographers to greet her with a kiss on each cheek (even though he'd been with her in the hospitality area twenty minutes before), and then she swanned off in Enrico's general direction. Relieved that she was occupied, I used the moment to focus on my job.

Vincent made space through the media wall towards Enrico, who was now in discussion with his engineer. I hiked the weighty handbag on to my shoulder and followed in his wake, loitering just outside their conversation. Martin Brundle arrived from the opposite direction, charging through the crowd at speed, followed by his cameraman, and thrust his microphone at Enrico.

'Enrico, what's your target today?'

The tight little circle of Enrico, Vincent and Rob, his engineer, opened for Enrico to reply. I looked up to see that I was in the back of the shot. And on BBC, too. I could almost hear the champagne popping in Shepherd's Bush. I had to concentrate hard on looking normal. On my belt my phone started to vibrate as text messages arrived. I had made it!

Then I remembered the handbag.

Dupont Lamborghini F1 Team

PRESS RELEASE

Malaysian Grand Prix
Sepang, Kuala Lumpur
Sunday

Race
Enrico Costa dominated the Malaysian Grand Prix, turning his pole position into victory. Marcel Müller came into contact with Sweeney's Martini Magna on the first corner, he was forced into the gravel and collided with Raikkonen's Lotus as he rejoined the track. The resulting rear-wing damage ended his race.

Enrico Costa – 1st
'I knew if I could keep the lead after the first two corners I could win this race. We had an aggressive race strategy and I just had to pray that nothing gave out in the heat. We had some cooling issues after my second pit stop, which meant I had to short-shift. It gave Santos a chance to close the gap, but it wasn't hard to hold him off.'

Marcel Müller - DNF
'Sweeney pulled alongside me on turn one. I was on the line and he didn't leave me enough space. We wheel-banged and he pushed me into the gravel. I managed to get the car back on track but one of the Lotuses clipped my rear wing, which effectively ended my race. I'm really disappointed, as it could have been a great race for me today.'

Vincent Dupont, Team Principal
'A flawless race from Enrico. He dominated from start to finish in a style we have come to expect. Sweeney's rear-ending of

I lost myself in the excitement of the race and the rush of our probable win. Glued to the timing screen I became obsessed, as each sector time appeared, with mentally calculating the differential between Enrico and second placed Santos, even though this figure was updated after each lap. On the penultimate lap I suddenly remembered the podium imperatives: I had to intercept the driver(s) with the Omega watch, team cap and interview jacket – a stiff version of the overalls which forced all the partner logos on the arms forward and flat for perfect TV exposure. And a clean shirt for Vincent.

I tore myself away from the screen and sprinted into action. I barged into Enrico's room, grabbed the cap and watch, and hurtled over to my office for the jacket and shirt. I power-walked to the top of the paddock, keeping my eyes down so as not to get caught into a conversation. Now, how on earth to get through to parc fermé?

'This way, Kate.' Lisa appeared behind me. She nodded at a security guard lifting up a pile of merchandise twice the size of mine for their second and third place, and he pushed the glass door open with an officious nod. We took the steps two at a time for the first floor, then both slowed to one step at a time for the second floor as we caught our breath. I followed Lisa into a small room that would have been nondescript if it weren't for a floor-to-ceiling window overlooking the pit lane. The crowd in the stands cheered. Rob's monotone voice came over the radio.

'Well done, Enrico. Really great drive.'

'Fantastic! Thanks, guys.' the noise of the engine drowned out the vowels. 'The beers are on … Vincent.'

A TV monitor in the corner of the room showed Enrico pulling in slowly to parc fermé. Vincent had somehow vaulted the barrier that kept the pit-lane crowds out, and stood with his arms outstretched towards the incoming racing car. The Dupont Lamborghini mechanics formed a cheering wall behind him with Adriana sandwiched in the middle, trying to look demure among the heaving mob. The barrier to Vincent's right held back a mass of camera lenses.

As the car came to a halt Enrico snapped open the seat belts, pulled off the steering wheel, and jumped up to standing. He roughly re-attached the steering wheel before leaping onto the white and silver monocoque and punching his fists in the air. Vincent turned to the cameras to echo the victory air-punch just as Enrico launched himself off the car, stage-dive style, towards him. Vincent's relaxed smile turned into an expression of alarm. His confident victory stance switched to an awkward semi-lunge as he braced himself to catch seventy flying kilos of helmeted twenty-four-million-dollar-a-year driver.

There was a collective sigh of relief in the room as, with a few steadying steps and an unhealthy back bend, Vincent successfully caught him.

'Jesus, that could have been expensive,' Lisa whispered. I laughed too hard.

Vincent and Enrico turned their celebratory embrace to the wall of photographers. Vincent's cheeks shone red; he'd taken quite a crack from the helmet.

Santos and Sweeney walked in behind me, extremely flushed, their hair and overalls sodden with sweat. They grabbed the water bottles, alternately drinking and pouring them over their head. Vincent and Enrico arrived, the former chest out and beaming, the latter sweaty and dishevelled. Sweeney shook Enrico's hand. Santos and Enrico ignored each other, stepping around each other for water and caps.

The Allsport Management rep delicately moved the drivers into line by the door and, on cue, sent them out on to the podium. Vincent buttoned up the clean shirt, tucking it in tight, smoothed down his hair, gently rubbed his inflamed cheeks, and then followed the drivers out to collect the constructors trophy.

The happy Italian anthem burst through the speakers. The team were chanting 'En-ri-co' just below the window. I was charged with energy; my legs pulsed to the anthem and I found myself mouthing along to the chants as I watched crowds of hot, elated faces staring up in awe at the podium. The osmotic effect of the victory buzz was as intense as it was surprising. While I had been trying to be professional I was overwhelmed by smugness, it was the playground value system all over again – I was in the winning team, and the victory was all the sweeter for the fact that so few got to experience it.

'Kate, we've got a problem.' Lisa pulled at my arm, turning me away from the window. 'I don't have many details, but there's quite a damning article coming out on Harry and Vincent and their antagonism.'

The buzz was gone, replaced by the familiar feeling of heart-quickening stress. 'Where? When?'

'Look, I don't know enough yet. I'm trying to find out more.'

'Can we stop it?' My breath was shallow.

'I'm pretty sure it's already being published. Listen, as soon as I know more I'll tell you and see what you can find out too. OK?'

'Of course.' I steadied myself on the back of a chair and forced a smile.

CHAPTER 5

Shepherd's Bush, London
Sunday, 10.10 p.m.

'*Arriba, abajo, al centro y dentro,*' Danny chanted, leading the ritualistic salute. He got especially creative this time round, incorporating some voguing. I swallowed and shuddered. The tequila burned, but with each round it was a bit less fierce. Emma waved the bottle over the shot glasses, creating a pool on the glass table-top.

'Woah, Em, slow down a bit. I'm just off the plane – these are going straight to my head.'

'Are you kidding? We haven't seen you since forever. There's so much catching up to do.' She gave up trying to aim into the miniature glasses and slumped back on the sofa, swigging from the bottle.

'Don't even think about using your glamorous life as an excuse now, dahling!' Danny shouted from the kitchen. 'Or it'll be double shots for you.'

'Ok, I've got one.' Em shot up her hand. 'George Clooney or Brad Pitt?'

'Too easy, Em.' Danny walked back in, carrying a huge bowl of popcorn and a plate of quartered limes. 'Clooney.'

'Clooney,' Em echoed.

'Pitt, of course.' I shook my head in mock despair.

'It's supposed to be a hard or unpleasant choice, Em.' Danny re-explained with forced patience the rules of his all-time favourite game. 'You know, like Osama bin Laden or Robert Mugabe?'

'Pass!' Em said. 'One of them's dead, for God's sake.'

'You absolutely can't pass. It's life or death. You shag one of them or you die.' He pulled out an old copy of *Elle* and flicked straight to the fashion pages at the back. 'A nasty, slow, painful, horrible death … evisceration or the like.'

'Ok, Batman or Superman?' I attempted to lighten the tone. 'You can tell a lot about a person from their choice of superhero.'

'Superman,' said Em.

'Exactly! Wholesome Superman is so you, Emma Peterson,' Danny said, throwing his arms up in triumph. 'It has to be Batman: he's more dark and brooding.'

'I have to agree with Danny, although I've always wondered – is that really his six- pack, or does it come with the suit?'

Em giggled. I could always rely on her to laugh at my jokes. 'Batwoman, that's Danny's new boss.' She elbowed me and gave a cheeky grin in our flatmate's direction.

'Yeah, but not because she'd look good in a PVC suit, cos she's a fucking evil old bat.' He flapped his arms and stuck his teeth out like fangs. 'A vampire bat feeding on the blood of young personal shoppers.'

'What happened?' I could tell by Em's face she was really familiar with the Batwoman story.

'She gave me a written warning on her first day. Very first day. I walk in, and bam!' He waved an imaginary letter. 'Here you go, Mr Matheson.'

'But what had you done?'

'NOTHING!'

Em's pursed lips, and beginnings of a smile, said otherwise.

'I was a bit late cos of the tube strike.'

'How late?'

'A couple of hours.'

'That's pretty late.' I imagined walking in two hours late to the TechQ. I wouldn't even get past the security gate. The work day officially started at nine a.m., but thinking about it, no one was ever later than eight-thirty, and the first person to leave, around seven p.m., always muttered some excuse like a doctor's appointment or off-site meeting.

'I had to walk from Notting Hill … it's a long walk in new Zegna loafers … passed that fabulous boutique in Kensington Church Street … that was having a clearance sale …'

'You went *shopping*?'

'I didn't *go* shopping. I just walked through and picked up two heavily discounted shirts, which I'll wear to work anyway.'

I turned open-mouthed to Em, who nodded and grinned as she topped up our glasses. 'Yeah, he arrived at work two hours late with a shopping bag.'

I shook my head and smiled. 'Oh, Danny, I've missed you.'

He stood up and stomped off towards his bedroom, muttering something about 'people in fashion should understand …' There followed a thud, the sound of opening drawers, and the clatter of falling CDs.

'Now, let me see the ring again.' I reached across the sofa and peeled Emma's left hand from the tequila bottle, the pathetically inadequate engagement present I'd just picked up in Bahrain airport, duty-free.

'Don't look straight at it or you'll be struck blind!' Danny shrieked theatrically as he pulled the cushions off the armchair in search of his iPod.

It was a beautifully elegant single Princess-cut diamond on a simple platinum band. 'Simple', not to be confused with 'cheap'. I had spotted the telltale Cartier box on her dressing table.

'No wonder you can't pour straight; that rock must set you off balance. How many carats is it?'

'Oh, around two.'

'Two point three, VVS1, E-colour diamond, to be precise. Practically perfection,' Danny announced proudly, as if he had mined the thing himself.

Em's ultimate dream had come true – well, the realistic dream, seeing as she wouldn't actually be able to cure world poverty. The first time we had met, at nursery school aged three, she had converted the Wendy house into a chapel and I was allowed to play on condition that I was the groom. From that day forward she was always the bride, whereas I doubled up as vicar and choir. The details had changed over the years, including fortunately her choice of groom, but her objective had stayed the same. I was mortified that it had taken over two weeks for me to be able to celebrate with her.

'How's Freddie? Will he be over later?'

'Oh, he's great, his usual sweet charming self. But flat-out on some merger or other, he's working round the clock, poor thing.'

My mobile beeped with a text message.

Sorry. Lisa x

I pressed 'Delete'.

'Round four,' Danny announced, grabbing the tequila bottle from Em's clutches and accurately pouring it into the glasses.

'Salt.' We clenched our left hands in a fist as Danny dropped a hefty pinch into the crook between the thumb and forefinger.

'Ladies, take your limes.' We did as we were told.

'To health, wealth and a fleet of private aircraft.' We swallowed, and Danny inverted the empty glass on his head.

'Right, Kate, I insist on some insider gossip from your fabulous Formula One jet-set lifestyle right now.' Having found the iPod in his jacket pocket, Danny was intently scrolling.

'Yeah.' Em joined in. 'I read that *Hello!* article set in Vincent's mansion near Oxford; it looks amazing. All old-school glamour with big chandeliers, one of those huge sweeping staircases, and something like fifteen staff. He was so witty in the interview, too – you must have had such a laugh.'

'He's my boss. It's not really like that.' I glanced at my BlackBerry screen. As a mark of defiance I'd turned it to 'Silent', but I found my eye drawn to it at ever-shorter intervals.

'He and his wife, she's a baroness isn't she, are like Euro royalty.' Em got that faraway look she always got when faced with great thoroughbred genes. 'Is it true Vincent's a French count?'

'I don't know, but I'm having to check it all out now for a CNN interview I'm preparing. He's pretty coy about his background, actually. It's hard to get any clear facts.' I had made a mental note not to talk about Vincent all night. I knew they would like the stories, but he had a tendency to dominate everything these days. I wanted to use the time to catch up with Em and Danny's lives. I'd missed so much, and I was in need of a solid dose of normality.

'By the way, what's that smell?' I screwed up my nose as I scanned the room, stopping at Danny's death-stare. 'What?' I whispered.

He gave a sideways nod at the dining table, which was covered in small strips of plaited leather with knotted attachments of various sizes and colours. 'Hey,' Danny said, with exaggerated spontaneity, 'did Em tell you about her brilliant new business idea?'

'Oooh, yeah.' Em hopped up and swayed her way to the table. 'Look at these.' She thrust a fistful of leather at me, and the stench intensified. 'Aren't they amazing?'

I separated one bracelet from the bunch in her palm. It had two small hanging green pendants and a thick white plastic thread braided through the centre. 'They're pretty; where are they from?'

'They're made by street kids in Mumbai from any and all materials they find.' She'd selected two, and was tying them on to my wrist.

'That they find where?'

'Anywhere, it's up to them. But, of course, most of it's reclaimed from the dumping grounds – there's a major waste problem in that city.' She held my arm up and twisted it, admiring her work. 'It's like a micro business for the kids, and it's recycling too. Every penny they raise goes directly back to them.'

'That's brilliant, Em.' I was in awe of her positivity; for that I could overlook the smell, although my fingers were twitching for Vincent's Viraguard. 'I'll take these, and give me a bunch more, I'll sell some at work.' I reached for my wallet and pulled out a couple of twenty-pound notes. It was doubtful I could shift any, but I was keen to compensate for all the weekends I hadn't been here to pitch in.

'Hey, what about Vincent?' Danny was tying a braid of tiny red metallic balls around his ankle.

'Oh, my God, yeah!' Em's eyes were wide with excitement. 'If he wore them during an interview,' she gasped, 'just imagine, everyone would want one. Kate, oh, please, we could help so many kids. He doesn't have to pay for them, you can let him have them for free!'

The collision of home and work worlds was sobering. How could I tell them I had a better chance of becoming the first female F1 world champion than getting Vincent to wear a bracelet made from trash? I couldn't. 'I'll do my best.'

'Thanks, Babe, you're the best.' She gave me a hug. I felt even worse.

'Right, D., rack up another round.'

'All right, but you've got to tell me about his clothes. It can't be true that he only wears his shirts once, then throws them away?' He handed round the glasses; we clinked and swallowed.

'His tailor flies in once a month from Milan and hand-makes everything. The shirts all get sent to charity after use.'

'Which charity? I feel the urge to volunteer …'

'Danny!' Em re-animated from her alcohol-induced trance.

'Yeah, yeah, but really. It physically hurts,' – he clutched theatrically at his chest – 'to think of some filthy down-and-out in Cardboard City, puking meths down a custom-tailored Italian shirt. There is no God. You've got to get me those cast-offs, Kate. I'm the same size, I swear. Christ, I'd even sleep in a tent if I had to.'

'Well, for a start you can stop hogging the popcorn,' – I reached as far as I could without moving my body from its perfect sofa position – 'and tell me what I've missed. How'za Paolo?' For some reason I always had to say his name with an awful Dolmio-advert Italian accent; Danny's boyfriend, while of Sicilian parentage, was born and bred in Hackney.

'Who?' he sniffed, sticking his head back in *Elle*.

'Pao- ...'

Em stretched her leg out to tap my shin. 'We don't talk about him.'

'Oh, OK … sorry,' I muttered. 'When?' I mouthed at Em.

'Three weeks ago,' she whispered back.

Three weeks! Usually I would have known inside of three minutes. Danny always told me everything. I felt a surge of indignation, and fought the urge to pout.

The violin intro started for Coldplay's 'Paradise'. We head-bobbed in silence.

A look was exchanged between Em and Danny.

'Guys, what's going on?' I tried not to sound accusatory.

Another look. Danny maintained his poker face.

'Go on,' Em said. 'You have to show her.'

I was bordering on a sense of humour failure when he finally cracked a mischievous grin.

'OK, OK, but my computer's at work.'

'Use my laptop.' I wrenched it out of my bag with unnecessary haste.

Danny used the double-page spread of Vincent and the baroness relaxing in the library to soak up the tequila, placed the Sony Vaio on top, and set to work with the familiarity of a natural-born nerd.

I rolled off the sofa to kneel in front of the screen, which was filled with the YouTube website.

'How did someone as good-looking as you get to be such a geek, by the way?'

'National Health specs and train tracks meant too long spent in my bedroom during my formative years. There was bugger-all to do in Tiverton. I couldn't even get *Vogue*.'

'Here we go.' Danny clicked 'Play' on a film entitled *George Michael's Secret Concert*.

A shower curtain came into view. A silhouetted man was swaying his hips. The 'Careless Whisper' saxophone intro was playing.

'Wait a minute, that's our ...'

Danny silenced me with his hand and a smirk.

The curtain was thrust to one side (thankfully the shot stopped at the chest), and a wet Paolo launched into the opening line, singing passionately into a shaving foam aerosol.

I only managed a sharp intake of breath as two faces stared at mine intently.

The voice continued, emotion distorting Paolo's handsome features as he improvised some sort of sexy peekaboo with the shower curtain. He was getting through the first verse, but the chorus was coming.

He threw his head back.

We all erupted. Paolo was achingly tone-deaf.

'Danny, you bitch,' I managed to splutter, when I'd just about regained control. Two and a half minutes later, and poor Paolo was still singing his heart out.

He faked offended. 'Oh, it wasn't me. Look, it was put up by someone called SinatraSings. It got 184,000 hits! He swung his legs over the side of the armchair with a smug grin. 'YouTube, the silent weapon … anonymous and yet so wide-reaching.' He was trying to be glib, but his eyes had lost their trademark sparkle.

'Hey, just imagine how he'll react when you're the next Mark Zuckerberg, or rather Natalie Massenet. You know what, we should organise a big PR launch for your website, like in a really cool bar. I'll invite the press – we can get a few celebs who're interested in fashion to come. Some of my old agency clients will turn up to anything … sorry, I mean … you know what I mean. They can sign up as your first personal shopping clients. It'll be a good start, don't you think?'

'Yeah.' Em nodded, and shot a nervous look at Danny. 'A guy from uni just opened that cool, futuristic bar in Knightsbridge. How about there?'

'The site's not ready yet, and you ate all the popcorn.' Danny picked up the bowl and walked out to the kitchen, turning the volume up on Lady Gaga as he passed the sound-dock.

'Kate, is everything all right?' I looked up from checking my BlackBerry and mobile screens to see Em peering at me.

'Oh, sure, yeah, fine.'

'You'd tell me, right?'

'I'm just knackered, you know. I haven't slept well in ages: jet lag is really screwing with my body clock.' I tried to avoid her gaze, or I knew I'd crack. It was so nice to be home again, getting drunk with my favourite people; I didn't want to burst the F1-free bubble.

She held my gaze and waited.

'I just had a shitty week, that's all.'

'Tell me about it. I want to know. We've hardly talked in ages.'

I flopped back into the outsize cushions. There was something confessional about this sofa.

'OK, well, it started with this terrible article in *Sport Business Europe*. I knew it was coming out, but there was nothing I could do to stop it. Which is a bad thing for a start, cos I'm supposed to have control of all articles written about the team.' I cleaned under my nails with the tip of the corkscrew. 'It listed, remarkably accurately, all Vincent's major spendings on non-race stuff like factory renovations, the launch, and even the new motorhome, which isn't even finished yet and is supposed to be a secret. It was meant to show the destructive rivalry between Vincent and Harry Bircher, that they're wasting the team's money in some petty image war. It's a respected magazine, so we couldn't just discredit it. And we're talking big money.'

'Like how big?' Sensing serious gossip, Danny was back in the room, tearing a packet of popcorn open with his teeth.

'In total, double figure millions. About a third of the team budget.'

They looked at me like I'd just flashed my boobs. Danny scrabbled to catch the open packet of popcorn that he'd let slip, and which was shooting its contents over the table and carpet.

'Well, this was bad on many levels. Vincent freaked out that we had a leak in the factory. He's paranoid about security, and ordered me to find it. The IT department were checking all emails and phone calls. I had to interrogate the staff. It was awful; no one was going to admit anything, and all it succeeded in doing was making everyone hate me.' Danny relieved me of the corkscrew: he hated it when I picked my nails.

'The designers, engineers and mechanics finally had hard evidence to back up their suspicions about budget-squandering, and the atmosphere in the team was just downright hostile. There were shouting matches between the technical director and chief designer in Vincent's office which half the factory could hear.' I massaged my neck to loosen a persistent knot. 'The partners all jumped in, saying that their money was being wasted and they invested in performance, blah blah. And then, of course, in the real part of my job, all the media wanted a comment on the article from senior team personnel. I issued a shamefully bland statement from Vincent, and spent the rest of the time dodging calls and coming up with crap excuses no one believed. It was amateur PR week.'

'Look, you've only been doing the job a couple of months; you can't be expected to know everything already,' Em said soothingly, leaning forward to take a handful of popcorn.

'Yes, I am. That's exactly the point!'

Em recoiled, dropping popcorn into her lap.

'Vincent isn't witty or fun to work with. In real life he's nothing like he appears, and he's absolutely not tolerant or understanding.'

'Listen, Kate ...' She put the hand with the rock on my knee.

'Em, stop consoling me, I haven't finished. It gets worse.'

'Oh, right, sorry.' She withdrew her hand and resumed her earnest expression.

'So, Lisa, she's Harry Bircher's PR, comes up with this idea to quieten the waters. Cos they've got a similar chaotic reaction on their side. Although technically, as they won the championship, no one can argue they're compromising performance.'

I looked up, and Danny nodded his head in agreement.

'The Bahrain Grand Prix was coming up. It has a vast paddock, and tends to be a bit actionless. She suggested we just get Vincent and Harry to sit down for a friendly chat in the middle of the paddock thoroughfare. Simple idea, and pretty brilliant I thought. It would show there couldn't be tension between them, hence the claim that they were spending out of a war was groundless. Of course we'd tip off a couple of photographers, who were always hanging round anyway, looking for something to shoot.'

'That makes sense,' said Danny. 'This Lisa girl, she's your friend?'

'I guess so, sort of. Well, she's been friendly to me, and quite helpful now that Helen's gone. Everyone is, really.'

'Go on, so what happened?'

I took a deep breath. Just recounting the whole thing made me cross. Mainly because I still couldn't tell if I'd been naïve, or if it had been a simple mistake. At the end of the day it didn't matter either way: the end result was the same, and was shit.

'Danny, let's do another round first. I can feel I'm bringing you all down.'

'Bollocks you are, but I shall oblige, as I heartily believe in the medicinal benefits of tequila for the soul.' He pulled the glasses into a line and knelt up to do his Tom Cruise cocktail-bottle spin. He never managed to throw and catch smoothly without fumbling crazily for the slippery bottle, but he always made Em and I crack up at the way he concentrated so hard.

'Girls, pull yourselves together,' he said after an awkward catch. 'What shall we drink to this time?' He handed out the limes and pushed the salt shaker across the table. We looked blankly at each other. 'I've got it. To your promotion, Kate.'

'What promotion?'

'You said your boss was fired and you had more work to do.'

'Vincent said there's no time to look for a replacement right now, but I've got the same job title and the same money.'

'Oh, you're so glass-half-full. To Kate's mach one rise up the career ladder.'

The doorbell rang as we sucked the limes.

'Pizzas; thank goodness – I'm starving, and can't eat another piece of popcorn.' I stood up too fast, and my head spun wildly. 'Wow, I'm going to have to slow down. I've got a big day smoothing egos tomorrow.' I struck a dramatic pose and strode off to the door, concentrating hard on avoiding the furniture.

'So this photo, did it work out?' Em asked as she sponged pizza topping off her pale pink jumper with the paper serviette. The stain had spread, and thin strands of paper were stuck on the fluffy fibres.

'We set it up for just before ten a.m. on the Saturday morning. Practice didn't start till eleven, and the photographers were milling about hoping something would happen. I'd told our photographer to have a couple of colleagues on standby, but in the end there were quite a few hanging around anyway.' I took a large swig from the bottle of Vittel that was delivered with the pizza. I needed to dilute the alcohol.

'Shortly before the agreed time Harry sauntered out from the back of the Martini Magna garage. He walked slowly, greeting the truckies who were hosing down the tyres, high-fiving the RTL film crew. I stood behind Vincent, who was watching from the window of his office on the other side of the paddock. Vincent waited another four minutes before heading to the door. It was all terribly contrived. He didn't want to just walk out on his own, so he tacked on to two gearbox engineers who were just heading back to the garage with a coffee. They were shock-frozen when Vincent appeared nonchalantly at their side trying to make small talk. I would have loved to eavesdrop.

'Anyway, the paddock was a good thirty metres wide, with a square of palm trees and a bench in the centre, where no one ever sat. When Vincent and his two "pals" were halfway across, Harry greeted him with a 'Hey Vince', and enveloped him into a hug. Harry's almost a head taller than Vincent, so he got a mouthful of chest hair.' I checked my audience was still awake. Danny was watching wide-eyed; Em's eyelids looked heavy as she melted into a particularly big cushion, but she was still conscious. It wouldn't have mattered; it was therapeutic just talking about it.

'So anyway, they sat down on this bench. Harry had his back to me and Vincent had a tight smile, but it was barely noticeable. Photographers started to shoot, some approached, some stayed put but crouched for a different angle. Others further down the paddock picked up on the scent of action and headed over. The cameramen followed suit. Harry was earning a BAFTA with his bursts of laughter. If it hadn't been for Vincent's rigid body language, even I'd have believed they were friends.'

Em's head swung into a sleepy nod, causing her eyes to shoot open again. She sat up into a cross-legged position.

'Sorry, Kate, go on.'

'Well, the whole thing was only a couple of minutes but it served its purpose – plenty of shots were taken.

They both stood to leave. Vincent clapped Harry on the arm: he doesn't shake hands. Then …' I sighed just thinking about it. 'Harry ruffled Vincent's hair.'

Danny snorted.

Em looked confused. 'He did what?'

'Ruffled his hair!' I waved my hand back and forth to demonstrate. 'You know, like a grandpa does to a cheeky child. Vincent's hair was slicked down with some sort of spray and so it stuck up vertically in two chunks veering off at different angles. The cameras caught it all.'

Danny was convulsed with giggles. Em's eyes were watery. She wanted to laugh but was trying to hold it in.

'It's not funny. It was awful. You don't know how obsessed he is with his image. He always looks perfect. This was all about protecting his image and showing he's in control, and Harry ridiculed him in the basest way possible.'

'I'm sorry, Kate, Danny doesn't mean it.' Em deliberately avoided looking at him as he thumped his chest to catch his breath. 'It just doesn't sound that bad. I guess we were waiting for something really terrible to happen, like a big crash or something.'

'This *was* terrible.' I was angry now. These were my friends. Why were they laughing? 'If it's bad for Vincent, it's *very* bad for me. There'll be jokes, and Bamber will do a cartoon in *Autosport*, and Vincent isn't someone who laughs at himself.'

Danny pulled himself up to sitting, wiping the tears away with his sleeve. Em still wasn't looking at him.

I was so mad I had to grip on to the sofa to stop my hands shaking. I was facing torrents of shit for this, and they just thought it was funny. They had no idea how hard it was, how hard I was working …

'This is my career that's on the line, every second of every day, depending on my boss's whim. I love my job and I want to keep it. Maybe it's hard for you to understand, Danny, but for me it's not all about bloody discounts and luncheon vouchers!' The words fell out of my mouth: they aimed to hurt. I felt a release; the blood that had been pumping so angrily gradually slowed. The rage had gone, to be swiftly replaced by regret. My hands released their clasp on the sofa. My body slumped.

The room was silent. I looked up slowly into two pairs of hurt, confused eyes.

'Sorry. I'm sorry, I'm just exhausted. I have to crash,' I mumbled as I pushed myself to standing; if I didn't get out of the sitting room fast I would definitely dissolve into tears. 'I have to leave at five a.m. Oh, can I still sleep in my room?'

'Of course you can, silly,' Em said, collecting the pizza boxes, making an exaggerated effort to look normal. 'We didn't touch anything in there until you gave us the say-so. But it's been three months now.'

'I know.' I picked up the glasses and followed Em into the kitchen. I had to get things back to normal before I could go to bed. 'I thought I might be able to commute, but there's no way, I'll fall asleep on the motorway. You're going to have to go ahead and find a new room-mate.'

'Did you visit Danny's aunt's flat?'

'What flat?'

'Apparently his aunt lets flats to students, and one was coming up free. He said he emailed you a couple of weeks ago.'

A bell rang somewhere in my exhausted tequila-sodden brain. 'I'll talk to him in the morning.'

'Ooh, I nearly forgot.' Em looked up from loading the dishwasher with a serious expression. 'Will you be my maid of honour?'

'Oh, my God, of course I will.' I enveloped her in an unco-ordinated hug, leaving two fat tears on her shoulder. 'I'd be honoured. What do I have to do?'

'Oh, not much. You need to plan the hen night, help me a bit on the day.' She looked down and fumbled with opening the dishwasher tablet bag. 'Oh, and it'd be great if you could come to help choose the dress. But no pressure, and we can fit it in on non-race weekends.'

'Stop it. Of course I'll be wherever you need me. Just say.'

Em grabbed my hand as I turned to walk to my room. 'Are you sure you're OK?'

'I work in Formula One and I'm Vincent Dupont's press officer. Of course I'm OK.' It sounded convincing, and she seemed satisfied with the reply. But she was drunk, and I wasn't sure it was just her I was trying to convince.

I set my alarm for five hours' time and flopped into bed. It was great to be home, even if this was probably my last official night. But the positive tequila buzz had worn off, and I felt a gnawing sense of dread about dealing with the photocall aftermath. Within a week Vincent's poor relations with the media, sponsors, public, and even the team itself, had been severely exacerbated. The only thing I'd succeeded in was leaving a wake of destruction.

I closed my eyes and put one foot on the floor. Apparently that stopped head spins.

CHAPTER 6

Dupont Lamborghini TechQ car park
Lower Bledcote, Oxfordshire, UK
Thursday, 8.25 a.m.

'Hi there, do you need a hand?' I crouched down to help pick up the wallet, tissues, hairbrush, butterfly clip, muesli bar, phone, compact and other extraneous items that were strewn across the car park tarmac next to the open car door. A young girl who I didn't recognise was clutching her handbag, desperately trying to reattach the flapping strap.

'Oh, is it broken?'

Lifting a big chunk of wiry black hair out of her eyes she looked up; her face was blotchy, on the verge of tears.

'I just caught it on the hook of the seat belt as I got out. I pulled too hard cos I was panicking because I'm late. It was so stupid because I woke up really early, but I spilled tea on my blouse so had to change, then I forgot I needed petrol. So now I'm late.'

I took the handbag to see if there was a quick fix for the strap. There wasn't, and there were no handles either.

'Ok, don't worry, you're here now, a couple of minutes more won't change anything. Here.' I handed the bag back. 'Hold it open, and let me put everything inside.'

She stood there helplessly, doing as she was told. I looked at her knee-length navy skirt, badly ironed blouse, new leather shoes a size too small. I had a flashback to my interview four months ago, remembering the terror this building inspired. I recognised it in her, the realisation that nerves and excitement had conspired against her, rendering her incapable of anything but the most basic of tasks. A lot had happened in these past four months.

'Look, I've just tucked the strap inside and you need to hold it like a clutch. Ok?'

'Ok.' She nodded earnestly. 'Thanks.' She slammed the car door, then looked alarmed for an instant before realising her car keys were hanging on her finger.

'I haven't seen you before; what department do you work in?' I said as we headed to the staff entrance.

With the hand that wasn't gripping the handbag she tried to flatten her hair, which was swelling in the wind to a sort of mane.

'I'm on reception. I'm covering the usual receptionist's maternity leave. I start today.'

'Well, congratulations, and really there's nothing to worry about.'

Recognising an unidentifiable female, Ivan was on full alert at the door.

'Ivan this is ... oh, sorry, I don't know your name.'
'Maria Hill.'
'It's her first day, Ivan, so be nice.'

Thursday, 8.45 a.m.

The phone console on my desk lit up with Natalie's name. My hand shot out instinctively to pick it up.

'Hi, Natalie.'

'Vincent wants you.' Click.

Argh. I hated it when she did that. Like her time was too precious to waste an extra syllable with civility. No hi, bye, thanks. Just three bloody words. Vincent did it all the time, but he was the boss.

I grabbed the handset, pad and pen and headed off at a trot to Vincent's office. I took the stairs two at a time, which meant by the time I got to the top I was bent double, panting, using the time I'd saved on recuperation. I used to be fit. It was amazing what fourteen-hour days and a few long-haul flights did for the physique.

'Hi, Vincent, you wanted to see me?' I said from the doorway.

Vincent was standing in the centre of the office with four men, all with their backs to me. He raised his hand to silence me as he screwed up his nose. 'Natalie, what's that smell?'

As Natalie pushed past me to search for the source of the stench, I looped my hands behind my back and wrenched at the leather, stretching the band enough to slide my hand out and stuff the offending bracelet in my pocket.

The consensus of suspicion having fallen on the gardener, who had just started to mow the lawn, I approached the group, recognising Vincent's VVIP.

'Ah, hello again, Mr Kato. How are you?' I thrust out my hand, which floated limply in the air as he acknowledged me with a curt head-nod.

'Keht, Mr Kato and his guests would like a factory tour.' Five pairs of eyes looked at me expectantly. *Christ, I'd only taken a couple of photographers around since I started, and they never needed to know facts.*

'Alrighty.' *Did I really just say that?* 'Would you like to follow me?'

One of the Japanese businessmen, with awful grey teeth, pulled out a small Canon digital camera, held it in front of my face and flashed. I gave a belated smile, turned and walked out. They all followed. Vincent included. *Since when did he come on a factory tour?*

Holding my ID card up to the door sensor, I scanned the merry band in to the design office. The tallest of the group, who was dressed in an ill-fitting navy suit, moved to the front and lifted a dictaphone to my mouth. *No pressure then.* I loosely described what went on in the office and did my best to throw in some interesting facts and figures, turning away from the dictaphone as I did. The tour group looked on with unreadable expressions, bursting into Japanese chatter at regular intervals. To compensate for their lack of feedback I got more and more animated, like a deranged children's TV presenter.

Vincent's hovering exacerbated the tension. Our arrival in the D.O. had triggered a general desk sweep. Pens, paper and crisp packets were subtly swept into drawers, conversations stopped, body language stiffened. Unable to stand still, he prowled, looking at screens and picking up stray documents at random. There was a collective sigh of relief as I led the group on to the next tour hot-spot.

As we continued our progress through the factory, I had a eureka moment of calling on departmental managers to present their area. After an initial look which warned me to expect to have my body parts fired in the autoclave, they usually spotted Vincent and obliged with an overly precise and fundamentally incomprehensible explanation.

The 'clean room' produced the only notable reaction in my deadpan audience. They pointed, flashed and upped the volume of 'Aww's as the staff, in emasculating pink plastic shower caps, fitted carbon fibre over moulds.

'So-called because it must be one hundred per cent clean.' *Oh, I was coming out with some gems.*

As we headed towards the race bay, Vincent found purpose and strode up to the chief mechanic and started talking intently. The instruction passed down the chain of command and the mechanics surrounding the car in the first race bay eased back in anticipation.

'So.' Vincent addressed Mr Kato. 'Would Yuji like to try the car?'

Mr Kato turned to the youngest of the group, who was much more casual than the rest in jeans and a tight, long-sleeved black t-shirt. 'Yuji.' The boy broke into a broad grin, nodded twice and walked up to the car, which stood suspended wheel-less on stands.

The chief mechanic gave him a professional once-over look and gestured towards Marcel's carbon-fibre seat which was propped against the wall, bottom-cheeks up. Another of the mechanics slid the seat into the chassis, while a third placed a small step on the floor beneath the raised cockpit.

The Japanese boy stepped up and confidently in, sliding into the low seating position. He wriggled as he tried to slot into a seat that had been moulded to fit Marcel's body shape, with not a millimetre to spare. A mechanic attached the steering wheel and Yuji turned it left and right.

'Put the front wheels on so he can see properly,' Vincent instructed, and two mechanics shot off to do his bidding, stepping carefully around the guests.

I eyed Mr Kato, who stood stiffly observing the scene; a few millimetres of teeth were revealed in what could have been a smile.

What did this po-faced man have that made him so valuable to Vincent?

To do my job well, I had to know everything that was happening, to have an answer, correct or circuitous, ready for every possible question. But Vincent was not one for sharing information. He always had a plan, that was all I knew.

'Ey ey ey, what's going on here, Kate?' I jumped as Dave's head appeared over my shoulder, close enough to hear my thoughts. 'That's Yuji Okada, who just won

Japanese Formula Three. He's supposed to be heading to the Indy Lights. What's he doing here? Are we getting rid of one of our drivers?'

This was exactly what I meant.

'No,' I replied with a feeble quash. 'It's just a courtesy visit. Mr Kato and Vincent are old friends.'

Dave sighed and walked off, shaking his head.

Even a truckie saw through my spin. Professionally I was a joke; I wasn't bending the truth, I was flat-out lying because I had no idea what the truth was.

Thursday, 10.30 a.m.

I grinned through the windscreen looking for Ivan, the surly security guard, as the front gate whirred to the side. It was pointless, but I'd amused myself for a few weeks already with the challenge of trying to make him crack a smile. And today I couldn't stop smiling. But as Vincent's car pulled out of the TechQ, instead of Ivan's tight jaw and battle-ready stance, Reg, his decidedly more combat-fatigued colleague, popped his head out from the booth with a smile, a wave, and what looked like half an egg sandwich.

I clutched the file of notes on the motorhome launch. My ticket to the Spanish Grand Prix aboard Vincent's private jet, as he wanted a briefing. I should have been on the excruciatingly early easyJet flight from Luton. Janey had struggled to express her joy at my alternative travel plans.

I was dangerously excited. There was a high-to-probable risk of embarrassing myself. I'd struggled to quell nervy giggles all day.

At Oxford airport the Mercedes cruised past the security control gate and straight on to the tarmac. It pulled gently to a stop next to a white jet with a fine silver and aqua stripe on the side, and Vincent's elegant personal Dupont script logo on the tail. The door was open and the stairs extended to the ground. Two pilots and a steward in a white shirt and aqua tie stood in a welcoming line. After they had greeted Mr Dupont and Miss Ellison, one of the pilots and the steward took Vincent's leather carry-on and my team-issued suitcase from the boot, and loaded it aboard. My request to 'please call me Kate' was politely ignored. They showed no indication of having sussed me as a private-jet virgin.

I was dying to show off. I'd been praying I'd see someone I knew at the airport. Anyone would do: friend, random acquaintance, the cashier at the supermarket. I should have had more self-respect but, my God, I was about to fly on a Gulfstream G200 jet.

I knew the details from Tuffy's private jet debrief over beans on toast in the canteen. He was pretty excited about the dual digital autopilot (sounded reassuring), mach 0.85 maximum operating speed, and something about high-thrust engines. At which I broke down again in girly giggles. It was going to be one of those days.

Tuffy also filled me in on what he called 'Jetiquette': firstly, not to sit in the owner's seat – Vincent liked to either lie on the sofa and sleep for the journey, or sit on the right side of the plane facing forward; secondly, not to drink on board small jets, as they didn't always have a toilet. Peeing in a bottle in front of your boss was not advised. (You said it, Tuffy). But, of course, there was a loo on a Gulfstream; thirdly, not to be late: time slots waited for no PRs; fourthly, it wasn't good form to panic or scream about turbulence in front of the host – that's what vertical seat belts and beta-blockers were for.

I let Vincent board first, then followed him into the cabin. It was bigger than I expected: I could stand fully upright. In the first row were two pairs of camel leather seats, two forward, two rear-facing. There was a further pair of seats in the second row, opposite a double sofa.

Vincent took the seat on the right, so I opted for the forward-facing left one. The attendant introduced himself as Marco, as he whisked away my coat and placed a cut-glass tumbler of iced water on a small napkin embroidered with the Dupont insignia on a pull-out polished table. He appeared again with a silver tray displaying the latest *Vogue*, *Vanity Fair*, *Elle*, *Wallpaper* and – my favourite – *Luxury* magazine. My hand hovered over the black and white Testino cover shot of 'Europe's Hot Young Royals', before I stoically declined. I had to stay on high alert for the motorhome quick-fire round.

Marco pulled the door closed and we taxied immediately to the runway, where there was no queue of aircraft. I quickly pulled out my phone and clicked on the text from Danny. He had never brought up my outburst at the flat again, just carried on as normal. I was grateful for that.

hey babe, got some news. u free to talk?
taxiing on gulfstream dahling, such a rock star! ☺

His reply beeped almost immediately.

wow, pj princess. d'ya think V will marry me?

no chance. i'll call when we land xx

Vincent was on his mobile from the moment we boarded: it was the baroness. I knew, because I could hear every word. She did the talking, and he did a lot of Uh-huhs and OKs. And then Vincent replied, with a surprising 'Maybe the chi levels need to be balanced. Why don't you call your feng shui guru to look at the stables?'

I had to bite down on my jaw not to show any facial reaction.

I was nervous about the flight. Apart from the odd car journey, where he was nearly always on the phone, all interactions with Vincent up to this point had involved going to his office, getting an instruction and leaving. Ditto a phone call. There was no chit-chat, small talk or superfluous dialogue of any kind. So what would happen when we were at thirty-five thousand feet and the phone didn't work? Should I try and chat?

I was thrust back into the soft leather as we hurtled down the runway. I still had my water on the tray table, Vincent was on the phone and, oh my God, he was lighting a Marlboro. I shot a look at Marco, who was unperturbed.

The jet tilted to a steep angle at take-off and an involuntary 'Oh-ohh' escaped me. I deflected this by picking up the file on the tray table and studying the to-do list intently. This was going to be one hell of a weekend. Vincent, the team and, above all, me, were in desperate need of positive PR. The fallout from the *Sport Business* article and the photocall disaster had been nuclear.

Vincent's image and ego had taken a blow which meant he'd responded by prowling the corridors of the TechQ between seven a.m. and ten p.m. so no one could go home, handing out written warnings like balloons at a kid's party, and calling in every department for a thorough bollocking. All because he'd had to fly to Lamborghini to smooth the waters with Signor Bertelli, and grovelling made him fearsome. Team spirit had haemorrhaged over the budget revelations and on-track performance was way under par, so Enrico, in particular, was becoming dangerously vocal. The whole team was under pressure, but no one more than Vincent.

If I let my mind wander with the ramifications I ended up paralysed over how to handle the escalating remit. So I focused on to-do lists. I made lists and I ticked things off. It staved off the panic.

We had a chance to silence, or at least distract, the critics with the motorhome opening this evening. It was a monument to Vincent's marketing foresight, and this time hadn't cost us a penny; it had even brought in some funds. But it was signature Vincent: incredibly ambitious, complicated and rushed. There were extensive teething problems, any one of which could succeed in ridiculing the whole endeavour. And it didn't solve the problem of on-track results.

'They finished building it?'

I looked up and realised Vincent was no longer on the phone.

'Er, almost. They worked through the night again and, the last I heard before take-off, the exterior was practically finished. Some of the construction team have worked forty-eight hours solid.' Vincent didn't need to know I'd had Bricky, so-called because he was 'built like the so-called shithouse', on the phone almost in tears at seven-thirty a.m. 'We drafted in most of the truckies to help.'

Vincent waved his hand impatiently; he wasn't interested in logistics.

'They've started much later than planned on the interior, so the air-con and most of the gadgets won't be operational by tonight, but we can do the opening without them. It won't be hot in Barcelona early evening, and we won't invite guests into the offices.'

'What about the guest list?' Vincent nodded to Marco, who shot over with two plates of artfully constructed canapés.

'King Juan Carlos's *aide de camp* has confirmed his attendance, and that he'll cut the ribbon. His security are camped out waiting to check through the motorhome, but they can't get in yet as there's no floor.' My laugh was greeted with a stony silence. Vincent was engrossed in picking the tops off the canapés.

I took a deep breath. This was probably a good moment.

'Erm, did you speak to Harry about tonight's invitation?'

No answer. He was scooping up a mini-mound of salmon eggs on the two-pronged fork. I ventured further.

'It's important we continue in this vein of truce or, um, friendship.'

Vincent scowled and pushed the plate away. Marco stepped forward to collect the plate and exchange it for a Dupont-embroidered velvet eye mask. The seat reclined and Vincent slipped on the mask, pausing while it was on his forehead.

'Oh, and deal with that witch on reception; I don't expect to see her there when I get back.'

Oh, no. 'Um, what do you mean, "deal with"? I talked to her, and I think she's very motivated.'

He turned to me and scowled. 'Keht, you're supposed to be in PR; do I really have to explain why *that* is not the first image we can project to TechQ guests?' He didn't wait for an answer, just pulled the mask over his eyes.

Of course he didn't have to explain: team image included everyone, and went down to the finest detail. Hair, certainly in any respect wayward, was one of his major bugbears. I knew that; I should have warned Maria to at least tie her hair back.

Bollocks.

To: patricia.markham@dupontf1.com
From: kate.ellison@dupontf1.com
Subject: Confidential

Hi Pat,

Vincent doesn't approve of the new receptionist, can you please let her go asap. I know it's your department, but was wondering if you could maybe say Kay changed her mind and will work to the end of her pregnancy...?
KE

The paddock was narrower than its Asian counterparts and instead of the standardised offices, outsized hospitality units jostled for space and attention. Now we were back in Europe, individualised and fully-branded motorhomes could be packed and driven in a convoy of trucks to all the European circuits. Although – and I had been corrected several times – they had got so big, they had outgrown the motorhome moniker. They were now 'energy stations' and 'brand centres', equipped with more flat screens than Currys, catering facilities to rival a Four Seasons hotel, and state-of-the-art 'relax zones' for the drivers.

But Vincent had gone one better.

I had spotted the glass feathers rising out of the paddock as soon as we pulled through the main gate. Once past the turnstiles, the soaring structure dominated the view, towering over its squat neighbours.

It was The Wing, a scaled reproduction of Qatar's first seven-star hotel which would be built on Palm Tree Island near Doha. The towering steel-and-glass structure was designed to replicate the form and elegance of an eagle wing. The real hotel would stand 276 metres high; our version was 12 metres, almost double the height of the previous tallest paddock building. It had four floors inside and a private viewing terrace for VIP guests, open but part-shaded by the curved feathers and reflective glass. It was accessed by an external lift that ran up the wing shaft.

The top two floors were long and narrow and had endless views across the track in both directions. Vincent's office and the drivers' suites were on the top for maximum privacy. Inside the drivers' suites, the glass wall could be used as a TV or computer game screen, or it could project views of rolling hills, the Indian Ocean or coral reefs to help relaxation.

The combined marketing and press office was on the second floor, with a big meeting room. There should have been a separate press office with a media lounge, but Vincent's peace deal with Lamborghini included the sweetener of the whole of floor three. The Wing widened at the ground to allow for a spacious partner and guest lounge.

When I started watching F1 on TV I clearly remember that a motorhome was a bus with an awning. Well, The Wing was transported to the circuits in fourteen trucks. Thirty construction crew were required to build and dismantle it each race weekend. In the media briefing sheets I had prepared, we claimed this could be done in under forty-eight hours, but the truth was, we didn't know. Once it was erected, four chefs and twelve waitresses (all model-pretty and at least trilingual) would cater for the team and guests.

It was Vincent's ingenious idea to create a replica of The Wing for the paddock. Not only was it a far stronger marketing vehicle than a sticker on the car, but it added a zero to the already significant sponsorship fee, plus the team got a free hospitality unit. The deal was signed before anyone actually looked at the feasibility.

As we rounded the corner into the paddock thoroughfare, the huge crowd of people swarming at the base came into view. Photographers and cameramen had set up tripods in a semi-circle around the base, while other team personnel and general onlookers hovered around. As we got closer I could see a bunch of workmen, sweaty and dirty, carrying white leather Barcelona chairs, rolls of cabling, two Gaggenau wine fridges, and something made of cow hide. And, oh no, Ivan was standing to attention at the unfinished door. *What was he here for? To tackle the media into submission?*

Mike appeared, running towards Vincent.

'Hi there, Vincent, I'm so glad you're here.' He was breathless and uncharacteristically timid. 'The sheikhs are here, and I'm afraid they aren't happy. They keep saying something about an agreement to land their helicopter on the viewing terrace. They won't be pacified. I put them in Marcel's suite, as it's the only one finished.'

Vincent studied the building, looking over Mike's head.

'Tell them five minutes.'

'Um, they told me not to come back unless I had you with me ...' His voice trailed off.

'Five minutes!'

Mike scurried back to his position of aimless hovering outside the building site.

I searched for a plug in the shell that was the marketing and press office. The lack of time meant that all the rooms not visible to guests, with the exception of the drivers' suites and Vincent's office, wouldn't be finished, as the workers had been sent home. The floor hadn't been laid, so I had to balance my chair on the horizontal struts, and the flat screens where I should have watched the sessions remained piled up in their boxes.

The sun streamed in through the supposedly reflective glass, and beads of sweat began to run down my back before my screen had even burst into life. The air-con wasn't installed, and the wireless was working intermittently. It was going to be a long weekend.

I went in search of one of the techies. I needed guarantees that I could go online all weekend. I also wanted an excuse to get out of the greenhouse before I sprouted leaves. I headed up to the top floor; the drivers and Vincent would definitely have technical priority. Enrico's door was open. I peered in and came face to face with a six-foot erect penis. I gasped, and Enrico and his cousins collapsed with schoolboy shrieks. There was no Wi-Fi, no air-con, and yet Enrico had already managed to convert his wall screen into a giant porn cinema.

The ground-floor lounge was cool, thanks to an intermittent current of fresh air from the sliding front doors. I nearly walked into Mike, who was skulking at the bottom of the stairs, half concealed by the Evian fridge.

'Hey, are you hiding?'

He nodded sulkily in the direction of Vincent and the three sheikhs, who were seated in the middle of the lounge, roaring with laughter.

'I need to know his secret.'

'What secret? What do you mean?' I asked. Mike was confident to the point of arrogant. It was strange to see him so deflated.

'Only Vincent Dupont can go into a meeting, get the other party to pay ten times over the odds, and then have them thank him for it. Look at them: "*Vincent, just tell us how much …?*" They love him.'

I stood in supportive silence, observing the scene.

'And he's keeping me out of the loop on the Kato deal. Kato's a seriously big hitter. He's the second richest guy in Japan and is seventeenth on the Forbes list.' Mike's usual aggressive confidence was surging back. 'But none of his technology companies advertise. So what's it all about?'

'I've no idea – all I did was a factory tour.' I leaned around him and pulled the fridge door open, taking out an Evian.

'Vincent must be selling the team.' He reached out and relieved me of the water bottle as I prepared to swig. 'I mean, I'm responsible for acquisitions; if it was about sponsorship he would have brought me in.'

In a way I had to admire Mike's absolute confidence in his own ability.

'You think he's selling the team to Kato?'

That would explain all the effort. But sell? I couldn't believe Vincent would walk away from F1 – the competition, the spotlight, it was his terrain. No, the Kato deal was about something else.

'Look, Kate, we have to watch out for each other in this one. Share info, ok?' He raised his hand for a street handshake.

'Yeah, sure.' I pushed my hands into my pockets.

'Your chef arrived, by the way. You should get in the kitchen. I think there's been a major fuck-up.'

'Ferran Adrià is here?' I was excited: it had been such a coup to get him to agree to cater the opening dinner. 'Great. What's the problem?'

'His team were bringing in loads of equipment. I'm not being funny, but there were nitrous oxide canisters. That's laughing gas. What's he going to do to our guests? Gas them?'

'It's for his foam – he's famous for it. He's like the top chef ever, Mike, and his restaurant, El Bulli, before it closed was widely considered the best in the Western world. I think we can trust him not to kill anyone.'

'Rice Krispies! They also brought in boxes of Kellogg's Rice Krispies, and a blowtorch. I've got the board of Lamborghini coming; I don't need to remind you how important they are right now, and we're serving them Krispie cakes.'

Out of the corner of my eye I noticed a tall, slim guy waving. I looked out through the sliding doors. He smiled and waved again.

'Oh yeah,' said Mike. 'That guy's been waiting for you.'

Maxed out on Mike tolerance, I stepped outside. My brain started the contact-card shuffle through the 'Who works in Formula 1?' pages, as I tried to match the scruffy blonde hair and wide-set eyes to a name. It was hard being the new girl. The journalists only had one new name to remember – I had about four hundred. But there was something different about this guy, not just because he was young and looked like he indulged in some sporting activity, but because his features had a sort of regularity that made him seem familiar, like he was someone I could have known from home.

He gave me the raised-eyebrow smile, the one that expects recognition.

'Hi, sorry for keeping you waiting.' *Give me a clue.*

'Oh, no problem, Kate. You said you'd arrive at three p.m.; you are in fact early.'

'Indeed. So how can I help?'

'First, I'd like to give you these very fine Polish chocolates. My father works for the company, so I can get the very best.'

Oh God: Tomasz, the overly diligent Polish researcher for Sport Heroes.

'Thanks, that's very kind. Did you get the in-depth version of Vincent's biography I emailed last week? I put in a lot more background about his personal life, as you requested.'

'I did, Kate, and I thank you. You'll have to forgive me, I'm new in this industry. I know you've got a lot to do, and I'm sure I'm starting to bug you …'

'Not at all,' I lied.

'It's just that *Sport Heroes* is an in-depth TV profile of the heavy-hitters. We want to show the real Mr Dupont, and most importantly how he became Vincent. It's a new angle, it'll show him in a way he's never been seen before.'

That's what they all say. I was starting to regret committing everything to this interview. Tomasz seemed too inexperienced, plus it was hugely time-consuming. I needed this interview to highlight Vincent's commercial successes, not check out his school report.

'So the biography wasn't sufficient?'

'If possible, and I apologise again. I'd need more information on the time before Dupont Lamborghini, before even Fontenay Paris, particularly late teens, early twenties.'

'Ok, give me a week or so.' Luckily for you, you have a nice smile. 'When have we scheduled the interview?'

'The Turkish GP, in four weeks' time. Kate, I'm really very grateful. This is a big break for me, I just want to do a good job.'

'I know.'

Hotel Arts, Barcelona
Friday, 6.50 a.m.

'Thank you,' I croaked at the automated wake-up call, dragging my leaden body up to seated and hitting the TV remote for wake-up noise. I forced myself out of the ultra-comfy bed and padded across the super-stylish room to the state-of-the-art shower. I wondered if there were guests who actually got to live the lifestyle experience the room promised or if, like me, their experience was limited to those small pre- and post-sleep comatose states when fiddling with little bottles of things fell into the 'too time-consuming' category. Who really had time to use hotel spas, order in-room fine dining, or work out how to order Box Office films? Actually, it was better not to dwell on the pay-per-view question in this overly testosteroned industry.

I pulled open the plastic bag that contained my team shirt and put it on, ditto the trousers. I had never associated wearing a uniform with any sort of job that involved satisfaction, but it turned out I was becoming unhealthily obsessed with vacuum-packing. Each day I threw the worn uniform into the laundry bag and at the end of each race weekend it was sent off, to return a few days later to the TechQ with each item cleaned, ironed and folded in a neat plastic sachet. Brilliant! In an industry where image was king, who could trust a mechanic (or a PR) to steam and starch? And for me, when the amount of time per day not spent working or sleeping could be counted in minutes, then little practicalities were sanity-savers.

As the lift door pinged open at reception, it dawned on me that for the first time I wasn't filled with dread about the forthcoming day. The Wing opening last night had gone smoothly. Vincent had sat between King Juan Carlos and the Crown Prince of Qatar. The food was excellent (from what I heard, and from the leftovers I tasted), the drivers behaved themselves, Enrico actually laughed at Signor Bertelli's jokes, and no one noticed that half the building was nothing more than an empty shell. TF1 did a live link into the evening news from the dinner, and I got a call during dessert from *Wallpaper* about doing a feature. The journalists enjoyed themselves so much we had to kick them out at midnight.

We did dodge one bullet. I was standing at the door scanning the guests who were congregated in front of The Wing, checking they all had champagne, and that the melon caviar canapés were being evenly distributed. Everyone seemed to be having fun, but then there was free booze.

I was also keeping a beady eye on Ivan, who had taken to following Vincent everywhere, two paces behind, and had even equipped himself with an earpiece. His 'security' presence was the opposite of reassuring, and just made Vincent look paranoid.

I had resolved to have a word when I spotted Harry Bircher heading down the Paddock 'riding' an ostrich. He'd squeezed his eighteen-stone frame into a Bernie Clifton ostrich puppet suit, obviously the closest thing he could get to an eagle, his nod to The Wing's origin. His heavy-set legs stretched the white tights to their denier limits and the puppet legs that straddled the neck of the bird dangled lifelessly, woefully skinny by comparison. His brown leather brogues protruded beneath the hairy, yellow-clawed feet. He lolloped his way towards us looking nonchalant, manoeuvring the ostrich head to peck the ground. I swung round to search for and warn Vincent. I spotted him about twenty people away, introducing the sheikhs to the King of Spain. I pushed my way through the guests, gently at first, then more forcefully when I realised my progress was too slow. Titters began to ripple through the crowd. I was debating how I could interrupt the king, when a voice boomed:

'Vince, mate. Is there anywhere I can park my bird?'

With perfect poise Vincent put his hand on King Juan Carlos's arm and looked up.

'Nonsense, Harry, you know your wife is always welcome.'

The guests laughed, and nobody seemed as horrified as I had expected. There followed a bizarre photoshoot: two team bosses, a king, four sheikhs and an ostrich.

Thankfully Harry then dumped the bird suit, which I stuffed in a corner of the kitchen in the hope that it would get blowtorched into a dessert.

So maybe I was finally getting my job under control. I was way off being relaxed but, well, this morning anyway, I didn't feel like I was a mouthful away from drowning. I'd even slept well, which was the first time ever on a race weekend.

Damnit. I cursed myself, realising I had never called Danny back to find out his news. As I clicked 'Compose text message' to send an apology, the phone rang; the caller ID flashing like a warning.

'Good morning, Vincent.'

'Come here.' Click.

I let out something between a sigh and a growl as I glared at the phone. I would have liked to maintain my high at least until after breakfast, but now I had to have it analysed, dissected and trampled on by Vincent.

I signalled to Janey who had just pulled up in the hire car, pointing at the phone and back to the hotel. She rolled her eyes and accelerated away.

The door of suite 914 was opened by an Asian man in a white cotton outfit. He nodded confirmation that it was indeed Vincent's room and I followed him in to find Vincent face down on a massage table, partly covered by a white towel.

There are people in life you just don't want to think could ever be naked, and my boss was one of those people. I decided the best approach was to pretend I hadn't noticed.

'Hello there, Vincent.' I overcompensated with cheeriness. 'How can I help?'

'What was the press feedback about the launch?' His voice was muffled by towels.

'Initial reports are very positive.' I pulled the copy of *El Pais* out of my bag, crouched down and held the front page under the breathing hole in the face support. It showed a quarter-page picture of Vincent and King Juan Carlos. '*The Times* called you a visionary, *Le Figaro* said it positioned Formula One as "the leader in corporate branding initiatives"'. I was winging it, as I hadn't received the full coverage report yet. Well, it was only seven-thirty a.m.

'Negatives?' He groaned as the energetic masseur dug in with his elbows.

I took a deep silent breath. '*Auto Moto* said it was "possibly the most elaborate smoke and mirrors attempt to distract from on-track performance ever", but that was to be expected.'

The masseur slipped one arm around Vincent's neck, pulling his back into an arch towards the opposing bent left leg. Fearing an imminent buttock-reveal from the slipping towel, I developed an intense interest in the ceiling light. I had to move Vincent off the subject of the coverage. Recently he had a tendency to fixate more and more on the negatives.

'Preparation for the CNN *Sport Heroes* interview is coming along …' I had to get the extra info for Tomasz. Vincent hated questions about his past, but at least now he couldn't stomp off.

Vincent let out an animal-like groan as the stretch was repeated with the right leg.

'I need to ask you a little more background on your life before Fontenay.' I chose the most bog-standard questions on the list. 'How old were you when you started there? Twenty-three?'

'More or less.'

'Were you studying or working beforehand?' I scribbled on the notepad.

There was a pause as he rolled over under the towel. 'Studying.'

'Right. Where was that? And what were you studying?'

'It was ... look, what the hell does that matter?' He jerked his head up to scowl at me, a movement mirrored by the masseur. 'What sort of ridiculous questions are these?'

Panicking, I appealed to his ego. 'It's just to get a clear picture of how you became the success that you are.'

'Well, it had nothing to do with reading books or sitting in cafés discussing philosophy.' He fixed me with a glacial stare. 'What sort of interview is this, anyway? Do you even know what you're doing?'

'Yes, of course.' He could make me go from capable to a jittery wreck in one sentence. I fumbled the pen and had to scrabble under the bed to retrieve it while scanning Tomasz's list of questions to see which might get a response. 'So maybe you can tell me about your parents?'

'My parents are dead.'

'Oh, ok, I'm sorry. I think that just about covers it.'

I practically ran to the door to get out before collapsing back on to the corridor wall to collect myself. I hated that I couldn't keep my cool in these situations. I hadn't done anything wrong; if he was upset by a question I should have just moved on to the next. But he was an expert at disconcertion. I'd seen the brightest and the best reduced to squirming messes in front of him. He almost seemed to enjoy it.

Circuit de Catalunya
Practice Session 2
2.05 p.m.

'I'm coming in.' Enrico's voice burst over the headset before he'd completed his outlap. 'This shitbox is undriveable.'

'What exactly is the problem, Enrico?' Rob replied. The mechanics on his side of the garage walked into the pit lane to await his arrival.

'No balance. Zero grip.' Engine noise drowned out some words. '... a fucking ice rink.'

He thundered to a halt in front of the garage. The mechanics pounced and wheeled the car back in. Rob crossed the pit lane with his clipboard, looking serious.

Enrico threw off his seat belt, pulling himself up to standing. Not a good sign that it was a quickly solvable problem, or that he was handling it well. This also deactivated the radio, which cut off my information source.

Gideon and Vincent headed over from the pit wall, Gideon plodding wearily, Vincent marching elbows-out.

Enrico pulled off his balaclava but remained standing in the cockpit.

'My sister could have designed a better car than this.' He jabbed his finger into Gideon's face, making the most of his height-assisted position.

I was getting nervous. Visible emotion in the garage was not good when the world's media were prowling at the front, alert to the slightest hint of the out-of-the-ordinary. Routine programmes were completed with bland professional expressions. Emotion meant things weren't under control, and as a team we had to look like everything was under control. Always.

The scent of drama had wafted fast down the pit lane, and photographers and cameramen multiplied in front of the garage.

'Step out of the car and let's go to the office, Enrico.'

Nothing much seemed to phase Gideon. He was the perfect embodiment of physical exhaustion, with his grey pallor, eye-bags big enough to double as carry-on luggage and a body that had long since given up the fight against gravity and had assumed a permanent slouch. Maybe twenty years of Formula One had consumed Gideon's fighting spirit. But I rather suspected he just saved himself for the battles that counted, and petulant drivers didn't fall into that category.

'No, no, no!' Enrico folded his arms in protest. 'I'm not going anywhere until you sort it out.'

Gideon turned and walked behind the screen at the back of the garage, as did Rob. Vincent, who was frowning and pacing, hesitated before following suit. Having lost his audience, Enrico stepped out of the car and stomped in their wake.

'We have to do something.' Vincent shook his hands at the group who had reconvened next to the bank of telemetry screens. 'Gideon?'

'We could take the fuel out to calm him down with some faster lap times and make a deeper analysis tonight. But there's no point making desperate changes.' Gideon spoke in a slow, measured tone. 'Until we get the new aero package next race, that's about it.'

Rob nodded in weary agreement.

'No. We must do better than that.' Vincent stood in battle stance, legs apart, hands on hips, right leg pulsating. 'The new aero package, why can't we use it now? You said the front wing lamination was finished yesterday.'

'Because quality control and load testing aren't complete.'

'But the results are positive?'

'Yes, well, airflow should be improved around the front tyres, but it's too early to ...'

'Right. So I'll send my plane to collect it tonight, and we'll use it for qualifying. We have to take action.'

Vincent swung his arm triumphantly on to Enrico's shoulder. It was shrugged off.

Saturday, 1.55 p.m.

As qualifying was about to start, I collected my headset and radio from the rack and took up my position at the screens in the back of the garage.

'It's your lucky day.'

I turned to see JB invading my space over my right shoulder.

'Shouldn't you be on the track or something?'

'No, today's my garage day. I get to hang around and shoot people looking pensive and experiment with making a cockpit shot look not like a cockpit shot.'

JB pulled up his camera at lightning speed, sweeping it in a horizontal arc, mirroring Enrico's trajectory as he strode past on the way to his car. We followed him into the garage, and took up a position on the edge of the pit lane.

'So why's it my lucky day?'

'Cos you made the paddock top five?'

The engine fired up on Marcel's car: a high-pitched noise preceding the mini- explosion. Talking was futile. I waited while the car was lowered off the rear jack and accelerated smoothly into the pit lane.

It was all very well trying not to be a fan, but it was impossible to be blasé in the garage. When the sessions were on the tension was palpable, and the intensity of the engine noise shook your bones. It was the most intense, physical, in-the-moment sensation. It was addictive.

'The paddock what?' I shouted over the deafening hammering of a wheel gun as JB sauntered back from shooting Enrico helmeting up.

'Top five. The top five working birds as voted by the prestigious F1 snappers.'

'Thanks, I'm flattered, but are you sure there are even five girls in the paddock?'

Enrico's engine fired up and JB held the camera low, clicking away as the car pulled out into the pit lane.

'Well, there are enough girls to justify a top five dogs list too. So think yourself ...'

'Yep, I got it. It's my lucky day.' For an industry so cutting-edge, the attitude towards women was lodged somewhere in the 70s – Benny Hill meets *Carry On Camping*. There seemed to be three choices: embrace, exploit or ignore. Lisa and her cleavage did the first, Janey and her notched bedpost did the second, and I (maybe in the absence of cleavage) took option number three. I figured my best chance to be taken seriously was to not draw any attention to the fact that I was a girl, so no flirting and absolutely no shagging. But in spite of myself I was a little flattered at JB's announcement, even though my scowl didn't show it.

Marcel's name hovered around the middle of the timing screen between positions eight and twelve, whereas Enrico didn't move higher than sixteen. On the pit wall, backs were hunched, comments exchanged. Silent looks passed in the garage.

The clock counted down to zero in Q1. Time up. Marcel was through, Enrico was out.

'That was the aero upgrade?' crackled over the radio.

Silence. Rob, Gideon and Vincent had their heads together on the pit wall, headsets pushed to the side.

'Talk to me, you motherfuckers.'

'In the garage please, Enrico.' Gideon rarely spoke on the radio.

Enrico sat stock-still as the car was wheeled into the garage. There was an eerie sense of calm before the storm. Rob, Gideon and Vincent crossed the pit lane.

I spotted the reporters from RAI and Premiere running towards our garage. I moved further inside and loitered as close as I could to Enrico's car, to overhear the argument and to hide from the media.

I hated this part. The media were looking for me to tell them the problem, and I had no bloody idea what to say. It wasn't enough to just ask someone and repeat it, as the official problem had to be carefully chosen to fulfil a raft of criteria:

- not to give away sensitive information to other teams;
- not to make the team look in any way less than one hundred per cent professional: we never made mistakes (nor did we introduce aero down-grades);
- not to admit fault on the part of any of our partners – engine or tyre manufacturers, for example – unless their culpability was blindingly obvious and therefore undeniable.

So if we couldn't blame the driver, it had to be an innocuous excuse. I needed Gideon for those, and right now he was busy pacifying Enrico.

Dupont Lamborghini F1 Team

PRESS RELEASE

Spanish Grand Prix
Circuit de Catalunya, Barcelona
Saturday

Qualifying

It was a mixed qualifying session for the Dupont Lamborghini team. Marcel overcame grip issues and made it into Q3 to qualify fifth, while Enrico suffered with balance issues in Q1 and posted the 19th fastest time.

Marcel Müller – 5th

'I'm very pleased with this position. The weekend started badly as we had no grip on Friday, but we worked hard on the set-up and as the track rubbered in, grip and balance improved. Hard work and patience really paid off today.'

Enrico Costa – 19th

'We've suffered with a lack of balance all weekend. We had no choice but to try a major change today, and it just didn't pay off.'

Vincent Dupont, Team Principal

'An extremely unacceptable session. Marcel is in a position to score points and the team will work through the night to work out an alternative and aggressive strategy for Enrico.'

Media contact

Kate Ellison – Kateellison@dupontf1.com

www.dupontf1.com

'Hey Tomasz, what are you up to lurking in the shadows?' I'd almost walked into the Pole, who was lounging against the cab of one of the team transporters. I was balancing two pairs of driver overalls and boots that I needed to get signed for a web competition, otherwise I would have swept my over-long fringe behind my ear.

'Good afternoon, Kate, I was hoping to catch you.'

'Hey, you gave me a week to get the extra biog info. I haven't got anything for you yet.' *Vincent was wonderfully forthcoming in response to your questions, though.*

'I know, Kate, that's not what I meant.' He was terribly earnest. 'I'm waiting for Enrico to come out ...'

'He's not with the engineers.'

'I know. He's in Harry's motorhome.' He nodded in the direction of the lurid purple and puce hospitality unit, at the top end of the paddock. Tomasz was perfectly positioned to see all traffic in and out of the entrance door.

An unanticipated face slap. I repositioned the pile of merchandise in my hands. I had to kill the story before my head had a chance to process the questions flying through it.

Why else would he meet Harry, if not for a drive? Did Vincent know? Was he bluffing? We didn't need this publicity right now.

'Oh, he's pretty friendly with Jake Sweeney: they often share a private jet back to Monaco. In fact, he mentioned he had to sort out his return trip.' I'd tried too hard. Truth was short, lies were long.

'No, Kate, he walked down the middle of the paddock and made sure the journalists and photographers saw him going in there. Harry met him at the door, they hugged and disappeared inside.'

'Well, that's all quite normal: you know it's a small industry, and everyone knows each other ...'

'Enrico was just trounced by his team-mate, and qualified on the back row. He's pissed-off and wants to make a point. Harry would like nothing more than to sign him away from Vincent, and Enrico knows that.'

'Listen, Tomasz, you're wrong. For a start, he's under contract ...'

'What does that ever mean to anyone in this industry? Anyway, you can relax, Kate, I'm not here for a quote or to make trouble.' He laid his hand lightly on my forearm. 'I just wanted to check you knew. Enrico's trying to make some noise, and he's succeeded.'

I looked over at the growing number of cameras collecting at the Martini Magna hospitality doors. I had to concentrate. I turned just enough so that Tomasz's hand slipped off my arm: that wasn't helping.

'Vincent is losing control of his team. Everyone's talking about it. The car's a dog, and he's spending like some maharajah on monuments to his ego. There's a joke in the media centre that he's planning Vincent World to rival Disneyland Paris. Seriously, though ...'

What, cos we were having such a laugh before?

'... now he's losing the best driver in the paddock. Vincent's not just slipping off his pedestal, he's bungee-jumping.'

I took a few deep breaths as I waited for the lift doors to open on to The Wing's top floor. I had to warn Vincent about Enrico as soon as possible: the whole paddock would know by now, so as well as media questions, angry sponsors would soon call demanding an explanation.

I knocked on the office door, which stood slightly ajar, and I marched in.

A visceral cry froze me in my tracks. A ball of light flew past, hitting the wall that overlooked the Martini Magna motorhome with a loud crack, and shattering into a rain of glass shards, cigarette butts and ash. I brought my hand up to my mouth to stifle a cry then stepped as motionlessly as possible back out of the doorway. From the corner of my eye, I could see a flushed and untucked Vincent standing over the desk, head hanging, hands clutching the corners as if it was the only thing keeping him upright.

I was too late. He already knew.

Dupont Lamborghini F1 Team

PRESS RELEASE

Spanish Grand Prix
Circuit de Catalunya, Barcelona
Sunday

Race

It was a disappointing race for Dupont Lamborghini at the Circuit de Catalunya. Marcel was set for a third place until Jake Sweeney's failed overtaking manoeuvre on lap 34 caused a slow puncture. Enrico stormed his way through the field from his back-row grid position to finish in ninth place.

Marcel Müller – 4th

'I got a great start pulling up to third behind Santos, who'd dropped a place. I couldn't get past him, though, but held my position despite pressure from the cars behind me. Sweeney was just overly ambitious; he didn't have the space to over-take but just dived in at the corner, clipping my left rear tyre, causing a slow puncture. He cost me my first podium.'

Enrico Costa – 9th

'Starting from the pit lane was our only chance, but this was never going to be any sort of race for me. Plus it's like bumper cars back there: you can't just race, you have to focus all your energy on avoiding trouble. I hope this is the last such week-end this season.'

Vincent Dupont, Team Principal

'A weekend that's best forgotten. The team let Enrico down and gave him no chance of a decent race. Marcel's podium finish was stolen by an act of stupidity.'

Media contact
Kate Ellison – Kateellison@dupontf1.com

www.dupontf1.com

CHAPTER 7

Heliair Monaco Flight YO1145
Nice Airport to Monaco
Wednesday, 11.45 a.m.

My stomach lurched into my mouth as the helicopter tilted perilously forward and pulled straight out over the Mediterranean. I was sitting in the row behind the pilot, between an Italian *grande dame* with a chihuahua and a middle-aged British banker who'd got his money's worth from the BA drinks trolley. The sun streamed through the full-length glass windscreen. It was hot and squashed, but wow, what an airport transfer.

We whirred past the jutting peninsula of Cap Ferrat. Even from this height the villas' pools looked Olympic-size.

'Enjoy those seven minutes, Kate,' Janey had said. 'It's the most amazing way to see Monaco for the first time, and it just has to be done. A small treat before the worst race weekend of the year.'

I brushed over her obligatory killjoy caveat. It was the Monaco Grand Prix, for God's sake. The most famous sporting event in the world. Ridiculous speed around dangerously narrow streets, a mythical land of celebrities, euro-royals and the ultra-rich. It was the high-cholesterol heart of Formula One.

I was flying in on a heli, staying on Vincent's fifty-metre luxury yacht, and Janey had wangled us invites to Elton John's ultra-VIP party on Saturday.

Of course I ignored her.

I walked along the jetty, pulling my suitcase with one hand and carry-on bag with the other, transfixed by the huge yachts gently bobbing rear-end next to rear-end. Janey's crazed waving from the middle deck of one such super-yacht broke my reverie, and I upped my pace. A young, tanned and unnervingly handsome man in a neat white polo shirt and grey shorts ran across the gangway.

'G'day, you must be Miss Ellison, I'm Aidan. Welcome to *Aqua Princesse*. Can I take your bags, please?'

'Oh, great, thank you,' I giggled. I didn't dare look up at Janey. She knew my type, and I knew exactly what face she'd be pulling. I stepped on to the narrow wooden gangway.

'It's a shoe-free yacht, miss.'

'I'm sorry, a what?' I turned gently to keep my balance. I was midway across the stretch of water between the dock and the safety of the yacht.

With a wide toothpaste-ad smile he pointed to a basket lying on the welcome mat. I recognised Janey's race pumps, our standard uniform issue.

'Oh, no shoes, right, no problem.' I backed awkwardly off the gangway. I steadied myself on the flimsy gangway support rail as I wobbled on one leg to remove my boot and sock. It was not the elegant way in which I had envisioned boarding a super-yacht.

It had been quite cold at home this morning and I'd had no time to do any washing in the last couple of weeks, so I'd resorted to an old pair of fluffy turquoise bed socks. One of them had a hole in the sole, but it was only for under my boots.

I looked up with a nervous smile as I tried to whip the sock off in one swift tug. Blue fluff balls had collected in the sweat between my toes, glowing almost luminous in the Côte d'Azur sunlight. They stood firm. I had to pick each tuft out individually and, for want of an alternative, wipe them on the lining of my handbag. Pure class.

'Good afternoon. I am Edoardo, the captain, and this is Kyla, our stewardess. She'll look after you during your stay.'

They wore the same style of neat white polo shirt; he had grey trousers and she a grey knee-length skirt. The silver- and aqua-coloured *Aqua Princesse* logo was embroidered on the chest in the same typeface as the Dupont logo on the plane. Vincent really did know how to own a brand.

'Can we get you anything to drink?'

I lounged on the white cushioned sofa on the middle rear deck. My luggage had been unpacked for me (I'd have washed more of it, had I known) and most of it had been whisked off for pressing. The twin cabin Janey and I were sharing was compact, but stylish of course, with polished maple wood everywhere and whiter-than-white bedding.

It was another world. A deep-pile, crisply ironed, stain-free world. I wanted to stay forever. I was in awe, but no longer so intimidated by the staff and the service. I was getting used to it, had come to expect it in Vincent's world. I knew it wasn't mine but I wasn't opposed to privilege by association. I gave Janey the eyebrows-raised look that says, 'Go on, we have to …'

'Well, it's past midday.' I made a show of looking at my watch, before remembering it was a chunky plastic freebie I'd got with my last tank of petrol. 'A glass of wine wouldn't be so ...'

'Two fresh orange juices, please Kyla,' Janey interrupted.

They disappeared silently.

'Hey, surely we could have had a little drink before it all starts?'

'Think about it for a second, Kate.' Cue the killjoy. 'This is Vincent's boat. They work for him, not for us. You really want him to know we were drinking at lunch? And at his expense?'

'Of course not, I just thought, well, you know, it is Monaco ...'

'I told you, sleeping on here is the worst bloody option. It's like staying in your boss's house. There's no escape from him. But I'm not missing the bloody party on Saturday, so for God's sake try and stay off his radar.'

'So I guess the jacuzzi's out of bounds?' I stretched my leg out, pointing an unpedicured toe in the direction of the raised whirlpool.

'As is the deckhand.' Janey relaxed back into her normal self. 'Well, you could always share the jacuzzi with Adriana and her two beautiful supermodel friends!'

'Oh God, she's staying here too?'

'Yeah, Enrico refuses to share his room with her here. And right now, to keep Enrico in the team, Vincent would eat glass to keep him placated. As for Adriana, the Monaco cocktail of celebs, megabucks and media goes straight to her head. Prepare to witness high-maintenance go stratospheric.'

'Christ, I'm going to need a hip flask.' I wasn't sure what was stranger, that I'd started to wish for a single room in any hotel, or that I'd begun to understand Janey.

Monaco Grand Prix Practice
Thursday, 10.45 a.m.

'Kate here,' I screeched into the radio mike, trying in vain to compete with the twenty F1 engines on maximum throttle a few metres either side of me.

'It's Captain Edoardo. Adriana is at the heliport; she wants you or Enrico to pick her up.' We had left a team radio on the yacht for emergencies, as mobiles rarely worked during the sessions.

'It's practice now. Enrico's driving, and I'm in the garage.' I tried to keep what my mum would call 'a facetious tone' out of my voice. 'I can't move for at least forty-five minutes. Please send the tender.'

'I did: it's there, but she refuses to get in it. She's insisting on a car.'

'The roads are all closed; she has no choice.' I was practically screaming, and getting filthy looks from the engineers.

'I know. Can you please call her?' Asking slipped into begging as stress trumped professionalism. Only Adriana was capable of reducing people to such abject desperation.

'I'm sorry Edoardo, the network's overloaded. I'll call as soon as I can, I promise. But there's no alternative: she *must* get in the tender.'

The second the session finished I ran across the bridge that linked pit lane and paddock. I hadn't got the post-session driver quotes, and the TVs were waiting for me to explain why Marcel had stayed in the garage for the whole session. Adriana was an infuriatingly badly timed distraction, but I also knew that every second I kept her waiting the problem, now my problem, would multiply tenfold. She was important to Enrico and he was important to Vincent, and those degrees of separation meant, annoyingly, that she was priority number one right now.

Janey was waiting for me at the foot of the stairs.

'You've got to call Adriana: she's stuck at the heliport.'

'I know. I'm ...'

'Kate!'

I looked up to see Mike hurtling towards me, waving a phone.

'It's Adriana – how could you forget to pick her up?'

'Blimey, is there anyone she didn't call?'

'She called me about twenty-five times, I swear,' said Janey, looking pale. 'She wouldn't listen, and just kept saying, "This is Adriana Oliveira – put me through to Kate at once", and when I said you were in the garage she hung up, rang again and said the same thing.'

Mike nodded with his best attempt at looking superior.

I broke into a trot, heading for the paddock gate. I couldn't physically get to the heliport any other way than by sea. Monaco was a street race, after all. Movement by road was impossible, even for one of the world's most beautiful women.

Through the turnstiles, I ran down the jetty past autograph hunters, wandering spectators, tourists and privileged yacht guests, to *Aqua Princesse*'s second tender, a smaller four-metre rigid inflatable boat which was hovering among the sea of other small boats, waiting its turn to pull up to the narrow dock. I waved frantically at Aidan, who was listening to his walkie-talkie. He clipped it back on his belt, scanned the surrounding rib gridlock, and – with no way of moving closer – cupped his hands around his mouth to shout:

'She got in the tender. She's on her way.' He gave a thumbs-up to add clarification.

'Thank God!' I shouted back, collapsing on to a stone bollard as my adrenaline levels plummeted.

A mane of chestnut hair bounced L'Oréal-like into view, flowing out the back of the *Aqua Princesse* custom tender, barely buoyant with eight passengers aboard. I squinted under my hand. Three extremely heavy-set men sat with their backs to me, and Adriana was roaring with laughter at something a black man with huge gold-rimmed shades and tilted white Panama hat had just said.

'Isn't that …?' I shouted to Aidan.

'ZeBeD, yeah.' He mimed the singer's famous rap pose before reversing out of the melée and accelerating across the choppy water.

In the world of celeb cool ZeBeD was definitely top five, with several number one rap albums and a new clothing line. Clearly megastar power created a protective aura, so Adriana no longer felt the four-minute boat trip to be life-threatening. I pondered the increased odds of sinking with the added ballast of six muscled security men.

'Kate …' Gideon's lifeless voice crackled over my radio.

'Yes, Gideon?'

'Enrico brought a group of girls into the garage, and they're getting in everyone's way.'

'I'll be right there.' I broke into another sprint to retrace my steps; snaking through the crowds, I attempted a short cut behind the Lotus motorhome. My phone beeped with a text.

i'm worried about danny he hasn't been home for a week. what to do? em x

As I pressed 'Reply' my hand smacked into the solid chest of a figure filling the narrow space.

'Hi, Kate.'

'Tomasz, er, hi, can we catch up later, I've got to get to the garage.' I flattened my back on the motorhome and shuffled sideways to bypass the roadblock without further distracting body contact.

'Sure, it's just we need to discuss timing for the interview.'

Why did people do that? Agree to talk later and then shoot the question anyway.

'How so? We agreed ten till eleven on the Thursday of the Turkish GP, two weeks' time,' I said, jogging backwards.

'I need more time: it's not nearly enough.'

The *Sport Heroes* interview was becoming my biggest headache. Tomasz was either incredibly fastidious or incredibly inept.

'That's the longest slot I've ever scheduled, Tomasz. It'll have to do.'

'One more question.'

'What?' I was late: I meant it to sound rude.

'How about a drink Saturday night?'

'I can't promise to have answers by then,' I snapped.

'I don't want answers.' He lifted his arm up and leaned on the back wall of the Lotus kitchen. 'I just want a drink. It's Monaco.' He shrugged and smiled. 'It's supposed to be social.'

He was calm and confident; it was unnerving. Where his arm was raised I could see the outline of his chest through the thin fabric of his t-shirt.

'Oh, er, right. I don't really have time to be social.' I'd forgotten how to have a conversation that wasn't work-related. 'And anyway, on Saturday, I actually have a party … to go to. A big one; should be fun. So no, sorry. But, um, thanks,' I shouted over my shoulder as I sprinted off as fast as I could, hopping over cables and storage boxes.

'Keht, join me for a coffee.'

I swung round full of the nerves that that voice instinctively triggered. 'Oh, er … hello.'

Did he never sleep?

I hadn't noticed Vincent reclining on the crushed-velvet taupe sofa, expresso cup in one hand, Marlboro in the other. I had run up the spiral stairs from my room below deck and was crossing the thick carpet on tiptoe, rubbing a toothpaste stain out of my shirt. Vincent had been out with the incongruous group of Signor Bertelli, Adriana and the ZeBeD posse at Jimmyz, the infamous nightclub, until about five a.m. I had heard Adriana shrieking about tangoing with Prince Albert when they came home a couple of hours ago. But there was no evidence of wild partying in Vincent's appearance. He was, as always, perfectly coiffed and perfectly tanned, and his white team shirt was open at the neck, revealing just enough chest to say relaxed, smart, and not trying too hard.

'Sit down.' He smiled and gestured towards the identical opposite sofa. Kyla appeared, her blonde hair in a neat French plait.

'Expresso, isn't it?' Vincent said.

'Er, yes, thank you.' I actually preferred a latte in the morning.

I perched on the edge of the sofa, and pulled a notepad and pen out of my handbag.

'How do you like *Aqua Princesse*?' Vincent swallowed his coffee in one go, placed the cup and saucer on the black lacquered coffee table, and relaxed back into the cushions with a deep drag on his cigarette.

'Oh, it's wonderful. Of course. Amazing.'

'Are the staff treating you well?'

Kyla had just placed my coffee in front of me on a small silver tray, complete with a mini-croissant and mini *pain au chocolat* on a white side plate.

'Of course, they're all fantastic.' I aimed a big smile in her direction, but she didn't look up.

Vincent nodded seriously, as if he was processing my inconsequential answer, and stretched out to tap his ash in the silver ashtray balanced on the sofa arm.

'You've been in Formula One for a few months now; what's your impression of the image of the sport as a whole?'

I had tried to imitate Vincent by slurping the scalding expresso in one go. I was caught with a mouthful of searing liquid and tearful eyes.

'Erm, well, it's the most glamorous sport in the world. The exclusive and elitist element is part of that attraction. The hi-tech factor interests some, but that's not the major sales point. Well, in my opinion.' I took a breath. I had to make a conscious effort to talk and breathe. 'In fact, I think the endless rejigging of the technical regulations just alienates all but the hardcore fans.' I raised a hesitant eyebrow.

Vincent distractedly smoothed down the velvet on the sofa arm.

'Hmm, the fans deserve more, don't they?'

'Definitely.' *Where was he going with this? I hadn't figured Vincent as a man of the people.*

'Formula One should be more responsible to the fans and its partners. We need to move on from this outdated view of an industry run by ex-mechanics and market traders.'

I nodded solemnly, slightly confused by the non-sequitur.

'Formula One is driven by image. The industry lives on its reputation. And this image must be spotless, not, how do you say, "grubby".'

'Hmm, absolutely.' I crossed my arms over the toothpaste stain. 'There's certainly a lot of corporate money riding ...'

'Bircher, he does things that are no good for the sport.' He got Kyla's attention with a small flick of the head, and with a second he nodded towards his expresso. She shot over and swept away the fine china Dupont-logoed cup and saucer.

'The parties, the playboy thing.' He waved his arm in a big sweeping gesture to encompass, I assumed, all Harry's legendary 'model' parties with his partner in crime, Sal Ovitz, the owner of *Lifestyle* magazine. 'That's part of his game ... but there's a legal line that can't be crossed.' He sat forward, fixing me with that penetrating stare that was painful to meet. 'Drugs, underage girls. Questions are being asked, and there's only so long secrets can be kept in an industry like this.'

He shook his head slowly with despair as he stubbed his cigarette out in the ashtray and leant forward to place it on the coffee table, shifting the corners until it was perfectly perpendicular to the table edge.

He was right: a scandal like that could be ruinous.

Kyla appeared back in less time than it took to make an expresso, and laid the next cup and saucer on the coffee table.

'I'm glad we see eye to eye on this. I need someone I can trust. Can I trust you, Keht?'

'Of course,' I spluttered, barely able to get the words out fast enough.

'We have a unique opportunity to preserve the future of Formula One. Tonight we can get the evidence to clean up the industry once and for all.'

He smiled as he stood up. I followed suit, swinging my bag on to my shoulder.

'You have a great future in F1, Kate. You understand the business, and not many do.'

'Thank you, Vincent.'

'So tell Aidan to have the tender ready to take us to Harry's Sin Palace at seven-thirty tonight.' He disappeared out of a door at the back of the room.

I walked out to the lower rear deck on air. I'd had a real conversation with Vincent. He valued my opinion, and said I had a great future in F1. A *great* future!

The media were crazy if they thought he was losing it. I had never met anyone so utterly in control.

'Where have you been?' Janey intercepted my lunge for the stylishly presented assortment of French patisseries, scooping me up by the elbow. 'We agreed to leave early to get everything done by tonight.'

'Sorry, Vincent cornered me ...' I successfully grabbed a brioche by swinging back with my left hand as Janey steered me towards the gangway.

'It's a horror day today. My VIP pass list looks like the effing Oscar guest list. But in five minutes I'm meeting the Chopard PR at Ferrari to get our invites for to-ni-ght.' She sang the last word, squeezing my arm unpleasantly tightly. 'What are you wearing? I've got this Roberto

Cavalli for H&M dress; it doesn't look cheap – well, I don't think so. It's a bit super-sexy, but hey, this is Monaco and anything goes, right?'

We picked our way around the edge of the port towards the paddock. The narrow walkway between the fence marking off the grandstand area and the water's edge was littered with hazards: thick boat ropes, leads of the resident toy dogs, and aimless stop-and-stare tourists. I wasn't really listening to Janey. My head was filled with a loop recording of 'a great future in F1'.

'Kate, what are you wearing?'

'Erm, my uniform, why?'

'For tonight, the party of the year. Earth to Kate …'

'Oh yeah, I'm sorry, I can't go.'

'You ARE kidding?' She spun round suddenly; I stopped short of walking into her and backed up so that there was enough space to speak.

'No, Vincent just told me I have to go with him to Harry's cocktail party.'

'No way, Christ, Kate. Just cos the baroness didn't turn up again he needs someone to hold his hand. For Chrissake, it's a team boss cocktail; what are you going to do there, chew the fat with Frank Williams?'

'I don't know, I ...'

'What have I been telling you all week? Keep Saturday free! It's only the ultra-exclusive VIP mega-bash I've sold my soul and your arse to get us invites for. Elton's hosting, Kylie's singing, Brad and Angelina are supposed to be going …'

'He's my boss, I can hardly say no.' It wasn't worth trying to tell her. She wouldn't understand. This was a job to her, not a career. 'Anyway, he needs me for a special project.'

'A what? Oh, for God's sake. You can do your job without behaving like a little lapdog around him. You just set yourself up to be kicked around.' She looked genuinely cross, and I was surprised at the vehemence of her reaction. 'What I can tell you for sure is that he certainly doesn't need you. He just hates walking into parties by himself, especially to those hosted by Harry Bircher; he'll forget you're there once he gets in the door.'

We scanned our passes at the turnstiles and carried on walking single-file to The Wing.

Saturday, 7.34 p.m.

I tried to maintain a dignified pose as the tender bumped over the criss-cross waves that scored the port surface, scars of the non-stop inter-yacht mingling. Harry Bircher's ferry-like yacht, *Seventh Heaven*, was moored on the Nouvelle Digue, the jetty reserved for the grossly oversize. One love to Harry in the 'mine's bigger than yours' game.

I forced Vincent's Nokia into my evening bag: a bag probably designed for a lipstick and instead containing two mobiles, one BlackBerry, business cards, Viraguard handspray, Marlboros, lighter, a lipgloss and my pass, it felt best to always have it. I had decided against the Zara dress I had bought for the party in favour of a pair of smart black trousers and a sleeveless cream satin shirt. Professional not social, so less visible flesh.

I looked down to admire my new, jewel-encrusted Sergio Rossi heels. I had decided my first Monaco weekend had merited the £300 splurge. I might have changed my mind had I known, when I paid with my over-the-limit Visa card, that they would spend the whole night in a basket on the dock.

Vincent sat next to Aidan, in a midnight-blue untucked shirt, white linen trousers and suede loafers, smoking and pointing out his route of preference. He was doing casual; still, Vincent was the only person I had met who managed to keep his linen crease-free. He leaned towards me, silhouetted by the evening sun.

'Hard evidence, Keht.' He jabbed his cigarette once again in emphasis. 'Do your job and we can get this industry back on track. I'm counting on you.'

I nodded several times.

I took a deep silent breath. This weekend in particular I had had the strange feeling I was watching myself in some film: the real me was watching this girl swan around on yachts, tenders and helis. But this was really me, here, right now. Nothing outside this moment was of any relevance. Those New Age *Chicken Soup for the Soul-*type books, which Em so loved, talked of living in the moment, and maybe I didn't realise what that meant until now. I was crossing Monaco harbour in a super-yacht tender to an even more super yacht for an evening with the most famous men in motorsport. Vincent Dupont had picked me. He trusted me. I looked up at the lights in the apartment blocks clustered around this, one of the most famous ports in the world. A Europop hit was blasting out from the speakers of one of the restaurant terraces, a girl's laugh punctured the excited chatter of a group of partygoers heading down a jetty, and multiple tender engines supplied the baseline buzz in the soundtrack to my wonderful life.

From sea level, the deep purple hull loomed ominously like a fantastically garish sea monster. While *Aqua Princesse* was a monument to old-school elegance, Harry's seventy-metre yacht screamed excess, or rather Essex. Since Wednesday the helipad had been in constant use and the whole port shook to the beat that emanated day and night from the upper party deck.

Aidan accelerated alongside the endless hull; we were close enough to get the full benefit of the chameleon paint which glinted from purple to pink. It was eerily quiet on board. My empty stomach contracted. I loosened my grip on the handbag to air my sweaty palms.

I hadn't dwelt on the details of my task aboard Harry's yacht. It would be obvious when I saw it. I'd take a quick photo on my mobile, and all done. Harry's parties were notorious; it wouldn't be tough to find something debauched or immoral. And Elton John's party was on the neighbouring yacht, so maybe I'd catch a glimpse of Brad after all.

Aidan threw the rope to the *Seventh Heaven* deckhand and Vincent hopped off.

I followed, stepping out onto the large wooden platform and crouching to undo the fine straps on my shoes before the audience of four smiling crew.

'This way please, ma'am.' A steward in a purple polo shirt and white trousers indicated the way up a curved stairway with his outstretched arm.

Vincent was long gone, and the knot of dread tugged at my insides. Three days on a super-yacht had sufficed to make me a little blasé. The yacht lunches, cocktails and parties for media, guests and sponsors spread an infectious feeling of merit, of entitlement, of belonging in this beautiful world. But now I was walking alone into a team boss cocktail party. My progress slowed to a stop halfway up the first set of stairs. I suddenly didn't want to be there. I wanted to be somewhere, anywhere else, with my peers. Smiling stewards waved me up a spiral staircase to the middle deck. There was no way back now.

The scene that greeted me was sombre. The men, the team bosses, stood together in a tight circle at the side rail. The women, the wives, ultra-elegant in real Dolce & Gabbana, Gucci and Prada cocktail dresses, and accessorised with diamonds equivalent in value to the GDP of a small African country, sat around a large dining table. Fewer than twenty people in total. Conversation was a murmur punctured by the odd polite laugh.

Where were the dancing girls? The crowd of party faithful? The infamous ice sculpture of a naked Harry for the obligatory vodka shot?

I froze. Janey's words filled my head: '*It's a team boss cocktail, what on earth are you going to do there, chew the fat with Frank Williams?*'

Vincent had his back to me and I realised it looked like I'd just arrived alone. I was shockingly out of place, and out of my league. This wasn't my world: I didn't belong.

At best I looked like some girl Vincent had picked up and couldn't even be bothered to walk in with.

'Hi, did you come with Vincent?'

A girl who looked very much like a glamour model, with a deep fake tan and a skimpy Pucci dress, appeared at my side. There was a hint of an Eastern European accent.

'Yes, I'm Kate, his press officer actually.' Relief made me gush. I felt a stab of guilt that I would usually have written her off as one of Harry's slappers, but right now I loved her more than I loved Em.

'I'm Annika. Come and sit with us girls; we're discussing the merits of having a genuine teppanyaki grill on board. It's Harry's thing: he has them imported from Japan for all his homes.' She rolled her eyes and linked her arm through mine as she led me to the 'girls' table'.

I sipped the glass of champagne that appeared in front of me, holding a fixed smile and contributing nothing whatsoever to the conversation. Out of the corner of my eye I could see the Elton John party starting up on the neighbouring deck. The first guests mingled among huge columns of white lilies and ornate glass chandeliers.

The minutes ticked by slowly. I sipped my second glass, trying to make it last. The canapés were beautiful mini-mountains of Japanese delights. They looked just too big to manage in one mouthful and, as I never was the tidiest eater and my top was ivory, I risked one and left it at that.

There was a lull in the table conversation as the women came to an impasse on whether Filipinas or Brazilians made better housekeepers. Vincent's voice soared above the voices from the other group, reminding me I had a job to do.

'Annika, where's the loo?' I whispered across the table.

'Eric, Kate needs the toilet!' she shrieked to one of the stewards.

I followed my guide down the side passage. Halfway towards the front he stepped through an entryway and pointed at a mahogany door with a number seven inlaid in the wood.

Inside I checked my 'natural' look in the mirror. Even with all the money in the world I would never manage to look as polished as those women out there: perfect hair, skin, nails and bodies. I bit my nails, never had time for a blow-dry and had some strange pore issue which meant make-up was just absorbed into my skin, and so the whole exercise was futile. It didn't matter: they were professional wives, and I was a professional press officer who had an important job to do (albeit nothing to do with press). I put on some lip gloss, flushed the loo for authenticity, and opened the door. If I was caught my plan was just to pretend I was lost – pretty credible on such a huge boat.

I scanned the corridor quickly and turned towards a set of descending mahogany stairs with a gold handrail. My limited yacht experience told me the master stateroom was usually towards the front. At the bottom of the stairs my feet sank into a deep cream carpet and I was momentarily entranced by a beautiful abstract artwork. I turned right, and through two heavy glass doors I could see a lounge with an enormous flat screen on the wall. It was empty and immaculate.

Vincent had alluded to 'illegal secrets'. The likelihood of walking in on an underage orgy within the next two minutes now seemed pathetically misguided. But I still didn't want to fail. Whatever Janey had said, I believed Vincent did have a higher ideal for himself and for the industry. Successful people made choices, took stands, didn't sit on the fence.

I took a deep breath, turned and quickly tiptoed in the opposite direction. Time was running out. My absence would start to look suspicious. The mahogany double doors were closed; I pushed hard on them, stepping over a small ledge into another cream-carpeted corridor. The whole interior was more tasteful than I had expected; I thought there would be leopardskin and leather. A room on my right had the door open; it was a small gym with a treadmill, rowing machine and Stair-Master. The corridor widened into what looked like a private office, with a heavy mahogany desk and studded leather chair. There were neat cupboards on one wall and a bank of four TV monitors on the other. Bingo! The double doors must be the master stateroom. I hurried forward and gently turned the gold door handle.

'What are you doing, Kate?'

I spun round with such force that I lost all composure and nearly my balance. Lisa stood with a man in a white shirt and epaulettes. The captain. They stared at me stony-faced. My mind went blank and blood rushed to my cheeks.

'Lisa, hey, I was hoping you were here …'

'Here? In Harry's private quarters?'

'No,' I laughed nervously, 'of course not, I mean, I was just lost, you know. The boat, I mean yacht, is amazing and huge and I just …'

Their expressions remained fixed. I couldn't remember how to act normal.

'The cocktail is on the rear middle deck. You've found your way to Harry's private deck, fifty metres in the wrong direction,' Lisa said, holding my gaze for a second longer than was comfortable. 'Come on, let's get you back to the party; they're getting ready to go.'

We walked in silence back up the stairs, out of a side door and along the length of the yacht. I was burning with humiliation. I kept my eyes on the deck and my mouth shut. What had begun with the promise of professional glory had ended in shame. I'd expected to feel righteous, but I was just full of self-disgust.

Just before we got to the cocktail terrace, Lisa turned to face me.

'I work for a ruthless boss too, you know. Everything is a competition to them. They'll do anything to defeat the opposition. Most of the time they don't even know what battle they're fighting, they're so obsessed with crushing the opponent.' She sighed. 'It's a job, Kate, that's all.'

I struggled to look her in the eye, forced a small smile in acknowledgement of her trying to make me feel better, and carried on to the guests.

The women were collecting handbags and wraps. Vincent turned and gave a very subtle questioning nod. I shook my head with as little movement as possible. He scowled and rolled his eyes, then turned and led the way down the stairs to the lower deck.

The shoes waited in a neat line on the decking in front of a row of chairs.

'We're going to the Elton John party,' Vincent said, looking round for an ashtray in which to tap a long curl of cigarette ash.

'Oh great, I did actually ...'

'You can go now.' He gave up and handed the burning stub to a steward, then sat on the chair, extending his foot. A steward obliged by slipping on his loafer.

I pretended to check my phone messages, as the guests started to leave. Then I sat down, taking my time to tie my shoes.

'Kate!' Vincent shouted from the dock.

'Yes?' I jumped up, hobbling with one shoe on, the other in my hand, over the walkway.

'My phone?'

'Oh yes, of course.'

I unclipped my handbag and pulled out the slim Nokia, so new it wasn't available for retail, and the Viraguard. He slipped the phone in his trouser pocket, spritzed his hands and upped his pace to catch the departing party guests.

I put on my other sandal, positioning the straps around the blister that had sprung up on my little toe on the trip over. Kylie's voice boomed over the microphone.

'Welcome to Monte Carlo – now let's party!' The neighbouring guests erupted into cheers and whoops.

I turned in the opposite direction, away from the party-of-the-year, and hobbled back towards *Aqua Princesse*. As I was about to mount the walkway I stopped. I was full of undirected anger and frustration, and the last thing I wanted was to sleep. I scrabbled in the handbag for my mobile, scrolled through contacts and hit 'Call'.

'Hi, Tomasz, it's Kate from Dupont Lamborghini. Do you still fancy that drink?'

Monaco GP paddock
Sunday, 7.40 a.m.

I was in the Paddock by seven-thirty. Janey had stumbled in around five, making a hell of a noise. She walked into the glass shower door and dropped her hefty washbag on the bathroom floor, shushing herself loudly. I couldn't face a party post-mortem before breakfast, especially today, so I'd slipped out leaving Janey flat on her back, snoring loudly in her red party dress.

Breakfast was laid out for the team in The Wing. The tables were full, with mechanics and engineers munching through full English breakfasts, cereal, toast and croissants. Avoiding any social interaction, I helped myself to a sausage, beans and a slice of toast, poured a mug of builder's tea, and walked up steadily to the office, trying to keep the thudding in my head to a minimum. My jittery stomach was vocal in its hangover protestations, and a fry-up was the necessary tonic.

I was relieved to be the first one in the office: I needed pre-race-day peace.

I leant forward to put the tea on my desk and a burning pain shot up through my already fragile body as trouser fabric chafed broken skin. My hand shot automatically to my hip in defence.

Standing by my desk, I scooped a forkful of beans on to the toast and took a bite. It had a familiar, reassuring taste: my stomach accepted it happily. It could have been any one of hundreds of hungover mornings at uni, or childhood suppers. Beans on toast – nothing beat it. Especially on a morning like this.

I shovelled in another large mouthful and lifted the napkin to wipe away some crumbs.

Then I smelt him. Instinctively I ran my nose along my arm; the foreign scent on my skin was like an intrusion, but at the same time familiar and instantly evocative.

The image of his chest arched away from mine, tiny droplets of sweat beading under the blonde hairs, Sergio Rossi heels behind his head, the cold of the glass desk on my back.

I shook the image away and stuffed in a big mouthful of sausage and beans. Looking through the window the paddock was deserted except for the real workers, the mechanics and engineers tramping in and out of the motorhomes for breakfast before a long day in the garage. The air-con was belching out glacial burps at waist height.

Limbs entwined on the carpet, the belt that wouldn't undo, his lips tasting of mint and lime, naked flesh on flesh, the liberation of being driven by feeling and not thought.

Which is exactly why it was a bad idea.

My mind was a fuzz of partial, occasionally acutely clear, non-sequential images and sensations. I closed my eyes and tried tentatively to put everything into some sort of order. By the third mojito our knees, as we perched on the bar stools in the American-style hang-out, no longer brushed, they touched. The rest of the punters, too many of whom were familiar paddock faces, had faded into the background. It was just a case of where? My room on Vincent's yacht was off-limits – thank God I'd retained that much sense – and Tomasz was staying in Nice. There was urgent hand-in-hand staggering past endless restaurant tables alongside the paddock, a fumbling for passes, tumbling into a kiss, clumsy and intense, against the glass wall of The Wing's lift.

Oh, God. No, no, no.

My hand found the sore on my hip. Carpet burn. Rare llama carpet burn from Vincent's office. *For Christ's sake, Kate!*

I stabbed at a soggy piece of toast with my fork; the stupid air-con had made it cold. Tannin floated on the top and inside of the mug; I slurped at it anyway. A phrase I had read somewhere, that a woman lost eighty per cent of her power when people knew who she'd slept with, surfaced tannin-like from my rum-sodden brain.

No one could find out.

I picked up my phone and clicked on the call list. Tomasz's name was still at the top with yesterday's date and 21.47 call time. My finger hovered over the green button. I checked for texts. Nothing. I put the phone back on the desk.

I swirled the last dregs of the tea and swallowed. Five or so photographers stood lethargically at the turnstiles. The fans on the outside were the only ones showing any early-morning enthusiasm. The party principality seemed to be suffering from one collective hangover.

It was Tomasz's fault: he had taken control. I'd just followed his lead, not unwillingly, not passively, but for once enjoying the lack of responsibility.

An image flashed up of me pulling his shirt off, actually ripping it. My subconscious wasn't buying it.

I forced myself down into the chair, yelping as a burning pain shot up and throbbed in my thigh.

Spontaneity, giving in to instinct, would be the death toll. Vincent would never act on impulse.

If only I'd just gone back to the yacht. If only I hadn't called. Damn Vincent. Damn Harry and his invisible whores.

'Whose invisible whores?' a voice croaked from somewhere under my desk.

'Aaaaagh!' I screamed and recoiled; the chair rolled back to the desk behind. 'What the …?'

A bundle of clothes that hadn't been visible before started to move, accompanied by a deep animal-like groan. With the clear lack of physical threat, my heart rate began to slow from imminent cardiac arrest and I began to worry how much of my internal monologue I had spoken out loud. I rolled forward on the chair and prodded the lump with my toe. It whimpered and rolled over, and a ghostly white unshaven face flopped on to the floor.

'JB! *What* are you doing here?'

There was a heaving sound that turned into a guttural cough.

'Did you sleep here all night?'

'Dedication, babe,' he said with a hefty stomach burp, as I swiftly withdrew my foot and moved it up on to the chair. 'Didn't wanna miss the photoshoot this morning.'

'It's at ten – you've got ages. The drivers aren't even here yet.'

'Also,' – he crawled on all fours at snail speed out from under the desk. I recoiled at the stale alcohol stench that accompanied him – 'I sort of got lost last night.'

'What do you mean? You had my invite for that party, didn't you?'

'Oh yeah, baby. I *love* Kylie. Really. I really love Kylie. *I'm spinning around …*'

'The yacht is just there.' I pointed through the glass window to the Nouvelle Digue, a hundred metres away. 'How did you get lost?'

'I sort of couldn't remember where my hotel was.' He slumped on to Tuffy's chair, his head collapsing on to his arms on the desk. 'I can't believe you missed it, Kate. It was the party to end all parties.'

To: daniel.mathers@harveynichols.com
From: Kateellison@dupontf1.com
Subject: Bonjour from Monaco!

I tried to call but seeing as it's not even 7 your time on Sunday morning I understand why you didn't pick up! How's everything? Feels like forever since we spoke. Em says she hasn't seen much of you. Have you been partying like it's 1999?! New man?
Monaco is exhausting and I got drunk and fucked up last night. Could really do with you making me laugh about it….
Send me your news. K xxx

To: Kateellison@dupontf1.com
From: postmaster@harveynichols.com
Subject: Delivery Service Failure

This is an automatically generated Delivery Status Notification.
Delivery to the following recipients failed.

daniel.mathers@harveynichols.com

The photoshoot JB was so diligently preparing for was with the drivers and ZeBeD. My objective was to show that Dupont Lamborghini was 'friends' with the hottest music stars, top supermodels, etc. All part of our quest to be brighter, better and cooler than our competitors. So in exchange for a priceless Monaco GP pass, the iconic rap star would stand for a few seconds next to our drivers. And thus, by PR osmosis, Dupont Lamborghini would become indisputably hip.

It was five to ten. The drivers were in their suites, but no sign of ZeBeD, or Janey for that matter, who had dealt with his 'people' about the logistics. I hovered in front of The Wing, scanning the crowds of F1 faces who mingled in the big open space that was the cross-section of entry to the paddock from the town and the port.

I couldn't concentrate. I was freaking out at the thought that I had left some sort of incriminating evidence in Vincent's office. It was hard to believe two drunken shaggers left it Vincent-perfect. I tried to word a text to Tomasz.

Hi thx for last night…
DELETE
Hi last night was nice but…

DELETE
Hi last night was a mistake. Pls lets keep btwn us.
SEND
His reply was fast.
Oh so they were screams of protest…? ☺
He was so arrogant.

'Hey, Katie.' Tuffy stepped away from his tour group, the family of Britain's most high-profile entrepreneur, whose wife was sporting a crocodile-skin handbag that would have Em throwing paint. 'You're either pretty stressed or practising for "Dance Dance Revolution". May I be of any assistance?'

'Have you seen Janey or ZeBeD? The drivers have an engineers' meeting in five minutes, and this is the only time slot they have today.'

'Yo.' He struck a clumsy rap pose. 'Isn't that Janey over there in that rabble at the turnstiles?'

I sprinted over to the gate where several extra-large people were jostling, some X-rated names were being called, and somewhere in the middle was a Dupont Lamborghini uniform.

I couldn't scan myself out of the turnstiles as the area on the other side was chock-full, so I leant across and pulled at the collar of Janey's shirt. She turned round; her skin was grey, hair dishevelled and eyes watery.

'What the hell …?'

'I've got two passes for ZeBeD and a guest. There are nine of them. He won't come in without his security.' Her voice was hoarse and defeated.

Fuelled by instantaneous outrage, I climbed on to a small table at the end of the turnstiles.

'Hey!' I shouted at the heaving throng. 'HEY!' I grabbed at an enormous bicep under a silk shirt and pulled. 'BACK OFF AND CALM DOWN.'

Incredibly, they did just that. I didn't have a plan as to what to do next, but something just took over. I had found my punchbag.

'There are two passes for ZeBeD and a guest. There is no flexibility and no negotiation. If you want them,' – I fixed a stare on the singer's diamond-encrusted shades – 'take them now, or go back to your yacht. This' – I circled my finger over their heads – '... this behaviour is unacceptable.'

Christ, I had just quoted Miss Franks, my odious geography teacher, to the world's biggest-grossing music star.

Nine tough faces looked up at me. I climbed awkwardly down from the table.

'Janey, over to you.'

With a weak smile, she fumbled in her pocket for the passes. I turned and marched back to The Wing. It seemed appropriate to follow up with a strong exit, even though my whole body was trembling.

As I approached I spotted Derek Capshaw, the dirt-digging journalist from the *Daily News*, slither his way in through The Wing's sliding doors. We had a semi-open policy towards letting the media in for hospitality, but it was an unwritten rule that it was only open to 'friends of the team'. Helen had warned me Capshaw was trouble. He thrived on gossip and scandal, and was one of the few who didn't care about being popular. Derek Capshaw was exactly who I didn't need near Vincent right now.

I ran towards the doors to see him disappear into the lift. *Where on earth did he think he was going?*

I took the stairs two at a time, glancing down the corridor as I passed each floor. Marketing all clear, Lamborghini all clear. *Shit, was he heading up to Vincent?*

Spurred on by the desire to redeem myself for last night's failed mission on Harry's yacht, I ran up to the fourth floor and straight into Ivan, the overzealous and of late omnipresent security guard.

'Can I help you, Ms Ellison?'

My lungs burned as I struggled to catch my breath. 'I've got to see Vincent, is he…?'

'Mr. Dupont is in a meeting.'

'Listen, did you see a scruffy-looking guy, wonky smile, just come up here? I think he's trying to see Vincent.' I tried to step past him, but he seemed to fill the corridor.

'Mr. Dupont is in a meeting. I can give him a message when he's finished.'

'Listen, this is no bloody joke, Ivan.' I pronounced it 'Yvonne', for my own personal satisfaction. 'If Derek Capshaw walks in on Vincent with no appointment, I'm in big shit, ok? He's bad news for Vincent and for the team. I'm not a security threat, so for the love of God will you stop being such a jobsworth and just …' I ducked under his arm, which was unsubtly barring my way, and sprinted to Vincent's door. Ivan's heavyset frame was against him in terms of nimbleness, and I got the door handle down before he reached me. I pushed the door, almost falling into the office.

'Vincent, I just …' I looked up to see Vincent with his arm around Derek Capshaw's shoulder, handing him a coffee. *Vincent serving coffee?* They were laughing. Both stopped and looked at me. Vincent shot a look behind me at Ivan, who filled the door frame.

'I'm sorry, sir, she slipped past.'

'Get out, Keht.'

Dupont Lamborghini F1 Team

PRESS RELEASE

Monaco Grand Prix
Sunday

Race

Marcel Müller claimed his first Formula One podium with a second-place finish at the Monaco Grand Prix. Enrico Costa crossed the line under a second later to claim third place.

Marcel Müller – 2nd

'This was an incredibly tough race. I just escaped the Massa and Santos collision, and when I read the pitboard said P2, I had to put it out of my mind and just focus on getting to the finish with no mistakes. To get my first F1 podium in Monaco is just an incredible experience.'

Enrico Costa – 3rd

'This result shows that the team has made progress, but we are just not strong enough in qualifying. It's practically impossible to overtake here so I just hung behind Marcel until the chequered flag.'

Vincent Dupont, Team Principal

'A positive weekend for the team with two strong finishes. Our hard work in the TechQ is beginning to pay off.'

Media contact

Kate Ellison – Kateellison@dupontf1.com

www.dupontf1.com

196

CHAPTER 8

Selfridges Bridal Suite
Oxford Street, London
Wednesday, 11.20 a.m.

'Hmm, upper arms on display ... there's a danger of bingo wings, don't you think ... Kate?'

'What? Sorry, oh, that's beautiful.' I looked up at Em in a strapless Vera Wang wedding dress. At least, it could have been a Vera Wang. She had tried on about thirty dresses. I was trying to keep up, and keep the impending *Sport Heroes* interview out of my mind.

'But do my arms look crêpey?' She pulled at the taut skin under her arm.

'I don't really know what that ... No, no they don't.'

'I prefer the Badgley Mischka.' Danny was flitting around pulling dresses off the rails, laying them up against Em or casting them away with a tut and a flick of his wrist as if their lack of perfection was personally offensive to him. 'The Mikado A-line highlights your curves.'

They might as well have been talking Urdu. Twenty-eight of the dresses looked great to me, all except for one with a meringue skirt and another with long lace sleeves. Emma had big boobs and long legs, so she looked good in everything. In truth I had never understood the whole fuss about wedding dresses. I was doing my best as it was so important to Em, but I could only say 'beautiful' so many times. They were madly in love, it was the big wedding she wanted, and Freddie was hardly going to change his mind over a dress. I pulled myself up straight in the hot pink Louis XVI armchair. I was here in body as moral support, but my head was racing with all things Vincent.

Had I covered all the questions for the interview in the briefing sheet? Were the questions suitably focused on Vincent as a successful businessman, and not on his lifestyle? Were any questions double-edged? Could any answer be misinterpreted? Did he sound capable but not arrogant? Preparing media Q&As were an endless worry. Journalists wanted spontaneity; a TV show needed personality and drama. While I needed predictability, even banality. Total control.

I also had to ensure everything was Vincent-proof. Would the DHL order of Viraguard (to replace the raspberry scent version) arrive at the hotel by tomorrow? Had I stapled his itinerary with one neat staple at a perfect diagonal to the corner? Would he prefer the corporate to the team shirt? It was a yes to all of these.

This part was getting easier. Most of Vincent's tics had become so ingrained that they had morphed into my own. I no longer used blue biros: I'd actually faltered at the bank last week when they gave me one to sign with. I found myself only buying Evian Sport water bottles at

Tesco, had started flushing public loos with my elbow, and was wary of touching loose change. But thankfully I was still blind to the grime in my apartment. Obsessive-compulsive behaviour required a level of energy I just couldn't summon in my limited free time.

'I'm not sure that these aren't all a little too glam for me. I mean, it's my day, I should be true to myself, right?'

Danny stared, a white fox-fur stole with diamante clasp hanging limply from his hand.

I jumped up, linking my arm with Danny's free one and holding it tight. 'Of course, Em, you've got to be comfortable.'

'Comfortable? What the hell ...?'

I sank my nails lightly into the flesh on Danny's wrist.

'We've been working with this programme in Brazil that supports budding designers who make outfits out of totally recycled materials.'

I kept a tight grasp on Danny.

'I know that sounds weird,' Em continued impassioned, 'but some of these guys are so creative it's amazing. They've got nothing, and yet they make the most beautiful pieces from things they've found.'

'Rubbish again? Come on! Oww, Kate!' He shook me off. 'Ok, Stella it is. She's ethical and into animal rights, and at least her dresses are beautiful.' He turned to the assistant. 'What are you waiting for? Go!'

Danny was always pretty hyper, but today he seemed especially wired. He'd ordered a huge rack of dresses and barked orders for shoes and accessories. The poor assistant was running around like a startled deer. He had taken over, to Em's and my relief, but his intensity was bringing an extra level of stress to the whole proceedings. I tried to zone back out behind a smiling and nodding mask while I discreetly checked my watch. T minus three hours till the flight to Istanbul and twenty-two hours until the interview.

Please, please, please, let it go well. It was exactly the profile we needed right now. Vincent among only stellar sporting names. An entire one-hour show. Global coverage. And after all, Vincent could handle it; he was born for TV.

When he came into F1 three years ago, everything Vincent touched had turned into trophies, dollars and acres of positive coverage. Now every comment was misinterpreted, good results ignored, bad results highlighted, and marketing foresight dismissed as examples of megalomania. A long, thorough interview was exactly what was needed to remind everyone why they had loved him in the first place.

I just hoped Tomasz was up to the task.

The interview had to be problem-free if I was to make amends for Yachtgate. My embarrassment and loss of dignity carried no weight with Vincent, who punished me for my lack of concrete results with what was tantamount to the silent treatment. In the meantime he was spending more and more time in chats with that creep Capshaw. I didn't understand why, and it didn't bode well.

Since Monaco, I had had a recurring dream that I was in the desert trying to escape (from what it was never clear) up an enormous sand dune in the Sergio Rossi heels. I woke up in a sweat every time.

My mobile beeped with a text from Tomasz.

Hi sorry but need 2 postpone iv. Will text new dates later.

My blood instantly started to boil. *Don't you dare, Tomasz!*

'These shoes won't do, they won't do.' Danny threw a nondescript white satin shoe on to the carpet. 'She might be an eco-warrior, but she won't be climbing any bloody trees.'

'Please, Danny, it's ok.' Em tried to pacify him.

I clicked 'Reply'.

No. the interview cannot be changed. not possible.

'I don't want to see anything that's officially a "wedding shoe".' He made quotation marks with his fingers, and the assistant recoiled as if it was a physical threat. 'Go and bring me every shoe that is white or neutral and elegant. El-e-gant. Go!'

New message.

No can do k, orders from cnn london.

Clutching the phone with enough force to crush it, I hit the call button. I looked up to see Em looking at me with pleading eyes and nodding in Danny's direction. Danny was pulling boxes from the middle of the pile the assistant was carrying.

I made a sympathetic face and held up a finger. 'One minute, OK?' I pointed to the phone. 'I've just got to do one quick thing.' I forced a smile, and her shoulders sagged as she turned back to the shoes.

'How can you not have the Dolce and Gabbana ivory and diamond-encrusted heels?' Danny screeched. 'Harvey Nicks have had them for weeks.'

The phone was ringing. I stood up and walked to the opposite side of the room where a window looked out on to the corner of Oxford Street: no surprise that it was teeming with pedestrians. I took a breath; the blood was pumping so hard in my head that I couldn't think. If I didn't solve this there would be no point flying to the Turkish GP this afternoon, because I'd be out of a job. I wasn't losing my job today.

'Hey, Kate, sorry about this, I know you're upset ...'

'Upset? Are you kidding?' I was trying very hard to whisper. 'We've planned this for months. This is the only hour-long interview Vincent has EVER given.'

'I know, I know all that.' Tomasz was annoyingly calm.

'If you're messing with me because of Monaco ...'

'I'm not. I'm gutted too – you're not the only one who's been working on it. But it's come from the top, and there's nothing I can do.'

'Do you have any idea who you're dealing with? You don't postpone Vincent Dupont.' I wasn't whispering any more.

'Of course, but this is CNN for God's sake, Kate. Tyler Moore, the presenter, is interviewing the president of some African country about a major breakthrough in Aids treatment. It's pretty big stuff.'

I took another breath. How would Vincent deal with this?

'This is what's going to happen. You are going to call your boss and tell him the interview is tomorrow as planned, or never. They either send another presenter or get someone else to interview the African guy. Christ, Aids and Africa, that's hardly a new story is it? Call me when it's done.'

I hit the red button and resisted the urge to throw the phone. I had dealt with it: tough but efficient. That was the only way to get things done.

I turned back to the room, ready to solve the shoe dilemma.

Three dumbstruck faces stared at me: the assistant open-mouthed, Danny confused, like he'd never seen me before, and – worst of all – Em's furrowed expression bordering on disgust.

'I, er ... sorry about that. All sorted, I think.'

'Yeah, sounds like it,' said Danny, 'otherwise you'll send the heavies round to kneecap him, right?' He let out a nasty laugh as he shook his head slowly. 'Who the fuck do you work for?'

'Do you think we could get another round of tea, maybe camomile?' I asked the assistant with a little laugh. She shot out of the door. I was scared by their reaction, scared that Em still looked scared.

'You have to play tough, or they walk all over you. It's a man's world.'

No one replied, and I caught a look between Em and Danny. I forced myself to be jolly.

'So D, why aren't we doing this at Harvey Nicks? Why did you send us to the competition? You always said there was nowhere else we should ever go for such an important occasion.' I smoothed out the train of Em's current dress and piled some cast-offs on to a sofa behind her.

Danny shrugged, 'Just fancied a change.' His voice was flat.

'Excuse me, I'm in 14A by the window – can I squeeze past?'

'Of course, Kate.'

'Oh, hey, Gordon, small world?'

'Not really,' he laughed. 'There are about a hundred and fifty F1 people on this flight.'

Travel was no longer an anonymous affair. The F1 world travelled en masse to most of the races, in fact many key flights in and out of London to the European races were booked out in their totality by the F1 travel agencies.

What I didn't learn until much later was that these travel agencies had long and complicated secret preference lists. X, who would on no account sit next to Y but absolutely had to sit next to Z, and so on. Nothing in F1, it seemed, was unplanned or left to chance.

But I was happy to be sitting next to Gordon. My initial intimidation in the face of such an industry legend had quickly evaporated: he was just too unassuming. He'd been in Formula One since teams consisted of a dozen people, as opposed to the eight hundred or so these days. He had seen it all before and was a mine of libellous stories. I looked forward to our Friday morning chats at the races as he slugged back heavily-sugared Nescafé. He knew everything about everything and everyone. That was not to be underestimated.

After take-off we chatted about the forecast heat wave in Istanbul, and Gordon warned me about the horrendous traffic jams as he folded his *Telegraph* down so that the crossword fitted on his tray table.

'So Vincent's really got his claws into Kato, hasn't he?'

'Oh, he and Vincent are old friends.' My denial retort kicked in on autopilot: I couldn't let my guard down. But I wondered, not for the first time, how on earth he could know about Vincent's priority number one.

Gordon smiled a sweet smile. 'Kate, someone like Vincent doesn't have friends. Well, unless they have multiple billions in the bank.' He chuckled. 'So, yes, maybe they are just that.'

I stayed quiet, rather than embarrassing myself with any more incredible excuses.

'This is Vincent's chance to get rich. He'll sell a big stake to Kato. Then he'll finally fulfil his wish to be independently wealthy.'

'He won't sell the team.' It came out as more of a question than a statement.

'No, no, of course not. He'll sell a stake. The biggest he can manage, but without giving up any control.' He scribbled with his ballpoint on the newspaper, but no ink came out. He rooted around in his inside blazer pocket for another.

'But what would be in it for Kato?' I didn't want to give anything away, but in truth, Gordon clearly knew loads more about both Vincent and Kato. I couldn't confirm anything, and he knew that. So I decided to listen and learn.

'He gets to part-own a team, rock up at races, strut about in a team shirt. It's amazing what people will pay for that privilege.'

'And Vincent would still make all the decisions in the team?'

'Absolutely. Vincent would rather hug a leper than relinquish control. Kato would be nothing more than a VIP guest in uniform. Oh, and he'd get a seat on the pit wall; there's a good twenty million in value just for that.'

'But Vincent's rich – he doesn't need the money.'

'Rich in your and my terms, but not in his terms. I can barely imagine what it costs to run a private plane, heli and yacht, let alone four houses. He must have a retinue of over forty staff.' He scribbled an answer into four across. 'And is he rich, or is it his wife's money? She's worth a tidy packet. Anyway, it doesn't matter. It's not about *need*, because there's never enough money, if there's a possibility to make more. Control freaks like Vincent only live for power and money.' He pulled a small pack of shortbread, which I had seen on offer in the BA lounge, out of another pocket. 'He'll have a plan for that money, I'm just not sure what it is right now.'

It did make sense. Kato was Vincent's number one priority VIP – I mean the gifts, the special TechQ tour, all the secrecy. And it wasn't a discussion about sponsor-ship, as Mike had pointed out, since Kato's companies didn't advertise. Could Kato really be about to invest so much, just for a paddock pass and some team merchan-dise? As for the money, I knew what he wanted it for. Vincent would be making that public tomorrow morning.

The irony of learning about my boss's intentions from a journalist was not lost on me. But Gordon was unfazed. He dipped the shortbread in his tea and carried on with his crossword.

The crew had set up their studio on the waterside terrace of our hotel. It was a stunning location, with the wide Bosphorus strait as a backdrop. Fishing boats and ferries crossed in the background on the river once travelled by Odysseus, and Jason and the Argonauts. I had learnt that factoid as I read the hotel's brochure last night to fall asleep. It also told me that Istanbul been named the 'World's Hippest City', but I knew by now not to expect my Turkish experience to be hip: it would be the usual round trip of hotel, airport and track.

In front of the neat lawn terrace the hotel's motorised launch bobbed on the water, attached by a rope to a small wooden jetty. Two black leather armchairs, symbolically chosen to denote a friendly chat, faced away from the water, angled towards each other, awaiting interviewer and interviewee.

I scanned the set for anything Vincent would hate. Three cameras were set up on tripods. One had a wide angle, taking in the whole scene and backdrop, and the other two were each directed at an armchair. On instruction from an excessively hairy man in a grey sleeveless t-shirt and combat shorts, a girl with a nose ring sat down in one of the armchairs as he focused the camera. There were about eight people busying themselves around the equipment. I nearly tripped over a guy who was lying on the floor collecting the cabling into a bundle with tape.

Tomasz hurried over, acknowledging me with a formal nod: no kiss on the cheeks. It was our first exchange since his curt, defensive text last night.

Iv on as planned. President delayed at home.

'It's important that both Vincent and Tyler are comfortable. I'm getting a small table brought out so there's somewhere to put two glasses of water for them. Do you think this set-up is OK for Vincent?' His pupils were tiny black pinheads, and his forehead sweaty. I recognised the familiar look of stress, adrenaline and borderline panic.

'It's a great location, Tomasz.' Technically, as it was our hotel, *we* should have been congratulated on the location choice, but he needed a boost and I wanted to make peace. 'It's pretty hot, though; do you think we could get some shade over the chairs, otherwise they're going to squint and sweat?'

As predicted by Gordon, the heat wave was in full force. The air was sticky and there was no breeze on the terrace. My designer uniform went clingy in the wrong places, and my feet slid around in my ever more putrid team-issue pumps.

'Yes, good point, I'll get that sorted. Anything else?'

We stood facing the scene.

'He needs to sit on the right-hand side.'

'Oh, but Tyler always ...'

'I'm sorry, but it has to be the right.' I had got better at being polite but firm. The trick was to just make the point and then stop talking – not so easy for a born silence-filler. Vincent's right ear stuck out minutely more than the left. The seating position was non-negotiable.

'Ok, then,' said Tomasz, looking like it wasn't. 'Now come and meet Tyler Moore, the presenter.' He dragged me by the arm to a table with a parasol where a blond man in his forties was having foundation sponged on his face.

'Hey there, you must be …' he shot a glance over to Tomasz, who mouthed my name. '… Kate!' He looked up with a TV smile, holding on to the white towel on his neck with one hand and extending the other. He had those classic American good looks: wholesome, clean, and totally unsexy. Chosen no doubt to up the housewife viewer quota.

His handshake was strong and firm. I expected nothing less.

'Great job on the biographical background, Kate. Is Vincent happy with everything?'

'Yes.' *Like he's ever happy with anything.* 'He'll be down shortly. Are there any last minute changes to the Q&A?'

'No, no, don't you worry.' The make-up artist finished and he sat up, checking his face in a hand-held mirror, and pulling individual curls of hair down on to his forehead with his fingers. 'It's a guideline, after all; we'll go with the flow.'

I caught my breath. *Go with the flow* was not a phrase I wanted to hear. The deal was that we had all the questions in advance to avoid any surprises. Everything was planned, anticipated and co-ordinated to render precisely the intended message. What could not happen was for the presenter to get creative once Vincent was in the hot seat.

I gave a tight smile and my best *don't mess with me* look, but he was too absorbed in his own reflection to see it.

'We know Vincent is tight for time, so we're filming as live. We'll run with no stops except to introduce the inserts, you know, the films.'

He walked over to the armchair and a technician came over to attach a microphone to his shirt.

'I'll go and get Vincent.'

'OK everybody, mobiles off. Tyler, I'm counting you in. Ten seconds. Five … four … three …' The producer finished the countdown in silence, making a slicing motion with his hand to indicate the final two seconds. He then swept his arm in a circle and pointed at Tyler, his cue to start.

'Good evening. I'm Tyler Moore. Welcome to *Sport Heroes*, where we reveal the men behind the myth. My guest tonight took the Formula One world by storm when he burst on to the scene two and half years ago and led the Dupont Lamborghini team to a double world championship victory in their first season: a feat unheard of in the ultra-competitive world of Grand Prix motor racing. He is as renowned for his glamour, style and taste as he is for his success. Please welcome Mr Formula One, Vincent Dupont.'

Vincent sat forward to shake Tyler's hand, showing no sign of how horrific he found the flesh-on-flesh contact, with a broad grin, seventy per cent friendly, thirty per cent modest, the perfect balance. He sat back in the armchair looking comfortable but not too relaxed: his posture said 'engaged and professional' rather than 'arrogant'. Spot on.

'Thank you for having me on the show, Tyler.'

I gave a little sigh of relief that he had got his name right. Vincent had called the host Taylor all week.

'So, Vincent, I'd like to start with the present and work backwards, if that's ok?'

'I'm in your hands, Tyler. Fire away.' Vincent leaned his hands on the arm of the chair. The corporate version of the team shirt, tailored, white with just the Dupont Lamborghini and Telsat logoes elegantly embroidered in silver and aqua on the breast pocket, had been the right call. Infinitely more stylish without the rainbow of logoes that featured on the team shirt, but still corporately correct, branded with our two biggest partners.

Tyler Moore: 'You appeared out of nowhere, taking on and defeating some of Formula One's most experienced and established figureheads. How did you do it?'

Vincent Dupont: 'There's no simple answer to that question, Tyler. Success in such a high-tech and competitive sport can't be defined by one single advantage, and in F1 the line between success and failure is exceedingly fine. Millions of factors come into play. You can have the most intelligent designers and engineers, the fastest drivers, the biggest budget, the most state-of-the-art wind tunnel, and then gusty wind, a faulty tyre pressure or a backmarker hogging the track can throw the most meticulous planning and strategy out the window. This makes it both exhilarating when things go your way, and extremely frustrating when they don't. That said, I think freshness can be an advantage in such an industry. Maybe an advantage we had was that being new we looked at problems in a different way, and that gave us an edge. That and an incredible team spirit.'

TM: 'What motivates you?'

VD: 'Winning. You can't work in sport and not admit to it. Somehow in society these days, we've come to see admitting ambition as a negative. It's our nature. And Formula One offers the toughest judgement. The results of your work are determined in front of hundreds of millions of people every two weeks. There's no grey area. You win or lose. Every two weeks there's another challenge, another chance. It is incredibly harsh, but somewhat addictive for competitive people.'

Good answer. Better than the one I wrote.

TM: 'But there must be a secret. What's the secret of your success?'

VD: 'There is no secret. It's hard work and a good dose of luck. Seriously, I've always been highly self-motivated, and somewhat of a perfectionist. I strive for the best in everything, and instil a similar work ethic in my co-workers.'

Co-workers … nice!

'But let's be clear, Tyler. I didn't win those world championships alone …

Good, a bit of humility.

… it was a team effort of nine hundred people, and Enrico Costa didn't do a bad job either!'

TM: 'What's the difference between a good boss and a great boss?'

VD: 'You'll have to ask my team if I'm a great boss! But I strive to listen and learn from those around me. I see my job as a people manager, channelling talent and energy so that it's used to maximum effect. We have six hundred members of staff in Lower Bledcote and three hundred working on the engine in Sant'Agata Bolognese with

Lamborghini. I'm not an engineer, I'm not a designer, but I understand their strengths and oversee output to achieve maximum efficiency while working within our budget. You could call me an engineer in efficiency.'

It was going well. Vincent was relaxed and chatty. As usual he was witty, but he never misspoke. I started to relax. I glanced over at Tomasz, who gave me a thumbs-up.

TM: 'What is Formula One for you? A sport? A business? A TV spectacle?'

VD: 'Formula One is many things. At its heart it's about state-of-the-art racing cars competing around a race track. It's also about the technology required to make a car cover three hundred and five kilometres in as short a time as possible. It's about the drivers, supremely talented sportsmen who embody the aspirations of many the world over. It's about the six hundred million viewers around the globe who plan their weekend around each Grand Prix. It's about the hundreds of millions of corporate dollars spent in pursuit of this goal and the raft of world-class brand names who commit to the challenge. Ultimately, it's about the relentless pursuit of perfection and the purity of the quest to win.'

TM: 'Tell me about working with drivers. You have a close relationship with Enrico Costa. Does there need to be a strong bond for success?'

Vincent's left eye twitched almost imperceptibly.

VD: 'Enrico and I came into Formula One together and won the driver's and constructor's titles together, so there is of course a strong relationship there. Drivers are an important part of the formula, but they aren't the only part required for success.'

He's still pissed off about Enrico threatening to sign with Harry.

TM: 'Are you still Mr Formula One, or has that title expired?'

VD: 'You'll have to ask *Time* magazine. But honestly, names mean little to me. Results are what count. That one was fun, but it did sound rather like a cartoon superhero, like I should have been running around in pants and tights. Which, believe me, wouldn't have been enjoyable for anyone!'

TM: 'The Dupont logo, independently from the F1 team, features on your stable of private vehicles: the Gulfstream G200, the Sikorsky S-76 helicopter, the superyacht. It's already become synonymous with your ultraglamorous lifestyle. Is Dupont becoming a stand-alone brand?'

VD: 'I am totally committed to F1. I still have a lot to do there. But I also love luxury and believe that everyone, whatever their financial position, wants and deserves a little luxury. I feel so passionately about this, Tyler, it's become like a calling: to create Dupont, a luxury brand for everyman …'

Blimey, Vincent is heading for a Tom Cruise jumping-on-the-sofa moment. Thank God Tyler's no Oprah.

'… My dream is to use what I learnt from Baron Fontenay, during my years at Fontenay Paris. There are many projects in development. The first Dupont brand announcement will be very soon, in fact.'

Tyler looked straight into the camera. 'Exciting news from Vincent Dupont. After the break we'll look at the private man: what really makes him tick. Don't go away.' He jabbed his finger at the camera with his all-American smile.

'OK, gentlemen. We'll just take a quick break, two minutes,' the producer announced. Tyler looked up at the make-up artist, who ran over with an open powder compact and sponge.

'Keht, cigarettes.' Vincent stood up, unclipped his microphone from his lapel and walked swiftly towards the river, like he was relieved to be in motion again. I handed over the Viraguard first, which was applied and returned. I then opened one of the two Marlboro packets that were a permanent presence in my handbag, pulled out a cigarette, and twisted it to hand it over butt-first. I then scrabbled in the inside zipped pocket for the lighter, which – despite being a solid platinum deadweight – always got lost between my house keys, lip salve, loose change and tampons. I pulled out the correct item, and the cigarette was lit.

'It's going well,' I said as I tried to subtly swerve from the jet of smoke Vincent exhaled. He stared out across the river. The sun rays off the water were almost blinding. A delicious spicy smell emanated from the hotel kitchen, wafting among the exhaust fumes of the fishing boats.

'It's too hot, the camera's too low, it's trying to shoot up my nose, and the presenter needs deodorant.' He dabbed at his forehead with a Kleenex, then stretched out his hand. 'Mirror and comb.'

'Ok, could you take your seats again, please!' the producer shouted.

Vincent passed me the half-smoked cigarette and walked languidly back to the armchair.

Tyler was cued back in.

'Two and a half years ago no one had heard of Vincent Dupont, and last year he ranked third among *Luxury* magazine's 'ten most alluring'. Let's have a look at Vincent off-duty.'

'Cue insert!' shouted the producer, his eyes fixed on the small TV monitor at his feet that indicated the camera angle. It showed the footage I had sent of Vincent and the baroness riding, his visit to Great Ormond Street Children's Hospital, him pointing out an Old Master in the Oxford mansion, and him reading in his wood-panelled study.

TM: 'We've talked about your successful career, now I'd like to take a look at the private Vincent Dupont. You've done everything well. You certainly married well. You married the daughter of your mentor, now the Baroness Fontenay.'

VD: 'Yes, I'm a very lucky man.'

TM: 'We don't see your wife very often. Does she travel with you?'

VD: 'Not very often. My wife is a very private person, and isn't comfortable with the media spotlight at the Grand Prix. She's also a devoted equestrian. We have a stable of twelve thoroughbreds at our home in Gloucestershire undergoing eventing training. That's her passion, and it's naturally very time-consuming. She's also a patron of several charities, including Great Ormond Street Hospital Charity and Medecins Sans Frontières. She's very committed to these causes, and she's a tireless fund-raiser.'

TM: 'How do you relax?'

VD: 'I don't think I ever do. But when we have time together, my wife and I like to go for a good hack on the horses, walk in the grounds, eat some good food, and drink a fine bottle of Bordeaux.'

TM: 'You worked for Baron Fontenay, your wife's father, for ten years. What was his role in your life?'

VD: 'The Baron was my mentor, and I feel privileged to have been able to call him a great friend. He was an inspirational man and businessman. He's widely known as the hugely successful founder of Fontenay Paris, which he built up to be the number two cosmetic and perfume company in the world, but few knew the private man who was generous, kind and a great teacher. He took me under his wing, and from him I learnt everything I know about business. If I can be even half as successful as he was, I'll be extremely happy. The world lost a truly great man when he passed away.'

I had never heard Vincent talk about anything personal. He seemed really moved; he spoke slowly, looking off into the distance as if trying to control the emotion. Tyler was working hard on his 'noddies', apparently living the emotion with Vincent through sympathy nods. It was an Oscar-worthy performance. I dug my nails in my thigh to quell a rising snigger.

TM: 'You rose through the ranks very fast at Fontenay Paris. In fact, I believe you were the only non-family member to reach board level. How did you get on the fast track?'

I had spent so much time preparing and editing Vincent's biography that I almost started lip-synching his answer. Looking over I noticed Vincent twiddling his 'D'-insignia cufflink: he was getting either bored or annoyed.

VD: 'I loved working at Fontenay, and worked all the hours I could. Lord Fontenay said he recognised the same determination and focus in me that he himself had.'

TM: 'It's a shame the baron didn't live to see your marriage to his daughter.'

VD: 'It was tough for both me and my wife to have such an important day without him. We always said he was there in spirit, and we toasted him several times. It was one of life's great ironies that, as he commuted from the UK for the working week, his family stayed in Britain, and so I only met Daphne after he passed away, when I attended board meetings with the family.'

TM: 'Tell me about your childhood. How did it shape your ambitions?'

VD: 'Paris is a beautiful city, a stylish, cultural, glamorous city. It was a fabulous place to grow up. There was always so much going on. I think growing up there, I got a taste for beautiful things. And I believe city life encourages ambition.'

TM: 'It must have been overwhelming for a young Polish boy from a small village. How old were you when you moved there?'

Vincent stared at the interviewer. The confident half-smile he had displayed throughout the interview sagged at the corners. He looked dazed, like he'd been put on 'Pause'.

Tyler gave a nervous laugh. 'Vincent, how old were you when you left Poland?'

'I … I …' He started to pull off his shirt mike. '… have to go.'

The sound man sat on the grass below me, holding his headphones and staring at a little box, started waving his arms at the producer.

Vincent stood up, pulled the mike cable out through the buttons on his shirt and unclipped the battery pack from his belt, dropping it all on the chair.

Tyler looked stunned, and looked between the producer and Vincent. 'We haven't finished, Vincent. Where are you going?'

Vincent walked slowly with his eyes fixed forward towards the rear of the hotel. I grabbed my bag off the grass and said the first thing that came into my head.

'Sorry, we have an important meeting.'

'Mr Dupont … we haven't finished …' shouted the producer.

I followed Vincent in through the terrace doors and to the lift as fast as I could walk, my heart beating so loudly in my ears that I was scared I wouldn't be able to hear him. The lift doors slid open as soon as I hit the button, and we both stepped inside. What the hell just happened? Why on earth did they ask him about being Polish? Why did Vincent leave?

As the lift rose, Vincent's breathing became audible; he exhaled heavily through his teeth, making a noise between a whistle and a hiss. The lift doors opened. He strode out, marching left towards the executive suite. His momentum stopped at the door and he stood rigidly in front of it, jaw clenched. I reached into the back pocket of my trousers and pulled out the duplicate small silver key ring. I had to lean around him to get it in the lock, careful to avoid body contact. As the lock released, he pushed at the door with force.

'It was a fucking set-up!' He wheeled round at me as the door clicked shut. I had only just cleared the threshold, and was pinned against the door. His flushed face was centimetres from mine. His breath smelt of stale cigarettes and coffee.

My heart thumped like it was about to break out of my ribcage, and my throat tightened. I looked past him to the wall of windows, desperate to avoid his burning stare.

He turned and marched away towards the fireplace that divided the semi-open-plan suite, only to swing round after five paces and march back.

'What are you here for?'

'I, um, wanted to check everything was all right ...'

'No,' he huffed. 'What are you here *for*? What is your *job*?' He was usually so obsessive about personal space, but he spat out the final words millimetres from my face.

'Erm, press officer.' My heart thundered in my ears. I was incapable of anything but stating the obvious.

'Yes, your job is to organise the press interviews? So why can't you do just that?' He paced, and waved his arms to an invisible audience. His rage was winning the battle for control. For the first time I felt scared.

'You find out the questions, so I can answer them. Is that so hard?'

'No, I did, it's just ...'

'Lazy, lazy, lazy attitude.' He marched across the suite, stopping at one of the windows and looking down in the direction of the crew.

'What's his name, that researcher?' He nodded in the direction of someone outside the window. I stayed put.

'Tomasz Ligas.'

He continued to stare out of the window, then nodded slowly to himself twice. He stomped into the bathroom, swung the door closed. I could hear running taps.

I leant on the door, resting my head back. I took a deep breath, then a second and a third. A dull ache behind my right eye swelled into a full-blown throbbing headache. My stomach was doing its best impression of a Moulinex hand mixer churning on the strong Turkish coffee and sickly-sweet pastry I'd stuffed down for breakfast. My mobile burst into *Making Your Mind Up* by Bucks Fizz. I grabbed it out of my pocket, as much to stop the nauseating noise as to answer the call. It had to be Tomasz.

'Yes!'

'Hey babe, Bill Gates or Bill Clinton?' Danny's chirpy voice filled my ear.

'What?'

'Gimme a Bill. Bill PC, or Bill BJ?'

The noise of running water in the bathroom stopped.

'For Chrissake Danny, I can't ...'

'Come on, Kate, it's life or death ... remember ...'

'Not now!' I pressed the red button, cutting Danny off, as Vincent hooked his elbow around the bathroom door and swung it open. He walked out, air-drying his hands. He looked annoyed, but not crazed like before. His shirt was undone. He walked past me to the walk-in closet then reappeared a few moments later, buttoning up a fresh team shirt.

So many questions swirled around my head. I couldn't help if I didn't know what the problem was. But Vincent was doing a mighty job of ignoring me. And I couldn't face another attack.

'Ivan!' Vincent shouted as he stuffed the papers from his desk into his briefcase.

The surly security guard appeared in the doorway of a side room. *He was bloody everywhere.*

'The car is ready, sir.'

'Let's go.'

I followed them out, opting to take the stairs to avoid an uncomfortable lift journey. As the lift doors closed I heard Tomasz's name mentioned again.

I was supposed to go with them to the circuit, but it was pretty clear I was persona non grata. Anyway, I needed a few moments alone in my room to get my head together. I'd find my own way to the track.

I got to the door of room 105, realising simultaneously that I had left my key at reception. I had taken Vincent's, of course. No risk that I would be caught without his key. Just as my handbag was never without three bottles of Viraguard hand spray, two packets of Marlboro Reds and a heavy platinum lighter. It was becoming a familiar pattern: I had everything Vincent needed, but I had travelled to Bahrain with no wash bag and to Monaco with no wallet.

I slumped to the carpet, with my back against the door. I didn't have the energy to run another errand. I needed a few moments of peace to clear the noise from my head.

It wasn't the travelling or the fourteen-hour days that were so draining, it was the permanent state of heightened alert. Always on the lookout for the next disaster. Checking and double-checking facts, details. Who said what? Who wrote what? Who promised what? Did I have guarantees in writing to that effect? What ulterior motive did X have? What did that question really mean? How could that sentence be twisted into a negative? Could any one of our partners be upset by that answer?

And still things seemed to go wrong.

In a neighbouring room a vacuum cleaner started up. I drew up my knees and lent my head on them. It was strangely comforting, and for a moment I felt quite relaxed.

'So I guess we're both in the shit?'

I looked up to see Tomasz standing next to me.

'I saw Vincent leave in his car with that beefcake. I guess the interview is finished.'

'You guessed right.' I couldn't look him in the eye; I was too drained for a fight.

'Kate, you know it wasn't my intention to piss him off.' He sat down next to me. 'CNN gave me the research job on Vincent as a test. If I did a good job it could lead to a full-time role.'

I stared at my shoes, retying the small useless bow on the right one, to avoid eye contact. Furious as I was with him, it seemed true: why would he risk angering one of the most important men in the industry he wanted to work in?

'I've wanted to work in F1 since I was a kid. I worked for Przeglad Sportowy last season for no salary, just to get my hand in the door.'

'It's your foot – to get your foot in the door. Anyway, at least you've completed a season. I'm not sure I'll make it that far.'

'I wasn't about to screw up my first big opportunity.'

'No, so you screwed up mine instead.'

We sat in silence. There was no way I was going to feel sorry for him. Tomasz pulled a crumpled red and white packet out of his pocket.

'Cigarette?'

'There's no smoking in the corridor, and anyway I gave up three years ago …' I sounded like a spoilt child. 'Fuck it, go on then.'

I reached for the packet. 'What are those?'

'Samsun 216, Turkey's finest. They were all they had at my B and B.'

'If I'm going to smoke, I'm going to do it properly.' I pulled my handbag open and brought out Vincent's Marlboros. 'This is a proper cigarette.'

I pulled a butt out half a centimetre and offered the packet to Tomasz, resisting the instinct to pull the whole thing out and hand it over, like I would for Vincent. I put a second one between my lips and lit both with the platinum Dupont-engraved lighter. I inhaled hard. It was harsh and bitter in my throat – satisfying and disgusting in equal measure.

'So, what the hell was that about Poland?'

'Vincent is Polish.'

'Don't be ridiculous, he's French. Does Vincent Dupont sound Polish to you?'

'No, but Wincent Ponieważ does.' He pronounced the surname 'Pon-yeah-vosh'.

I swivelled round to face Tomasz. He looked back from under his floppy fringe, exhaling away from me out of the corner of his mouth.

'You're just making that up.'

'Look, he moved to Paris with his parents when he was about twelve. They were very poor and he obviously didn't want to be stigmatised, so at some point he changed his name to something very French. He cut 'Ponieważ' down to 'Pont' and, I'm guessing, added the 'Du' to suggest semi-noble roots. 'Vincent' is almost the same: he just changed the first letter.' Tomasz opened a matchbox and laid it between us on the carpet as an ashtray.

'How would you know this?'

'Well, in what I previously thought was a lucky coincidence, some hand of fate playing finally in my favour, I come from Gorlice in the south of Poland, which is about thirty-five kilometres from Jaslo, where he's from.' He took a serious smoker's drag on the cigarette, turning a good half-centimetre to ash in one toke.

'After high school my first job was working on the local newspaper.' He paused for a second, as if he was trying to gauge how much background info I needed. 'I got given all the really mundane stories to look into. One was about the standard of care in a local nursing home. I went to interview the old people there, one of whom was Mrs Ponieważ.'

'Vincent's mother?'

'No, his aunt. His father's sister. His mother and father went with him to Paris. Anyway, she talked a lot and I felt sorry for her as she was clearly lonely. So I sat with her for a whole afternoon, as there was nothing else to do, drinking *czwórniak* mead as she went off on tangents about the past and her family. Then, some time after the fourth glass, while we were sharing a plate of pasties I'd brought, she started saying how proud she was of her nephew. How he was a big successful businessman in Paris.' He stubbed out the cigarette and rubbed his eyes with the palms of his hands. 'Then the photo albums came out, and I swear there was no question it was Vincent. I mean, he was twelve in the photos, his hair was lighter and of course he didn't have the tan, but the erect posture was the same: the piercing green eyes, the hook nose. She didn't know about Formula One, I doubt she'd had any contact since he left. I tell you, I nearly choked on my Pierogi …'

I leant my head in my hand and frowned.

'… the pasty. Anyway, I looked into some records after that and it was all true. The trail went dry when they left Jaslo in 1970.'

'So you found out four years ago; why did you wait until now to say something?'

'I was waiting for my big break. *Sport Heroes* was supposed to reveal "the Man behind the Myth", so it was a perfect chance.' He spun the cigarette packet absent-mindedly between his fingers. 'But listen, you have to understand, this wasn't supposed to be some sort of exposé to ridicule or embarrass Vincent. Quite the opposite: it's an inspiring rags-to-riches story. He's an amazing figurehead for Polish people, a shining example of achievement through ambition.'

'I'm pretty sure he wouldn't agree with you.'

'He was really pissed-off?'

'He doesn't like surprises.'

Tomasz let out a big sigh, tilting his head back on the wall and closing his eyes. 'Figurehead he may be, but seems like a hellish boss.'

'Not at all; he just likes things done properly – you know, thoroughly. I know it looks extreme from the outside, but it works.' I sighed. 'It's just not the best timing, there's, well, he's under quite a lot of pressure at the moment.'

'No results, no money and a number one driver off to the enemy. I see what you mean.'

'Enrico's not going anywhere.'

'Not yet, anyway. Rumour is if Vincent can't secure a major cash injection the whole team is going under.'

Christ, I had no idea things were that bad. I took a stiff drag, watching the ash hit the butt, and stubbed it out in the matchbox. 'Look, there's no way.' I tried to sound convincing. 'Does Vincent look like a guy who'd let that happen?'

'No, but well, as we just found out, appearance and reality are two very different things.' He stood up and stretched out his hand to pull me up. 'Hey, Kate, cheer up. We're partners in shit right now: let's at least climb out together'.

'I just remembered: on top of everything, I slammed the phone down on my best friend.'

'It's always the loved ones who bear the brunt.'

I looked down at my watch. 'Damn, I've got to get to the track. Vincent is en route, so that makes me late.'

'Grab your stuff. I'll give you a lift.' He smiled the smile, the one that got me last time. 'Unless, of course ...'

'No.'

Dupont Lamborghini F1 Team

PRESS RELEASE

Turkish Grand Prix
Otodrom Istanbul Park
Sunday

Race

Dupont Lamborghini F1 dominated the Turkish Grand Prix, with Enrico Costa taking his second race win of the season and Marcel Müller claiming second place. Enrico has taken the lead from Riccardo Santos in the Drivers' Championship.

Enrico Costa – 1st

'Race weekends don't get much better than this. From the moment we hit the track in practice on Friday, the car felt fantastic. I got a good start off the grid and kept my lead, so it was just a case of not making any mistakes, and I didn't!'

Marcel Müller – 2nd

'It was a tough race today. I got wheelspin on the grid and was down to sixth at the first corner, but I attacked immediately and got past both Ferraris by lap two. Our three-stop strategy worked well and the boys did a great job to get me out of my second pit-stop ahead of Massa. I'm very happy to bring home 18 points for the team.'

Vincent Dupont, Team Principal

'Enrico drove an outstanding fault-free race to a very well-deserved win. After his terrible start, Marcel put in a strong performance to claw his way up to second. The 1-2 result was a satisfying end to a weekend of great teamwork.'

Media contact

Kate Ellison – Kateellison@dupontf1.com

www.dupontf1.com

CHAPTER 9

Le Manoir aux Quat' Saisons
Great Milton, Oxfordshire
Sunday, 10.45 p.m.

Our table collectively gasped as four waiters arrived with quite the most spectacular birthday cake, presented on a huge black board. A circular central cake had been covered in liquid milk chocolate. The surrounding sixteen mini-circles, in milk, dark and white chocolate, rose on tiny individual podiums around the central cake like a Busby Berkeley sweeping staircase. Finely sculpted chocolate flowers intertwined around the podiums, bearing mini-bunches of redcurrants in their petals. All it missed were a hundred tiny chocolate showgirls. A single red candle burned in the corner.

'Happy birthday, your lordship,' the head waiter said with a small bow of the head.

'Thank you, François. But how many times do I have to tell you to call me Tuffy? I *love* this cake.' He clapped his hands together in delight. 'I've had the exact same one for thirty of my thirty-five birthdays. Raymond Blanc designed it for me.' He grinned like the over-aged child that he was.

'Ha-ppy birth-day to you …' Mike led, and Janey and I joined in an out-of-tune, painfully slow and semi-hushed rendition of the birthday song. It wasn't really appropriate in the Manoir's elegant conservatory dining room, but that cake, and our bubbly birthday boy, demanded some sort of climax.

Tuffy had invited his 'work chums' out for a small birthday dinner. It was good timing as we were all stressed pre-Silverstone, a notoriously guest- and VIP-heavy Grand Prix, and it was a rare treat to be invited somewhere so utterly wonderful as Raymond Blanc's Manoir aux Quat' Saisons. But I hadn't been able to relax during the dinner for fear that we would have to pick up the bill. Tuffy had invited us, but it was his birthday. My measly salary and maxed-out credit card weren't prepared for Michelin-star prices.

'Excuse me a minute.' I stood up to go to the bathroom. I also wanted an excuse to have a quick nose around.

From the moment we had driven through the gated entrance, I had fallen in love with the fifteenth-century manor and its perfect British garden with sweeping lawn, lavender bushes and little gated passageways. I had zoned out of Mike's monologue on the Superhawk's bow thrusters to envisage doing cartwheels on the grass, drinking old-fashioned lemonade and maybe even reading poetry. But for now I'd suffice with just checking out the loo.

I made a small detour across the wide oak floorboards of the lounge, where guests relaxed in armchairs enjoying post-prandial drinks. From somewhere across the corridor, a familiar voice with its trademark Essex lilt boomed.

'… and that's why I love Russian birds! Show me a Svetlana who won't …'

A door closed and the voice became muffled.

It was just impossible to have an F1-free evening in Oxford, although who'd have thought I'd frequent the same hang-outs as Harry Bircher?

I made sure I tested the soaps and hand creams in the toilet, drying my hands on the beautifully soft white towel before tossing it into the discreetly placed wash basket. I swung open the heavy oak door and stepped out on to the flagstones, considering an alternative route back to the restaurant, when I almost collided with a guest exiting the male toilet.

'Excuse me,' the man muttered.

'My fault … Oh, Mr Kato, well, hello there.' I beamed, and realised I had actually had too much to drink.

He looked up with saucer-like eyes, froze for a second, then scuttled off down a wide set of stairs.

That man had no social skills.

It took a few more seconds for my alcohol-sozzled brain to realise the blindingly obvious. Harry was meeting in secret with Kato, Vincent's priority number one. That could not be good. I had to tell Vincent.

'Tell me again. Tell me everything.' Vincent fixed me with his unnervingly penetrating stare, far more powerful than any lie detector, as I recounted for the third time what I had seen at Le Manoir the night before. He was mid-breakfast; an expresso, a small glass of wheatgrass juice (the sight of it almost made me redeliver the scrambled eggs I'd just bolted in the canteen to feed my hangover), and a white saucer with about ten different vitamin pills in a variety of colours and shapes, all laid out on a small silver tray. Next to the healthy tray, in a cut-glass ashtray, awaited a packet of Marlboros.

'So, Bircher not only wants my driver, he wants my partner as well.' He picked up a large handful of vitamins, tossed them into his mouth and crunched.

'It would seem that way, Vincent,' said Mike, who had invited himself to the meeting.

'Well, it's not going to happen.'

As I closed the door to his outer office I heard: 'Natalie, get me that Capshaw guy on the phone – and I want Gideon in my office in five.'

British Grand Prix, Silverstone Circuit
Saturday, 8.30 a.m.

I squelched into The Wing and slumped down on the chair opposite Janey.

'Traffic?'

'Shit.'

'Soaked?'

'Uh-huh.'

'Tea?'

'Please.'

When Janey had announced in the British GP marketing meeting that we all got to sleep in our own beds for the race, I did a one-woman Mexican wave. Seven races into the season, and I was fed up with hotel rooms. Of course, I enjoyed coming into a perfectly tidy stylish room every night, using three fresh fluffy towels for a shower, and swiping the trendy bath products, but I rarely got a good night's sleep. My shoebox-size one-bed flat, on the other hand, although starkly, rather than 'Starckly', furnished, was home for the past two months, and there I slept like the dead.

The furniture was sparse: a bed, chest of drawers, sofa, TV and two foldaway chairs. The other surfaces were made up of the cardboard boxes I hadn't yet unpacked. But it was my retreat for the micro work-free window. I paid the same rent as in London. Danny's aunt, my landlady, hadn't heard of 'mates' rates', but as I had so little time to myself, I was glad to live alone.

What I hadn't counted on, when I saluted the British Grand Prix home commute, was the horrendous traffic that solidified every main and back road into the Silverstone circuit. This meant I had to leave my flat at an offensive five-thirty a.m. To add to the growing list of negatives, an unanticipated cold front had descended on Northamptonshire for the weekend, bringing uninterrupted rain. It was only Saturday but – tired, cold and wet through – we'd all had more than enough of this Grand Prix.

'They said they won't fly in unsuitable weather conditions? What's the definition of "unsuitable"?' Janey leant her elbows on the table, head in hands, as she studied her minutely detailed helicopter programme of twenty arrivals and departures.

I gave Gareth, The Wing's 21-year-old gofer, a sympathetic smile. His job was to keep the mirrored Dupont Lamborghini-logoed floor tiles, directly inside the entrance doors, polished at all times. Vincent's orders. Every wet foot that entered left its print. Every day there were at least a thousand comings and goings over that tile. Gareth had assumed a permanent crouch at the entrance. In Vincent's value system, a smudge-free arrival trumped stepping over a squatting man.

When I started at the team I regularly found myself open-mouthed at the irrational, inflexible and, quite frankly, often ludicrous demands that would issue from Vincent's office. I wondered how someone so busy had time to worry about staff mugs, mechanics' haircuts and perfume bans? Why did he bother? Was it even possible to have so many pet hates? But then I saw how each demand was implemented immediately and without question, and realised – it was because he could. Because power and tolerance were incompatible, and it was the ultimate ego trip to be able to eliminate every slight annoyance.

'I have car companies on standby in Battersea, Paddington and Oxford. I'm in touch with the weather station at Oxford, the coast guard and the team satellite.

They think the rain'll ease off at nine.' We both leaned forward and looked up through the window at the dark grey clouds blanketing the sky. Janey groaned. 'Do you think Adriana would share a car with the Telsat CEO?'

'If he's not famous, then no chance. By the way, when can I get the Paddock Club pass for Danny?'

Janey sighed, pulling a pained face to hammer home how enormous the favour was she was doing me by letting me use one of her precious passes. 'Tomorrow, first thing. You must have done something pretty bad?'

I didn't take the bait. 'Thank you.' It was my peace offering for slamming the phone down in Turkey. When I eventually called back he never picked up. But the way to Danny's heart was through a VIP pass and unlimited bubbly.

A huge, dripping cagoul-cum-poncho appeared next to our table.

'Ladieez, ladieez, why so glum? At least you're inside.'

Wet layers were flung off, selflessly caught by Celine, the Wing 'hostess', who was losing the fight against floor puddles, and JB was revealed.

'I know just what you need.' He pulled two chairs over from the neighbouring table, loaded cameras and zooms on to one, and plonked himself, legs spread, on the other.

Janey and I looked up unconvinced as he whipped off his wet hunting cap and slapped it down on Janey's heli programme.

'Hot fudge sauce, nipple clamps, and an hour of semi-exclusive JB lurve.' He leant back, flicking his unnaturally long tongue.

'Eeww!' Janey and I screeched in unison.

'You are truly gross, JB,' Janey added, picking his hat up and chucking it at him.

'I know.' JB caught the hat and grinned, showing too many yellowing teeth for one mouth, delighted to have revolted us once again. 'All part of my irresistible charm.'

I pressed the blue button outside Marcel's suite. It was designed for minimum disturbance, and a blue light lit up on the inside to inform the driver that someone was at the door.

'Come in.'

Marcel stood in his fireproof underwear, which looked remarkably like my Grandad's thermal long johns, holding different helmet visors up to the light.

'Hi, Marcel, sorry to bother you. I wanted to run through the promo for this afternoon.'

'No problem. I have to choose a visor for this weather, which is a joke as we aren't going to be able to see anything through the rain whatsoever. Ah, have you met my parents, Ilse and Harald?'

'Nice to meet you.' I shook hands with the couple who sat on Marcel's massage table, legs dangling above the floor. 'Is this your first race?'

'Ja,' said the father, his brow knitted with concentration. 'We don't like to travel. But we are so proud of our son.' He leant over and ruffled the driver's dark blonde hair. Marcel rolled his eyes and smiled.

'If you like, I could take you into the garage to watch qualifying. We can give you a headset to listen to Marcel's radio.'

They conferred in German and broke into smiles.

'If it's not too much trouble, that would be wonderful.'

'Great. So, Marcel, the promo. Playstation have a new game called The Racer. The concept is to start at karting and race through the Formulas until Formula One.' I tried to keep the description as short as possible, as Marcel had that common driver trait of an acutely short attention span. He picked up his iPhone and started texting.

'We'll set up two game consoles in The Wing's lounge and use the whole rear wall as a screen. You'll play against Enrico: ideally three races – one in karting, one in Formula Three and one in Formula One. There'll be about forty media present: ten have been invited by Sony.'

'Which circuits will we race?'

I shuffled through my notes. I'd had this question earlier this morning already. 'Karting track will be Parma, Formula Three at Macau and F1 at Monza.'

'So Enrico got to pick the tracks?' he challenged. 'I want F1 at Spa.'

Damnit, I'd been rumbled. Enrico had already set his ultimatum, and had refused to appear unless they were the tracks of his choice. Marcel was right, Enrico did always get what he wanted. 'The Sony CEO particularly requested Monza as Italy is, well, a very important market.'

'Enrico always gets what he wants; well, this time I want Spa.' He stood with hands on hips, looking as determined as was possible in baggy white underwear.

'Marcel!' his father reprimanded. They broke into heated German.

'OK, I'll do Monza, but Kate, it's not going to always be me who compromises.' He resumed his texting. 'Please have a game delivered to my room so I can check it out.'

Practice, more like. Enrico had asked for the same thing. Drivers were competitive in everything.

'Will do, and thank you.'

Qualifying, Q3
1.50 p.m.

The Dupont Lamborghini cars pulled out of the garage into the pit lane, forming a queue with the other eight contenders at the red light. In seconds it would turn green and Q3, the qualifying 'final', would start. The rain had eased up mid-morning, but dark clouds now hovered menacingly over the start/finish straight.

Green light.

Ten impatient 750-horsepower engines on slick tyres accelerated deafeningly away.

I stood next to Marcel's parents watching the timing screen in the middle of the garage, making sure they didn't get in the way. They held on to their headsets with both hands, shouting occasionally to each other.

'According to the data, we're pretty sure it won't rain in Q3, Marcel.' Our headset was filled with the voice of Anton, Marcel's engineer.

The first car of the pack crossed the start/finish line, beginning the first timed lap. The cars had spread out, and there was a rhythmic roar as each passed just metres in front of us.

'It's raining at Stowe. Shall I come in?' Marcel shouted over the thundering engine.

'Stay out, stay out. Try to keep temperature in the tyres. It's a light shower, it won't last.' Anton and all the other seven backs on the pit wall were hunched over the twenty screens, showing all the fundamental information the driver needed and couldn't see: car telemetry, track position, timing, and – crucially – a real-time weather map.

'The data is crap. Look at the sky!' Marcel shouted.

A huge crack rocked the sky, and the clouds dumped their load on the tarmac.

Marcel had just passed the pit-lane entrance and so had to make it once more around the 5.14-kilometre circuit before he could change to wet tyres. The TV images showed the track to be more like a fairground log flume than a circuit.

A high-pitched horn sounded the arrival of multiple cars in the pit lane. Truckies flew by carrying tyres in warming blankets; mechanics ran into position as Enrico roared to a halt in the white painted box in front of the garage. I pulled the Müllers to the back wall, out of the way.

'Fuck, I'm off.'

Marcel's mother winced, and the TV screen filled with a replay of our number six car aquaplaning and sailing off into the tyrewall at Becketts.

On the pit wall of immobile backs, Vincent threw his hands to the heavens.

At the end of the session I ushered the parents out of the garage through the flurry of mechanics, who were high-fiving Enrico's pole, and directed them towards The Wing. My babysitting time was up, and I had the press release to do.

Marcel was stuck at turn four and awaiting a scooter ride back. Enrico was on pole, so had been whisked off to the FIA press conference. I looked for Vincent. I checked the pit wall, walked through the garage, and was on my way to the engineer's office when I spotted him on the steps of The Wing. He was gesticulating to a group of dictaphones all huddled under the glass porch sheltering from the rain.

Why the impromptu press conference?

I walked as fast as a surface calm demeanour would allow, and squeezed around the side of the pack. Vincent was animated and enjoying his pulpit.

'It's a ridiculous, immature mistake. You don't take risks in the wet. He should have done like Enrico and pitted to change tyres, before driving like a lunatic.'

'Did the team have bad weather information?' an *Autosport* journalist shouted.

'We have the most sophisticated weather-tracking system in the paddock.' Vincent waved his arms in despair.

I stood as close as I could to Vincent, trying to get in his line of sight so that I could interrupt, but he was not to be deterred.

'He needs to learn he isn't on the Playstation now!'

Everything about this was wrong. We didn't attack our drivers in the press, and we didn't address the press when we were visibly emotional. I scanned the crowd, who were locked on their target, nodding supportively or scribbling notes. My eyes caught Harald and Ilse Müller, stuck behind the group, unable to get past into The Wing. I quickly looked away.

The Ferrari drivers darted across the paddock towards their motorhome; catching sight of them the journos set off in pursuit. That was one of the only windows in the day for them to catch a driver directly for a quote – a chance not to be missed. I said a little prayer of thanks to the prancing horse.

Vincent finally noticed I was standing at his elbow.

'Kate, good, come with me, we're going to do the press release.'

We? I followed him into the lift. He clapped his hands together several times. The glass capsule rang out with *Mambo Number Five*, and I shot my hand into my pocket to grab my phone.

'Hello.'

'Kate, it's Tomasz.'

At the sound of his voice my heartbeat quickened, and feelings of guilt, embarrassment and annoyance all fought each other for supremacy. That was way too many emotions to deal with. I shot a glance sideways to see if

Vincent could somehow hear his voice. It had been a trying two weeks but, on Vincent's command to 'deal with it', I had finally managed to calm the waters after his spectacular exit from the *Sport Heroes* interview. The best excuse I could come up with was that Vincent had had an aggressive attack of food poisoning and couldn't control his bowels. (Of course I hadn't told the whole truth to Vincent: announcing that my master-of-control boss had shat himself wasn't the key to career longevity).

I sent a sports bag full of merchandise as an apology, and snagged a couple of British GP Paddock Club tickets for Tyler Moore and his wife. The producer agreed that the interview would suffice for a programme if they could pad it out with some more films, so I sent the footage I had hoped to keep back of Vincent on *Aqua Princesse* and flying his heli. I had wanted to keep the focus off his Euro-jet set image, but the goalposts had moved and now it was just a question of getting the programme finished and 'dealt with'.

Vincent had stayed furious with me over the Turkish GP weekend, but I had redeemed myself with the Kato-Bircher discovery. I really hoped that would be the last I would hear about *Sport Heroes*.

'Oh, hi, it's not a good time …'

'You won't believe this. I'm at the Paddock Gate and my pass has been stopped.'

'What do you mean?'

The lift doors opened and I followed Vincent to his office.

'My pass doesn't work. It comes up as no longer valid. I can't get in, Kate. And if I can't get in, I can't work!'

Vincent stood behind his desk and stared; he was ready to begin.

'I'll call you back.' I clicked off and pulled out my notepad.

I left Vincent's office with the sick feeling back in my stomach. It was a ball of stress that never seemed to disappear. Sometimes I could forget about it, but other times it felt so big and tight I could barely stand upright, like a giant fist clenching and twisting my gut.

The quote Vincent had just dictated and reworked for ten minutes was horribly harsh on Marcel. It was practically a professional disownment. This was not what we did. We didn't show the cracks to the outside world.

I didn't get it. Why was he so pissed-off at Marcel? I'd heard the radio: the poor guy had asked to pit, to change tyres. It wasn't his fault.

Dupont Lamborghini F1 Team

PRESS RELEASE

British Grand Prix
Silverstone Circuit
Saturday

Qualifying

Enrico Costa claimed pole position for the British Grand Prix today in a qualifying session beset by heavy rain. Marcel Müller will start tomorrow's race from the fifth row of the grid after aquaplaning into the tyrewall at Becketts and failing to set a time in Q3.

Enrico Costa – 1st

'It was tough out there today but we all had the same conditions in Q3, so it was just a case of keeping on the track and hoping the rain would ease off. Once I changed tyres I could push a bit more, and on my last lap of the session I just went for it. I couldn't be happier with pole.'

Marcel Müller – 10th

'When the heavens opened I'd already passed the pit entrance, so I had to try to complete another lap. The quantity of rain on the track was incredible. I had zero grip, and just sailed off at turn four. Luckily there was no serious damage to the car.'

Vincent Dupont, Team Principal

'Enrico showed his supremacy among the drivers today, with faultless judgement and a superb lap in tricky conditions. Marcel demonstrated that speed alone does not suffice to make a great driver in Formula One. Great drivers read the car and the conditions, and constantly adapt their driving to these factors. The team cannot do all the thinking for a driver.'

'You've got to be kidding, Kate.' Gordon Barry held out the press release I had just laid on his desk between two fingers, as if it was too toxic to touch.

Distributing the press releases by hand to the three hundred print journalists sandwiched next to each other in long rows in the media centre was one of the jobs that hadn't changed over the years. It was a task generally loathed by the press officers as

time-consuming and embarrassing for all but the super-skinny. The rows were only wide enough for a size ten bottom: anything larger ran the risk of sweeping laptops and cables with it as it progressed down the row. It did, however, serve to maintain that ever-rarer human contact between press officer and journo. The journalists all received a press release by email to their inbox, but this gave both sides a chance for a brief moment of face-time and a quick question or clarification. Exactly what I wanted to avoid today.

'How could you let Vincent say this?' He looked at me with disappointment, the worst kind of look, over his black-rimmed glasses. 'Marcel was on the podium in the last two races.'

Blood rushed to my cheeks, and I struggled to look him in the eye. Did he really think I could say no to Vincent? I thought Gordon at least would understand. His expression just hammered home what I knew – distributing this release was tantamount to professional suicide. It proved that either I had no idea how to write a press release, or that I had zero influence in PR matters, so I was nothing more than Vincent's typist. Unfortunately the latter seemed to be true.

My phone rang.

'Yes.'

'You didn't call me back.'

'Shit, sorry Tomasz, look, I'm in the middle of something …' Standing in the middle of the full F1 press pack, I had to choose my words with care.

'In the middle of *something*! Kate, if I can't get in the paddock my life is over. No job, no money, everything I've worked for down the drain. You have to help me. Can you get me a pass?'

Guilt that I had totally forgotten about him, and resentment at being told what to do by one of the few people who actually had no right to boss me around, made my tone more aggressive than I intended.

'I don't *have* to do anything, Tomasz,' I said, semi-hushed, as I shuffled down the row to an exit door that led out to a less public corridor. 'Listen. One: Dupont Lamborghini has team, not media, passes; two: I have no say in who gets what; and three: we just said no to Ronan Keating, so you can pretty much assume we don't have a pass for *you*!'

In the silence that followed I heard my bitchy tone repeated in my head.

'Kate, I just thought you could help, that's all. I thought we … well, forget it. You're right, why should you help me?'

'Wait, I'm sorry, but really, why don't you just talk to the FIA media office? It'll be a logistical matter.'

'Kate,' he sighed. 'Your boss did it. I don't know how, but Vincent had my pass stopped. He's punishing me for the interview.'

'That's ridiculous …' I wasn't going to be drawn into his imaginary problems.

'It's ok, I have to go.' He clicked off, and I felt immediate relief. I could ignore the niggling thought that Tomasz was not just paranoid; besides, I still had the press release from hell to deliver.

I handed out the rest of the releases at speed, responding to the quizzical looks and the 'What on earth?'s with an unprofessional shrug and an apologetic smile. There really was nothing to say.

Kate's flat, 14a Waverley Road, Oxford
Saturday, 10.50 p.m.

With my hands full with my race file, team jacket, handbag, and car and house keys, I hadn't seen the hunched figure on the doorstep when I pushed open the rickety gate with my knee. Today had been one of my worst in the paddock. Vincent's bewildering treatment of Marcel had resulted in an industry-wide trumpeting of my PR incompetence. I would deal with it the only way I knew how: with denial, wine and bed.

Luckily, the figure stirred before I trod on him.

'You worked late. I'm bloody freezing, been waiting for hours.'

'Tomasz, what on earth are you doing here? How do you even know where I ...' I side-stepped him and fumbled with the key in the lock. I was too tired for confrontation.

'I missed my flight after waiting all day to hear about my pass. Don't suppose I can sleep on your couch?'

I let out a loud sigh. 'If you promise not to say another word, which includes any sort of pass-related moaning, *and* you don't look at the mess, then OK. I'm too tired to speak, let alone argue.'

He nodded, made a zipping-of-the-mouth gesture, and followed me inside.

'There's not much to eat, but there's always wine,' I said as I dumped my stuff in a pile by the door ready for tomorrow. 'Mugs are on the draining board.'

I headed to the bathroom to wash my face, the first step of my accelerated night routine, where the aim was to get from front door to bed in under five minutes. I usually completed the routine on autopilot, numbing my brain into a pre-sleep fuzz, but trying to do this while stepping round a lanky Pole in a hundred square feet was close to impossible. It was too weird having him in my flat, my private F1-free haven; rather than zoning out I found myself trying to remember the last time I'd shaved my legs, and wishing I had less childish pyjamas.

I rooted around in the bathroom cupboards for a clean towel, finding one under a bumper pack of loo roll.

As I sniffed it for mildew, a thought surfaced: I had no spare bedding; no duvet, sheets, or even a blanket.

'Right.' I took the Snoopy mug of wine, leaving him with the 'World's Best Granddaughter' one. I summoned my most businesslike tone to prevent any ambiguity in meaning. 'There are no sheets, so you'll have to sleep on the right side of my bed. I've got to crash, as I've got an early start. Watch TV if you want, but please be quiet.' I handed over the towel, avoiding any eye contact.

Wearing the baggiest t-shirt and the only pair of pyjama bottoms without cartoon figures I possessed, I lay on my back, duvet pulled under my chin, staring at the ceiling. Having been certain of crashing out within a minute, a quarter of an hour later my mind was bright and active, providing in Blu-ray quality the images to fit the sounds emanating from the paper-thin walls of my bathroom. To the brushing and spitting noises that could be heard over the running taps, I saw Tomasz diligently carrying out his teeth-cleaning ritual. The taps stopped and the showerhead spluttered into action. There was a dull rustling noise, and a light thud of belted jeans hitting the floor. Oversize colour-saturated images of Tomasz naked in my bathroom, a few feet away, flashed up in my head. A rattling and a forced sliding sound meant he was in the shower.

Wet, naked and soapy.

To stop my inner soft-porn cinema, I opened my eyes and stared at the bare bulb in my ceiling. The bedside clock read 23.20; I had to be up in six hours.

The running water stopped. The shower door slid forcibly open. A couple of minutes later the bathroom door opened and a band of steam-filled light illuminated the foot of the bed. I quickly closed my eyes and made an elegant sleeping face.

23.50. The clock's digital red numbers glowed mockingly. My mind was torturingly alert.

Tomasz lay on his side, facing away from me. The duvet tucked under his naked shoulders rose and fell gently; his breath was quiet. *Was he seriously sleeping already?*

He stirred and began to shift position.

Elegant sleeping face.

I could feel his warm breath on my face. I squinted my right eye open. Two pale brown eyes, at very close proximity, smiled back.

'Couldn't sleep, eh?' he chuckled.

I tried to purse my lips into a scowl, but it was defeated by a smile.

'I'm waiting for one of your speeches,' he said, his face so close I could only focus on a single feature. I chose his left eye.

'What do you mean?'

'About how this isn't a good idea, and that we should definitely not do it again.' He smelt of my coconut shower gel. I had an overwhelming need to touch his skin; the top half of his chest had fallen free of the duvet and was just inches away from my fingertips.

'That just about covers it; now shut up and kiss me.' I took his arms, pushing him back on the bed, and swung my leg over to straddle him. 'I've got to be up in five hours.'

My morning glow had long since passed by the time I finally got into the paddock. Danny had kept me waiting for forty minutes in a layby on the A43 so I could give him his pass. Time enough for endless self-flagellation over my lack of self-control. It wasn't like everybody else in the paddock wasn't shagging. Married or not, travel was the ultimate moral vacuum. But Tomasz and I, well, it just crossed too many lines. Ignoring the fact that it broke Vincent's 'no sex' rule, Tomasz was a journalist – and one Vincent hated. Work-wise his disingenuous act was wearing pretty thin, but he had a knack of appearing all smiley, insouciant and nice- smelling when my professional resolve was impaired.

It was hard to stay mad at Danny when he shimmied over to me doing his Carmen Miranda impression, with a plastic punnet of Waitrose grapes on his head. He looked too rough to be moaned at, ghostly pale with big grey circles under his eyes. He never was a morning person.

I hurried head-down through the paddock so I could dump my laptop in the marketing office and pretend I had been there for hours. I swung past the breakfast bar and grabbed a mug and a Tetley teabag. As I reached out to the hot water dispenser another hand got there just before me, pressing down as a few drops of water splattered out.

'Ah, it's empty again.' I turned to face the last person in the world I wanted to see. 'Oh, hello, Marcel's dad, er, Mr Müller.'

'Kate.' He acknowledged me with a curt nod.

Celine whisked away the hot water canister. I really wanted to escape to the office, but was holding an empty mug with a teabag in it.

We stood in silence side by side, awaiting the refill. It was understandable that his parents blamed me. I wrote the press release, after all. Marcel had done nothing wrong. I knew that, and I had professionally crucified him. I still didn't know why Vincent had reacted so extremely.

I stared at my shoes, for want of a better idea for looking busy.

'You've forgotten how to make tea, or what?'

I looked up to see Gordon Barry smiling. He scanned the area immediately surrounding me, clocking Marcel's dad and a couple of photographers piling toast and croissants on to their plates, and tilted his head in the direction of the quiet corner table where his mug of tea was steaming. I followed him with my empty cup and we both sat down.

'So, when is Yuji Okada scheduled for a seat-fitting?' He looked at me pointedly, unable to hide an air of self-congratulation.

I tried to keep my face as neutral as possible, as my caffeine-deprived brain played mental dot-to-dot. Yuji Okada: that name rang a bell – the young driver who toured the factory with Kato ... he sat in the car ... but it wasn't a seat-fitting ... a race seat wasn't moulded for him ... so the answer is no. But why is Gordon asking this?

'What do you mean?'

'Well, I'm getting old, Kate. The old brain isn't as sharp as it used to be, so it took me until last night to work out Vincent's plan.' He smiled.

'What plan?'

'We all know Vincent doesn't do things by accident. There had to be a reason for that horrific press release yesterday. I listened to the radio transmissions, and it certainly wasn't Marcel's fault.'

'How did you hear the ...'

'Never mind. The point is, Vincent's partnership deal with Kato is threatened somehow, isn't it?'

'Look, I ...'

'And now more than ever, with Enrico threatening to leave, he needs to secure the team with a major cash injection. Plus he needs a serious amount of money behind the launch of Planet Dupont.'

'It's Dupont the brand. But honestly, Gordon, I don't think ...'

'Forget about the denial; it's clear ...' he said gently. 'Okada is Kato's protégé; he's not a bad driver either, although personally I rate Marcel higher. Anyway, Vincent is finding a reason to oust Marcel – there'll be a performance clause in his contract – and put Okada in the car. Kato would be over the moon, plus he'd have to close the deal with Vincent.' He sat back, looking satisfied. There was nothing a journalist liked more than solving a puzzle.

The Paddock Club was where the teams entertained their sponsor guests.

Commandeering the best position on the circuit, the Paddock Club suites were air-conditioned, carpeted rooms usually with a viewing window over the pit lane – bringing the well-heeled close to the action without heat, deafness or dirt. A five-star catering service ran non-stop, and champagne flowed from breakfast onwards.

These luxury pods did, however, have a downside: they were cut off (by security-manned turnstiles) from the paddock: the real heart and soul of the circuit, and more importantly where the drivers hung out. And what self-respecting VIP could accept going home after a Grand Prix unable to boast a budding friendship with the team's drivers? So twice on a race weekend, once on Saturday and once on Sunday, I had to escort the drivers up to the Dupont Lamborghini suite for Show and Tell, aka the Paddock Club appearance.

At Silverstone, as was par for this race, everything was more complicated. There were two major issues. One, we had loads of guests; whereas at some races there might be only fifty, this weekend there were three hundred and forty. This meant we brought out the big guns, and Vincent came over for the appearance too. Secondly, the Paddock Club wasn't situated above the pit lane but in a 'village' – a group of tents in the circuit grounds.

'It's out with the general public?' Vincent stared at me like I'd just stabbed one of his horses.

'I'm not going. The drivers can go.'

'They're going as well, but we've announced you're coming. The CEO and CFO of Telsat are there with a hundred staff, a big Sony delegation…'

'OK.' He waved his hand to stop me talking. 'And how am I supposed to get there?'

'We have three team scooters waiting at the turnstiles for you, Enrico and Marcel. Ivan, Janey and I will drive you there.' I turned to Ivan, who was in his ever-more-regular position by Vincent's door; he nodded in agreement. 'It's no longer than three minutes on the scooter, straight to the entrance of the Village.'

Now Janey was on standby at the paddock exit with the scooters, I was waiting outside the drivers' suites and, as Ivan was never further than a few metres from Vincent's side these days, he was to escort the boss.

'Ivan to Kate.' His voice crackled over the radio.

'Yes, Ivan.'

'I have the package, proceeding to rendezvous point.'

'What? Ivan, have you left with Vincent?'

'Affirmative.'

Fuck, Ivan was supposed to wait for my call when I had the drivers en route before he left. *Vincent wouldn't wait.*

'Walk slowly, Ivan.'

'Copy that.'

I hit the blue button on Marcel's door; it swooshed open almost simultaneously and he trudged out stony-faced, headphones on, nodding to the beat. I ran down the corridor to Enrico's room, hit the button, and slid open the door manually. A more forceful approach was required for our star driver, who made a point of ignoring the flashing-light warning system.

'Enrico, we have to ... Oh ...'

There was a profusion of flesh and limbs. I was way too close to a pair of taut, writhing female buttocks, and had an eyeful of frantically jiggling breasts. There were too many legs, only one set hairy. A grunt told me that Enrico was somewhere underneath.

I slapped my hand twice on the button to reopen the door that had swooshed closed so swiftly behind me, but it chose this moment to glitch. I also had to disentangle my feet from a heap of grid-girl dirndls, the bodice of one having hooked itself around my heel.

My presence hadn't dampened their enthusiasm, which was intensifying to a frenetic climax of thrusts, gasps and wails. I thumped on the door release with my fist; it responded by sliding open at snail-speed. I had one leg in the corridor of freedom when Enrico emitted a guttural groan then sat up, shaking the girls off him. He looked me in the eye with a what-do-you-want shrug, as if I had interrupted him drinking tea.

'Paddock Club appearance. I'll be out here.' I squeezed my way out of the narrowed door space.

My radio buzzed into life. 'Ivan for Kate. What's your twenty?'

Christ – give an ex-soldier a radio … 'Ivan, what are you talking about?'

'Where are you, Kate? Over.'

'Leaving the motorhome.'

'Ten-four.'

I half-trotted next to the drivers, trying to get them to speed up their deliberately languid pace. These moments of multiple ego-juggling were the worst part of the week-end. Once a certain level of success was achieved, a code of conduct kicked in where tolerance for others was no longer an option. The code seemed to be:

(1) Important people didn't wait – they were in a hurry because they were very busy and time was money, blah, blah.

(2) However, on no account would they hurry for someone else,

(3) unless, of course, that someone could bestow money/power/status, in which case the speed of movement would be in direct proportion to said benefit.

I had mentally sorted them into a Vincent–Enrico–Marcel order on the basis of ego priority, and of whose wrath I feared the most. I spotted Vincent about to exit the turnstiles. Right now it was not looking good.

There was probably a *Nota Bene* at the end of the code that said:

'N.B. A potential waiting situation may be deflected, by finding and engaging an important third party in a discussion of the utmost urgency (where no such third party is present, a phone conversation may act as a substitute).'

Mercifully, Vincent paused to chat to Stefano Domenicali of Ferrari in front of a bank of photographers, so we caught up and a scene was avoided.

Ivan took the scooter on the left, and Janey sat on the middle one and held out the key to the right-hand one for me.

She whispered out of the corner of her mouth, her eyes brimming with tears of laughter. 'Affirmative, twenty-four, got the package, check! Someone needs to tell old Andy McNab that we aren't actually on the front line.'

I smirked as I took the key. I'd driven a scooter once, about two years ago. I bent down to look for the keyhole.

'*Stai scherzando?*' Enrico whipped the key out of my hand and sat down, revving the fifty c.c. engine.

I sat on the back just in time as he accelerated away full-throttle. Hundreds of spectators milled about looking for lunch, swigging beer and buying merchandise. The pathways were solid with people walking in different directions. Enrico didn't ease off the throttle as he snaked through the crowds, finding spaces where none existed. I sat rigid on the back, my palms clamped around the bar behind my seat, trying to make myself thin.

Marcel appeared out of the crowds at our side, with Janey riding pillion and looking decidedly more relaxed than I felt. He accelerated, cutting through a group of lager-drinking Button supporters in outsized Union Jack hats. Enrico upped the pace. We hurtled towards a Champagne Mumm tent, where a solid queue of well-heeled fans blocked the road.

'It's there!' I yelled, pointing to the Paddock Club entrance on the right, immediately before the Champagne queue.

He turned sharply, the rear (and my rear) flying round three hundred degrees to stop exactly in front of the turnstiles. Marcel affected a similar manoeuvre, stopping a few centimetres to our left. They all dismounted and headed towards the entrance. I tried to will my body to move as my brain did its best to catch up.

Ivan arrived, hunched over the handlebars. Vincent hopped off as soon as he stopped, without touching the scooter, and put his hand out for his comb, which I produced from my back pocket with still-trembling fingers.

We crossed the communal garden that separated the team tents, to Dupont Lamborghini's marquee with its silver and aqua interior. Mike waited on a small stage, microphone in hand, looking like Alan Partridge on a Radio Norwich roadshow.

'Please welcome the Dupont Lamborghini stars, Enrico Costa, Marcel Müller and the man who has it all, Vincent Dupont!'

I made a mental note to write a script for Mike, which would definitely not include the words 'stars' or 'the man who has it all'.

The guests applauded and there was a loud 'whoop whoop'. I looked up to see Danny standing on a chair, a glass of champagne in his left hand, his right one punching the air.

'Vincent, it was a bittersweet qualifying yesterday. How important is strategy when the weather is so unpredictable?'

Mike thrust the microphone at Vincent.

'Well, strategy doesn't count for much if the driver can't keep the car on the circuit,' Vincent smiled as he answered, but the undertone was clear. Damnit, why couldn't he back down?

'Vincent, Vincent, he's our man, if he can't do it no one can!'

I looked over in horror as Danny led a one-man chant, swinging his hips and circling his arm in the air.

Mike gave a nervous laugh. 'You've certainly got some loyal fans, Vincent. Now, we're six races into the season, and Dupont Lamborghini are second in the constructors' championship, behind Martini Magna and just ahead of Ferrari, and Enrico has just taken the lead in the drivers' table. How confident are you of winning both titles?'

'We're never confident, and we never stop pushing. In F1 you can't afford to relax ...'

'Vincent, we love you, Vincent we do, even when you're far away, we think of you …'

Danny had emptied his glass, and now swayed with both hands over his head. He waved at the other guests, indicating they should join in his version of the St Winifred's School Choir's nauseating hit.

Vincent shot me a sharp look. He didn't know I knew Danny, but it meant I had to stop him. What was Danny doing? Why did he want to humiliate me? This was my boss, for God's sake. I needed someone else to deal with it. I looked around for Janey but I had seen her slip out into the garden with a glass of champagne and a *pain au chocolat*. If I sent Ivan, then he was bound to overdo the whole security risk thing and pin Danny's head to the floor with his boot. There was no choice, I'd have to go.

There were thirty-four tables of ten, tightly packed in the suite, all laid up like a wedding with elegant silverware and multiple glasses. Most guests were seated as there wasn't the space to stand. Danny was on the opposite side of the tent from me. I took a circuitous route around the outside of the room to draw as little attention as possible.

The guests were murmuring among themselves and throwing unsubtle glances at Danny. Mike was trying to hold the audience's attention and moved on to question Enrico, just as Danny started a cheerleader cry, shaking his hands by his toes and bringing them up vertically as he increased the pitch to a climactic 'Oooooooooooh … Vincent!'

I stepped over handbags and squeezed through chairs until I could finally grab his leg.

'Danny, get down.' I prayed he would listen and disappear quietly.

'Hey! Ooooooooooooh … Kate!'

'Get down, please. Now!' I was talking as quietly as I could, but nearly everyone had turned to look. Vincent was shooting daggers, and Ivan seemed to be deep-breathing to prepare for an attack.

'For God's sake, what is wrong with you?' I pulled Danny's arm hard; the chair rocked and tipped sideways. He fell, arms and legs flailing; there was a thud as he hit the table. Glasses shattered, the women on his table shrieked, a pashmina was ripped, and Paddock Club security, who were all ex-Foreign Legion, appeared with cheetah-like speed at the entrance.

'Kate, what are you doing?' Danny looked at me with wide eyes, seemingly oblivious to the chaos he had caused. His shirt was soaked with orange juice and champagne, and a lump of chocolate cream slid down his temple as he pushed himself up with one arm to a seated position; the other hand was clamped tightly to his nose.

'Do you need some help here, miss?' the Paddock Club security guard asked.

'Yes, this guest is just leaving.'

Danny, still in a seated position, was lifted under his arms by the two neat navy-blazered guards. As his hand fell away from his nose, blood spurted out, turning the bottom half of his face into a solid red mask. I instinctively took a step back. Danny read the horror on my face.

'Kate, I think you broke my nose.' He looked down at the red hand that dangled, dripping, in mid-air, then back up to me, eyes wide. 'Tell them to stop. It was just a bit of fun.'

I turned back to the stage, where a nervous Mike was trying to crack a joke.

'Kate, Ka-te, why are you being like this?'

I wanted him to stop saying my name. I didn't want anyone to know he was with me.

Dupont Lamborghini F1 Team

PRESS RELEASE

British Grand Prix
Silverstone Circuit
Sunday

Race
Enrico Costa was leading the British Grand Prix when a gearbox failure on lap 49 effectively ended his race. Marcel Müller pulled up two positions to finish eighth, scoring four points for the team.

Marcel Müller – 8th
'This was an extremely frustrating race. On this circuit, where it's notoriously hard to overtake and everyone is on an identical two-stop strategy, it was the best I could do to pull up two places to eighth, and bring home four points.'

Enrico Costa – DNF – Gearbox
'There's nothing more frustrating than losing the lead due to a mechanical failure. After the second stop I had a good few seconds' lead on Santos, and then coming out of turn 3 I suddenly lost drive: I guess it was the driveshaft. At this position in the championship I can't afford to lose 25 points like that.'

Vincent Dupont, Team Principal
'Unfortunately we were racing with only one car this weekend, which is not an acceptable position for a team fighting for the world championship. Enrico could have won had it not been for the driveshaft failure. We've identified the problem, and modifications are already in production at the TechQ.'

Media contact
Kate Ellison – Kateellison@dupontf1.com

www.dupontf1.com

CHAPTER 10

14A Waverley Road, Oxford
Friday, 8.45 p.m.

I opened the fridge door for the fourth time, leaning my head on the top as I stared inside at the empty shelves. Half a pack of Sainsbury's organic butter, a bottle of soy sauce, Dijon mustard, a jar of Hartley's strawberry jam three months past its sell-by date, half a pint of long-life low-fat milk, three carrots, some Philadelphia cheese and a bottle of Chablis. I would defy any *Ready Steady Cook* participant to make a wholesome three-course meal out of those ingredients.

I grabbed the bottle of wine, pushed the door closed and rooted around in the cutlery drawer for the bottle opener. It would be Cheerios and milk again.

Work took one hundred per cent of my energy and, pathetic as it sounded, I couldn't even be bothered to buy food in the small amount of time I wasn't actually running around double-checking, briefing, writing or pacifying.

I put the cold Chablis down on Mike's proposal while I opened the corkscrew. The bold red headline screamed

'How to Save the Kato Deal'. A drop of condensation turned his arrow bullet point to a watery purple blob. Mike had forcefully requested my feedback 'by end of play today' so that he could present his 'Saviour of the Team' document to Vincent.

Isn't gonna happen, Mikey. Nothing is delaying my rendezvous with the Chablis. He didn't really want my feedback, he wanted me to check he had guessed the details correctly, as he was out of the loop.

I pulled out his papers and slid them back into my laptop bag, with a mental promise to look it over tomorrow.

Placing the wine bottle between my knees, I screwed in the imitation Swiss Army penknife corkscrew and pulled. The cork didn't budge. Placing the bottle on the floor, I secured a purchase between my sandals. I yanked hard and the bottle shot out from between my feet, throwing me backwards. I steadied myself just before hitting the bedroom door frame.

For Christ's sake, I just wanted a bloody glass of wine.

The pace hadn't let up after Silverstone, not that that was unusual. I was back in the TechQ at eight a.m. on the Monday morning, ducking and swerving in Tuffy's rubber band-flicking championship and working flat-out on the logistics for the Dupont brand launch at the weekend.

It was like sitting next to Just William. While his continual changing of my ringtone was infuriating, Tuffy had quickly become my favourite person in the office. He was the only one to offer advice without a lecture, or help where there was no personal benefit for him. It was true he didn't do much work and Vincent loved blue blood, so his job was never under threat, but I envied his calm.

The Dupont brand launch event was taking place at Vincent's chateau and the first official announcement would be of his purchase of a prestigious St Emilion wine. The event fell into the realm of Vincent's personal activity, so technically it was not my responsibility; instead Natalie had to finally move her grumpy arse on to a plane, and do her job as his PA. I wasn't taking any chances, though, and double-checked the guest list and travel logistics, reworked the timing programme at least fourteen times, wrote multiple versions of Vincent's speech until his long-overdue OK, and finalised the press release. I had more than covered my back, and so I more than deserved the two Ws: wine, and a weekend off.

Putting the bottle back on the floor, I pushed all my weight down on the red plastic handle. I'd just push the damn cork inside.

Nothing.

A bottle opener that doesn't open bottles. Fucking perfect.

I untwisted the corkscrew and took a kitchen knife out of the drawer. I stabbed at the infuriating cork. Small flakes crumbled. I twisted and pushed.

A two-tone ring similar to my doorbell sounded in the distance. I wasn't to be distracted. I thrashed with renewed vigour; larger chunks of cork broke free. I wiped away the loose ones and kept slicing at the remaining plug. I was starting to sweat, and the knife handle was hard to grip in my damp palm.

I was having a glass of wine, chunks of cork or not!

The cheap knife buckled as I increased the force, so I took off my sandal and whacked the heel down hard. A millimetre of movement. Another two-tone ring. I swung at the knife again. Two millimetres more. Spurred on, I thrashed away with the shoe. My heart was racing, and beads of sweat pricked my forehead and coursed down my flushed cheeks. A last-gasp strike, launched with a primeval grunt, released the seal and the knife handle clattered on to the empty bottle neck.

'Kate?'

I pulled the knife out, collapsed triumphant on to the foldaway chair, and took a big cork-filled swig of Chablis.

'Kate!'

My victory grasp on the bottle neck was vice-like.

'Are you ok?'

I turned to see where the voice, Em's voice, could possibly be coming from.

'Are you going to let me in?'

I stared with disbelief at the letterbox and the two concerned eyes looking through.

Oh my God, Em!

I had completely forgotten her hen-night planning visit. This was my first free weekend in weeks. I really wanted to see her and to catch up, but even more I wanted to spend the whole weekend in bed, watching the *Grey's Anatomy* DVD box set.

With an exaggerated effort to look unfazed, I pulled myself up off the chair, rather too quickly, and sprinted to the door.

'Em! Sorry, I was just … Welcome to the countryside.' I swung one arm around her, cranking up the positive energy and taking care not to clunk her with the bottle in my other hand. Out of instinct I glanced behind her, expecting to see Danny grinning, but there was nothing but the rickety wooden gate hanging on its one lower hinge.

'I brought chicken tikka.' She held up two white plastic bags with a smile that didn't spread to her eyes. 'I had a feeling if I didn't, it'd be Dairylea on toast.'

'Yeah, but without the toast.' I grabbed her carpet bag, avoiding her eyeline, and walked the couple of paces to the kitchen counter.

On the other side, I pulled out the second foldaway chair, placing it next to the cardboard-box table. Em discreetly scanned the bare room.

'So Freddie went to the Silverstone Grand Prix with some guys from work, and got soaked.'

'Yeah, it was a seriously miserable weekend.' Feeling suddenly defensive, I picked up two wine glasses and plates off the draining board, and placed them carefully on the unsteady table.

Em nodded sympathetically, tilting her head to let me continue. It was my cue to bring up the Danny disaster. She knew something – she was his room-mate, after all. She gave up waiting and prompted me.

'You know Danny hasn't been back to the flat all week. What on earth happened?'

'He was seriously out of order, to be honest. He should be hiding in shame.' I filled the wine glasses and forced a smile.

She sipped at the wine and resumed the sympathetic head tilt.

'He could have got me fired, Em. I just don't know what got into him. Doesn't he know how important this job is to me?'

'Of course he does, we all do.'

'I mean, I'm clocking twelve- to fourteen-hour days, I haven't had a day off in weeks …' My voice caught in my throat. I reached for the wine bottle to top up Em's glass, but just a dribble trickled out.

'Is it true you broke his nose?' she asked gently.

'No! No way.' I stood up and started flinging cupboard doors open on a wine hunt. 'I had to get him down off that chair; he was fan-chanting Vincent in front of our top sponsors.'

Seeing Em's face, as she leant on her elbows nodding, brow knotted in sympathy, knowing she wanted to believe me, I lost my conviction. I hadn't thought back over what had happened, it had been easier not to. Anyway, there was no doubt that Danny had behaved outrageously – it wasn't a bloody football match. He could have enjoyed the free drink without getting hammered. And I'd had to stop that stupid chanting. Maybe I had pulled him too hard. I could still hear the thunk as he hit the table.

'To be honest, this is what I wanted to talk to you about. I'm worried about him. I mean his behaviour, it's so erratic. He disappears for days at a time … I have no idea who he hangs out with, or where he goes. I think he actually times it so he's never at home when I'm back from work, so I can't confront him.'

'You don't think he's just enjoying being single? He never does things by halves.'

'No, it's more than that. It seems like that time he went AWOL at uni just before finals and hitched to Calais with those travellers. You had to go and bring him home, remember?'

'Of course I do. I never got the stench of joss sticks properly out of my clothes, and I only sat in that caravan for an hour. I'll talk to him. OK?'

'You will? Oh, thank you.' She clapped her hands together, looking genuinely relieved. 'I'm worried, you know, that things are changing …'

I was waist-deep in the cupboard under the sink, searching for a bottle of wine I vaguely remembered seeing behind a stack of kitchen roll.

'Our lives, yours, mine and Danny's, are heading in such different directions …'

'Whe-hey – found it!' I held a bottle of rosé aloft. Em didn't match my delight. 'I'll call Danny, I promise.' But not before I'd let him stew for a while longer. I still couldn't get that bloody *Grandma, We Love You* song out of my head.

Em took the bottle and decorked it with minimal fuss. 'Let's eat the curry before it gets cold.' I opened the plastic pots and poured the red liquidy gunk on to each plate.

'So, more importantly, tell me about the wedding plans. Have you found a venue?'

'I've got so much to tell you.' She reached into her carpet bag and pulled out a solid A4 binder bursting with swatches of fabric and magazine clippings. I felt my heart sink; there were hours of discussion right there and I was too exhausted, and now too drunk, to concentrate.

'But I propose ...' she delved into her bag again. I feared a second file, but she pulled out a DVD case. 'Tonight, let's get up to date on *Mad Men*, and then get down to business tomorrow.'

I gave a victory air-punch, trying not to look too relieved. 'Great plan. After a hearty breakfast of Cheerios, for forty-eight uninterrupted hours, this here' – I tapped the cardboard table – 'is hen-night HQ.'

My legs were like dead weights. I willed my right thigh to lift and propel the calf forward. My foot plunged deep into the burning sand, the sandal straps tearing at my raw, blistered skin. The heat of the sun was relentless; the air burnt my dry throat.

I have to move faster ...

I squinted up the mountain of sand to find the peak, but it just rose without visible end. My pursuer was closing in.

... and not look back.

I had to keep on, but the damn shoes weren't helping. The burning sky started to pulsate with *A-wimoweh ...*

That meant something important.

Ignore the heat and concentrate ...

... A-wimoweh ... the two-tone catchy refrain continued to ring out.

I had to ... Oh crap, phone, where was my phone?

I thrashed around on the bedside table. My wrist looped around the bedside light cable, dragging a magazine and eventually the whole stand to the floor.

Open your eyes, Kate. A call in the night is always important.

My fingers slapped down on the cold metal handset. I dragged my sleeping body up to semi-vertical and coughed my voice into action.

'Hello.'

'Keht, Natalie is sick, you must come to Bordeaux. The slot is at eight-forty a.m.' Click.

I looked down to check the time on the phone screen, my pupils recoiling at its brightness.

Seven-thirty a.m.! It wasn't night, but neither was it the Saturday lie-in I'd planned and so desperately needed.

I sat bolt upright and pulled off the duvet, hoping to jump-start my brain with the cold air. To get to Kidlington airport by eight-thirty (allowing a ten-minute safety window) I had to leave home at eight. Which left me twenty-seven – the phone clock clicked over to seven-thirty-four a.m. – or, rather, twenty-six minutes to get ready.

Shit! Shit! Shit!

I jumped up to standing to ready myself for the next twenty-six minutes of hell. My body was not designed to shift painlessly from deep drunken slumber to Vincent levels of intensity in a matter of minutes. I was still seventy per cent asleep as my brain desperately sucked on its first dribble of adrenaline like a junkie two days post-fix.

Step by step.

What was the absolute minimum I had to do to get ready and out of the house? Face, teeth, clothes, pack. But what? Christ, as it wasn't a race weekend I had to plan outfits: I couldn't get away with just throwing my uniform on. Outfits! Two days and one night at the Duponts' chateau garden party. Of course everyone would be wonderfully glamorous and expensively casual.

I ran over to the mountain of dirty laundry in the corner of my bedroom. I hadn't done any dry cleaning in months. Tossing the dirty garments one by one to the side I pulled out the cream blouse from Harry Bircher's dreadful yacht party. I held it up to the window. It was really creased, but no stains – it'd have to do. Vincent would have hundreds of staff I could ask to iron it. The black trousers smelt of cigarettes and stale champagne, but they were in too. At the bottom I found the little black dress I'd bought in five minutes at Kuala Lumpur airport for the last-minute gala dinner invitation. That would suffice for the evening dinner.

Now something for today. I pulled open my closet; there were two pairs of scruffy jeans, a nasty long navy skirt that was only just preferable to going naked, two pairs of shorts, a couple of roll-necks and a Rolling Stones 'The Licks Tour' t-shirt. I had a vague recollection of some summer clothes still unpacked, and pulled open the cardboard box that functioned as my bedside table. I emptied out the contents on to the carpet. Under the DVDs and unused running trousers were some white jeans, purchased last summer. Hallelujah!

Vincent hated jeans and had banned them from the TechQ, but I decided white didn't count, and hell, they were better than shorts. I threw them on. The creases from being folded in the box for four months were pronounced. I still didn't have a top, and only twelve minutes till departure. I bundled the other clothes under my left arm, grabbed the Sergio Rossi heels and the Zara sandals, and went in search of my team carry-on, which was always where I'd dropped it at the front door.

I passed Em splayed out on the sofa in her pale blue Gap pyjamas. Damn, hen plans and swatches would have to wait. My feelings of guilt were put on pause as I spied the pretty sheer blouse with pink and black flowers she'd been wearing last night, hung neatly over my foldaway chair.

It was perfect. She wouldn't mind. Of course not. I wouldn't wake her, I'd just text later.

I slipped on the blouse, dumped the clothes in the small suitcase, and ran into the bathroom to wash my face. I pulled my hair up into a French pleat (a Godsend for unwashed hair), brushed my teeth, put on some mascara, swallowed two mouthfuls of cold chicken tikka, and was out of the door at four minutes past eight a.m.

Clutching the steering wheel like Dick Dastardly, with my foot as flat as I dared, I horned a cyclist who was hogging the centre of the country lane. He visibly jumped and swerved into the roadside bushes before giving me the finger.

Damn Natalie, I bet she wasn't sick at all. This was my one weekend off. I did not want to be going to Vincent's chateau launch. The guest list was teeming with A-listers, which meant Vincent would be charged like some handmade bottle rocket.

I jogged into the small Oxford airport terminal with five minutes to spare. The gate to the tarmac was closed and the stairs were down on Vincent's plane, so I was guessing he hadn't arrived. There were two sets of automatic glass doors. The first set slid open and I marched through, scanning the waiting room for the white shirt and aqua tie combo of the pilots and crew. Three people were chatting on the sofa.

Oh my God, JUDE LAW!

I stood stock-still, aware that I was no longer in control of my body, which wanted to yelp, wave and giggle all at the same time.

'Ow!' The glass door closed on my shoulder. The sensor had run out of patience with my immobility.

The three people turned to look at me, bemused.

And Keira Knightley, and the butler from that period film!

Pull yourself together, Kate.

My star-gawping attack was interrupted as I caught the reflection in the glass door of Vincent's Mercedes pulling past the barrier on to the tarmac. The co-pilot appeared in the waiting room, greeted the seated guests politely, and moved me out of the doorway.

In spite of the odd wobble, like in the lift in Melbourne when I had rambled incoherently to Alonso about 'a friend being such a fan', or when Jenson Button appeared in our office looking for Vincent and I burst out in a pneumatic-drill laugh, I thought I had tamed my inner groupie. One, it was extremely unprofessional, and two, it suggested a mental imbalance, neither of which was acceptable behaviour for a career-focused press officer.

The professional thing to do would have been to introduce myself politely to the three guests with no sign of recognition whatsoever. But I felt compelled to share with Jude how insanely gorgeous he was, how I could quote all his lines from *The Talented Mr Ripley*, and how I was considering a career as a nanny, should a good opportunity arise.

The trio walked towards the small X-ray machine and I walked behind, staring fairly subtly at his bum and breathing out laterally to avoid asphyxiating him with tikka breath. I punched out a text message to Danny, the only person to appreciate the full weight of the situation.

Jude Laws arse in groping range – should I?

Outside a Mercedes Vito waited with the side door open and engine running, to drive us the thirty metres to Vincent's Gulfstream where the Baroness waited, smiling beatifically. Vincent, until now the master of the stroll, appeared, jogging over.

'Keira! Jeremy! Jude!'

He made an exaggerated gesture of kissing the actress's hand. She giggled and gently reprimanded him. Vincent shook hands and backslapped the two men as he tried to behave like a fellow thirty-something film star.

They'd probably never met before.

From Bordeaux Airport we boarded the Dupont-branded Sikorsky heli for the short transfer to Chateau du Pont de l'Evêque. The event had been named the Dupont Garden Party. As the pilot circled the Chateau, I realised what a colossal understatement that was. The 'garden' was about the size of Oxfordshire.

The location was jaw-droppingly beautiful. It was a true fairy-tale chateau, making Disney's look council-estate. The walls were light sand-coloured brick with a slate-grey roof and real conical turrets. The main chateau stood perfectly in the centre of an enormous square of bright green lawn. Down the long pebble drive about fifty elegant cypress trees stood to attention. The whole plot was, apparently, a whopping two hundred and fifty hectares.

To the right of the entrance, after a wide patch of lawn, the vineyards extended in endless undulating lines. At the back of the chateau, around a small lake, stood four cottages built in the same style. The lawn was peppered with perfect topiary, pergolas and canopied seating areas. Several white tents were erected close to what I assumed was the polo field, and tiered seating bordered a tennis court.

'We had to move the helipad to the other side of the lake so as not to disturb the polo ponies,' Daphne Dupont announced to the guests. She didn't have to shout over the noise of the heli. Her voice had a natural built-in loudspeaker, like the Queen amplified. Vincent just kept grinning, in a way that made him look slightly deranged. I probably didn't look much more intelligent.

We landed on the big white 'H' on the lawn. Awaiting us was a welcome line of four pairs of handsome young things, the girls in white Prada-like shift dresses and the boys in crisp white shirts and trousers. (For a party celebrating Bordeaux wine, I thought white was rather optimistic, but then in Vincent's world no one spilled.) They each stood next to a golf cart. The chief greeter was dressed in the traditional butler suit with pinstriped grey trousers, a white shirt and fitted black jacket. He was, of course, English, and almost as posh as Mrs D.

'Baroness, Mr Dupont, welcome home,' he said obsequiously, taking Mrs D's hand to help her down from the heli.

'Chester, it's so good to be here,' Mrs D boomed.

Still grinning, Vincent leapt energetically down on to the grass, ushering the guests out to the golf carts. The three carts containing Keira, Jeremy and Jude peeled off towards the lakeside cottages. Mine followed Vincent's, bumping over the narrow gravel path up to the chateau. Final touches were being applied across the perfect lawn – pergolas polished, topiary trimmed and staff smartened. Paul, the event producer, was co-ordinating the party and was barking something about 'refined elegance' to a female violin quintet seated under a lilac-entwined gazebo.

I found myself drifting off into the thought that I was somehow a part of this beautiful setting, one of the privileged guests at this exclusive party. I pictured myself relaxing on one of the sofa sets, sipping wine and applauding the quintet. Maybe it wouldn't be such a terrible weekend.

The golf cart pulled to a stop in front of the chateau.

'Come on, come on, Keht, for goodness' sake.' He all but pulled me from the cart.

'You.' He flicked his fingers at a man in white. 'Take her things to the staff quarters.' He swung back to face me. 'Drivers – visible but not social. Seat them centrally,' – he gestured vaguely towards the lawn – 'but they shouldn't mingle.' He marched towards the sets of tables and chairs on the gravel, and fingered the white linen table cloth.

I fumbled in my handbag and pulled out the event running order.

'I have Enrico's arrival times, but not Marcel's. I'm not sure ...'

'It's not Marcel, it's Yuji Okada,' he said in a tone that didn't leave any opening for questions.

Oh no, please don't say you've replaced Marcel. The press will eat us alive.

'So I've decided *Paris Match* can't talk to anyone but me. I'll do the sit-down interview we agreed tomorrow, but that's it. They can take photos, but they talk to no one. You understand? *NO ONE.*' He spotted something in the flower-bed by the main rear door and set off at a pace. I followed.

'Um, but we did agree with *Paris Match* that they could talk to the drivers and get sound bites from the guests ...'

And we had a long contract to that effect. That was why they paid so much money. The guests were the hook, not the wine.

'Today is about Dupont, and only Dupont.' He stopped at a perfectly pruned bush then wheeled around, brandishing a dead rose. 'The message must not be diluted.' Snapping his fingers at one of the many cloned tanned men in white standing at intervals around the lawn, he handed over the wilted stalk. 'After this weekend, anyone who's anyone will have heard of Dupont. It will be a brand more exclusive and more sought-after than a sleepover invitation at the White House.'

His eyes darted around the garden. Heaving a sigh he headed off towards a canopied bar that seemed to be made entirely of ivy and tiny blue flowers. I trotted behind.

'Pope, God and Allah for you this weekend is Kato-san.' About two hundred large red wine glasses were laid out on the semi-circular bar top. Six waiters in white were pulling glasses from a box and polishing them with white cloths.

'Next to me, he must be the happiest man at this party.'

I sniggered, seriously misjudging the undertone.

Vincent glared, pupils dilated, wine glass still raised to the light for inspection. I couldn't be sure he wouldn't clunk me with it.

'Of course.' I segued into a solemn nod. 'Definitely.'

Kato was the most deadpan man I had ever met. I suspected he was physically incapable of cracking a smile. 'Happy' was downright impossible. Every time I had met him it had been an exercise in social awkwardness. And still too fresh in my mind was the encounter at Le Manoir, when he looked like he'd have preferred to de-skin himself than chit-chat with me. Of course, it had been a stretch to hope I was on Jude- or Chilean Polo team-watch: they each had a pretty white Prada-ette to cater for their every need.

The butler appeared at the bar. 'Monsieur Dupont, the Casiraghis are arriving.'

Vincent flung the glass at one of the unsuspecting waiters and ran back towards the golf cart, shouting at no one in particular, 'The Casiraghis are coming!'

I crouched at the edge of the tennis court with the *Paris Match* photographer, waiting for the players' arrival. The sun was high, there was no breeze, and the guests were getting fidgety. The start had already been delayed by thirty minutes while Bill Clinton's secret service agents secured the pool house (I was assuming they didn't mean in case it flew off in the wind), before his heli would land.

Kato, seated in the front row with his four male assistants, was looking bored and not happy. Neither had he heeded the 'refined elegance' dress code, with baggy orange and white striped shorts, a lemon polo shirt, and a floppy, rather feminine, sun hat.

Apart from the 'happy' mission, all my responsibilities were under control. I was trying to stay off Vincent's radar as he was wound up to the point of self-combustion.

Applause started up from somewhere, and the players walked on to the court. Serena and Venus Williams accompanied by Enrico Costa and Yuji Okada. It was a moment of pure comedy. Enrico, 1.67 metres, was paired with Venus, 1.85 metres, and Yuji Okada, 1.62 metres, partnered with Serena, 1.75 metres. While the drivers had strong upper bodies, their skinny legs were less than half the length of their partners'. And next to these superhuman sportswomen, they looked like hobbits.

For PR activity, I tried to keep the drivers in their environment. Drivers were perceived as fearless, cool and heroic in the cockpit. In reality, outside the car, they could be somewhat of an anti-climax – short, sulky and, more often than not, monosyllabic.

The tennis match hadn't been my idea, and I had voiced my concerns futilely to Vincent. So, my back covered, I could relax and join the rest of the audience, who were struggling to stifle their giggles.

The match was one in a series of five-star diversions for the garden party guests, to be followed by a polo match with world champions Chile against Brazil.

The coin was tossed and Venus prepared to serve. Yuji, who'd taken a leaf out of Rafael Nadal's book and was bouncing up and down like Tigger, returned the gentle serve with a lunge and an animal-like groan. Kato erupted in solo applause. Enrico hit a baseline backhand which crossed the net to bounce right at Serena's feet. As she prepared to strike the ball, Yuji appeared flying almost horizontally in front of her, racket outstretched. The ball hit the rim of his racket and flew into the net. Yuji landed from his lateral leap racket-first with a yelp and a crack. The audience gasped Wimbledon-style and Yuji delivered a Japanese monologue which sounded pretty profane.

'I think his wrist is broken,' Serena announced to the circle of well-wishers.

Polo was delayed while Yuji was helicoptered to the Institut de Médecine de Bordeaux.

Kato-san was even less happy.

'Your Serene Highnesses, Mr President, friends ...' Vincent stood on the small stage, addressing the increasingly inebriated audience.

Seated on an incredibly long dining table in the Salle Vendange, the hundred guests turned politely towards their host with pre-paid smiles. The barn-like room had been transformed into a white wonderland, a childlike view of heaven, for the evening dinner. White silk drapes covered the walls; soft dream-like clouds seemed to float below the ceiling, interspersed with tiny silver stars. The floor was a blanket of fake snow and the table was set with the finest white linen, white Meissen porcelain and crystal wine glasses. Even the guests, who had rested and changed in their sumptuous guest accommodation, were all dressed in white. The only colour in the room was the Chateau du Pont de l'Evêque Bordeaux in the wine glasses, and me. Being so caught up in the event logistics I somehow hadn't registered the all-white dress code, and was wearing my cheap Malaysian black dress. Vincent's look informed me that I had hit an unprecedented low, and would have no doubt made me eat in the kitchen had I not been the only sucker available for Kato-sitting.

I didn't want to be here. I wanted to be at home with Em, eating cheese on toast and making outrageous hen-night plans. I was too tired to make an effort with people too famous for friends; fed up with faking friendly to Kato; and pissed-off with looking so ridiculously out of place.

'It is an honour and a pleasure to be able to welcome such distinguished and dear friends to the beautiful

Chateau du Pont de l'Evêque for this most special of occasions.'

I looked across the table at Mr Kato and the two assistants flanking him. I was stuck between the other two, who I had nicknamed (in my head) Lanky and Bad Teeth. They had spoken across me in Japanese and chain-smoked for the three courses, while I had sampled and re-sampled the Premier Grand Cru Classé B. Which, it had to be said, was improving as the evening progressed. Vincent's careful table planning meant Kato was close enough to the host to feel special, but not so close that Vincent had to actually talk to him. That privilege was reserved for me. Adriana and Enrico sat opposite Vincent and diagonally opposed to Kato, who had stared unashamedly at the model's Dolce and Gabbana-framed cleavage for the past two hours.

'I thank you all from the bottom of my heart.' – he put his hand where his heart would be if he had one – 'for joining me at the launch of Dupont, a new group of luxury brands, to indulge and inspire.'

Vincent had told me to make the speech 'emotional'. I had struggled as I usually got emotional with wine rather than about it. I thought by the time he had finished pulling it to pieces it was as cheesy as an over-ripe Camembert, but, as always, it was his call.

'Dupont has been very many years in the making. It started as a dream when I was a young boy …'

A large screen appeared from the clouds above Vincent's head. Black and white photos of Vincent in his twenties looking pensive or smiling, clearly strictly edited, flashed up. A further nine screens appeared in similar celestial positions around the hall, so no guest could escape the magnified smile of their beatific host.

This had been part of Paul's plan, and it caught me off guard. Whether it was the ethereal setting, eerily reflecting Gordon's predictions of Planet Dupont, the wallpaper of grinning Vincents, or my total exhaustion, I felt the powerful and uncontrollable tsunami of rising hysteria: one of those waves of physical laughter that rocks your body and over which there is no control.

I tensed my jaw and glanced up as a two-metre-high close-up of a young but surprisingly similar-looking Vincent in a straw boating hat and clichéd Parisian striped t-shirt beamed back from some sort of punt.

There was a fine line between a good image presentation and a display of shocking megalomania. Vincent had long-jumped over that line.

'… turning the vision of a young Parisian boy into reality.' Chest puffed out, Vincent performed for his glassy-eyed public.

I felt strangely detached from the scene, like I was watching it on an old black and white TV. Once I'd got past the stellar but arbitrary guest list and the no-expense-spared set-up, all that was left was something rather pathetic. Vincent, this man I had worshipped for his consummate professionalism and media nous, was subjecting his uninterested audience to a king-size slide-show, as if size alone would make them care.

Look at me! Love me!

It was just so needy.

It was at about this moment that I belatedly remembered red wine didn't agree with me.

A snort escaped my mouth. I brought my napkin up to my face and pretended to blow my nose, which was the first time I got any attention from the Japanese delegation. I was teetering on the edge of the danger zone: I was on the limit of losing control of my bodily functions and my job. I kept my eyes fixed on the thread count of the white linen table cloth, and dug my right thumbnail hard into the left palm.

'Dupont is about the best, and I have waited a long time to purchase what I'm sure is the best Saint Emilion Chateau, which by beautiful coincidence also shares the name "du Pont" …'

'Dupont', which isn't even your name.

'… Chateau du Pont de l'Evèque is currently a Premier Grand Cru classé B, but will soon be rightfully recognised as a classé A.'

On cue, the merry guests erupted in cheers.

The photos jumped to Vincent in his thirties in an 80s double-breasted blazer and baby yellow slacks. It was the slacks that did it.

Oh, no. No. No.

The dam was broken. My whole body started rocking as tears of laughter careered down my cheeks. My lower lids became two infinity pools. I could barely see through the torrents of water flowing out of my tear ducts and forming multiple black mascara rivers down my face, nose and napkin. Snorts persisted in breaking through the napkin sound barrier. I could feel I was getting some sideways glances, but if I didn't move, didn't look up and absolutely didn't try to speak, I might just survive the two paragraphs until the end of Vincent's speech.

Vincent was building up to the climax of the 'One Man, One Dream' speech. I was bolted to my chair, clenching the frame with my fist to resist the silent shudders, when Kato noisily pushed his chair back, got up and walked out of the Salle. Each of his steps echoed around the celestial space. Shockingly bad timing, for which he went up in my estimation. Vincent paused for a microsecond, before continuing undeterred.

My napkin was sodden and streaked with zebra Maybelline stripes. I shot a glance at the screen, where we were in the safer territory of Vincent's forties.

I should have checked on Kato, but as soon as I tried to compose myself a shudder rippled up my spine, reminding me that the hysteria had not yet relinquished control. I gave myself a stern talking-to.

For Christ's sake, Kate, you are the peddler and protector of this image, slacks or not. Pull yourself together.

'So, friends ...'

YOU'VE NEVER EVEN MET THEM BEFORE!

'... to christen the first steps of this epic Dupont journey, no one less than a legend would do. I am immensely proud to welcome, and if I wasn't married already ...'

I knew without looking that Vincent and Mrs D exchanged a look of love.

'... I would worship the ground she walks on. Please, friends, welcome Miss Diana Ross!'

And I could now say something I wouldn't have ever dreamed possible – my career was saved by Diana Ross. In the movement and excitement she generated, no one noticed the snivelly streaked wreck I had become.

The guests jumped to their feet and about fifty waiters appeared, gracefully separated the table into components and swept the chairs aside to form a dance floor. Twenty-five mirror balls descended from the ceiling, filling the room with sparkly disco light. Vincent stepped off the stage and spotlights circled on the shimmering backdrop, lighting a slim silhouette.

The inimitable voice filled the room, speaking the opening lines to 'Ain't No Mountain High Enough' and sending the atmosphere electric with anticipation. The screen seemed to evaporate and Diana Ross stood centre-stage in a long white sequinned dress with outsize white fur cuffs.

As she launched into the chorus the guests screamed, whooped and jumped up and down. The power of a diva to get a party started. Or the relief that Vincent had finally shut up.

Adriana leapt to the front of the dance floor, bouncing in her barely-there dress.

Pull yourself together, Kate.

I wiped my face with someone else's clean napkin and downed a glass of Evian. I was dying to dance but had to retrieve the *Paris Match* photographer from the staff kitchens for photos of dancing celebs. He had controlled access and I had to be vigilant so that the shots showed an amazing party with guests having sober fun. Nothing embarrassing, damaging or sue-able. I scanned the room for my other charges. Enrico was half-engaged in a conversation with the actor from *House* and half watching his boogieing girlfriend. Where was Kato?

I grabbed a second glass of water from a circling waiter, and edged my way through the pulsating guests towards the steel kitchen doors.

I had completed half a lap of the dance floor when I spotted what could only be described as 'white Elvis': shirt undone to the waist, tight white trousers, and a previously unspotted pair of white Swarovski-studded cowboy boots. Kato thrust his hips and jabbed his finger in the air like a *Saturday Night Fever* extra. What on earth had happened to the deadpan dinner guest? He jerked and thrusted, creating instant space around him. He used a distorted medley of all the classic disco moves, getting closer to Adriana, who was oblivious to the advancing Travolta.

One trip to the loo and he'd returned with a personality transplant. But, well, he was happy and that was what Vincent had ordered. Another box ticked.

Diana Ross followed with 'Upside Down'. Every time she sang the title words, Kato threw his head towards the floor and stuck his bum in the air. He also experimented with some moonwalking.

'Ok guys, I'm going to slow the tempo down a bit now,' the soul diva announced before breaking into my all-time favourite, 'Touch me in the Morning'.

With the speed of a chemically enhanced ferret, Kato pulled Adriana into a slow dance hold, resting his head on her boobs.

Then everything happened very fast.

Adriana screamed and tried to push Kato away. He clung on like some Greenpeace activist to a protected tree. Enrico pushed his way aggressively past the dancing guests, elbowing The Edge in the ribs and spilling Bordeaux down Elle Macpherson's Valentino. Bill Clinton's secret service homed in on the scream. I was still trying to find somewhere to put down my glass of water when Enrico swung his fist into Kato's temple, and he collapsed in a slump on the floor.

The *Paris Match* photographer looked triumphant.

'I don't care 'ow fucking much you're taking the guy for, my girlfriend is not included,' Enrico yelled at Vincent, as Adriana lay on the chaise longue in the chateau's magnificent sitting room, pouting and fanning herself with a copy of *Architectural Design*. 'The guy snorted half of Colombia.'

'Oh!' Adriana perked up. 'Do you think he …' and then petered out.

I walked in, sober and exhausted, after a lengthy, impassioned plea, which encompassed threats and outright bribery, to the photographer to delete the final shots. I had finally won after agreeing to an 'at home' shoot with Enrico and Adriana. They didn't need to know that right now.

Kato was being cared for by the housekeeper in the library on the other side of the wide entrance hall. Vincent was caught between two evils: siding with his beloved and valuable driver, or the inestimable financial value of Kato's partnership. I lurked just inside the door, sure that in some way, as both Enrico and Kato were my responsibility, this would all end up being my fault.

The guests had proved to be pretty unshockable and like the star that she was, Diana Ross hadn't stopped singing. I was too drained to tap my feet to the muffled beat of 'Why Do Fools Fall in Love'.

'I'm sick of this whoring bullsheet. Harry has offered me double money, so give me one good reason why I shouldn't sign?'

'Because with Kato's money, my team is unbeatable,' Vincent said with one hundred per cent conviction.

I lay on the narrow single bed in the spartan staff quarters. I had had to clamber across a small building site to get there. It turned out that while the central part of the chateau was exquisitely decorated, the side wings were just empty shells of rubble.

I checked my text messages inbox and winced when I saw Em's name.

Gd job im yr best friend cos not many would 4give abandonment & clothes theft!

I thumped my head backwards on the pillow. *For* … thump … *Fuck's* … thump … *sake* … thump. This job so engulfed me, I could no longer function in the real world.

CHAPTER 11

Nürburgring Circuit, Germany
Sunday

Dupont Lamborghini F1 Team

PRESS RELEASE

German Grand Prix
Nürburgring Circuit
Sunday

Race

Marcel Müller claimed his maiden Formula One victory at The Ring to the delight of legions of countrymen who had turned out in support. From pole position he drove a faultless race, holding off attacks from both Martini Magna cars. Enrico Costa was involved in a coming together with Felipe Massa at Turn 2 that effectively ended his race.

Marcel Müller – 1st

'This day is so special I can barely put it into words. I grew up only 25 km from this legendary circuit, and always dreamed of one day standing on the podium. Winning at my home Grand Prix in my first F1 season, is just amazing. It's the best day of my life!'

Enrico Costa – DNF

'I got a great start and got past Sweeney off the grid. I was alongside Massa going into Turn 2 when I felt us touch, and then I was off. That was it. Race over.'

Vincent Dupont, Team Principal

'A great result for Marcel who has delivered on his promise with a superior drive and a well-deserved win. Enrico did not even get a chance to race, which is unacceptable.'

Media contact

Kate Ellison – Kateellison@dupontf1.com

www.dupontf1.com

There were many things Vincent could and did control, but the Nürburgring result was not one of them. Due to Yuji Okada's broken wrist from the tennis match, Vincent couldn't follow through on having him replace Marcel. Thankfully, because that would have been a PR nail bomb. Gordon Barry had worked out Vincent's plan in fifteen hours, so it wouldn't have taken long for the rest of the paddock media to catch up. Marcel was liked and rated as an up-and-coming talent by many of them. A change like that would not have been put to bed with two lines in a press release.

I was really happy with the result but, until I could gauge Vincent's reaction, I did my best to conceal my whoops and cheers under my gradually thickening professional skin. A team win was of course great, but when a good guy won, on his home turf (the Golden Globe for a driver), it was like a rare moment of motorsport justice.

Also, on a selfish level, I felt his win offered some sort of redemption for my Silverstone press release that could easily have put an end to his career in a few keystrokes, had it not been for a women's tennis champion and an ambitious but stupid Japanese driver.

Vincent seemed caught between celebrating a team win, taking the credit for discovering the new Senna-Schumacher-Alonso (depending on the nationality of the quoted journalist) and dealing with the Calabrian wrath of his number one driver. Enrico had been so enraged by Marcel's pole position that he attacked at the race start, attempting an ill-judged move on Massa into turn two which resulted in a damaged front wing, a spin and a stall. Totally his fault.

Vincent had to do the traditional congratulatory display in parc fermé as Marcel pulled in triumphant. I was interested to see whether he'd do his customary leap over the barrier for a sweaty driver hug. Or whether, considering his less than cordial treatment of the race winner, he'd keep his distance, fearing a helmet headbutt. Vincent opted for a toned-down handslap-cum-hug and Marcel, who was flying high on his first F1 win, would have hugged anyone.

So, another PR nightmare averted.

'Kate, are you welling up?'

Lisa appeared at my side in the podium anteroom as I watched Marcel pull off his cap, clench his jaw and look out over the crowds as the German national anthem sang out over the circuit. The fans had gone crazy, and had somehow vaulted the barriers into the pit lane.

'It's one of those rare nice moments, don't you think?'

'Nice moments are when Martini Magna wins.' She nudged me in the ribs. 'Wow, Marcel is so damn young. Listen, I wanted to mention,' – she leant in to whisper, although there was no one standing nearby – 'I've had my fill of F1; I've had a job offer from Champions League, so I'll be off at the end of the season ...'

The 'Marseillaise' took over the anthem baton. Despite being based in the UK, Vincent was resolute that Dupont Lamborghini was a French team.

'... If you fancy jumping ship, I'll put in a word for you. Harry thinks you do "a good job, considering ...". His words not mine!'

I dragged my eyes off the screen to look at Lisa, who was at my right shoulder. Formula One never ceased to surprise me. Since she had caught me red-handed snooping on Harry's yacht in Monaco we hadn't talked much, just the usual greetings in passing. I'd been too embarrassed to try to clear the air.

I had no plan to change team, but it was really nice to know I was rated. My fragile ego swelled instantaneously, like a corn kernel in a hot pan.

'Congratulations to you. And thanks, that's really kind, but I'm happy where I am for now.'

She looked at me with a confused smile.

'I know Vincent makes Harry out to be Dr Evil, but he's a good man, Kate. It's true he has a flexible moral compass. But as a boss, he trusts and empowers his staff, and pays well.'

I wasn't really listening. It would take more than a couple of sentences to swing me pro-Bircher. His constant attacks on Vincent had caused most of my PR headaches and I credited him with the ball of stress that constantly knotted my intestines. So, as I did more and more often these days, I exercised selective hearing, while uttering a non-committal, 'Oh, yeah.'

'Formula One is just like a big playground for him. He finds Vincent an easy target because he's so, you know, well, anally retentive. Harry can't help himself, he loves to wind him up. And the rest of it is just business.'

I was saved from another neutral retort as the podium music finished and the drivers and Vincent appeared, champagne-drenched. I quickly stuck my dictaphone in front of Marcel to grab his quote for the press release before he was whisked off to the press conference.

'Sorry I'm late.' I flew into the stillness of Vincent's office and plonked myself on a chair between Tuffy and Mike. Janey gave me a wide-eyed 'you're-in-trouble' look. My other marketing colleagues were all transfixed with various parts of the table surface, in the bollocking pose, the inevitable outcome of an early morning summons. I tried to discreetly tuck in my shirt.

Vincent paced at the head of the meeting table under the *Last Supper* painting.

'This is *exactly* what I am talking about!' He stopped pacing to point at me, and ten other pairs of eyes followed suit. 'I made it very clear that this meeting was to start at seven-thirty, not seven-thirty-two or seven-thirty-four or whenever you could be bothered to drag yourself out of bed …'

His eyes were burning into the side of my head: '… or finish getting dressed.'

I stopped tucking in.

In spite of the hour, Vincent was fired up and on a roll. The reason why was still a mystery. Everyone else sat slumped, red-eyed and unkempt. It was an example of the differing lives of boss and employee. Vincent flew home from the German Grand Prix last night in his private jet. He would have been home for an aperitif with the baroness by eight p.m. Followed, no doubt, by a fine three-course meal prepared by their highly-acclaimed French chef, a good night's sleep, a nutritional breakfast and a chauffeured ride to the TechQ in his Mercedes S-class.

We, the staff, had on the other hand got home between one-thirty and two a.m. The ten p.m. flight from Frankfurt had been delayed for forty minutes, then followed the usual seventy-five-minute journey in the team bus to the TechQ, from where we took our own cars back home in the direction we had just come from. There was an unidentifiable sandwich on the plane and, well, personally speaking, a pack of Walkers Builder's Breakfast crisps at six forty-five a.m. And I could bet large sums of money I didn't have, that his outfit was not recycled from his dirty laundry pile.

'Success depends on order, precision, discipline.' He strode to his desk and picked up a document between his thumb and forefinger. 'There is no flexibility. And I do *not* want creativity.' He waved the document in the air, plain side towards us, so we were still none the wiser. I just prayed, as I'm sure the rest of the table did, that the document wasn't mine.

'So what the hell is this?' He slapped the document on to the desk and I heard Mike's sharp exhalation. I recognised the page.

'Actually, Vincent,' Mike ventured with suicidal boldness, 'I thought I could make a valuable contribution ...'

'Whose name is on the letterhead?'

'Vincent, if I may just defend ...'

For crying out loud, Mike. Shut up!

'Does it say Mike F1?'

Now my mum would definitely call that tone 'facetious'.

'No,' several voices mumbled.

'Dupont F1.' Vincent dragged out the syllables like a boxing commentator. 'My name. My team. My way.' He leant on the table with his knuckles, fixing each eyeline in turn. 'So let's be clear. On no account get clever, creative, or show initiative.' He sneered, managing to make 'initiative' sound like something truly disgusting.

His attention switched to a flake of ash of the table. Pinning it down with his index finger, he walked to the bin by his desk, flicked it in, and Viraguarded his hands.

There was a rustle of movement around the table as the bollockees believed the meeting was over. But Vincent hadn't finished: he marched back.

'And the next person who produces a multi-coloured scrapbook of a document on my letterhead, will be stacking shelves at Tesco before the ink has dried in the printer tray.' It was an example of how ingrained in us Vincent's '46 Rules of Presentation' were (black ink only, Garamond font, one staple, no paper clips, etc) that no one sniggered. 'In fact, as of now, I want all coloured print cartridges removed from the building.'

Natalie walked in with Vincent's expresso. I had hoped for some croissants, but it clearly wasn't that kind of meeting.

'Presentation is as fundamental to success as car performance. You are not working for Harry Bircher, where memos are signed with handprints.'

As Natalie held the saucer, Vincent swallowed the coffee in one and replaced the cup.

'You have all let standards slip, and given that slob Bircher the advantage. That is unacceptable. Now get to work.'

We filed out. Every meeting, bollocking or interaction with Vincent in the past week had somehow ended up being about Harry Bircher.

'He's bloody well losing it,' Mike huffed when we had barely cleared the stairwell.

'I've seen him stressed before, but this is borderline psychotic,' Janey added, her heels clip-clopping on the tiles. 'Mike, have you got a death wish or something? I mean, purple bullet points!'

'Vincent is screwing up the Kato deal.' Mike pushed open the marketing door with ninja force.

'Why do you even care?' I said, protecting my face with my arm from the forceful return swing. Mike had stomped off.

'Because he's finally put down the deposit on the Sunseeker Superhawk he's buying with the commission,' Tuffy said, a cheeky glint in his eye. 'He'll finally have the boat, not just the keyring.'

'But he had nothing to do with the deal.' My mind began to churn through the calculations. If Kato was buying into the team, it wouldn't be for less than a hundred million dollars. Fuck! If Mike got only two per cent, that was two million dollars.

Tuffy looked at me with a bemused smile. 'You finished the maths yet, Kate? Tidy old sum, eh?'

'But … he's done fuck-all of nothing.' I felt a surge of anger. I thought back to Mike's pity speeches about being 'out of the loop', his bloody proposal I'd carted with me to Bordeaux, and his crashing the post-Manoir meeting.

'Cheer up, Vincent will never fall for it,' Janey chuckled at my open-mouth stare. 'Mike's just trying it on. And for that sort of money, why not?'

I shrugged, feeling a black mood settling in. I had neither commission deal, nor menial-task-threshold clause. Out of the marketing team I was working the hardest, but somehow reaping the least rewards. And I wasn't sure that wasn't totally my fault.

'I don't want to be the one who breaks the bad news.' Janey looped her arm through mine. 'Father Christmas, happy-ever-after, team spirit ... it's all the same fairy tale.'

The German and Hungarian Grands Prix were what was called back-to-back races or double-headers. These harmless-sounding names belied their true horror. Race weekends were physically draining in their intensity and, while I tried to plan a few GPs in advance, in truth I never managed it, so I used the ten days between races to (a) tidy up loose ends and reply to questions from the previous race, (b) recover, and (c) prepare the next weekend's programme. On a back-to-back the GPs took place on successive weekends, so this ten-day cycle was compacted into three days. You had to fight against the Monday post-race coma to crank up the same pace worked on a weekend. Having had the chateau launch the weekend before, this was an exercise in futility. I sat in front of my laptop, staring trance-like at the Sony logo. There were no reserves to draw on.

With minimal index finger movement, I scrolled down to the red-flagged email from my dad. Received three weeks ago, it was a lengthy text formatted like a letter. I clicked on 'Reply'.

Can't wait. C u then. K x

I clicked 'Send'. Hungary was the crunch point for mid-season fatigue, but after this race there would be a heavenly three and a half weeks until the European GP in Valencia. I was taking the full allotted seven-day holiday and flying to my parents' cottage in Normandy, where I would do absolutely bugger-all each and every day, except lie in the garden and read Dad's paper.

Budapest, Hungary
Thursday, 11.30 a.m.

'Ah, Miss Ellison, it's a pleasure to meet you. I am Robert, the manager of the Kempinski Hotel Corvinus.' He was strange to look at, somewhat reptilian, tall and very skinny; his head hung to the left as if it was too heavy for its lanky frame. He seemed to be aware that his limbs were unfeasibly long, and he kept his arms folded in close to his waist.

'Thank you, Robert.' I shook his clammy hand. 'I just need to prepare Mr Dupont's suite, if someone could accompany me.' I never called him Mr Dupont, but found hotel managers reacted better to the formality.

'Yes, miss, I'm afraid there is a very slight problem with Mr Dupont's suite.' He twisted his mouth into a pained pout, which drew attention to his pitted skin.

'What problem?'

'We do have a presidential suite available for him, just not his usual one. It is our other one.' He looked relieved to have got it off his chest, and looked at me optimistically for a positive reply. No such luck.

'Robert, this isn't good, really, it isn't good.' In life pre-Dupont Lamborghini, I would have been intimidated by five-star hotel managers, especially since, well, in life pre-DL I'd never even met any before. Hell, even a snotty waitress in Pizza Hut could have me apologising for ordering something on the menu. But I had got used to, and was no longer embarrassed by, presenting Vincent's precise, bizarre and uncompromising demands. At the end of the day, it was them or me who was going to get it if everything wasn't perfect. And I was pretty fed up with it being me.

'There has been extensive correspondence between the Kempinski and Mr Dupont's office, where his request for his usual suite was very clear. I have confirmation here.' I started to pull files out of my laptop bag, laying great wads on the reception desk. My heart rate was quickening as my adrenaline started to spike. Vincent would be arriving soon. I already had a very small window to prepare his room and luggage, so that everything was sterile and pressed.

'Miss Ellison, I can assure you, it is an equally magnificent suite. Heads of state have marvelled at its opulence, and it also shares a magnificent view of the Danube.'

'But it's not his suite!' My panicked voice rang out around reception as several heads, including many I recognised from F1, turned in my direction.

Robert's stance changed from grovelling to seeing me as a potential public liability. He took my elbow, trying to usher me into a quiet corner at the end of the long reception counter. I decided to switch tack.

'Look, Robert, I understand you must be flat-out with the Grand Prix and everything.' – I put my hand on his bony shoulder – 'and I realise you're in a tricky situation, but Mr Dupont is a precise man who is very specific about what he likes and dislikes. He will be here very shortly and, believe me, he will not accept change or compromise.'

'Miss Ellison, if I could change the situation I would. Mr Dupont is an extremely valuable client, but so is Mr Bircher.' He spoke in a hushed whisper, his forehead concertinaing with worry lines. At the mention of Bircher's name the giant fist reappeared in my gut.

'I don't know how it happened, but Mr Bircher was let into the wrong suite when he arrived an hour ago. I explained that the suite was reserved for Mr Dupont and he was very gracious and understanding, but said that he suffers from a condition where if he doesn't sleep in an east-west direction he suffers extreme nausea. He said Mr Dupont and he were great friends and that he would understand.'

Bullshit, you gullible idiot, I wanted to shout, but was interrupted by: 'Oi, Vincey!' It was Harry's voice booming across reception. I cringed and turned slowly to see Vincent, preceded by a crowd-scanning Ivan, stepping out of the revolving door.

M3 en route to the Hungaroring circuit

'Marina, Marina-ah,' JB sang out from the back row of the Peugeot Tepee, parodying the Santana hit. 'Oh, Marina, Marina-ah …'

'Hey, Carlos, I think you'll find it's Maria,' Mike corrected. 'I mean, think about it, otherwise the *West Side Story* reference doesn't work.'

'Mike, my pedantic friend, it was most definitely Marina.' JB followed up with his filthy laugh.

'Bloody hell, JB,' Janey said. 'You don't waste time: you only arrived last night.'

'You're right on the button there, Janey. At twenty thousand forints an hour, time is one thing I did not waste.' JB jabbed me with his elbow.

'Well, there certainly are a lot of attractive girls here.' I leant my head on the car window, replaying Vincent's reaction to the suite debacle in my head. Something was going down. I didn't know what, but I didn't have a good feeling.

As I'd Vincent-proofed the suite on tiptoe, the maniacally pacing occupant kept muttering 'last straw' while pressing the redial button on his mobile. I was waiting for the tongue-lashing, but his full focus was on whoever should have picked up that call. Just as I was Viraguarding the last TV remote, he got through.

'Have you got it? ... You have ...' He exhaled loudly, high-fiving the window. 'Great, great job ... As soon as you can ... At the circuit, my office.'

He hung up, visibly calmed and, exhibiting all the layman signs of schizophrenia, gave me a huge smile and a slap on the back as I left the suite.

'Great job, Kate, see you at the track.'

My attention drifted back to the car, where a pregnant silence lay heavy in the air. I turned away from the window. Janey, Mike and Tuffy looked at each other and burst out laughing. JB reached around the headrest and put his palm on my forehead.

'What?' I shook him off.

There had been a big crowd of fans at the entrance to the hotel, who had been cordoned off by a couple of black-suited hotel security. More than half were girls with long hair and long legs. And now, as we skirted the circuit, there were more of the same.

'They'll be a fan of yours if you want,' Tuffy said, and they all cracked up again. I felt like the only person without the translation headset as the Kyrgyzstan delegate addressed the United Nations.

The Tepee pulled up to the track entrance and the needle swung from 'attractive' girls to 'decidedly more obvious'. One even held up a sign with a list of services available.

'Oh, ok, I got it.' The headset had just kicked into action.

Vincent's office, The Wing
Hungaroring Paddock
Saturday, 4.10 p.m.

'Kate,' – Vincent leant back on his chair, swinging on the rear legs, – 'what medium would you use to get a film out to the widest possible audience?'

Vincent's extreme moods were all-pervading. I could usually sense, from the door, a storming black mood, or the rarer and more disconcerting bright bubbly mood. I picked up on the latter as I stepped through the doorway, squeezing to the side to let Mike Capshaw out. This time I didn't have to be a genius reader of minds: Vincent was actually humming.

'You mean a promo – I assume not a feature film?' I smiled to show I was on board with the jolly spirit as I tried to gauge what he was really after.

'A short film, Kate.' He tapped his fingers on the desk in time with the DJ in his head. It sounded like the theme tune to *Dad's Army*. Good mood notwithstanding, he wasn't verbose.

'This film is for media use, or general public viewing?' I was pushing it with the extra questions, but I'd have to stand by whatever answer I gave.

'I said the widest possible audience.' Vincent took a swig from the Evian bottle and replaced it on the round silver coaster. He held the mouthful in an exaggerated pout, then sucked some air through it with a gurgling sound before swallowing. He was getting bored.

'Erm, well, YouTube. It reaches an international audience, and billions of films are viewed each month.' He gave an almost imperceptible nod. I got the impression this was the answer he expected. 'We could issue a simultaneous press release with a link to encourage viewing.'

'No.' He rocked forward, tapping his index finger on the desk. 'No press releases. It would be anonymous.'

'Really? Oh, right, well, that's definitely possible, in fact a friend of mine did just that …'

I petered out. The jovial atmosphere had caught me out. Vincent would not have been interested in how Danny paid back Paolo's betrayal.

Vincent stopped humming, and his beady black pupils locked on mine.

'Take a seat, Kate.'

I perched on the edge of the small black leather chair facing his desk, and pulled out my pad and pen to take notes.

'The future of the team is at stake.' He leaned his forearms on the desk. I was leaning forward to take notes. I couldn't hold his unblinking gaze so looked down to my pad and scribbled 'stake'.

Is he finally going to tell me what's going on?

'Dupont Lamborghini is hanging in the balance between a great future and no future.'

This was a sudden shift in mood from the hummer of a few minutes ago. I felt proud he could be so honest with me.

Vincent slid the heavy ashtray across the desk as he lit a Marlboro, all the while fixing me with his stare.

'In this industry, nobody likes a winner. Because if you're winning, then they aren't. And that's all they exist to do. It's what we all exist to do. But some of us do it better than others.'

He smiled and I smiled back, holding my breath until the cloud of Philip Morris's finest dispersed.

'They especially don't like someone new who comes in and wins off the bat, following their own way, with new ideas and not kow-towing to the old school.'

I knew who he meant by 'they'. It wasn't really a 'they', just a 'him', a two-metre-tall Essex lout called Harry Bircher. Vincent was using the US presidential campaign tactic of not naming 'my opponent'.

'I am a hair's breadth away from securing the finances to ensure Dupont Lamborghini can continue to dominate Formula One and retain the best driver in the world.'

He tapped the non-existent column of ash on the chunky glass edge of the ashtray. 'This deal has to happen, Keht. Dupont Lamborghini is not a team that can be beaten into submission. Great teams don't give up without a fight.' Vincent clenched his hand into a fist to show he was serious about the fight part.

Working for Vincent was intense and stressful, but it was also somehow liberating. He lived in a world of perfect clarity: black or white, friend or foe. No need for me to think, evaluate or deliberate, just to act on the conclusion.

'Unfortunately there's only one kind of fight these guys understand.' He rested his head in his hand and sighed. I had stopped taking useless notes, and just clutched my pad on my lap.

'I appreciate that you've shown loyalty and dedication to the team.' He pulled his head up straight and smiled. My cheeks flushed instantly as my popcorn ego inflated on impact again. It was ninety degrees Fahrenheit in the shade outside, but chilled to a polar sixty in Vincent's office, and I was sweating.

'It hasn't gone unnoticed.'

I looked down awkwardly, as externally I didn't know how to behave in the light of this rare praise. Internally I was beaming and doing handsprings around his office.

Balancing the half-smoked cigarette in the ashtray, positioning it with precision so the butt didn't slip down into the curls of ash in the base, Vincent reached down and opened the left-hand drawer below his desk. There must have been very little in the drawer, or he had literally just placed the item in there, because he pulled out a transparent CD case without looking down, and placed it on the desk.

Vincent waited for me to look up, and then smiled as he let out another sigh. I glanced down at the black marker scribble on the disk, but couldn't decipher it upside down.

'Put this on WhoTube, tonight.' He slid the plastic box across the desk with his perfectly manicured finger.

'It's, er … YouTube.' I reached to take it, but his finger remained in place.

'But it *must be* untraceable to me and the team.'

He released his finger and sat back in his chair, hands clasped on the desk.

'Tag it with the key words "Bircher" and "Formula One".'

For someone who called it WhoTube, that was a remarkably precise request.

The hotel phone trilled with a staccato ring. I woke up with the bolt of stress that goes hand in hand with a call in the night.

I was still in my team uniform, on top of the bed, all the lights were on and CNN blared out from the TV. Big black mascara streaks decorated the pillow, and the TV remote had left a complete imprint on my upper arm.

Germany? Hungary? Turkey? Where am I? The neutral but expensive fabrics, polished wood and satellite TV were the worldwide five-star standard.

The nauseatingly impatient ring trilled through my brain. I scoured each bedside table for the antidote to the instrument of torture.

'Hello!' I pulled the TV remote out from the folds of white duvet and muted Richard Quest.

'Kate, it's JB.'

Relief, trumped by annoyance.

'JB, what the …' I caught sight of the digital clock on the bottom of the television screen: 23.45.

'Kate, I'm here with the hotel manager,' JB continued in an exaggerated tone, as if my English language skills had become sub-standard, 'and he would like to check that Marina is here to pick up her guest pass for the race tomorrow.'

The manager's voice came on the phone. 'Miss Ellison, I apologise, but the hotel has a strict policy on guest visits.'

Damn JB. It had taken me a while to catch on on Thursday, but even half-asleep I could read between the lines on this one. The 'guest visit policy' was a 'no hooker' policy.

I just wanted to sleep.

'Yes Robert, I understand, but I was in a meeting until now.' I threw in a note of frustration to add authenticity. 'Miss, er, Marina is indeed a guest of Dupont Lamborghini tomorrow. I must give her the pass tonight.'

'Very well, Miss Ellison. Thank you.' He hung up, not believing a word of it.

'JB, you deserve all the knobrot Eastern Europe can offer!' I shouted into the dead handset.

Now that I was fully awake, I swung my legs over the side of the bed to undress and wash off my congealed make-up. My right leg retracted as something sharp dug into my inner thigh. I slid my hand across the thick down duvet, pulling out the clear CD case with the illegible writing.

Christ, I must have fallen asleep before I uploaded it. What on earth was I thinking? I took back part of that curse on JB.

I flipped open my laptop on the nightstand and booted it up. While the black screen whirred into life I went into the bathroom, washed my face, changed into the big white dressing gown and scraped my hair into a ponytail. Under the spotlights over the mirror in the white marble bathroom every blemish was highlighted. I had dark grey shadows under my eyes, and even with the bit of tan that stopped at the collar of my shirt, I looked washed-out. The face that looked back at me in the mirror looked old and drained. Already a casualty of Formula One's accelerated ageing.

I curtailed the downward spiral into depression by switching off the floodlighting and heading back to the bed, where the Dupont Lamborghini logo screensaver shone back at me.

Sitting cross-legged on the bed, with my back against the headboard, I swigged at the day-old Diet Coke bottle on the bedside table before pulling the laptop on to a pillow on my lap. The CD case lay next to me on the duvet, looking unremarkable. I picked it up, turning it over in my hand. In the case was a bog-standard Tevion recordable compact disc in a silvery-gold finish.

Did the black scribble say '*Victoire*'? French for 'victory', or 'video'? It was pretty illegible.

How could I have fallen asleep?

I was nosey by nature, which wasn't a negative in this job, as I needed to know everything all the time. And this disc contained a lot of answers.

Whatever was on it would ensure Enrico re-signed with the team.

Whatever was on it would make Kato hand over large chunks of money to be Vincent's partner.

Whatever was on it would secure the future of Dupont Lamborghini F1.

Whatever was on it was causing Vincent's freakishly happy mood.

But somehow, I didn't want to know what was on it. At the track I hadn't been able to view the CD for risk of being overseen. Vincent had been clear about being discreet. At least I had had an excuse to escape from the track relatively early, at seven-thirty p.m. But then, was it the combination of permanent exhaustion and a comfy bed that meant I'd crashed out?

Now I was awake and alone, and yet I still didn't want to view it.

I clicked on the network icon and waited for the hotel wi-fi option to appear. I typed the username and password the manager had given me. The two mini-screens on the bottom toolbar lit up with the world icon.

I was online.

I wasn't sure I'd remember how to upload the film. I'd been pretty tequila-sodden when Danny showed me. I wanted to call him. I looked at the digital clock, which flashed 00.04. It was three weeks since Silverstone and we still hadn't spoken.

I clicked on Internet Explorer and typed in www. youtube.com.

Sign In or Sign up

My attention kept being drawn to the muted images of international weather maps on the TV. I reached for the remote and started to channel surf. I watched a few minutes of *House*, but couldn't lip-read over the Hungarian. I forced my focus back on to the computer screen.

I clicked 'Sign Up'. I needed a spoof account. I clicked in the username box and Danny's 'Sinatrasings' account name appeared, with his asterisked password. *What to do? Vincent said 'not linked to the team or F1'. Danny wasn't, plus he would have made it anonymous so Paolo couldn't directly blame him. I just wanted it over with.*

I clicked 'Sign In'.

I was in.

My deluxe room in the Kempinski Corvinus had nifty buttons on the bedside table to turn on the lights, and one even opened the curtains. I pressed and watched the Basilica appear as the yellow gold drapes slowly whirred apart, reminding me that I was actually in Budapest rather than an international hotel vacuum.

The digital clock glowed 00.27.

Just do as you were told. Upload the film, then go back to sleep. Stop procrastinating!

Christ, this wasn't the hardest job. It was a lot easier than asking the kids from Oxford hospital on a special TechQ tour to wear a paper face mask before entering Vincent's office.

I opened the case, took out the CD and inserted it in my disc drive. I clicked on 'Play'.

The image was very grainy. Certainly not shot with professional equipment. The light wasn't great, but neither was it dark. There were a few people milling about on a yacht. It was a party; a dance track with a heavy bass was playing in the background. I recognised one of the staff; I recognised the deck. It was Harry Bircher's *Seventh Heaven*. The camera swung across the dance floor, where Riccardo Santos was spinning a girl in a tiny Samba outfit and huge feather headdress.

The camera zoomed behind the dancing couple to a young girl lying on her front in a white string bikini on the wide sunbeds. A hand extended towards her carrying a small silver tray. She pulled herself languidly up to a half-seated position, picked up a rolled-up note from the tray, held it to her nose and bent over the tray for a couple of seconds, before pulling herself abruptly upright. She repeated the action with her other nostril. Then she tossed her long blonde hair back, pulled off her bikini top and threw herself on top of a balding fat man, the tray holder. As they were kissing, the camera got jolted and the film was over.

Vincent was right: this was not what Fi needed. Rich old men abusing their power with clearly underage girls. Harry Bircher and his fat friend should be ashamed.

Upload.

Click.

I selected the G:/drive. A single file name appeared. 'Victoria'.

I clicked on it. A timer bar appeared and the block of blue colour filled the box surprisingly quickly.

Add video name and description and edit privacy settings.

I typed in 'Victoria' and then 'Formula 1' and 'Bircher'.
Share your video with the world.
Click.
Upload video.
Click.

Dupont Lamborghini F1 Team

PRESS RELEASE

Hungarian Grand Prix
Hungaroring Circuit, Budapest
Sunday

Race

The Dupont Lamborghini cars finished a disappointing 8th and 9th in the Hungarian Grand Prix. A wheel-gun malfunction on Enrico's first pit-stop meant he had to complete a slow lap before coming in again to have the tyre refitted. Marcel was given a drive-through penalty after cutting across the white line on the exit of the pit lane.

Enrico Costa – 8th

'I had a great pace at the start of the race and was close behind Santos before my first stop. In the pit stop my right rear tyre wasn't fitted properly. I realised the moment I went out, I had to drive ultra-carefully to complete the lap and get the car back to the pits to fit a new tyre. We just threw points away today.'

Marcel Müller – 9th

'Our race strategy was based on me exiting the pits ahead of Sweeney after my first stop. I knew it was going to be close. When I saw him in my mirrors pulling up alongside me, I accelerated and must have crossed the line too early. I apologise to the team. I lost out on a great result today.'

Vincent Dupont, Team Principal

'An unacceptable result. The race was marred by amateur mistakes at a critical point in the season. These were errors that Dupont Lamborghini will never make again.'

Media contact
Kate Ellison – Kateellison@dupontf1.com

www.dupontf1.com

CHAPTER 12

The Ellisons' very well-maintained garden
St Gatien des Bois, Normandy, France
Tuesday, 3.30 p.m.

'Darling, I'm making shepherd's pie for dinner. Do you want peas or carrots?' my Mum shouted through the kitchen window, peering over a thick clump of rambling rose.

'Either's great.' I swatted a fly, which kept landing on the paragraph I was reading. It was a perfect sunny day, with just enough breeze to make sitting immobile pleasant and not sticky. I had been sitting on the sunlounger in a Speedo swimming costume, a relic of the inter-school swimming championships, for five hours solid (bar pee and tea breaks). And was already halfway through the trashy novel I'd picked up at Luton airport.

'Your father prefers peas, but I know you like your carrots.'

Leaning on the garden table, his glasses balanced on his nose as he tackled the Sudoku challenge from yesterday's *Telegraph*, Dad rolled his eyes.

'Peas would be lovely, Mum.'

'You know what, I'm going to do both. These carrots came from the garden, and they really are tasty. I've been using a new organic peat. Did you tell Kate about the organic peat, darling?'

'Not yet, dear.' Dad and I smiled, falling into our lifelong habit of placating her in the name of peace.

'I want to make sure you get a good meal inside of you – you're all skin and bones.'

'Hardly,' I replied, grabbing a chunk of thigh flesh.

'You don't eat, and you never return my calls.' Mum's voice had a brief wobble of hysteria. 'You can't expect me not to worry!'

'I don't, and I'm very happy with the pea and carrot combo.'

'Are you being facetious, Kate? Is she being facetious?'

'No!' Dad and I chorused.

I was loving the idea of a home-cooked meal: anything that didn't come out of a packet with a free kids' toy was a delight. And I was blissfully happy catching up on a healthy dose of chick lit with, almost, no interruptions.

On arrival last night, I'd slept for eleven hours solid, awaking in a panic that I was late for work. I had defiantly left my mobile and BlackBerry in my bedroom for a good half hour, before deciding to at least bring them downstairs in case of emergency. I finally conceded shortly after breakfast to keep my mobile with me by the sunlounger (to avoid the instinctive sprint inside every time I imagined it ringing), and to leave my BlackBerry on the kitchen table. As Mum was forever misplacing her glasses, I half-hoped it might end up minced into the shepherd's pie.

My parents' cottage was just outside the village of St Gatien des Bois, near Deauville, in Normandy. My grandfather on my mother's side had bought it after the war, and we had spent all our summers here. Once my father 'retired' from the accountancy firm, my parents surprised me by moving straight out, the sole unconventional act of their safe surburban lives.

The cottage was small, with just two bedrooms in the large low roof, but as the French rightly said, it had '*beaucoup de charme*'. There were exposed beams inside and out, a big old fireplace, stone floors, and loads of surfaces for Mum's dreaded knicknacks. There was a neat grey stone patio where lunch and dinner were eaten almost every day, and a long garden with a great lawn and herbaceous borders that kept my parents endlessly busy.

'So how is everything in the world of Grand Prix racing?' Dad laid his glasses on the puzzle, resting his hands on his hard-earned paunch.

'Fine, Dad.'

'Just fine, Kitkat?' He peered at me in a way I didn't want to be peered at.

'It's great, just the travelling is exhausting, you know.' I stuck my head back in the book.

'You know we're very proud of you, even your mother.' He smiled sweetly. 'Now that she sees you on TV occasionally, she seems to have finally understood you have a proper job. Press officers are the new lawyers, apparently.' He chuckled, and his shoulders shook in support. 'She's not so keen on your boss though, thinks he's Lucifer in a suit.'

'How so? Last time we spoke she was totally taken with the suave thing.'

'Well, that was until she tried to call him.'

'What? She did what?' I was sitting bolt upright now, and my book had fallen on to the grass, the page no longer saved.

'Shh, keep your voice down.' Dad looked nervously at the kitchen window. 'She tried to call three times but never got past the secretary – said she was quite the rudest girl she'd ever spoken to. She had to have a large G and T each time she put the phone down.' He gave a nervous laugh. 'Which at ten a.m. is something even for your mother.'

'Dad, why the hell did Mum call Vincent?'

'Oh you know your mother, when she gets something in her head …'

'Dad …'

'Oh, it's a long time ago now, Kitkat. It's really nothing to worry about …'

'Dad!'

'It was for my birthday back in April. She planned a big surprise party, which of course I knew about, so it wasn't really a surprise; still, she really wanted you to come.'

'But I told her ...'

'I know, but well, you know your mother, she thought you were too afraid to ask Vincent for time off, what with it being a new job, so she thought she'd call him and explain it was a special occasion.'

'Too afraid? For God's sake, I'm not twelve. This is my career, my life. Why can't she just butt out?'

He rubbed the arm of the chair like he was sanding it with his hand. 'Come on now, Catherine ...' He only ever called me that when he was angry, which was really rare. 'She is your mother, she only has your best interests at heart, and in her defence, she wanted it to be a great party.'

'I'm killing myself to be professional, and then my *mother*' – I spat the word – 'takes it upon herself to stalker-call my boss. How childish do you think that makes me look?'

His eyes were fixed on the grass; he wouldn't look at me, wouldn't engage. 'You're overreacting. She tried to call and was unsuccessful. And I don't think it makes you look childish, it makes you look like you have a family who cares.'

'Yeah, that makes all the difference.' I laid back on the lounger and pulled my sunglasses from their hairband position on to my eyes.

Dad exhaled loudly; he sounded exhausted. 'I think you're tired, and saying things you don't mean.' There was a clatter of pans, and he shot another nervous look at the kitchen window. 'This isn't like you at all.'

We sat in silence; I scowled and brooded. What was it about visiting my parents that brought out the sulky, argumentative teenager in me? I knew I should snap out of it; Dad hated conflict. I wasn't quite sure why I was making such a fuss; of course they wouldn't understand Vincent, so why ruin the few days I had here? But I wasn't quite ready to grow up. Maybe I wanted them, or at least him, to know how hard it was, how every misstep could have colossal ramifications. A lawnmower started up in a neighbouring garden, and a small flock of birds sheltering in the apple tree took flight.

'So was it good?' I asked, retrieving my book from the lawn and thumbing through for the lost page.

'What?'

'The party.'

'Oh yes, very good. Your mother worked herself into a tizz and there was some crisis with the quiche, but I had a wonderful time; cracked open a marvellous Scotch.' His voice brightened with relief that the conversation was back to safe ground. 'Nearly fifty people came out from the UK; it was great to see Em and meet Freddie, too.'

'Em was there?'

'Mm, you didn't know? She drove out with her parents.'

'I didn't really know it was such a big thing.' *I don't think I sent a present. Shit, did I even call?*

'Well … you know your mother.' He smiled and shrugged. 'I'm going to stroll into town to get today's papers; they only arrive after lunch out here. Do you fancy coming?' Dad rocked himself up to standing, hitching up his shorts, which were struggling to cling to his lack of waist.

'Thanks, but I'm pretty much fused to the sunbed. Could you get a good selection please, though: not just the sensible papers, some red tops too.'

'Right you are, Kitkat.'

'Oh that's sad, so very sad.'

I woke up from a snooze to hear that Mum had joined Dad at the garden table. The rustling of papers accompanied the clinking of china.

'I wonder if Kate knows her?'

'Knows who?' I stretched my arms over the back of the chair and yawned loudly, repositioning my bottom where it had seeped between the lounger's wooden slats.

'This poor girl who attempted suicide.' She started collecting the pages together to pass it to me. 'It's that Harry Bircher's daughter.'

Like the ball in a pinball machine, hurtling at random across the playfield, neurons in my brain darted between this new and stored information. Red lights flashed across the board.

'She's so young. What does it say, sixteen?' Mum was making a meal of folding the paper back together.

'For Chrissake, just give it to me.' I snatched the paper out of her hand, and ignored their silent stares.

Did they say 'attempted' or 'committed' suicide?
Was she dead? Oh my God, was she dead?

I was breathing, but couldn't get any air.

His daughter? Harry's daughter? I didn't know he had a daughter. Only sixteen.

I got up off the lounger and laid *The Sun* on the grass, kneeling in front of it. I had to see every word, every fact, clearly. The front page screamed 'F1 Bircher's Daughter in Suicide Horror'. There was a full-page photo of a stretcher being rushed into the sliding doors of a hospital, a tiny body under the sheet. In the back of the shot, behind the ambulance men, was a dazed- and distraught-looking Harry Bircher.

My fingers moved insufficiently fast to flip to the inside page.

'The daughter of Formula 1 boss, Harry Bircher ... in ... suicide attempt. Victoria Bircher, just 16 ...'

'Victoria' … Oh, Christ.

I skim-read the article, which continued on three pages inside the paper.

'… is in intensive care after swallowing a quantity of unspecified pills. Victoria, on summer holiday from prestigious girl's boarding school Benenden, was saved by her F1 supremo father, who received her apologetic text message while dining close by their Belgravia house …'

They even had a photo of the text message.

daddy, Ive let u down, ive let u all down. sorry v xxx

There was a photo of her and Harry with their arms around each other, smiling. She looked incredibly young, and must have inherited her mother's delicate frame as she was tiny next to Harry. And there was a grainy close-up of her smiling wildly, lifted off the YouTube film.

'… a wilder side of the softly-spoken public school girl was recently revealed in a YouTube video filmed during one of her father's infamous yacht parties …'

I crawled to the edge of the grass and threw up on the organic carrots.

I took the late flight back from Charles de Gaulle to Heathrow. There was nothing to do in the UK but I couldn't stay at my parents – they had questions I didn't want to answer. I needed to move. I had to be busy. I used the excuse that Vincent would be upset, and we'd have to make a media statement. I didn't know if they bought it. Unlikely.

At the airport I headed straight to Relay to buy all the papers, but the *Sun* had the exclusive, so that was the extent of available news. I called Vincent under the pretence of preparing a statement for the media, to see how he'd react. What he'd say. He was cruising the Med, so maybe he hadn't heard. The call went to voicemail.

14A Waverley Road, Oxford

I got to my flat at two-thirty a.m. and turned on Sky News, where the same footage had no doubt been looping for most of the day. McLaren's Martin Whitmarsh had been in the studio and spoken of how the thoughts of the paddock were with Harry. How he was such a devoted family man. I didn't even know he had a daughter. Or a wife, or rather ex-wife. But then again, I didn't know him at all.

Some of Harry's Belgravia neighbours had been interviewed too.

'Harry and Victoria are devoted to each other.'

'She's a wonderfully polite and well-brought-up girl.'

There was new footage of girls from Victoria's class holding a candlelit vigil outside the hospital entrance.

The YouTube film had been successful – well, in terms of what I assumed to be Vincent's objective, which was to make as much noise as possible and discredit Harry by showing his debauched parties. Derek Capshaw lit the match, and by lunchtime on Sunday in Budapest news of the film had raged its way around the paddock. In a restricted environment of inquisitive people, paddock gossip travelled faster than swine flu at a pig farm. The paddock media were pretty unshockable, there wasn't much they hadn't heard before, but everyone was aware of the dangerous impact of an illicit scandal in a PR-led and blue chip-funded industry.

Sky News' refrain of 'All the news in fifteen minutes, every fifteen minutes' sang out as I stared trance-like at the screen. I realised my brain had compressed the information and questions into a tortuous 60 second loop that was spinning at warp speed in my head. The images of the stretcher, rushing ambulance men, crying teenage girls with candles, a pretty young girl on a pony, an anguished Harry, flashed up to a soundtrack of questions: *Why Harry's daughter? Is she ok? Please God, let her be ok. Vincent couldn't have known it was Harry's daughter. Maybe the film wasn't the trigger?*

Even in this state of suspended self-denial I couldn't ignore the name scribbled on the DVD, '*Victoria*'.

If I didn't speak to someone soon, I would go insane.

I needed a non-judgemental friend. I glanced at the digital clock on the top of the TV screen, who I could call at three a.m. I grabbed my mobile and speed-dialled Danny. He picked up on the fifth ring.

'Kate! Whassup, ba-aby?' he yelled over a deafening background noise of hardcore house music.

'Danny, I need to talk to you!' I shouted back.

'What! Wait, I can't hear you. What did ya say?'

'I need to talk to you. Can you talk?'

The track changed and a pumping bass filled the receiver. Danny let out a howl of delight.

'Course, Kate. Go ahead.'

If anything, the music was getting louder.

'I'm in the shit, Danny!' I yelled. 'Forget it, I'll call later.' I hung up, exhausted, frustrated, and now confused: why was he clubbing at three a.m. on a Tuesday?

I needed a focus. The news cycle was hauntingly addictive, but it gave no new information. I didn't dare call Lisa for fear she would catch me out again. I decided to concentrate on identifying the hospital. Then maybe I could find out if Victoria was all right. Fuelled with a fresh motivation, I checked Google maps to see what hospitals were near Belgravia. There were about six potentials. I searched for photos on the web to cross-reference with the *Sun* photo. Victoria was at the Chelsea and Westminster.

'Hello, I'd like to enquire after the status of a patient admitted today by the name of Victoria Bircher.'

'Are you family?'

'No, but my boss is a colleague of her father ...'

'I can't help you.' Click.

I was logged on to *The Sun*'s website and Martini Magna's site, and ran a Victoria Bircher search on Google, refreshing the windows every few minutes, but there was no news on her progress. I learned that she was Harry's only daughter and the product of his eight-year marriage to the fairly famous 80s model, Shebah Sangster. After the divorce Harry was given sole custody of Victoria. She had been educated at Britain's most exclusive schools, Kensington Prep and Benenden, was a talented violinist, had a horse called Bella, and got six As and four Bs in her GSCEs. I also read that Harry had gone to great lengths to keep her out of the public eye. A photo of her at a gymkhana showed a pretty, delicate-featured girl with almond-shaped grey eyes and long blonde plaits. Harry was a devoted single dad.

The clock on the bottom of the computer screen said 06.17. My stomach made a loud gurgle. I hadn't eaten since last night's shepherd's pie, and I'd only managed to get a few mouthfuls of that down to avoid parental grief. I felt like I had had four expressos; my body was exhausted, but my mind was still racing with relentless questions. I walked into the kitchen and filled the kettle.

I didn't remember falling asleep, but I lifted my head up from the sofa cushion and a double page of *The Sun* rose with it. The sun streamed in through the sitting room window and there was street noise of car engines and chatter. Exhaust fumes and fried garlic from the Italian restaurant next door mingled in the stagnant sitting room air, a stomach-turning combination.

I reached for my mobile. '10.10 a.m. No Messages'.

Under the feeble spray of the electric shower, the citrus shower gel did not fulfil its advertising promise to refresh and invigorate.

I had to get a grip. What was I going to do? What could I do?

Sleep hadn't cleared the mental quagmire. But a new factor shot to the front of my mind. This was a huge media story now. It was no longer a subject of paddock gossip. If it was in *The Sun* yesterday it would be all over the UK press today, and the F1 media would pick it up internationally.

I pulled on a pair of denim shorts and the 'The Licks' t-shirt, and strode the hundred yards to the 7-11.

'Morning, young lady, I thought you was on yer hols.' Di seemed to work the full seven a.m. to eleven p.m. shift every day: I'd never been in here when she wasn't. The archetypal tough old bird, she was solid flesh from bust to hips, aged anywhere between forty-five and sixty-five years old. Always friendly, she took no shit. Wasted students and thieving kids had long since taken their business elsewhere.

I replied with the 'You know how it is' shrug.

'Bloody typical, innit. To get sick on yer week off. You should get yerself back to bed, love. You look like a piece o' shit.'

I dropped the heavy pile of papers next to the till and pulled out my wallet.

'Yeah, bloody typical.'

The story was indeed everywhere.

The Sun had dug up loads of Bircher family photos and background information, taking the angle of troubled celebrity kids growing up in the glare of the media. There were no quotes from Harry or Shebah, and it said Victoria's condition was 'critical but stable'.

Thank God!

The man in the film, Victoria's love interest, had been identified as Harry's party pal, Sal Owitz, owner of *Lifestyle* magazine.

The *Daily Mail* had chosen the angle of our nation's youth being corrupted by drink and drugs and a *Daily Express* editorial questioned the role of YouTube in personal privacy. YouTube had reacted swiftly with a statement saying the film violated YouTube's community guidelines, which clearly condemned the posting of illegal activity. They went on to say the film had been removed and the account terminated.

I pressed 'Speed dial #1'.

'Vincent, it's Kate, thank goodness. I wanted to check if you'd heard, something terrible's happened ...'

'Keht, good.' I was expecting the usual crackly line when he was at sea on *Aqua Princesse*, but it was clear. 'Right, you must do the following ...'

I fumbled for a pen, flipping to an ad page in the *Express* to write notes. In the background I heard a woman's voice.

'Sir, mobile phones are not permitted in the ICU.'

'Shebah Sangster is landing in the Gulfstream at Farnborough Airfield in one hour; she was stuck in Fiji and impossible to reach. She needs a car waiting to bring her here.'

'Sorry, here?'

'The Chelsea and Westminster hospital,' he snapped. 'Keht, you work in media, have you been living in a bubble for the past twenty-four hours? The number one priority right now is to support Harry with whatever he needs.'

Once again my brain was playing catch-up, this time not with the facts – I now knew who Shebah Sangster was, I knew about the hospital – but with Vincent's latest persona. Could he really have re-invented himself as Harry's loyal and trusty rock in his time of crisis? Did he really just speak to me as if I had no idea what he'd done, what he'd made me do, in Hungary four days ago?

'Then get Jefferson from the London flat to pack four sets of shirts and trousers for me, not too smart. Tell him 'informal wear'. Then he should drive via Harry's house in Belgravia, where the housekeeper has prepared a bag of Victoria's favourite possessions. He needs to bring everything here asap.'

'OK.' Eloquence failed me.

'Then call my lawyer, what's his name, Rupert Shearing at Shearing & Dunthorpe, and tell him I need him over here for a meeting now. Make sure it's clear: this is for me personally, not for the team. I'll need his best people on this.'

Or could this be how he dealt with his guilt? Was he trying to make amends?

'I want everything they can get on Sal Owitz. I will not rest until that sick paedophile is behind bars.'

He hung up. I stared at the phone.

At least one of us was losing their mind.

European Grand Prix, Valencia
Saturday, 8 a.m.

Valencia was a street circuit and the paddock was set up around the port where the America's Cup teams had had their base. Boutique hotels set on the beachfront were the place to stay and, while it didn't touch Monaco for glamour, Valencia buzzed with a sunny holiday atmosphere.

However, what the European GP gained in personality, it lost in logistic simplicity. The route from our hotel to the paddock was by shuttle boat, which was a novelty for the first day until hundreds of Paddock Club guests joined the party, forming solid queue blocks and potentially fire-able delays.

Just as the boat was about to depart, I spotted Lisa doing her best to queue-barge, mobile clamped to her ear, waving her free arm.

'Stop!' I yelled too loudly at the boat driver, who was unhooking the rope from the cleat.

I had been trying to see Lisa since I arrived, but she had understandably been busy as hell since Harry wasn't attending this race. I already knew that Victoria Bircher was recovering well, and had been out of hospital for over a week. It was hard to express how enormously relieved I felt when I heard she was out of intensive care. I ran to the TechQ loos and dissolved into tears for more than half an hour. I realised I had been holding my breath for days; stuff was going on as it always did, but my ability to think and feel was on pause. Then the crippling feeling of guilt, and an inescapable sensation of having descended to a previously unimaginable murky moral depth, engulfed me. Followed by an overriding feeling of loneliness. There was no one to talk to. No one but Vincent knew, and he was acting as if he had had a lobotomy. Even if I had managed to speak to Danny, I didn't know if I could have brought myself to tell the whole truth, and it wouldn't be fair to burst Em's wedding bubble. Janey would probably understand, but I wasn't up for a lecture on my stupidity.

I felt as if I had been standing on the set of an ultra-glamorous, big-budget film, and bit by bit the props were removed, the costumed actors disappeared, and finally even the walls were picked up and carried away by stage-hands. The next scene was in preparation and was set to be equally spectacular, but it was too late because I'd seen the empty, ugly warehouse, and suspension of disbelief was no longer possible.

So I was stuck in no-man's-land, paralysed and scared shitless. There was no way to just carry on, and yet neither could I just renounce everything and go back to a nine-to-five commute. I'd worked too hard; I couldn't just give up, but I couldn't take much more of this either.

I tried to catch Lisa's eye as she carried on her phone conversation perched on a narrow bench, as the boat pulled out into the harbour waters. I was clinging to a weak sense of solidarity as she was suffering from the situation too, albeit due to a heavy workload. I was staring and grinning rather intensely. She eventually looked up and acknowledged me with a nod. She looked exhausted.

Lisa was always perfectly presented in an Essex kind of way. Big blow-dried hair, flawless French manicure on UV Gel nails, and smart-sexy secretary clothes (she even managed to make her team uniform flattering). But today her nails were bitten down and her big hair looked slept-on.

'If I die, I wanna be reincarnated as her boulder hold-ers.' JB leaned his head on my shoulder and swiped at a bit of dribble just before it hit my shirt.

'… and his name's Thorsten, isn't that just sexy?'

I realised Janey was talking to me, and had been for some time.

'... I think he's Austrian – well, the Red Bull marketeers all are, pretty much. He hasn't got much of a sense of humour, but he's fit, fit, fit.' She held her mobile in front of my face with a blurry photo of a shirtless man. 'Oh, it's so exciting to have some paddock eye candy at last. Eew, JB, you're dribbling again.'

I scowled and swatted him off my shoulder.

'Oh, Kitty Kat, don't be dejected.' JB contorted his face in mock sympathy. 'I love your chesticles too!'

Nothing and everything had changed.

Dupont Lamborghini F1 Team

PRESS RELEASE

European Grand Prix
Valencia Street Circuit
Saturday

Qualifying
Marcel Müller qualified fourth and Enrico Costa sixth on the Valencia Street Circuit. They will start the European Grand Prix tomorrow respectively from the second and third rows of the grid.

Marcel Müller – 4th
'I had a fuel pump problem this morning so didn't run at all, which meant I went into this session pretty much blind. I like the circuit, but it just doesn't seem to fit our car. I think P4 was the best I could have hoped for today.'

Enrico Costa – 6th
'We've struggled for speed here all weekend. We just don't seem to have the pace. It also didn't help that Santos blocked me on my last run. If we can pull something out of the bag overnight, maybe we have a chance of a decent race.'

Vincent Dupont, Team Principal
'An unsatisfactory qualifying session. The engineers will work through the night to maximise strategy for the race.'

Media contact
Kate Ellison – Kateellison@dupontf1.com

www.dupontf1.com

I completed the press release distribution in a respectable time, fourth out of the ten press officers, and walked back to The Wing past the wonderful brick arches at the back of the pit lane.

'Mike for Kate,' a voice crackled over the radio.

'Yes, Mike.'

'FOM Security just called: you have a major delivery at the turnstiles.'

'But I'm not expecting anything.'

'Not interested. Deal with it.'

I stomped to the gate, praying for a mistake and for Mike to be the real recipient. I approached one of the interchangeable turnstile security guys in neat blue suits.

'Hi, I'm Kate from Dupont Lamborghini; I was told there was some sort of delivery?'

'Ah, here she is.' The band of three security men and three girls looked at each other and shook their heads. 'Deliveries to the circuit have to be made prior to Wednesday. They aren't permitted during the race weekend.'

'I'm sorry, but I'm not expecting anything.'

'Now, we can overlook it just this once if the packages are taken in immediately, as they're blocking access.'

'Sure, I'll carry it back with me now.'

Another set of looks was exchanged, this time with smirks. The security guy pointed at a mountain of about thirty half-metre-square boxes.

Half an hour later, with platform trolleys borrowed from McLaren, Mercedes and Lotus, Gareth, Celine,

Janey and I were wheeling perilously stacked loads to The Wing. The sender's address was Paris, and I was indeed the addressee. It was obviously some monumental mistake. The next challenge would be where to store the boxes. Space in The Wing, like in all motorhomes, was calculated with millimetric precision.

'Keht, mhkhghg.' An intelligible message on the radio had to be Vincent.

'Sorry, guys, can you deal with this?' I said to the horror-struck faces of my not-so-willing volunteers. 'Vincent just called.'

Finally! I hadn't seen him since Hungary, although he'd been on the phone twice a day with Victoria-related instructions. He'd kicked off a massive media attack on Sal Ovitz, who, despite being the owner of the prestigious *Lifestyle* magazine, and recently launched Lifestyle TV channel, had a history of chasing underage girls.

The stories couldn't avoid Sal and Harry's ten-year party partnership, and details of the *Seventh Heaven* 'model' parties were trickled out over a week, horrifying mothers with teenage daughters across the UK. In contrast to Vincent, who was giving interviews and quotes to all who asked, Harry maintained a dignified silence throughout the public flogging.

Then, just before this race, Vincent had gone off the radar for two days. Totally unreachable.

I knocked on Vincent's smoked-glass office door. Smoked glass meant he was inside: when it was empty the glass became transparent – one of the many nifty and no doubt excruciatingly expensive design features. I waited for the 'Yes' and pushed it open.

Vincent and Enrico were standing at the window to the left of his desk, the same one Vincent had stared blankly out of when he watched Enrico disappear into Harry's motorhome at the Spanish GP. Vincent had a pair of binoculars trained on the paddock as Enrico hung on his shoulder, bouncing up and down on tiptoe.

'Oh, oh, ooooh, nearly, nearly, go oooon.'

'Give them to me, give them to me,' Enrico squealed, practically mounting Vincent's hip.

'Wait a minute, I need to zoom. Do these things zoom?'

I stood bewildered as the *Wayne's World* spectacle played out. Eventually Vincent passed the binoculars to Enrico, who continued the animal noises of appreciation, before catching sight of me.

'Keht, there you are. Where have you been?' He turned back quickly to the window, pointing directions out for Enrico. He looked different, a bit bloated with some small yellowish bruises on his forehead.

'Sorry, I was bringing in a big delivery from Paris. Were you expecting something?'

'Si, Si,' Enrico shouted, the binoculars clamped to his eyes, triggering some sort of sensory confusion. 'It's from Adriana for you.'

'For me?' I addressed the jiggling backs.

'She's moving, I can see right down. *Santo Cielo!*' Enrico pretended to swoon, and Vincent made a lunge for the binoculars.

'It's 'er new perfume. You 'ave to give it to the media.'

You've got to be fucking kidding.

I prayed Vincent would intervene. I had read about the launch of Love Blossom in *Heat* magazine. Just the name made me want to hurl all over the llama carpet.

'*Madonna mia,*' Enrico sang out.

'Yes, Keht, talk it up, you know the thing,' Vincent said, still glued to the window. 'Maybe think of an event or cocktail around it.'

I forced myself out of my standing coma. 'Did you want something else, Vincent? You called me on the radio.'

He stopped giggling for a moment.

'Yes. Go down to the paddock and talk to those girls. Bring them closer to the wall below.'

Dupont Lamborghini F1 Team

PRESS RELEASE

European Grand Prix
Valencia Street Circuit
Sunday

Race

After a hard race, Enrico Costa finished in third position. Marcel was unable to improve on his qualifying position and finished the race in fourth. Dupont Lamborghini remains in second place in the championship with 207 points.

Enrico Costa – 3rd

'I was stuck in traffic for the whole of my first stint. Once I changed to the harder tyre compound I was able to make up some ground and fight through the field. Our performance level is not where it should be at this stage of the championship.'

Marcel Müller – 4th

'This was one of my toughest races to date as I fought as hard as I could, but the pace just wasn't there. We must improve for Spa.'

Vincent Dupont, Team Principal

'This was not a top team performance this weekend. We are already hard at work in the TechQ, focusing on Spa.'

Media contact

Kate Ellison – Kateellison@dupontf1.com

www.dupontf1.com

I sipped at the Love Blossom cocktail, swiftly concocted by The Wing bar staff, from the only shadowy corner of the lounge as I looked over the group of media, guests and random hangers-on who were merrily swigging the pale pink drink. A Beyoncé track played in the background.

In the interests of career longevity I had duly organised a 'Cocktail Party hosted by Adriana Oliveira' (it would take a man of steel or of a different persuasion to turn down her invitation, professionally relevant or not, especially given the pink negligée she had chosen to wear). But in the interests of career credibility, I failed to mention Love Blossom anywhere on the invitation and scheduled the get-together after the race when most of the media were flat-out writing. I did not want to be remembered as the press officer who attempted to make the hard-core petrolhead paddock media include a mention of 'the fruity-floral bluebell note and feminine jasmine heart of Love Blossom' in their post-race reports.

Nothing had changed and yet, for me, everything was different. Formula One, the race weekend, the people – it all seemed more banal. I overheard Adriana asking Vincent how he had got on in the clinic. It turned out Vincent had prepped for his next media sound-off about the black hole of modern morality with a comprehensive dose of Botox. Maybe they threw in a personality Botoxing too, which would explain his pre-pubescent behaviour.

Feeding off the crowds and the jostling clutch of photographers, Adriana leapt on to one of the round tables and started a poleless pole dance, swinging her tiny hips and twisting her endless legs.

Even Adriana was less beautiful.

Unfortunately, that wasn't exactly true.

CHAPTER 13

Zigfrid von Underbelly
Hoxton, London N1
Saturday, 6.30 p.m.

I was hot and sweaty; the straps on the Sergio Rossi heels were cutting into my feet. This time there was no sand dune to climb, but a pole to spin around. I was wearing a leotard – it had been many years, although not enough, since it had last been worn – insufficiently covered by an old tennis skirt. This time it wasn't a dream. Unfortunately not. I really was pole dancing in north London. And what's more, I had organised it.

It was Em's hen night, and eight of us were trying to master the Fireman Spin, in our own private pole dancing lesson. Tuffy had provided the idea ten days ago, on a tip from his sister, saving me from best-friend purgatory. I had had to redeem myself after never rescheduling the hen-planning weekend. I had played for time by announcing that it would be a surprise hen night. Then I almost blew any goodwill by announcing the location only three days ago.

As with everything that fell into the 'personal life' category, there was no time or energy to spend on it. I was too ashamed to tell the truth, so what was worse was that I had starting making up little lies of elaborate hen-party plans that I had had to cancel due to train strikes in France and hotels booked out in Monaco. I hated the deceit, but the truth was equally unpalatable. What upset me even more was that over the years I had come up with, and stored away, some inspired hen-night plans for Em – and now they just served as fodder for the lies.

Vincent, post Victoria-gate, had been insatiable in his Kato-Enrico-Sal Ovitz quests and had accepted every media request, from Bulgaria to Bali, for modern morality quotes and interviews. There had barely been time to breathe. So, yet another reason to be thankful for Tuffy.

David Guetta's *Delirious* blasted out of the speakers in the subterranean private (thank God!) Underbelly room as legs looped awkwardly around poles on the velvet curtained stage. Aside from Em and I, there was Natasha, one of her charity colleagues, and Sally, Lou and Erica, old friends from Cambridge Uni, and Beth, her cousin.

'I did it!' Em shrieked, her face flushed with blotches of exertion.

'Everyone stop!' shouted Natasha. 'Time for an Em Wave.'

We duly detangled ourselves from the poles and, led by Natasha, who in a past life must have sparkled as a majorette, counted us in.

'And a one, two, three ...'

Fists in front of our chests we punched out to the right, and with a sweeping motion swung jazz hands over to the left, bringing them into our chests and finishing with an optional yelp.

With a grin Prit-sticked on my face I had embraced my inner stripper and tried to look like this wasn't my idea of personal hell. Maybe I was too much of a tomboy but hen nights, like all-girl trips to Magaluf, or anywhere for that matter, made me want to run like Paula Radcliffe in the opposite direction, leaving high-pitched screams, feather boas and t-shirts with nicknames a good marathon distance away.

All in all though, I was pretty proud of the day, and Em seemed to be really enjoying herself, which of course was the whole point. I didn't understand why Natasha felt the need to add what she called her 'henifications'. What particularly grated was that her contributions were excessively girly and made everyone, including Em, who was not a giggler, feel that if they didn't join in they were somehow ruining the fun. The Em Wave always ended with a hug between Natasha and Em, and now an En (for Natasha, of course). The Wave had had to be invented, which was even more Morecombe and Wise and involved leaning forward sideways on one leg, jiggling a non-existent top hat.

Two glasses of Moet had helped anaesthetise my reticence, but I felt like only two bottles could see me through to the end. With Em enveloped in a permanent En Hug, I found myself looking more frequently at the door for my other partner in crime. Danny, self-appointed queen hen, had not yet arrived. He had replied to my text with a *c u there x*. Not unfriendly, but not his usual loquacious self either.

I tried to focus on the lesson to take my mind off the En Hen; the Back Hook Spin looked so easy and elegant when Jenni, our instructor and ex-British gymnast, did it. I reached high up the pole with my right arm, swung my right leg out and round where in the rotation my left leg should have somehow hooked on to the pole. Instead, my sweaty arm slid down the pole until I sat in a tangled heap at the bottom.

'You need to try and relax, Kate.' Jenni stretched out her hand to help me up. 'You attack the move with so much aggression; just let it flow.' As she pulled me up I caught a flash of Jenni's incredible abs in close-up. Life could be so cruel.

'OK girls, let's have a break and a drink,' Jenni announced, as a waiter arrived with a fresh bucket of Moet on ice.

'Kate, this is such fun; you're the best!' Em flopped down on the floor next to me with two full flutes.

'Yeah? Are you sure? I didn't want it to be a total oestrogen overload.'

'It's perfect.' She linked her arm through mine and leaned a sweaty head on my shoulder.

A sense of calm cancelled out my hostility. I hadn't let her down. 'I tell you, I hereby swear to never mock the fine art of the pole dancer. But I'm definitely more Fireman Sam than Stringfellows' Angel!'

We clinked glasses and leaned back on the stage rear wall. Natasha appeared and flopped down on the other side of Em, proffering a plate of chocolate-covered strawberries.

'Did Danny leave a message?' Em asked, munching on a strawberry while looking into the bottom of the glass.

'Fraid not. But you know, he's always late for everything.' I tried to keep my voice light-hearted. 'What did he say when you left the flat this morning?'

'I didn't see him. I told you, he's hardly ever there. He still keeps such anti-social hours.' She wrinkled her nose, the way she always did when she was trying not to show that something bothered her. I nodded supportively.

'It didn't seem to do any good,' she said.

'What didn't?'

'The chat you had with him after Silverstone. That's usually enough to sort him out when he goes off on one. Did he give any sort of explanation?'

Realisation, and then guilt, must have flashed fleetingly across my face. I definitely did try to call Danny a couple of times and an email I'd sent to his work was returned, but I had neither spoken to him nor confronted him about his behaviour. The important tasks on my to-do list were constantly being replaced by ever more important and urgent ones: it was a never-ending cycle.

I thought out a lie; I didn't have to hurt Em with the truth. Not today. I'd deal with it right away, as soon as the hen night was over.

'Umm, no not …'

Then I saw Natasha who, unlike Em, who was picking through the strawberries, was fixing me with a pursed, superior look. She had seen my reaction. She knew I'd forgotten. She raised her eyebrows, challenging me to lie.

The silent showdown was interrupted as Sally, Lou and Erica appeared before us with nine presents wrapped in pink tissue. The largest one had a big silver ribbon tied in a bow on the top. They beamed as they handed it to

Em, before passing around the packages among the other girls.

'Thanks, guys,' Em said, looking truly thrilled.

'Oh, it was all Natasha's idea,' said Sally.

Course it was.

'Oh, I *love* it,' Em squealed as she pulled a glittering silver tiara out of the paper. She put it straight on her head, so we could all read the 'Hen' spelled out in crystals on the front. Ours were pink and all said 'Chick'.

I downed my flute in one.

Belgian Grand Prix, Spa Francorchamps Circuit
Thursday, 2 p.m.

I sat at the head of the production line that we'd set up on the meeting-room table. In front of me were four boxes of twenty-five team caps and a big wedge of team posters showing both Dupont Lamborghini cars angled into a 'V', and the drivers sitting on the respective front wheels. With the fat black marker pen I signed above Enrico's car and slid the poster to Marcel, who was sitting next to me nodding to his iPod. He signed on his car and handed the poster off to Mike, who collected them all in a pile. Every time ten posters were completed, Mike rolled them into a cardboard tube, which he placed on its end on the table. Four tubes stood to attention, but the poster pile in front of me did not seem to be diminishing.

I had forced Mike to take part as punishment for dropping this boulder on me only last night, and on this of all weekends. He announced blithely that in view of the announcement we should reward the Paddock Club guests with a little extra something: which meant a hundred posters and a hundred caps signed by the drivers by Sunday.

This was absolutely my least favourite job, as I'd learnt a few things about drivers and autographs:

* Drivers disliked PR work: interviews (unless post-victory), photoshoots, appearances, all of it. But *la grande bête noire* was the autograph session.

* Should the autograph request exceed two (even for a proper and good reason like for charity or the son of the Lamborghini CEO) flat refusal and/or wrath ensued.

* The Squiggle (i): at some point, on the rise up the fame ladder, a driver's signature morphed into a squiggly line that could be reproduced while walking at speed and without looking.

* The Squiggle (ii): a secondary function was reproduction capability by managers, PRs and relatives. NB: Unless dangerously dumb, the driver had a second, real signature for his credit card.

* The flip side of having a manager, business advisor, physio, PA and expanding post-success family, was that a driver eventually suspected that everyone was getting rich off him. The knock-on effect was even less PR co-operation in the paranoid belief that flogging a poxy poster on Ebay would pay off my mortgage and buy me a spanking new Beamer.

My list of reasons to hate Mike was now two pages long.

'You know it's very good of you to actually sign these all yourself,' I said to Marcel, who was still nodding to what sounded like The Kills. He had a new trendy haircut for this race; he looked rather like a blonde Jonas brother, his thick short curls perfectly tousled. I had noticed a change in him since the beginning of the season. Looks-wise he was getting cooler, or certainly trying harder. When I first met him at the launch, he had been goofy and a bit too smart in a neat polo shirt and sensible jeans, but he'd adopted that designer-scruffy look of skinny t-shirts, expensive Japanese jeans and vintage Converse shoes. His attitude had changed a bit, too. He was still pretty easy and willing with PR work, but, certainly since the British GP, he smiled less.

Contrary to the aforementioned points, when I had announced the mammoth signathon, Marcel had merely sighed before trudging after me. Enrico, on the other hand, had laughed, told me in Italian to go and do something to myself (I was getting better at picking up the gist, but not all the vocab), and had flicked me away with his fingers.

Noticing me looking at him, Marcel pulled out one of the headphones.

'What?'

Even when polite, Germans didn't mince their words.

'I said it's very good of you to sign these yourself,' I said as I held the pen in the tips of my fingers in an attempt to reproduce Enrico's loop-and-squiggle signature.

'It's just correct,' he shrugged. 'But in five minutes I have an engineers' meeting, then I'm off.' He plugged The Kills back in.

'Mike, in future, let's agree to a maximum of five signed items, eh? Then at least we can deliver. If you really need them all, you're going to have to sign the caps and the rest of the posters as Marcel.'

'I just really don't have the bandwidth to deal with your inefficiency right now, Kate. This is a huge weekend for marketing and an even bigger one for Me Plc, so just do your job.'

Was he bloody kidding? This deal had haunted my every working hour in F1. I was cripplingly aware of the many casualties, my integrity included, of this bloody result. He didn't realise how lucky he was to have Mike Plc uninvolved and unscathed.

I tried to verbalise this mental tirade.

'Piss off, Mike.'

For once he did as he was told.

As I stared, defeated, at the pile of posters, my mobile rang out with *Oops upside your head, say oops upside your head. Say oops upside ...*

'Kate speaking.'

'Kate, it's Tomasz.'

'Hey, are you at the track?' My voice went up an octave. Once I'd slept with someone my voice refused to perform predictably in conversation. It was nothing to do with whether I particularly liked them or not. Sex with Tomasz had been great – well, the one shag I remembered – but I was absolutely not interested in a repeat or a relationship. My priority was to be ultra-professional, and that was hard when the person on the other end of the phone had seen me naked. 'Did you get your pass situation sorted?'

'No, and not exactly, but I'm working on something very exciting, and I need your input.'

'OK, shoot.'

'No, not now, I'll be in Monza. Can we meet there? I'll buy you dinner.'

'Really, can't we just meet for coffee … it's always hard on a race weekend to …'

'You'll want to hear what I have to say.'

'You can't just email …'

'Kate!'

'Oh right. OK, then. Pasta and hot news, how can I refuse?' Well, now my curiosity was piqued.

Hostellerie Le Roannay, Spa
Saturday, 7.30 a.m.

Anyone who thought Formula One was glamorous had not been to Spa.

It was a serious circuit, beloved by drivers, who got a mystical look in their eye when they talked of Eau Rouge. But like Nurbürgring, it was a circuit for the hard-core enthusiast, who liked camping and staying up all night singing German drinking songs.

Set in the Ardennes mountains, it was cold, wet and, seeing as I didn't even like Moules Frites or Leffe beer, pretty bloody grim.

I opened the curtains and was greeted by a solid grey block of sky-to-earth. Sleet cut diagonal lines through the fog.

I checked my watch. Damn, I had to shift to get into my uniform and down to reception, as I was getting a lift to the circuit with Enrico. It was the only chance I had to brief him about the announcement and tonight's event. And the lift was dependent on being within grabbing distance of the car door when he pipped the alarm.

But the greyness was pervasive. My limbs felt heavy, leaden with apathy. I forced my body into the security of routine.

At the two-tone beep, I jumped out of my trance and lunged at the handle of the canary yellow Lamborghini Gallardo, on loan from our engine partner for the European races. Having slid unelegantly into the bucket seat to a snug, almost horizontal, position, I realised Vincent's polite refusal of supercar travel hung on the fact that he just wasn't supple enough to pull off a cool car exit.

I piled bags and coat into the footwell, and had barely swung the door closed before Enrico accelerated away. It was a very short drive from the hotel to the circuit entrance. The route was lined with merchandise stands, hot dog stalls, beer bars (with deep queues at seven-thirty a.m.) and hundreds of fans in various team kits, jumbo fun hats and airhorns. To the chants of 'En-ri-co' as he pulled out of the hotel gates, Enrico floored it, and fans and autograph books scattered to our left and right.

I pulled the small card out of my bag and tried to hold it steady as g-force took control of my arms. He turned up the stereo, adding the challenge of competing with Jay-Z, and the 550-horsepower engine, for Enrico's limited attention.

'*A-ri-ga-tou Go-zai-mas*,' I said slowly. 'Do you want to repeat it after me?'

Enrico rapped back to the lyrics blasting out of the car speakers. Jay-Z with a heavy Italian accent.

'Look, it's quite simple, if you take it step by step. *ARI-* it's like Harry without the H.'

'The what?'

'The H … forget it, it's how you say Harry anyway. *ARI-GATOU.*'

'What's this, like school? *Minchia*! Look over there.'

Enrico laughed as he pointed to a jumble of khaki, orange and navy blue tents squashed on a patch of land bordering the track entrance. Confused and dirty fans were stepping out into the grey daylight, untangling themselves from ropes and lines. I glanced up the once-grassy hill, now covered in solid muddy tracks. A couple of lone tent pegs were the only clue as to where the fans had begun their night.

'I'm sorry, Enrico.' I took a yoga breath. 'But it is important, please try. *ARI-GATOU.*'

'*Gatto* is cat in Italian.'

'Great, yes, so think "Harry Cat". OK?' I was buoyed by the minuscule victory of feedback.

He was rapping again, or singing, or talking to himself.

My window was closing. 'Then it's *GO-ZAI-MAS.*'

Enrico braked at the front gate, millimetres before a beautiful girl with a blonde ponytail and knee boots. They locked eyes, he opened the car door and she climbed in giggling, stepping over him slowly then perching her mini-skirted bottom between the front seats. That had to rate as one of the fastest pulls in history.

So Enrico was even more distracted, but I had to persevere because Vincent wanted this and hadn't considered that his champion driver couldn't retain seven syllables. With Enrico, Vincent never could see past his speed.

'Can you try *GO-ZAI-MAS*?'

Enrico swerved into his personally named car park place, and I was still collecting my face off the central console when I realised he was halfway to the turnstiles, arm in arm with his spellbound temporary girlfriend. I unclipped my seat belt and pulled on my non-existent abdominal muscles to sit up, and then forward, to collect my bags and coat. With legs extended it was harder than it appeared. I opened the door and chucked my stuff on to the asphalt so that I had both arms free to lift me out of the snug racing seat. Today I could do without a reminder that my bum was expanding. I pulled hard, and succeeded in raising my hips to an inverted plank position. Now what? I flipped myself over and crawled out, practically on all fours. Some people were not made for supercars.

This weekend called for a big entrance, so Vincent had delayed his arrival until Saturday morning. The Gulfstream landed at Liège airport at eight forty-five a.m., full to bursting with Vincent and Daphne Dupont (self-appointed orchid manager), Mr 'Elvis' Kato, two deadpan assistants, world-renowned chef Nobu Mat-suhisa, Sogetsu artist Manami Kinjo, one ton of bamboo, and a hundred rare Vanda orchids.

I had sent three cars to pick up the guests, and the catering bus to pick up the luggage and accessories.

After a spirit-lifting cup of Tetley and a breakfast of Marmite on toast, I picked up the box of invitations in their delicate envelopes and carried them to the media centre. Each one was handwritten with Japanese callig-raphy on mulberry paper, with English text on the back. We had invited sixty of the most important journalists, plus key team partners and paddock friends (Bernie Ecclestone, Jean Todt, the team bosses Vincent spoke to). Eighty guests in total.

I had sent a save-the-date email, in the vain hope of retaining some element of surprise but ensuring that the guests were free. Naturally, most of the journalists had a pretty good idea of what was going on by the time I arrived with my big invitation box. We were going to announce something big: now it was just a question of whittling it down to what.

'Here you go, Gordon,' I said poking the envelope under the side of his keyboard, where he was furiously typing with both index fingers.

He raised an eyebrow, not even bothering to open it or look up from his typing.

The five thousand-plus pounds we'd spent on the invitations, not including the man-hours of Vincent's never-ending changes, were a total waste of time and money. Journalists didn't decide to come based on the quality of the calligraphy or the authenticity of the mulberry paper. Although I did receive some positive nods from the Japanese media contingent, which was somewhat gratifying. Vincent had declared that we were pulling out all the stops, and by now I knew what that meant. The baroness had muscled in, declaring an extensive knowledge of all things Japanese. The event budget stretched to include her orchid recce to Tokyo last weekend.

I decided to lie low in the garage for most of the day.

Qualifying Q3
3 p.m.

The timer on the top of the live feed showing the track action read 00.00. The session was technically over but eight cars were still on flying laps including ours, the Martini Magnas, the Ferraris, Raikkonen and Button. As long as the car crossed start/finish before the timer expired, the lap was valid. Everyone aimed for the latest possible lap, as that was when the circuit had the most grip.

The timing screen was a rainbow of colour. In the three columns reserved for the sector times, green 'personal best' sector times flashed up for the remaining runners. The coveted pink times of the overall fastest on the track jumped from driver to driver as each outdid the other. In the garage, thirty-five mechanics, fifteen truckies, four engine engineers, two physios, two managers, four Costa cousins, the girl in the boots and myself stared transfixed at the timing screen.

No one breathed.

No one moved.

An FOM cameraman focused his camera in from the pit lane, in anticipation of a big reaction. His colleagues would have been standing in similar positions in our rivals' garages.

You could get a good idea how quick the lap was, certainly if there were some pink fastest-sector times, but you couldn't do the mental calculation, not helped by nervous excitement, without the final sector. The time for this third and final sector of the lap never appeared on the row you had been staring so hard at while your eyes begged to blink. Once the driver passed start/finish his name (and times) shot up the screen to his new finishing position. While you were hurriedly searching for it (either top-down or bottom-up, depending on whether you were an optimist or a pessimist), the times continued jumping around the screen as other drivers finished their lap. The last fifteen seconds of qualifying were the most intense on the heart rate. And in front of your sixty team-mates and millions of viewers you did not want to make the mistake of an ill-judged premature cheer.

Santos took pink for the first sector for several seconds, then it jumped to Enrico. Marcel was flying and had the pink second sector, which jumped to Alonso and almost immediately to Enrico. It was incredibly close.

Marcel crossed the line and jumped up to the top of the time sheets. A lone cheer escaped me. Alonso finished second. Santos came in on top, shuffling everyone down a position. Massa split Marcel and Alonso. Enrico popped

364

up at the top of the screen with three pink sector times. The garage erupted with cheers and high-fives.

'Enrico, great job, can I get a quick quote for the press release?'

'Big fucking balls! I've got the biggest fucking balls!' He grabbed them and thrust them forward. '*Come si dice "acciaio"!*' he yelled to one of his many cousins. 'Yeah, steel. You write this: "Enrico Costa has balls of steel: he took Eau Rouge flat, unlike the other pussies."' The testosterone crew butted chests and Enrico strutted off to the FIA press conference.

'Great, thanks.'

Dupont Lamborghini F1 Team

PRESS RELEASE

Belgian Grand Prix
Circuit de Spa Francorchamps
Saturday

Qualifying
Enrico Costa claimed pole with a faultless lap in the dying seconds of Q3. Marcel Müller posted the third fastest time, under a tenth of a second behind his team mate.

Enrico Costa – 1st
'This was a perfect lap. There's no better feeling than when everything comes together. I can't wait for the race tomorrow.'

Marcel Müller – 3rd
'I'm satisfied with third today. It was an incredibly tight qualifying session, and while it's frustrating to have just missed out on second, or even pole, I'm very happy with the car and feel we're in a strong position for the race tomorrow.'

Vincent Dupont, Team Principal
'A good qualifying session from both drivers. The team did a great job of preparing the cars and we are in a strong position for the race tomorrow. Now we have to capitalise on this advantage.'

Media contact
Kate Ellison – Kateellison@dupontf1.com

www.dupontf1.com

'It all looks amazing out there, Kate: well done!' Janey flopped into her chair, counting passes. She was always counting passes.

'Thanks, I had no idea bamboo was so versatile. This afternoon I seriously thought it was starting to look all *Blair Witch Project*, but I take it back. That artist – she's amazing.'

'Ka-ate.' When she dragged the vowel out, she was after something. 'Do you re-eally need me at the sushi thingy?'

'Well, it's sort of like a major deal for the team. Vincent wanted everyone there. He'll notice if you're not.'

'You can cover for me, right? He'll be so busy showing off, he'll never notice me, and if he does, just say I've got dermatitis and it's flaky and contagious.'

'Come on, I could really do without lying for you. I'm going to be flat-out.'

'Oh go oooon, puh-leeease. Thorsten and I are going for moules frites in this little bistro near the hotel. So damn romantic. You know, he's got a cute friend he could bring … he's tall and dark, and just your type …'

'The one with the stubble he was escorting down the paddock earlier? He's exactly my type, except he was bald and about five foot five.'

'Well, his name's Tim, and he works for some agency. Go on, you could seriously do with lightening up!'

'In another life, great, but you know I can't tonight. You bugger off, and I'll cover your flaky back.'

367

'Thanks, K. Now I feel guilty for slagging you off to Thorsten.' She blew a kiss into the air and flounced out of the door.

I had to question whether Vincent had some divine leverage. It had been grey for the three days since we landed in Brussels. Now, fifteen minutes before our soirée was due to start, the clouds were thinning out, revealing the previously unseen pale blue sky. Not that the weather was fundamental to our event. It was inside and everyone would attend out of curiosity, hunger, and a lack of better offers. But a hint of sun would certainly brighten the mood. I hoped it would brighten my mood.

On strict instructions that he was to smile and be welcoming, to which he nodded seriously, mentally preparing himself for the mission, I'd allowed Ivan to man the door, primarily because I wasn't in the mood to chat with every guest. Bang on the dot of seven the German media contingent arrived, and over the following twenty minutes all the guests came in, followed finally by the Italians – in double the numbers we had invited.

Everyone, without exception, paused in wonder as they stepped through the glass doors (and this was a tough audience to impress).

The Wing had been transformed into a beautiful, almost surreal, corner of Japan. In the central column of space below the atrium, rare blue Vanda orchids were suspended freely at varying heights. Under the beautiful deep-blue petals, each stem extended for at least a metre before splaying into aerial roots. (The petals weren't exactly aqua, more of a purply-blue, but I wasn't going to be the one to tell the baroness.)

The esteemed artist, Manami Kinjo, had created a unique installation of bamboo sculptures, circling the lounge, in the Japanese art form Sogetsu Ikebana. Individual poles rose from the floor, and at about two metres high the bamboo was thinly sliced, curled and intertwined with the neighbouring shoots. It was simple, organically beautiful and totally unique. It fitted perfectly with The Wing's modern glass structure.

In front of the central bar a gaggle of geishas (there was probably a collective noun, but I wasn't the expert on all things Japanese) came and went with trays filled with tiny glasses of sake, delicious soft-shell crab rolls, rock shrimp tacos and sea urchin tempura.

The baroness had been pushing for a shamisen player, but luckily we were out of passes. I always thought traditional music could tip the balance from cool to awkward. I opted instead for a Buddha Bar album.

Vincent, Kato and Enrico sat on the high stools, each holding a microphone. We'd opted for the informal approach; unfortunately that meant I had to sellotape Enrico's flashcard vertically to the microphone. I was staring, willing him telepathically to read the words.

'*Irasshaimase*,' Vincent said, with a little bow of the head.

The Japanese media led a gentle flutter of applause that was picked up and rippled around the other guests.

'The Wing has become a little Japanese tonight, as Dupont Lamborghini has also become a little Japanese.'

I cringed. Vincent didn't have the latest draft of the speech. I had replaced 'little' with 'a touch', as it was a bit too close to the bone. Kato was about five foot four.

Thank God they were sitting down.

'Shinsei Kato is a business pioneer. The technology empire he has built has become a model for aspiring entrepreneurs the world over.' He paused, giving a meaningful look to Kato, who replied with a curt nod. The silent language of important businessmen.

'Kato-san and I share many values ...'

Cue the ubiquitous 'We're so alike, I'm obliged to take his money' partner speech ...

'Striving for excellence in business, a commitment to perfection ...'

I zoned out and scanned the room. The guests were politely listening to their host. None of the journalists were taking notes: they knew there would be a press release. Vincent was in his element, speaking from his faux-casual pulpit to his congregation. For once, Enrico didn't look bored. Kato sat looking serious in his crisp new team shirt, complete with packing creases.

'SORRY I'm late,' boomed that Essex voice as the doors slid open, to be filled by Harry's large frame. 'Sorry Vince, sorry guys.' He took in the decoration, gave an impressed nod, and concluded by lifting his hands in the air and doing a strange karate kick.

'Hii-ya!'

Vincent forced his mouth into a tight smile, and waited until the chuckles died down and the guests returned their gaze to him.

'So I am extremely proud to present my new partner and shareholder in Dupont Lamborghini, Mr Shinsei Kato.'

Polite applause was accompanied by some low muttering among the guests. Then came the death knell for an event.

Kato made a slow expressionless speech in Japanese, that Bad Teeth translated in staccatoed and grammatically bizarre English. The guests looked on politely, but their eyes started to dart around the room looking for distraction. Thank heaven Kato had heeded our request for a two-minute speech (even though that doubled with the protracted translation).

Vincent shook hands with his new partner, holding the pose and the smile while the photographers captured the moment.

'Kato-san and I are delighted to be able to follow up with our first major announcement for the Dupont Lamborghini team.' The audience woke up again. 'Enrico Costa has signed a five-year contract extension …'

Enrico, read the card, read the card.

Enrico lifted up the mike and for a split second looked like he was actually concentrating.

'Ari … er… Arry-Bircher, *Go-zai-mas.*'

His Italian media fan club burst into spontaneous applause, which would have happened even if he'd just burped. The rest of the guests looked confused.

For fuck's sake.

As the guests started to search for their place settings on the horseshoe-shaped table, I mingled with the stack of press releases.

'Hey, Gordon, here you go.'

'Kate.' He looked up from close study of a place card. 'All the details here, then?' He started to skim-read the release.

'Of course.'

Gordon pulled the sheets up to his glasses. 'What's the share split?'

'Lamborghini forty per cent, Vincent thirty, Kato thirty. It's all in the release.'

'How about management structure?'

'It stays the same. It says so there.' I pointed to the third paragraph in a vain attempt to ignore his smirk.

'Hmm ... Vincent retains management control. The sum Kato paid?'

'I'm afraid that's undisclosed.'

'I heard a hundred million dollars.'

'Did you, indeed?'

'So?'

'Gordon ...'

'I see he got the uniform.'

'Yes, he did.'

'The seat on the pit wall.'

'Uh-huh.'

'I'm guessing this'll be the only team press release with a quote from him on?'

'Probably, well, as a shareholder it's ...'

'You've got to hand it to Vincent: he pulls it off every time. God knows how he does it.'

He rolled the release up, stuck it in the inside pocket of his blazer and went back to lifting up each place card five centimetres from his glasses.

Dupont Lamborghini F1 Team

PRESS RELEASE

Shinsei Kato becomes Dupont Lamborghini shareholder

Japanese entrepreneur and businessman Shinsei Kato has acquired a thirty per cent stake in the Dupont Lamborghini F1 team.

Kato is founder and owner of SK Technology Enterprises, a Japanese conglomerate corporation headquartered in Tokyo. SK Technology Enterprises is one of the leading manufacturers of electronic and information technology products, and specialises in developing networking hardware, software and services.

The shareholding structure of Dupont Lamborghini F1 Team is 40% Lamborghini, 30% Vincent Dupont, 30% Shinsei Kato. The current management structure remains unchanged.

Vincent Dupont

'This is an historic day for Dupont Lamborghini F1, and I'm delighted to welcome Shinsei Kato to the team. His record of business success is impeccable, and his skills and foresight are invaluable in making Dupont Lamborghini F1 simply the best team in the world.'

Shinsei Kato

'I am very proud to become a shareholder in the Dupont Lamborghini F1 Team. Vincent Dupont and I share a common vision for the team and I look forward to a successful future together.'

Spa Francorchamps, Belgium, 28 August.

Media contact
Kate Ellison – Kateellison@dupontf1.com

www.dupontf1.com

Dupont Lamborghini F1 Team

PRESS RELEASE

Dupont Lamborghini F1 extends Enrico Costa's contract

Dupont Lamborghini F1 has today extended Enrico Costa's contract for a further five years.

Vincent Dupont, Team Principal

'I am very happy to announce a five-year contract extension with Enrico. He has been with the team since its birth three years ago, and his exceptional commitment and outstanding talent have been instrumental in the team's success. This is a partnership that works, and I look forward to many competitive seasons together.'

Enrico Costa

'Stability is important in a driver's career and I'm really happy to know I will be working with the same team of friends for the next five years to win as many points, podiums and championships as is humanly possible. Dupont Lamborghini is a great, highly motivated team, and what is more they know how to win. And that is all I live for – to win!'

Spa Francorchamps, Belgium, 28 August.

Media contact

Kate Ellison – Kateellison@dupontf1.com

www.dupontf1.com

Vincent was still striding aimlessly around The Wing after the last guests had gone. Like the child who couldn't come to terms with his birthday party being over for another year.

'Keht, Keht!'

I waved away the last two Belgian journalists, who had locked horns over Jackie Stewart's Spa crash in 1966. I turned to find Vincent invading my personal space.

'Oh, hello, is everything all right? Do you want your car?'

'Listen, great job tonight, great.' He wagged his finger in my face, which sort of contradicted the positive statement. 'You've been working hard. So I've decided … you can fly home with the baroness and I on the plane tomorrow.' He smiled an unnatural smile of polished incisors.

'Thank you, that would be great, er … very kind.'

'Right, where is my car?'

Flying back on the Gulfstream was a total luxury, and above all meant I was home hours earlier.

But somehow it didn't feel like a treat, or a bonus: more like a pay-off.

Dupont Lamborghini F1 Team

PRESS RELEASE

Belgian Grand Prix
Circuit de Spa Francorchamps
Sunday

Race
Dupont Lamborghini F1 dominated the Belgian Grand Prix, with Enrico Costa and Marcel Müller claiming a 1-2 at the chequered flag in spite of heavy rain in the last laps of the race.

Enrico Costa – 1st
'I enjoyed this race, but it wasn't easy. The team kept saying it might rain, but when it suddenly chucked it down in the last 15 minutes I was seriously worried. I saw a load of cars fly off at the exit of Eau Rouge, so I just focused on keeping the car on the track.'

Marcel Müller – 2nd
'I had a long battle with Santos for this second place. I got past him at the start, and then he was right in my mirrors all the way to the first stop. He got past me in that stop, but I kept on his back. I finally made my move into turn four, which was just before the rain started. I saw him aquaplane off in my mirrors a few corners later.'

Vincent Dupont, Team Principal
'A great result for the team in a tough race.'

Media contact
Kate Ellison – Kateellison@dupontf1.com

www.dupontf1.com

CHAPTER 14

Autodromo Nazionale di Monza, Italy
Thursday, 12.20 p.m.

My dad's favourite film was John Frankenheimer's *Grand Prix*. I had seen it more times than I could count on rainy Sunday afternoons, and my earliest memories of watching Formula One were a confused mix of reality and fiction. The Italian Grand Prix was a major part of the film, including the scene of Jean-Pierre Sarti's fatal Ferrari accident. Monza was burnt into my memory, and part of my emotional core.

In reality it didn't disappoint.

The *tifosi*, head to toe in Ferrari red, were everywhere: outside the hotel, lining the roads to the circuit, inside the great park, crowding every security checkpoint to peer into each incoming car. They waved flags, held up banners, pounded their airhorns. The atmosphere was intense, vibrant and infectious.

There was a strong showing of Dupont Lamborghini fans – we had the Italian driver and engine after all – in silver and aqua caps, and the hi-tech merchandise version of the team shirt. But they didn't make up more than a quarter of the fans.

The message was clear: we were all invited to join the fun, but this was Ferrari's party.

I became obsessed with people-watching. The Monza paddock was like nowhere else (Monaco had the A-list talent, but lacked the central thoroughfare for unrestricted scrutiny). The women strutted in expensive, perfectly co-ordinated outfits, beautifully thick hair and oversize sunglasses. Striking the right balance between sexy and stylish. The men wore jeans (often red) that were cropped just above the height-assisted Hogans, a Dolce & Gabbana-style fitted shirt and the obligatory bright cashmere jumper, thrown over the shoulders or rolled and tied around the waist. Accessorised with cool sunglasses and a perfect tan. Whereas this outfit would get you beaten up at a football match in the UK, Italian men somehow pulled it off.

I peeled my face off the office's glass wall, my big screen on the paddock, frowning at the greasy mark left by my forehead. I wiped at it with my fist, spreading the smear to twice its original size, before turning my attention to my laptop, where the inbox filled with the rolling bold type of new emails. Without spam there were sixty-five new messages since I'd left the office last night. Some of the interview requests I'd rejected had replied with ever more aggressive and threatening demands.

I knew journalists were under pressure from their editors to get an Enrico interview in Monza – an Italian driver at the Italian Grand Prix was a must – but it wasn't feasible for him to do all of them. There had to be a selection, and that was decided by a combination of factors:

i) Readership and viewership – big figures were obviously best;

ii) Type of feature – with preference given to a ratio of many gushing pages to little interview and photo time;

iii) Trustworthiness of journalist – so that what we agreed was what happened;

iv) Credibility of publication – although in truth this was somewhat trumped by (i), as

Famiglia Cristiana (top-selling Italian Catholic magazine) and *Playboy* were both equally revered in press officer land for their incredible reach.

However nicely you tried to deal with it, you always had to piss someone off. But those who tried to threaten bad or unsubstantiated stories only succeeded in getting on my blacklist – until, of course, they got a job at *Famiglia Cristiana* or *Playboy*.

Janey let out a squeal as she hung up her mobile and ran over to perch a bum cheek next to my keyboard.

'How much do you love me?'

I looked up at her face, pursed in anticipatory self-congratulation.

'No way? You are unbelievable.'

'Unbelievably ingenious, more like.' She flicked her hair back and stretched out her legs in a mock 1950s beauty queen pose.

'Who's paying?'

'Thorsten – well, Red Bull, of course.'

Thankfully she couldn't see my mind working full-time to remember he was her 'sort of' boyfriend.

'He said he can get it through on expenses. He'll just claim we were a new potential sponsor. Red Bull are more chilled about exes than Vincent.'

'Wow, I can't bloody believe it. We are really going for dinner at the Villa d'Este?' I had read about this fairy-tale hotel on Lake Como, complete with George Clooney-sighting possibility, in the in-flight magazine on the way over. Janey and I had gone off on one of those 'if only' conversations.

'Sure are, babe. Eight p.m., be ready, be smart and be hungry.'

'OK. I'll just have to check Vincent is settled in his dinner with Signor Bertelli at the Derby Grill, then I'm there.' I ignored her eye-roll. 'You know Janey, if you looked after your Paddock Club guests half as much as you looked after us, you'd be one shit-hot hospitality manager!'

I swerved to avoid the tip of her shoe, which shot out in a kick.

Da Beppi Pizzeria
8.30 p.m.

I was tired, starving and looking for an argument by the time I pushed open the glass door into the strip-lit pizzeria.

Vincent, Signor Bertelli, Lucilla, an apparently famous Italian TV presenter who looked like a man in drag, and her AC Milan footballer boyfriend, were quaffing Sassicaia and tucking into the *amuse-bouche* at the restaurant in the Hotel de Ville. I had checked that they had the best table, the head waiter knew to sprint to their every command, and the bill should be added to the Dupont account, so Vincent didn't have to deal with anything messy like money.

Janey was speeding in the hire car with Thorsten and one of his Red Bull colleagues to one of the most beautiful hotels in the world on the banks of Lake Como. While I was stuck with the Italian equivalent of Pizza Hut.

My heart had sunk when Tomasz's email had popped up in my inbox with one of those red exclamation marks, annoying in itself as I felt qualified to draw my own conclusions on an email's importance. The exclamation mark was up there with the 'Read Receipt' option, which screamed sender paranoia. I already worked for one obsessive control freak, wasn't that enough?

Janey was probably right, I should have just cancelled the dinner with Tomasz. I wasn't even sure what compelled me to disregard the once-in-a-lifetime opportunity to eat at the Villa d'Este. This was another example of sex complicating things. I couldn't trace the origin of the twisted feeling of guilt and responsibility I felt towards this punctilious Pole. He was a journalist with no F1 access and on Vincent's blacklist, so there was no reason for me, as Vincent's press officer, to meet him for dinner. Professionally Tomasz had caused me nothing but trouble, and personally, well, that was just an additional nuisance.

But in some dank, dark corner of my mind, an area I wasn't keen to frequent, lurked an unwelcome but persistent thought that my boss *was* responsible for both Tomasz's loss of job and his paddock ban.

'I've ordered a carafe of house red. OK, Kate?'

'Fine,' I said with minimal effort, in order not to sound petulant. I squeezed through the narrow space between the neighbouring table to sit on the straight-backed wooden chair. Tomasz slouched on the opposing banquette in a navy blue polo shirt, pushing his fringe out of his eyes to view the menu.

Halfway into the carafe, and after a good bruschetta, I was feeling less hostile.

'So you said you have a new project? Will it get you back in the paddock?'

Tomasz looked furtively over each shoulder to the neighbouring tables, where loud animated discussions in Italian were taking place. He crossed his arms and leaned forward. The table wobbled towards him.

'Quite honestly Kate, the last couple of months have been complete hell. Maybe I crossed some line in terms of self-preservation in the *Sport Heroes* interview, but as far as I'm concerned, if you're a public personality, you put yourself out there: your life isn't private any more.' His intonation was bizarre; he accented the wrong vowels, and his tone went up at the end of the sentence even though it wasn't a question.

'I didn't do anything wrong and Vincent had no right to stop my pass, to try and ruin my career …'

'To be fair, you don't know that he did that,' I said half-heartedly.

He gave me a long, searching look. It was the same look that I'd been getting more and more often recently. I picked up the plastic-covered menu.

'But anyway, I've learned my lesson, and the gloves are off.' He mimed throwing something over his shoulder. I resisted the urge to roll my eyes. 'I'm a curious man – I'm a journalist, for God's sake – and I figured if Vincent reacted so strongly he must have something to hide. So I did some more digging.' He took a swig of wine. 'Do you remember before the interview I kept asking you for more details in Vincent's biography?'

'Oh, yes,' I replied, not disguising how annoying his request had been.

'Well, there was, is, a hole of four years, between the ages of nineteen and twenty-three.'

I hadn't noticed; his youth had seemed pretty irrelevant.

'And there were so many questions. I mean, how does a poor farmer's son from south Poland end up even meeting Baron Fontenay, one of Europe's most successful men, let alone become his prodigal son? How did he rise up the ranks at Fontenay Paris so quickly? Vincent's obviously very smart, but he wouldn't have had a privileged education living in the immigrant-filled twentieth arrondissement. So no bespoke fast track.'

He left these question marks floating in the air as the waiter, in the classic garb of white shirt, black waistcoat and trousers, reappeared with a small white pad. I ordered a *pizza regina*, and Tomasz a *quattro stagione*.

My ravenous appetite was beginning to wane. This dinner was not about friendly professional advice, nor was it an excuse for a bit of flirting. The conversation had veered in an unexpected and uncomfortable direction. Tomasz was here as a journalist, one with a grudge against my boss, and I was Vincent's media security buffer. And once again I was working blind, as I had no information or pre-prepared answers about Vincent's youth.

'So after Silverstone, when I couldn't get into the paddock, I decided to go to Paris and sniff around. I had no job any more, so nothing to lose.' He left a weighty pause. Tomasz was quite the storyteller, hooking his audience, reeling them in slowly, keeping them dangling as long as possible.

'And?' I attempted nonchalant but polite interest.

'Well, when they got to Paris in 1970, Vincent's father got a job washing dishes at the Hôtel de Crillon, and his mother was taken on as a chambermaid.'

'That's that amazing hotel on Place de la Concorde, isn't it?'

'Yeah, that's the one. Anyway, his parents are the lowest of the low rungs on the ladder, working all hours, so Vincent spends hours on end hanging round the back of the kitchen and in the staff quarters.'

Two large, delicious-smelling pizzas arrived on the paper place mats in front of us.

'*Buon appetito, signori*,' said the cheery waiter.

Tomasz watched the waiter leave before resuming.

'This part wasn't so hard to find out. I mean, his parents were illegal when they first got there, but eventually they got all their papers in order, so they crop up on official documentation. The next part was the tricky bit.'

There was a disturbance at the door as a group of rowdy Ferrari fans burst into the restaurant. I turned to see that the place was now full, and about ten people were waiting at the door to be seated. I turned back to my plate and sawed off a triangle of pizza.

'OK, I can see how he'd develop a taste for nice things, even from the basement of one of the most majestic hotels in the world, but that's just healthy ambition.'

'He took it way further than healthy, but wait: let me get to that part.' He took a large mouthful of pizza, struggling with some resilient strings of elastic *mozzarella*, which eventually broke off, swinging back and forth in mid-air before latching on to his chin.

'Now the baron, while running an international cosmetic empire, was living the archetypal French businessman's dream. He had the baroness and their beautiful daughter Daphne at the Gloucestershire mansion where he lived at the weekend. During the working week he was based in Paris, where he had a long-term mistress and son. *À la* Mitterrand, although with Mitterrand it was a daughter.'

He finally wiped his mouth with his napkin and topped up our stemless glasses from the carafe.

'So he had an illegitimate son.' I shrugged. 'That's practically a must for successful businessmen these days.'

'This isn't a quick affair, this is a whole second-family scenario. The affair went on for some twenty to twenty-five years, during which time the baron housed his mistress at the Hotel de Crillon.'

'How on earth would you even know this?'

'I found her. The mistress. She's pushing eighty now, but still very lucid. Unfortunately his parents wouldn't talk to me.' He continued to eat as he told his story. I was treated to a front-row seat for the digestive journey of the *quattro stagione*.

'Of course not, they're dead.' I cringed at the memory of the biography Q&A in Vincent's suite in Barcelona.

'No, they aren't. They live in a small flat in La Villette, in the nineteenth arrondissement.' He drained his water glass. 'Anyway, so what you've got is two pre-adolescent social misfits, admittedly from very different backgrounds, hanging round the Hotel de Crillon. Nicolas, the Baron's son, is a difficult boy, always playing truant from school, finds it hard to make friends. And then there's our social chameleon, the young Vincent, or rather Wincent Ponieważ, who skives off school, preferring to hang around the hotel.

I became transfixed by his hands, which danced around as he talked; the freckles on the back; the long, almost feminine fingers; the habit he had of repositioning his watch.

'*Tutto bene signori?*' The waiter topped up our water glasses. We both nodded.

'I'm skipping chunks, otherwise the story is too long, but you get the picture. Nicolas's mum said at the beginning she was wary of this boy her son found in the kitchens, but in the end she was relieved he had a friend, and young Wincent was so incredibly polite and well-behaved she was won over by him.'

Tomasz continued to eat voraciously. I prodded at the three-quarter pizza on my plate, which looked overwhelmingly big, before putting down my knife and fork.

'From what the mother told me, the baron was very attentive, and pretty much idolised the boy. It was his only son, after all. But Nicolas was wayward, always getting into trouble, drinking too much and getting into fights. Wincent, already a gifted *charmeur*, usually managed to talk them out of any serious trouble.'

Pushing the last large piece of crust into his mouth, Tomasz pushed his empty plate to the centre of the table.

'Fast forward to 1977: Wincent is nineteen, Nicolas twenty. They "borrow" the baron's Daimler for the usual night of partying. Now you probably won't have heard of it, but there was a very high-profile incident in Paris where a young couple on their honeymoon were killed by a hit-and-run driver who mounted the pavement below the Arc de Triomphe. It horrified the nation and dominated the media for weeks, as the driver was never found. A police investigation went on for months.'

'Go on,' I said, wishing he wouldn't.

'Apparently, Nicolas was driving the car. Wincent was the passenger.'

'Apparently?' I seized on the only potentially positive word.

'For Christ's sake, Kate, just wait!' He brought his hand down on the table, catching his fork, which clattered to the floor. The neighbouring guests paused in their chatter to look. Tomasz lent in closer. 'Wincent claimed he wasn't driving. But then Nicolas received a fatal head injury, so could hardly contradict him.'

'*Gradite un dolce, signori?*'

We sat back to allow the waiter to collect our plates.

'Do you have a *panna cotta*?' Tomasz looked across the room to the glass-covered dessert trolley.

'*Si signore*, with strawberries.'

'Kate?'

I gave a 'whatever' shrug.

'Two, please.'

The waiter disappeared and Tomasz resumed his inclined story-telling position.

'So what does Vincent do? His best and only friend is dying or dead next to him, and a young couple are splattered all over the pavement. Does he call the police? Does he call the ambulance? No, for a nineteen-year-old boy he shows inhuman *sang froid*. He calls the baron. The cold, calculating bastard is already thinking of the PR implications of the accident, and how to turn the situation to his benefit. He apparently pulled his dead or dying friend out of the driving seat, took the wheel and drove to the baron's apartment, hiding the car in the underground garage.'

'Why do you keep saying "apparently"?'

'Because his mum says Nicolas couldn't have been driving.'

'She's his mum, of course ...'

'He was born with nyctalopia, otherwise known as night blindness. He couldn't see well after dark and so never drove at night. It was diagnosed when he was ten, and Nicolas had insisted the baron wasn't told as he didn't want him to know he was less than perfect.'

The *panna cotta* arrived. A solitary white island in a blood-red strawberry sea.

'The baron, it would seem, was distraught, but also savvy enough to want to avoid a scandal: the illegitimate son, his car, a terrible murder. He's well-connected, of course, pulls some strings, and no evidence is ever found.'

'What about Vincent?'

'He disappears, literally off the face of the planet, for four years, and reappears in 1983 as Vincent Dupont, sliding into a junior but fast-track position at Fontenay Paris. In the position the baron always wanted for Nicolas. Vincent stepped straight into the shoes of the prodigal son, his dead best friend.'

Tomasz sat back, still holding my gaze. My head was spinning with words, images, questions. It was too much to take in. I didn't want to take it in.

'It's a terrible story, but it's in the past.' I fell into 'kill-the-story' defence mode. 'A grieving old man wants to support his son's friend, who turns out to be a talented businessman. Is that really so bad?' I should have gone to the Villa d'Este.

'Kate,' Tomasz said patiently, 'you've got very good at spinning the truth, but' – he stretched his hand across the table to mine, which I retracted into my lap – 'don't be blinded by your own web. Wincent or Vincent does not have a shred of human sentiment in his body. He is brutal ambition and re-invention personified. He was fully convinced that he had whole-heartedly become the prodigal son until the baron died, leaving him not a penny of inheritance. I mean, many would argue that the chances and support he had given Vincent way outweighed any duty, but not our friend. No, he promptly set about wooing the sole inheritor, Daphne Fontenay.'

We sat in silence. I stared at the food-splattered place mats as the waiter cleared away Tomasz's empty plate and my untouched *panna cotta*. After what seemed like an endless silence, I spoke.

'Why are you telling me this, Tomasz?' My voice had an involuntary tremor.

'I have to publish this. I'm talking to a couple of tabloids in the UK, and *Bild* in Germany. It's going to run as something like "Vincent Dupont: The Ugly Truth", or maybe "The Monster behind the Mask". The newspapers have started a bidding war – it's insane, the money they're talking about.'

'I'm going to have to tell him. You know he'll attack you with the whole weight of his hot-shot lawyer team. It'll never happen.'

'Come on board with me. If we do it together we can double the money. The papers are hankering for current evidence, and stories to go with it. I know you have some, Kate. Guys like him don't change, especially when they find an approach that works.'

As Vincent's press officer, I should have said no immediately. I should have told Tomasz he was crazy to think I'd take his side. I should have stood up in protest and walked out to call Vincent and his lawyers. I did none of this. I just sat, leaning my elbows on the table. I felt like the zip that had been holding everything inside had been yanked down. I desperately wanted to talk, to tell him about the YouTube film, about Victoria. I needed to let out this horrible truth that was rotting me from the inside out. But if I started, I wouldn't be able to stop. And then what? All I ever wanted was to do a good job and that meant being loyal, protecting Vincent, the drivers, the team from damaging media. The last thing a press officer could ever do would be to co-operate with them, co-operate in his downfall.

Tomasz was a good journalist. He knew when to shut up.

The silence was suffocating.

'*Signori*, would you like some *grappa*?'

We watched the waiter place two shot glasses in the middle of the table, each containing a coffee bean, and fill them with the clear spirit.

'Why should I trust you, Tomasz?'

'No. Why should you trust him? People look up to him – he presents himself as an aspirational leader. Christ, now he's on that sanctimonious mission to bring down Sal Ovitz, and he's getting praised for his moral upstanding ...' Tomasz tried a new tack of moral outrage.

I sipped the harmless-looking digestive. It was take-your-breath-away strong. I'd never liked *grappa*. I downed it in one, coffee bean included.

'We both know this wasn't a one-off. He won't suddenly become good or moral. It's too late. But you know that, don't you, Kate? You know him much better than me?'

Did I? Did I really? My head screamed. *The longer I worked for him, the more I realised I had no fucking idea who he was.*

I let out a snort of derision. I could feel Tomasz's eyes boring into my forehead, but I refused to look up from the safety of the table surface.

'Work with me, Kate. The money is great – you could set up on your own.'

'It's not a question of money.'

'You're right. It's bigger than that. People deserve to know who he really is. The truth must be told.'

I had always hated that line, used by hacks the world over to make a target confess some lurid celebrity bedroom secrets. Tomasz had moved into the hard sell.

'Vincent Dupont is one of the most recognised people alive. That level of profile confers exceptional power. And he thinks he's above the law. That's what's scary.'

I knew Tomasz was manipulating me. He was trying every angle – moral, financial, emotional – to get a rise, to get me to agree to work with him. But what he said made sense. Vincent should be accountable for his actions, and who knew at what point he would stop. If he'd stop at all. But was an exposé the right way? Of course Tomasz was convinced, he had nothing to lose. I had everything to lose.

I needed fresh air.

'Kate, why are you protecting him?'

Looks from neighbouring tables were becoming more frequent, no doubt due to Tomasz's escalating tone and insistence on banging the table.

'He's a murderer, Kate.'

I pushed back my chair and ran out of the restaurant.

Monza Circuit, Biassono Corner
Sunday, 10.35 a.m.

'Today the *Autodromo Nazionale di Monza* would like to honour a very special man. His commitment to performance, to presentation, and to Formula One in general, has already made an indelible mark on the sport.'

One of the ten grey-haired dignitaries in dark suits and large ties standing solemnly either side of Vincent on the asphalt addressed the crowd. I had lost track of all their job titles. On Vincent's left was the *Sindaco* or Mayor of Monza, next to him were a couple of local government officials. Then there were at least two presidents of the circuit, and a whole raft of directors. I hoped they weren't all going to make a speech.

Facing this delegation on a hastily erected tiered platform, the F1 photographers jostled with cameramen, and about forty journalists stood around the edges, dictaphones outstretched.

The wind had picked up and was blowing away from the audience, carrying the speech with it. The fans supporting with airhorns from the grandstand didn't help. The besuited band battled the elements stoically.

'He is at the forefront of a new era in Formula One: where the team boss is no longer just an acute businessman and sporting manager, but a philanthropist: a beacon of honour and responsibility.'

God knows why he chose the word 'beacon', but in a divine nod to the overall irony, the wind changed direction on that very word, relaying it with full diaphragmatic power to the cataleptic audience. A titter rippled through the crowd.

'He was responsible for bringing the legend of Lamborghini back into Formula One, and for giving Italy its first world champion since Alberto Ascari in 1952 and '53. He may not be Italian, but no man better sums up both '*lo spirito italiano*' and '*lo spirito della Formula Uno*'.'

Some serious nods of agreement Mexican-waved down the line. Vincent stood stiffly in the centre, chin raised. Proud and worthy.

I looked at the boss I had worked for for nine months. It was not an excessive history, but I could recognise a lot of his body language. Certainly the performance poses.

Tomasz said that I knew Vincent. What did I really know about him? I knew that he was hating that he would have to shake all those sweaty hands at the end of the speech. I knew that while he was standing there looking proud but humble, he had moved on in his head and was already working through his next strategic play. I knew that he was about to give a great speech in Italian and English, which would win over the unbelievers in the audience. I knew that he was wanting Harry Bircher to see him right now. I knew he would ask for a cigarette the second this was over.

But more than that, what did I know? Who was the real Vincent Dupont or Wincent Poniewaz? I had seen a chameleon who adapted to his surroundings, becoming whoever he needed or was expected to be; a randy adolescent with Enrico, a spiritual horse-lover with the baroness, a smiling friend to the media, and, almost always, a perfect walking, talking Dupont brand example.

'... so the committee was in no doubt that' – the speaker's voice rose in crescendo as he finally reached the climax – '*La Curva Biassono* be now known as *La Curva Dupont.*'

There was polite applause and the click and whir of multiple cameras, as Vincent walked to the kerb and lifted a small silk tent to reveal an anti-climactic plaque in the grass.

Gordon Barry's voice in my ear brought me back into the moment, where Vincent was thanking each of the dignitaries in turn in Italian.

'This whole bilingual speech thing is starting to look a lot like showing off.'

I sighed. 'But you'd expect nothing less.'

Gordon had the uncanny ability to say the unsayable and make me smile at the same time. No small feat, especially today.

'Listen, I need a comment.' He scooped me by the elbow, steering me away from the crowd towards the gravel bed. 'I'm hearing that in spite of the Kato deal, the aero budget is still severely limited.' He raised his eyebrows in a question. I kept my expression neutral, waiting for the question. 'The only update before the end of the season will be a new front wing package for Japan. But they only have enough budget for one. Is that true?'

'Let me get back to you.'

'Asap, Kate.'

Dupont Lamborghini F1 Team

PRESS RELEASE

Italian Grand Prix
Circuito di Monza
Sunday

Race

It was a very disappointing race for Dupont Lamborghini, with both cars failing to finish. On lap 27 Enrico Costa spun at the second Lesmo corner, hitting the wall on the inside. Marcel Müller was running in second position when he suffered an engine failure on lap 41.

Enrico Costa – DNF

'My start wasn't good, and I lost two places by the first corner. I was pushing really hard to catch up every tenth. Then coming out of the second Lesmo I lost the rear end and hit the inside wall. This is very frustrating, as at this point of the championship it's all about points.'

Marcel Müller – DNF

'What can I say? This was a great race until lap 41. I was lapping faster than Santos and could have caught him. I would have liked to have given Lamborghini a win in Monza, but it wasn't to be.'

Vincent Dupont, Team Principal

'An extremely frustrating result for the team and drivers at this stage in the season. Enrico was pushing 110%, but that's motorsport. Lamborghini's engines have been ultra-reliable to date, so it's a shame their first failure was in Monza.'

Media contact

Kate Ellison – Kateellison@dupontf1.com

www.dupontf1.com

CHAPTER 15

The TechQ, Lower Bledcote, UK
Tuesday, 10.15 a.m.

'There hasn't been a season this close in years. Two races to go, and five potential world champions and three potential constructors' champions,' said the prolifically-haired Brazilian journalist as we walked down the stairs into the race bay. South America was a target market for Kato's SK Technology Enterprises, so a new addition to our media priority list. I was only half-listening, as I was torn between keeping a beady eye on the photographer who was swinging his camera nonchalantly with his finger on the shutter release, and staring in horror at a solid ring of black back hair that had burst free from the back of the journalist's shirt.

The new front wing package was being packed up. One single wing, the sum total of the team's final aerodynamic push for the world championship. It was a meagre and, if I listened to the engineers, pathetically inadequate development, especially from a team whose coffers had just been boosted by a hundred million dollars. If the news that we could only afford one wing got out, it would be impossible for me to stop Gordon running his article on the team's money problems.

'So there must be some tension in the factory right now?'

No kidding. Come on, you could do better than that.

'Oh no, it's just business as usual. The guys are one hundred per cent focused on Singapore right now. So, as I was saying, the team travels about a hundred thousand miles around the world each year to races and tests, so freight logistics are a mammoth task. Sorry,' – I put a restraining hand on the photographer's left arm to disturb camera stability – 'you need to wait until we're in the freight preparation area before taking any shots.'

'What about between Enrico and Marcel? There must be some tension there. I mean Enrico is the champion, Marcel the newcomer: I bet he didn't expect to be only eight points ahead so late in the season.'

'It's just healthy competition.' It was scary how well I lied these days. 'They push each other, which is very positive for the team. So, some facts for you: Dupont Lamborghini ships about twenty thousand items – cars, parts, equipment – to each race. They're packed into specially designed cargo crates, which travel on cargo planes chartered by Formula One Management.'

I stifled a face-distorting yawn. Since Tomasz's declaration I had hardly slept. An endless rehashing of allegations and limited facts had made for debilitating insomnia.

What was I supposed to do now? How on earth was I supposed to process that information? Vincent, the consummate businessman, PR ideal, marketing visionary, one of the most recognised faces in the world, Mr bloody Formula One, was a double killer.

Why me? Why did Tomasz have to tell *me*?

I did not need to know that my mentor was a murderer. That everything he had achieved stemmed from absolute moral bankruptcy. And that if I didn't stop him, he would continue trampling more innocent victims in his endless quest for power.

I had done my best to believe that Vincent hadn't been truly aware of the content or implications of the Victoria Bircher film, that he had needed to destabilise Harry and Derek Capshaw had provided the tool. The unscrupulousness was classic Capshaw. Vincent's post-trauma support of Harry and his media attack on Sal Ovitz had surely been his conscience showing through.

It was supposed to be all over. Vincent had got what he wanted: the multi-million-dollar deal with Kato, and a long-term contract with Enrico. OK, so it looked unlikely Dupont Lamborghini would win the championship this year and there was still an alleged debt issue, but Vincent had secured a strong future for the team.

'Enrico isn't clamouring for team orders?'

'For Chrissake, this is supposed to be a story on freight!' I was too easily irritated these days; it was becoming harder and harder not to speak my mind. 'Sorry, I mean Dupont Lamborghini don't do team orders.' I hurried over to the logistics manager, who was bent over a multi-page checklist. 'Ah, Jim, this is Luiz from *Folha di Sao Paolo*. Can you talk him through freight preparation?'

My mobile sang out with Kylie and Jason's *Especially for You*. Silence swept over the race bay while I scrabbled to answer it. Just not fast enough to avoid ten truckies and eight mechanics sing the chorus, complete with theatrical gestures of love, all directed at me.

I knew it and I expected it: outnumbered by so many lads, one toe-curlingly embarrassing incident per day was mandatory, and yet my cheeks still flushed red as they finished up with laughs, whoops and applause.

'Yes?' I barked into the handset, in an effort to retrieve a little professional authority.

'Yes? Christ, Kate, whatever happened to hello?'

'Oh, Em, hey, sorry about that, I'm a bit stressed, as usual. What's up?' I jogged out of the huge roller door to the truck bay outside, in an effort to minimise the background noise, but where I could still keep an eye on my charges.

'Are you busy?'

'Always,' – I meant it as a half-joke but it came out rather curt – 'but go on.' The photographer was loitering by Enrico's car; the chief mechanic threw me a 'do something' glare.

'The thing is, I need … Danny needs …' It was quite hard to hear her against the noise of truckie banter and crate lids being bolted down. I pressed the phone harder to my ear. 'You've got to come to London.'

'Fat chance: my schedule over the next few weeks is hell and Vincent has an intensive media programme – you probably heard, he's on a bit of a quest right now.' One of Enrico's mechanics looked like he was in a stand-off with the snapper; I headed back over. 'Is it about the hymn choice, because I really haven't had a chance to look at the email, but honestly, I don't remember any except for *Morning has Broken*, and that's a terrible choice cos no one can sing that high.'

'No, Kate. You have to come *now*.'

'There's no way … I'm flying to Japan this evening, and Vincent has a fitting for the *GQ* shoot this afternoon.' I took the photographer by the arm and led him over to the photographic wasteland of two three-by-three-metre freight boxes.

There was a long pause on the end of the line; I started to wonder if Em had hung up. Then she spoke, her voice quiet, but imbued with an unfamiliar steely quality that made me finally give full focus to the conversation.

'I don't even know how to talk to you any more. I refuse to make a sales pitch for your time. This is the situation: Danny is in intensive care. He got himself into some serious trouble. He made me swear on Freddie's life not to tell you but, well, I'm in Hereford meeting with the bishop about the wedding, and I'm stuck here till tomorrow.' She let out a weary sigh. 'Quite frankly I'd rather call anyone than you right now, but clearly I have little choice.'

'But … what happened?' I couldn't understand why she was so cross.

'I don't know any more than that, except that he's got in with a pretty dodgy crowd and did something stupid with YouTube. He's been on a mission to self-destruct for months.' Her voice started to trail off, or maybe I just stopped hearing her clearly, because once she'd said YouTube a siren started somewhere in my brain, and escalated in volume. '…

he's got a broken jaw, ribs, I think he said a punctured lung. God, Kate, it sounds so awful.'

'You said YouTube?' Guilt, responsibility, panic were all confusing my thought process; I had to stall. 'You don't think Paolo did this cos of the George Michael film?'

'No way, he could never do something that ferocious. This attack was pure evil.'

I'd sent out the Victoria Bircher film from Danny's account. My computer had saved the details after he'd showed me Paolo's film. It had been quick and easy, and I had wanted my hands clean of it.

Now Vincent's top lawyers, international press and even YouTube's directors had got involved. Vincent was lobbying for a new internet law, for Christ's sake.

My gut tightened in a wince-inducing spasm, and my free hand moved instinctively to the source of the pain. I might as well have beaten him up myself. 'Did he say if it was some sort of payback?'

'He can barely speak, Kate!' She was impatient now. 'Anyway, what does that matter, getting Danny better and away from this crowd is the only thing that matters.'

'Of course it is.' But I had to know. Was this my fault? Shit, did I do this to him? 'Is that the reason he said not to tell me? I mean, why would he say that otherwise?'

She was silent again. 'Oh, I dunno,' – her voice was tight, quiet, angry – 'maybe cos you never have time for anyone but you, or he didn't want to interrupt your flour- ishing career wiping Vincent Dupont's arse, or it could be that the last time you saw you had him forcibly removed for drinking at a party. Just pick a reason.'

Formula One had made me tougher. I had been subjected to Vincent's forthright roastings, dressing-downs by journalists with decades more experience, and expletive-laden rants from Enrico. I'd sucked it up, as the Americans would say, and where necessary I'd defended my corner as professionally as I could. I'd had to be resilient to do this job. It was very much a man's world, and those were the rules it played by. So I was resistant to shouting, swearing and screaming ... but not to the quiet, considered hostility of one of the few people who really knew me.

'If you can't go then Natasha has volunteered, even though she only met Danny about twice.' Em moved on in a business-like tone: she wanted the conversation over.

'Oh, right, now Natasha is everyone's best friend ...' – I couldn't help myself, it was the time to be mature, but I was wounded and that girl was prowling around like some scavenging hyena.

'Don't! Don't you dare. She has a job, a very good job, where – you know what? – she save lives every day: abandoned babies in China are rescued and given a home thanks to her. But of course, your time, topping up Vincent Dupont's spray tan and sharpening his pencils so two cars can drive fast is *so* much more important.'

'Oh, you had no problem with Vincent when you thought he could model your Indian junk bracelets. You can ridicule my job, but Vincent's profile makes him more effective than ten Ban Ki-moons!'

'Yeah, I know,' she sighed. 'And while we're being honest, those hotel managers who jump when you call, the yacht captains who call you Miss Ellison, the raft of professionals who don't blink at your eccentric demands, aren't doing it because they respect you – without Vincent's name they wouldn't even answer your calls.' She gave a snort of disgust. 'The sad truth is, you're becoming more and more like him, and he's not someone I would ever want as a friend.'

I couldn't think of anything to say. On her end of the line, hushed voices pleaded in the background.

'So, yes or no? I can't keep the bishop waiting any longer. Are you going or not?'

'Of course I'm ...' But she had already hung up.

M40
11.05 a.m.

With the accelerator flat to the floor I hogged the fast lane on the M40, pulling over only when the occasional Audi, Mercedes, or any car with a half-decent engine, filled my rear-view mirror. There was little traffic as it was the middle of the day. The air inside the Fiesta was fermenting on two-day-old Big Mac detritus. I switched the fan to 'Max'. Tepid, dusty air blew out, forcing my tear ducts into overdrive.

Incredibly, it had taken me only eight minutes to get out of the TechQ. I dragged Janey off a tea break to step in on the Brazilian story before she could think of a get-out clause, and emailed her the *GQ* brief. I'd grabbed my files for Japan, and my laptop, and run to the car. Thank God I'd already put Vincent's suitcase in the boot.

I was firing on conflicting emotions; concern and guilt about Danny, defiant exhilaration at leaving the TechQ, and anger and surprise at Em's outburst.

Of course I wasn't saving lives: I never claimed I was in it for the Nobel Peace Prize. She was the one who wanted to save the world, I just wanted to work for someone who mattered, someone influential whose image needed protecting – that was where the challenge lay.

Protecting from what? Influence to achieve what, exactly? What was he prepared to do to get that much power? Murder?

In the twenty-three years I had known her, Em had never sounded so let down.

I hunched over the steering wheel, trying to minimise the loss of power on the long climb up through the Stokenchurch Gap. The steep chalk cutting was the mental gateway from the countryside to the city, in normal circumstances my destination of choice. A heavy grey cloud parked itself in front of the sun. Even the weather was ominous.

So much had changed in the past few months. The five post-uni years in London had followed a cyclical pattern of hellish commutes, microwave meals and raging hangovers. But Em, Danny and I had been an impregnable unit and through in-jokes, piss-takes and drunken character assassinations we were impervious to stagnant career paths, ever-extending overdrafts, and train-wreck relationships. Then my gift, or curse, to strive higher, faster, longer, and my innate fear of habit and routine, had pushed me into an industry where higher, faster, longer would never be enough – all the while pushing me away from the very people who could help me cope.

I overtook a Volvo with an overloaded roof rack; a little boy in the back seat stared out the window. When he saw me looking, he stuck out his tongue. I sneered back.

The thing was, the five-star hotel rooms, super-yachts, heli rides and Gulfstream flights weren't so amazing if I had no one to tell about them: friends who knew me well enough not to consider it showing off, who loved the details and shunned the blasé. Friends who were as excited by the contents of in-flight wash bags, who appreciated the embarrassment-slash-frustration of stumbling in on Patrick Dempsey changing into driver overalls in Vincent's office. Not to mention the twisted satisfaction of spotting a cold sore on a supermodel. And I guess they were also the ones who reminded me it wasn't my world, it was something I visited, and could even enjoy elements of, but it was not nor ever would be mine, and that I was all the better off for that.

Vincent's sordid secret, Em's disillusion, Danny's attack, Tomasz's article – it was too much for my head to process; every one presented a problem that needed decisive action. Decisions. Solutions. I didn't have any.

I pushed the button for the lighter and pulled a cigarette out of my bag. I had slipped seamlessly back into a ten-a-day smoking habit, and it was increasing daily.

Intensive care. Those were two scary words.

I picked up the phone and hit 'Speed dial #3' before I lost my nerve.

'Hey, Kate, you'd better not be calling with another job for me? You're all out of favours.'

'I need to delay my flight to Japan. I'm going to go tomorrow, instead of today. Can you change it?'

'Hmm, probably.' She paused, no doubt as her brain worked through various hypotheses. 'Has Vincent got himself in a bit of bother?'

'It's personal, Janey.'

'Oooh, even better. So Miss Super Spod is finally bunking off. Love it. Do spill?'

'I've got "Call waiting",' I lied. 'Tell Vincent I have athlete's foot, and text me the flight details, please.' I hung up fast. I felt nervous, but a bit better; I was doing a good thing, the right thing.

I turned right on the M25, exiting on the M4 into Hammersmith. This was my corner of London. I repressed an instinct to drive to Shepherd's Bush and turned off on to the Fulham Palace Road and the inevitable stop/start traffic.

My phone lit up with an sms. I clicked on it, expecting the details from Janey. It was Tomasz. He had texted me every day since Monza. This time the content was different.

I think u fear losing your job more than knowing the truth about Vincent.

I reached over to pick up the mobile from the passenger seat and deleted the message, as I had all the others.

If only life was that simple. That we could delete the parts we didn't like. For a start I'd delete the picture of Victoria Bircher's tiny body on that stretcher, which was a constant, haunting image every time I closed my eyes. In Vincent's world everything was black and white. In mine it was all increasingly grey.

I reached for the radio knob and turned it. A woman was screaming. She'd won tickets to a show, no doubt because she'd been vetted as a screamer. I turned the radio off.

Pedestrians were making faster progress as I advanced at a crawl through Fulham Broadway. A huge poster informed me that my ex-client, the repugnant reality TV star, had landed herself a role in *The Vagina Monologues*.

What was Vincent prepared to do to succeed? What was I prepared to do? Because my tally no longer consisted of just one innocent girl; I had dragged my best friend with me down this moral black hole.

I wound down the window and the car filled with the smell of exhaust fumes and the sweet nuts served on every London street corner. I forced myself to concentrate on the road as motorbikers with a death wish looped in and out of the traffic. The hospital was supposed to be coming up soon.

I eased over the Edith Grove junction, and then I saw it. The steel struts and arched canopy roof of the Chelsea and Westminster Hospital. *Déjà vu. Victoria on the stretcher. Harry grief-stricken.* The backdrop to the images that now lived in my mind. I was paralysed: my limbs disconnected from my brain, my lungs shallow, I couldn't get enough air. *The ambulance door, hurrying doctors, her tiny, tiny body.* I had to breathe. The back of my head felt light, like it was filling with a cloud ... it was inexorable and strangely peaceful.

A gob of glutinous liquid splatted on my cheek, just below my right eye, and started a slow slithering descent. Startled, I turned, alert now, to face the irate eyes of a cycle courier screaming 'Fucking tourist!' Then I could hear the noise: a cacophony of pounding horns, shouts, and a variety of profanities. I was stationary in the fast lane.

I wiped the spit with my sleeve and turned the key with jittery fingers to restart the engine. It stalled in third gear. I tried again: brake, clutch, neutral, turn key, clutch, first gear, ease off clutch, accelerate. I took a right into the hospital car park, pulled into the first space, emptied the contents of my handbag on to the passenger seat and lit a Marlboro Red.

With my eyes closed and head tilted back on the headrest, the harsh intoxicating smoke filled my lungs, providing an instant head rush.

I had to make this better.

With each drag came greater clarity.

This job had taught me how to get what I wanted done. I would make it right, and Danny better.

Em had lost faith in me and I couldn't blame her. Right now I wasn't sure I had much faith in me either. But I had a full twenty-four hours to dedicate to Danny. They would both see who was important to me.

Chelsea and Westminster Hospital, London

I strode into the hospital, brimming with renewed confidence from having a clear purpose. I could almost ignore the smell of disinfectant as I breezed through the atrium, following signs for the ICU and trying not to stare at the tubes, bags and drains emanating from shuffling patients. Hospitals made me uncomfortable. I did not react well to visible sickness and hated the sense of powerlessness they gave off, as places to just wait and hope. I pressed on down the wide aseptic corridor, eyes fixed on a point in the middle distance, breathing through my mouth rather than my nose.

When I had called the ICU for Vincent to get news on Victoria, I had been summarily dismissed as I was not family. I wasn't going to let that happen this time. I didn't risk stopping at the nurses' station, just walked past at a confident pace.

I carried out a visual scan of the ward and, not finding Danny, was about to reconsider asking when I did a double, then triple, take at a small figure in a bed to my right. The left side of the face was swollen in a purply-blue shapeless pulp. One eye socket was protruding, distorted, the lid puffy and closed, like some gory latex Halloween mask. Bandages covered the top and side of the head and from the powder-blue gown, tubes with coloured plastic attachments emerged, taped down on to a small free space of skin on the neck. At the top end of the bed various machines beeped and flashed graphic information.

My stomach was flipping on nausea-inducing acid. I steadied myself on the footboard of the bed. The unswollen right eye opened and proved what I knew already: it was Danny.

'Oh … Oh, God!' I moved around to the right-eye side. I was revolted, horrified and terrified all at once. This was Danny, my best friend. I had no idea what to do. A big part of me wanted to run away, like I had from Tomasz in the pizzeria. But just as that hadn't succeeded in making Vincent not a murderer, nor would it make Danny better.

'Excuse me, you can't be here.' A nurse with a no-nonsense face and hair scraped back in a bun appeared next to me.

I turned to her, my mouth still hanging open. *Pull yourself together, Kate.* 'I need to speak to the … head nurse, or erm, intensive care boss.' I was using my most authoritative tone, together with strong eye contact; it was usually infallible.

'Only immediate family are allowed in the ICU. Please step outside.'

'Now, listen to me …'

'My shis …,' a small, hoarse voice whispered. 'She's my shister.'

The nurse and I turned to Danny, who managed a sort of smile with the right corner of his mouth. He was looking at her, though not at me. She nodded as she took the IV drip tube, checked a small dial, and rotated it. 'Don't tire him out; he needs rest.'

Once she was at a safe distance I leant in to Danny. 'Unbelievable, the attitude on that one!'

'Please, Kate. They're really helping me.'

The exchange had succeeded in making me feel a bit more in control, but Danny was still not looking at me. I smiled in a way I hoped looked natural, and pulled up a small stool. I looped my hand around his fingers, which was the only clear patch of skin available.

'Shit, D.' I had planned a positive speech about being strong, that things would be better now and just allowing time for the healing process, all the while looking like I barely noticed any injures; but faced with so much distortion and damage, where I could only identify my friend by the three-centimetre-square space of his eye socket, it was pathetically trite and inadequate.

We sat in silence punctuated by the rhythmic ventilator of the patient in the next bed.

'Looksh worsh than it ish.'

'I'm not sure that's possible.' I brought my forehead down to lean it on his fingers. It felt reassuring to have some manner of body contact, but his hand smelt clinical. 'Does everything hurt?'

'They've got me on shome pretty good drugsh. That' – he nodded up at the IV bag – 'is my new best friend.' That he was trying to be chipper just made me feel worse. My eyes welled, but I swallowed the emotion back down.

'So what actually happened?' I said gently.

'Picked on the wrong guy. Musht've been an ex-featherweight or shomething.'

'What, he attacked you, just like that?'

'Look, it's a long shtory and I'm tired. You should get back to work.'

'It's ok, I don't ...'

'When's Em coming?'

'She's ... look, I'm here. Please, D., I want to help.' I took a deep breath. 'I need to help. I think it ... it was my fault.' I brought my other hand up to grasp his fingers in a double clasp, as if to ensure his attention. 'I posted an awful film on YouTube using your account, I didn't think it through. It was just there, and I wanted the whole thing over with. I never thought there would be so many ... ramifications.'

His eye was closed, and his breath was laboured and heavy. I thought he might have fallen asleep.

'I know, you idiot. YouTube cancelled my account and sent me a really shnotty email.' He squeezed my fingers. 'You bloody Luddite.' He repositioned his head carefully on the pillow, then met my eyes; his look was flat, resigned. 'It wasn't your fault, so you don't have to worry.' He turned away as if the conversation was over.

'Thank God. But, wait a minute ...' I realised what he was saying; like Em, he thought I was interested in no one but myself. 'No. You've got it wrong. That's not why I came. Please D., tell me what happened?'

He let out a sigh. 'It was a game that got out of hand.' The words came out slowly as he struggled to enunciate through the swollen lips. 'There's a gang of ush, but me and Tariq are the front men. We pose as rent boys on the Common, offering like fifty quid a blow job.'

There was a sudden flurry of activity as several nurses hurried to a patient two beds down. Danny glanced over in the direction of the movement. I kept my eyes fixed on him, trying to find the Danny I knew inside the bandages, bruising and story about strangers.

'There are another couple of guys in the bushes filming the exchange. Once we have enough footage we change the terms and shay five grand or we put the film on YouTube.' He closed his eye for a couple of breaths. 'It usually works pretty well, but last night I picked the wrong guy ... had one motherfucker of a left hook.'

I had so many questions I didn't know where to start. There was no relief in knowing it was not my fault, just too much difficulty in understanding how so much change of which I was totally ignorant could happen to my best friend. And I was still reeling from the fact that the two people who knew me best fully believed I had become a self-absorbed egotist. I wanted to be back on Em's sofa with a pitcher of margaritas, with Danny mimicking the *X Factor* contestants and Em knitting Bolivian finger puppets. I wanted everything to be how it was before Em was so disillusioned with me, before Danny looked like an extra in *Thriller*, when morality was still instinctual. 'Why? Why did you do it? Why risk everything?' I shot a glance at the nurse's station; the urgency dealt with, I was back to receiving withering looks. I lowered my tone to a whisper. 'Your boss is going to have a bloody field day.'

Danny nodded towards a plastic cup and straw on the bedside table. I lifted it to his mouth so he could take a sip.

'What, the boss that fired me five months ago?'

'What? Oh my God, why didn't you say?'

He closed his eye in a long blink. 'Listen, I'm getting pretty tired. Thanks for coming, though. They're moving me out of the ICU soon. Apparently I'm no longer critical.'

I started to panic. I couldn't go yet. 'Listen, I'm going to make this right. Last night you got it on film, correct? Well then, we can see the guy who did it. Now we can really make him pay for what he did. We can embarrass him publicly ...'

'Kate ...'

'I can take a still off the film and send it out to the media ... I'll write a press statement with a link to the rest of the film. He isn't going to get away with this. How do I find the guy with the film?'

'There's no way ...'

The nurse appeared by my side and put a firm hand on my shoulder. 'He really needs to rest now; you need to step outside.'

'No! I haven't finished.' I shook her off. 'Danny, I know what I'm doing, I'm good at this. He's a thug and a bully, he needs to pay.'

'Kate, I don't want your strong-arm techniques; not everything can be solved by sheer force of will. Just leave it. Please.'

'I want to make it better.'

'I want you to leave.'

The Chapel
Chelsea and Westminster Hospital

The pew was hard, the air slightly fetid from a decaying flower arrangement, and the small stained-glass window brought in no light as it was backed by black clouds. The tears had come suddenly, abundantly: sweeping up, overwhelming and incapacitating me. I had been gathered up by a kind old lady with a Salvation Army pin, who – no doubt fearing the worst as I was outside the ICU – had ushered me into the chapel. I didn't, couldn't put her straight. She stroked my hair, saying, 'Don't talk, dearie, just let it out.' So I did, into the shoulder of her hand-knitted cardigan.

And as I leaned snivelling, wet-faced and sore-eyed on this stranger, it dawned on me. It wasn't the feeling of guilt that I had got Danny in so much trouble that was so scary, it was the fact that I knew, I didn't suspect, that Vincent and the people he dealt with would easily have been capable of it. I had thought I couldn't be sure if Tomasz was telling the truth, but I realised now that I had known he was, all along.

Japan Airlines Lounge
Terminal 3, Heathrow Airport
8.55 p.m.

I sucked hard on the straw, my cheeks concave, eyeballs bulging under the strain; the cube on the other end rose hesitantly from the clear liquid. All my concentration was focused on maintaining enough suck for the straw not to buckle under the strain. That was the key to success.

'What are *you* doing here?'

I swung my head up in the direction of the voice, a movement my head and brain found tricky to co-ordinate. The ice cube made its escape, leaving splashes of vodka tonic on my cheek.

'Thought you were doing a cheeky bunk.'

Ah yes, the voice belonged to Janey. I gave her a winning smile. 'Janeeeey, have a seat. I'll get you a drink, it's my round, ha!'

'Oh my God, are you wasted?' She was whispering now.

I stood up and my chair rocked over backwards with a thud. Some heads moved in response to the noise. 'Oopsy.' I was about to pick it back up, when it somehow righted itself and, responding to heavy pressure on my shoulder, I found myself sitting down again. Janey disappeared for a while, and reappeared with two coffees and a strangely pursed expression.

'What are you thinking? The lounge is full of paddock personnel; there are two team bosses at the table behind you!'

I started to twist and see, but she grasped my elbows tightly enough to leave finger marks, and held them firm. I reached for the vodka to take a sip, but it had gone.

'Oh, come ooon, Janey. You're always telling me I take life too seriously.' Somehow the last word came out with five syllables.

'Not like this, you idiot. This is just professional suicide.' She pushed a small plate of triangular cheese sandwiches towards me. 'Why are you even here? You're supposed to fly tomorrow. You took a day off, remember?'

'Ooh, these are great sandwiches. Look how neat they are. Perfect little triangles. I'm actually starving; think I skipped lunch.' I stuffed a second one in. 'I wonder whose job it is to make these? *My job is to make perfect right-angle-triangle sandwiches ... I can also do equilateral and isosos ... isoss ... isosceles ...*' I broke down in a fit of giggles, my head collapsing on to the remaining sandwich.

A really hard pinch on my upper arm brought my head up, sandwich included. Janey flicked it off and forced some uncomfortably intense eye contact. 'It's nine p.m., and you've clearly been drinking for a long time. What the fuck happened?'

Everything that was funny drained away. 'I had nothing else to do. I had a day off and no one to spend it with. I am officially that sad.'

'Drink the coffee.' She pushed the saucer towards me. 'What about Danny?'

'I think our friendship was just annulled.' The world outside of the small silver table was coming back into focus: the travellers with their wheelie bags, folded newspapers, mobile conversations, furious typing on laptop keyboards, a nascent headache behind my right eye, the feeling of being totally alone. 'I've had my head up my arse and neglected Danny and Em both, big-time. He got into some really bad shit and I didn't even have the faintest idea. Plus I must be the world's worst maid of honour: I even got the date wrong the other day. They seem to think I'm turning into Vincent and he, on the other hand, is turning out to be someone seriously scary.'

'I tried to tell you a hundred times, but you don't listen. You have to be ruthlessly selfish in this job, or you just end up burnt-out and alone.'

I snorted at the belated truth.

'Stop hanging on Vincent's every word, expecting him to have all the answers for you. You've gotta get your own agenda, no one else is going to look out for you.' She waved to a couple of new entrants to the lounge, but looked back quickly to me to avoid conversation. 'If your friends are important to you then you've got to make time for them. This job will take everything you've got: it's up to you to set the limits.' Janey was on a roll – another speech, what she did best. But this time, it seemed to make sense. What I'd always put down as lazy freeloading was maybe just seasoned cynicism after all. 'It's what I've been trying to tell you from the start. You're still too much of a fan, of Fi but, more than that, of Vincent Dupont. You spend way too much effort trying to pretend he's a good guy. Get that bloody Dupont-branded noseclip off, and smell the genetically-modified roses.' She stood up and collected a bowl of cashew nuts and a can of orange juice from the buffet counter, then plonked them down on the table. 'Drink that, and eat those.'

'Really? I don't think that's a good idea ...' My stomach was making some worryingly loud gurgling noises.

'Just do it. We've a way to go to make you plane-ready.' She scooped up a handful of nuts and dropped them into my palm. 'So what does Danny like?'

'What do you mean? Apart from cute Italian men?'

'Yeah, I'm not renting him a boyfriend. I'm trying to think how you can make it up to him. We'll deal with him first, Em later.'

'Designer clothes, anything five-star and luxury, really. If I can make it up to him, Em will forgive me. She's been trying to get me to help him for months.' I took a large sip of the orange juice, as instructed. It's acidy pulp made an uneasy addition to my volatile stomach contents; I hoped a burp would suffice to calm the waters and render vomiting avoidable. I was in Janey's hands, and relieved to have someone take control who seemed so sure of how to mop up the mess I'd made.

'Thank God for that, because I've got no leverage with UNICEF or Angelina Jolie.' She scrolled through her Black-

Berry, hitting the touch-screen a couple of times, then looked up smiling. 'You're going to give Danny the ultra-Fi VIP treatment. This, my dear, is where I seriously excel. But just so we're clear, I'm prepared to use some hard-earned credit and sexually-accrued favours, just to stop those pathetic red-rimmed puppy eyes from bringing me down and ruining a great party at the Log Cabin on Sunday. But I will expect a full season of back-covering: no favour will be too big.'

'Done. So what's the plan?'

'First I need to know when he gets out of hospital, and where he'll go.'

I took a deep breath and hit 'Compose text'. I didn't know if Danny would have access to his mobile in the hospital, or even if he had the same number; and where did I start with only 160 characters?

D, pls trust me to make it up 2 u. when do u get out of hospital? k xxx

Janey was typing intently, occasionally smiling or giggling to herself.

'1 Message received
Monday 12 pm'

I showed Janey the screen. 'We'll be back from Japan, so I want him to come to my flat. I'll look after him, help him recuperate.'

A brief sceptical look flashed across Janey's face; it seemed not even she had that much faith in me. 'OK then, so Vincent's car service will pick Danny up from … Where is he?'

'Chelsea and Westminster.'

'OK.' She typed again. 'Is chauffeur garb, you know, peaked cap, too much?'

'No, no, it's perfect.' Even I found myself starting to smile.

'Dom P. on ice?'

'Nah, I think he's been partying enough.'

'Fortnum and Mason's hamper?'

'He prefers Domino's pizza.'

'OK.' She looked dejected for a minute. 'Ooh, wait a minute, I can get the guy who was Britney and Rihanna's security guard. Do you remember, he's massive and kept filling all the paps' photos? He can go from the hospital to the heliport.'

'Heliport?'

'Nothing less, dahling, flying straight into Oxford, followed by a second chauffeur to your poky flat. Should I send in a cleaning service? It's going to be one hell of an anti-climax.'

'Nah, it's good enough.' The objective of an apology to Danny had been superseded by Janey's desire to show her ultimate hospitality prowess, but it didn't matter: I was hugely grateful to her for taking over, and knew it would do the trick.

'Has Danny put on weight recently?'

'Er, no, if anything he's lost some.'

'Good, so what you need to do is save one of Vincent's spare suits and shirts from this weekend – I mean the smart stuff, not team kit. Take it into the hospital; whatever he was wearing will have been trashed. Hmm, Danny will look great in them.'

'That's funny, that's what he's always saying to me.' I fingered the handle of the Louis Vuitton keepall lying safely next to my chair. 'But, you know, I think I'd prefer to buy him something. I can up my credit card limit …'

She looked up with a scowl of disbelief.

'OK, OK! Vincent's hardly going to ever bump into him, I suppose.'

'Good, so all done.' She threw her BlackBerry into her handbag with a smug grin. 'If you'll excuse me, there's a hot but lonely-looking businessman over there who's also in need of some Janey magic, and' – she leaned in closely – 'some in-flight experience. See you on the plane.'

I smiled at the space she had left. Some people really were full of surprises. The headache had swelled to a pounding spike in my right eye socket, but the vomiting threat had subsided; all things considered, I felt much better. I picked up the phone to reply to Danny.

Pls let me pick u up on Mon. I lost my way for a bit but I'm back now & am going to make it up 2 u xxx

'1 message received'. I clicked on it nervously, but it was from Tomasz.

Deadline 4 publication set for final GP in Brazil. I know u want 2 do the right thing.

Vincent Dupont's image had not had its corners buffed and polished from several years in the media spotlight. It wasn't a coat of varnish designed to enhance his attributes and appearance. No, Vincent's image was a total construction, a new-build of all the most opulent materials, to hide the fact that there was no heart or soul inside, just pure unqualified ambition.

Maybe it had taken me so long to realise this because I considered myself an expert in image management, or maybe it was so convincing because Vincent believed it himself.

Anyway, Vincent was the common denominator to all my problems. I had to get out from working for him before it was too late. There were other teams; there had to be other chances. I had two races until the end of the season, and hopefully that was time enough to line up another job.

I highlighted Tomasz's message. 'Ruthlessly selfish', Janey had said, and that's what I would be. I had to help myself.

I clicked 'Delete'.

Flight JL402 London Heathrow-Tokyo Narita

I'd just put Vincent's bags and mine in the overhead locker, when my phone beeped with a 'Received' text from Danny.

OK c u Monday, Em will b here 2

I smiled as I settled into my business class seat, leaning over to swipe Mike's in-flight wash bag (Danny wouldn't have wanted my girl's one) and hide it in my carry-on, while he chatted up the stewardess.

Despite an early-onset hangover, characterised by exhaustion and a raging thirst, I felt like I was more or less back on track. I had deviated on to some badly lit country lanes in a storm with faulty windscreen wipers, but now I was back on the motorway and the wipers were working. I could see more clearly and knew where I was going, but it was raining heavily nonetheless.

CHAPTER 16

Lovenet Karaoke Bar, Roppongi, Tokyo
11.30 p.m. Japanese Standard Time

'Kate, your dress is soooo pretty.' Adriana leaned over the pink basin, applying lipgloss to her bee-stung pout.

'Oh thanks,' I said, smoothing the clingy black fabric over my thighs as I stepped out of the cubicle door, hesitating as a hunched figure hurried past to the exit. I was absorbed in checking that the unanticipated post-pee 'cleansing jet' hadn't left a visible trace. Japanese toilets hid no end of surprises. 'It's just an old ...'

'And I like how you've done your hair.'

Ok. Two compliments too many from someone who has only spoken to me to order tea.

'You know, some people say that once you do Victoria's Secret your career as a top model is over, you know, you don't get any more offers ...'

Oh, I get it, she was preparing the way for some ego-stroking story.

'But it's definitely not true for me. I'm, like, inundated.' She shook her hair back and it tumbled in perfect bouncy curls.

'I bet.' I rifled through my hefty handbag for my BlackBerry to keep my eyes off the mirror: sharing it with a supermodel was not an uplifting experience.

Since we had touched down at Narita International, Kato's office had swept us up into a minute-by-minute itinerary of obscurely intentioned activities in Vincent's honour. It included a supposedly secret evening programme for the men to which I was not invited and which the Japanese went to great lengths to pretend didn't exist. But they were less familiar with our drivers who, over breakfast, recounted and acted out in every detail their experience of guiding Momoko and Ayaka to the Love Hotel using remote-controlled vibrators. It was the first time I had actually wished for Adriana to hurry up and arrive.

I had two priorities at this race: to corner as many press officers as possible to check out job opportunities – I had spoken to three at the airport with no luck so far – and to suss out where Gordon was with the article I'd spent weeks trying to kill. Janey had reminded me to get my focus back on the proper part of my job, dealing with the press. If I wanted a new job I had to show I could do this one well, and a major article about Dupont Lamborghini's debt crisis would not be a CV plus point.

I punched out a text to Gordon while nodding along to Adriana's long and lazy vowels.

We want to co-operate on the financial questions, what info do u need to put the matter to rest?

I had pondered ways to self-inflict laryngitis to get out of the evening karaoke programme, but for a lack of medical know-how and the stronger desire to see Vincent belt out *Smoke on the Water*, here I was in the day-glo pink ladies' toilets of the Lovenet bar, complete with sparkly-heart mirrors and multiple TV screens in the loo door. And if this sensory overload wasn't enough, it would appear Adriana and I were bonding.

'You know, I didn't get Shin-sey before, but he's such a sweet man, and so enthusiahh-stic.'

Shinsei, aka Mr Kato, had bounced up and down clapping his hands like a deranged wind-up monkey, flushed and sweaty, as Adriana had belted 'Hit me baby one more time', complete with improvised pigtails and microphone at cleavage height. It had instigated a cringingly embarrassing display of pubescent lust in a middle-aged businessman, and Adriana had lapped it up.

'You know, Shin-sey's company has never advertised in its forty-year history. He said it's because he never found the right face for the brand. Now he wants me to front a global campaign,' – she let out a squeal – 'with the photographer of my choice!'

I followed her tiny hips towards the exit. She waltzed out of the heart-shaped plexiglass door and, lulled into a false sense of sisterhood, I failed to anticipate the force of an unsupported, and surprisingly heavy, swing door which thumped into the flesh of my non-model-size hip.

We were in the Candy Suite, one of many individually themed private rooms, which in our case was decorated in Liquorice Allsort colours and had glass display cases filled with sweets along the walls and inside the table top.

When I re-entered the booth, Vincent was perched on the pink and purple leather sofa having his cigarette lit by the suite hostess (in candy-coloured skating outfit). He exhaled a thick cloud of smoke.

'Where's Bertelli?'

'I just had an email from his PA.' I scrolled down my BlackBerry. 'His board meeting ran late and he's missed his flight. It's unlikely he'll make the race now, I'm afraid.'

'He never misses this race.' Vincent stared into the middle distance, then stood up and pushed rather roughly past a line of Kato minions.

'Enrico, let's go.'

'*Grazie al cielo!* Adi, we're off, baby.'

Adriana, who had settled herself in next to Kato and was studying the playlist on a small screen, looked up and wailed.

'No, Ricky, puh-lease. I can't go yet, Shinsey and I are going to do *You're The One That I Want* in duet.'

Vincent, who had a lot less patience with all things Japanese since the Kato deal was signed, was already half-way out of the door.

'Adi, I'm going *now*.'

'Oh baby, you're no fun.' She pouted and got up, squeezing slowly past a seated Kato, who looked like he might cry.

I read Gordon's reply as I jogged behind them to the car.

I want a sitdown with VD about the budget & don't give me proof on track I can't ignore.

Dupont Lamborghini hospitality area, Suzuka circuit
Friday, 9 a.m.

'Enrico has pretty much got to win both races if he wants to be sure of the title.' The journalist from *Het Laatste Nieuws* raised a gnarly finger. 'It's so close, if he's second to Santos or Alonso even once he'll lose the advantage.'

I was enjoying a trance, staring at a space above the white plastic table top. The PR line was that we were focused on Sunday and not on the championship, but in truth, Vincent was wired like a Mumbai taxi driver on speed.

The difference between winning and not winning the world championship was somewhere between sixty and a hundred million dollars in actual money and two hundred and fifty million in brand value. There was the big chunk of Formula One Management earnings that rewarded first place, sponsor bonuses tied into the contract small print, revenue from special edition books and merchandise and, of course, new sponsor money from companies keen to surf on the wave of victory for the next season. And, in Vincent's case, invaluable and well-timed publicity for the fledgling Dupont brand.

On top of the considerable financial reward, there was the official stamp of recognition as World Number One. The lifeblood of the egotist.

So it was anything but Just Another Race. The whole team was on edge, even the catering staff. No one wanted to be the one who made the mistake that cost the team the championship. The wheel nut not perfectly screwed, the tyre pressure a quarter of a bar out, the weather forecast miscalculated, the undercooked chicken. There were thousands of potential pitfalls. And the precision of Formula One meant every mistake could be traced to its source, so survival instinct reigned.

I became aware that the conversation pause was too long. 'Uh-huh.'

'And Enrico is just too hot-headed under pressure. If he has Santos and Alonso behind him on the grid, I tell you, he'll just overdrive and put it in the wall on the first corner.' Régis from *Le Soir* took the reins with the bad probability combinations required for Dupont Lamborghini to win the constructors championship and Enrico the driver's title. This Belgian media breakfast had turned into a painful exercise in team-flagellation.

'Harry's aero upgrade is apparently the dog's bollocks, could well blow the competition away.' *Het Laaste Nieuws* was back: was it Jens or Jan?

'Oh yeah.' Maarten from *Het Nieuwsblad* let out a deep, dirty laugh; aero upgrades were petrolhead porn. I checked everyone's hands were visible on the table. 'Vincent has been uncharacteristically monosyllabic about his upgrade.' He smiled knowingly, whether he actually did or not. 'I reckon Enrico's best chance is to get pole, and for Marcel to take the other three out.' The six journalists chuckled into their notebooks.

I jumped to the defence of my team. 'Coffee?' I steered the conversation to neutral ground and quickly scribbled WS on my to-do list. A coded reminder to call Lanvin about the special-edition aqua winner's shirts, which were in secret production should we, against all the odds, actually win.

Two heads nodded.

'Do you remember 1983 was an incredibly close season between Ferrari, Renault and Brabham?'

'You're forgetting '82 with Ferrari, McLaren, Renault *and* Williams.'

I drifted off again. Historic F1 debates were a powerful sedative. Plus the Bullet Train trip yesterday had been draining. For an engineering brain, the high-speed journey might have been fascinating, but I was underwhelmed by what was, in fact, just a train. Plus the nerves and patience required to get two bumper egos like Vincent and Enrico across Tokyo, through a station and on to a train, could not be underestimated. (For the first and only time, I thanked God for Kato, who had offered Adriana a flight up on Saturday in his heli.)

For a start, even in our five-star hotel, the level of English spoken was limited and had to be undertaken face to face with hand gestures, diagrams and absolutely no raised voices. Outside the Conrad Hotel cocoon, there was no winging it, ad libbing, or playing it by ear. I gave the suited taxi driver a piece of paper written by the receptionist and prayed that it did indeed say Tokyo Station.

Twelve minutes and 22,000 Yen later, the driver pulled his immaculate Toyota Crown to a halt. As I handed over my entire envelope of expenses, my charges marched at full speed towards the building entrance, heads down, no idea of their destination, and drawing attention to themselves by trying too hard to look unrecognisable.

Running like Usain Bolt in kitten heels I caught up with them and, in the longest ninety seconds of my life, found the correct platform, the correct carriage and our more than ordinary seats. A tantrum was brewing as there was a seven-minute wait until departure, and the only refreshments I could find were two iced green teas from the distributor on the platform. (Japanese iced tea, it transpired, was nothing like its sugary, peach-flavoured European cousin.)

Then, with two minutes to go, the carriage filled with twenty pretty grid girls who giggled behind their hands when they spotted their fellow passengers. Vincent and Enrico broke the ice by Kampai-ing their fellow travellers with the green tea and swigging happily at the contents (naturally after having Viraguarded the lid).

'Oh, Harry's meeting the press in five minutes. We need to go,' Régis announced.

The journalists stood up and moved as one. Taking my tea-stained mug, I headed to the breakfast bar for a refill. I picked my way through the plastic garden chairs crammed into the small space between the freight boxes that defined the Dupont Lamborghini hospitality area. Definitely the grimmest of the flyaway locations.

I tilted the display case of Lapsang Suchong and organic peppermint tea to find the Tetley bags hidden underneath.

'Keht.'

I swung round to see that Vincent had taken a seat at the table behind me.

'So what did they have to say?' He gestured with his half-smoked Marlboro in the direction of the departing Belgians.

'Oh, er, just, you know, facts and stats.' 'Of what?'

'Whether we can win?'

'And?' He exhaled, letting the smoke creep slowly out of his mouth through his teeth, curling up towards his nose.

'Well, if Enrico keeps his head, then yes.'

'Everyone's an expert.'

The front wing package was the elephant in the room. *Don't be intimidated.* 'As you are here, there is something I would like to discuss …' My voice had gone all squeaky.

He stood and started to walk towards the garage. I followed.

'Gordon Barry is writing an article provisionally titled "Where Did all the Money Go?" He believes the money from Kato's investment has been spent already and that the team is bankrupt.' My voice was shrill. 'Once Enrico runs with the single front wing package in practice today his suspicions will be confirmed.'

He altered direction to a corner of freight boxes, consulted his watch, the über-bling new Dupont prototype, and turned to me. Practice one would start in ten minutes.

'He just can't let it go.' He shook his head crossly. 'Get that has-been here now.'

'Oh, good, that's what I was going to suggest. If you can just talk him through the financials, clarify the misunderstanding, we can put this whole issue to bed.' I consulted my Timex: I knew what the time was but needed a break from his stare. 'It's probably too close to practice for him to come now, but how about straight after?'

'No.' A long curl of ash fell on to the astroturf. 'Go and tell him' – he stopped speaking but kept staring at me, like he'd been put on 'pause' – 'that he must be getting old-age dementia. He should be retiring, not wasting his time printing such fiction.'

'No! I can't! Gordon's always well ...' And then it dawned on me. 'I'm not threatening him. That won't stop him printing it, just the opposite.'

'Just do your job.'

Just do as you are told is what he meant. He walked into the garage, picked up his headset, and headed off to the pit wall.

I looked down at my hands, where I'd unconsciously shredded the Tetley bag, and at my shoes speckled with loose tea.

Lisa Bates Fan Club Reception
Orchid Suite, Suzuka Circuit Flower Garden Hotel
Friday, 7 p.m.

I knocked twice, shouldered the heavy fire door open, and slipped in through the gap. I couldn't risk waiting in the corridor for an 'OK' to enter, not when the hotel was full of F1 personnel and Vincent was due back for a dinner at seven-thirty p.m. I had planned to be discreet, but I hadn't expected to be at my last resort so soon. Between Narita airport and the first day in the Suzuka paddock I had managed to corner all of the team press officers, bar Lisa, and there were no imminent job vacancies, or maybe just none for me. So the vague job offer I had scoffed at a few months ago had taken on a new significance. I tried to block out of my mind how quickly, by applying to work for Harry Bircher, I was jettisoning the moral high ground, and reminded myself that my absolute priority was just to extricate myself from Vincent Dupont's web.

The first thing that hit me was the intensity of high-pitched chatter and the sheer mass of bodies in the room. Then, as I took in the environment, I saw voluminous blonde perfectly coiffed bobs, fitted puce Martini Magna team shirts, tight purple pencil skirts and French mani-cured hands holding flutes of pink champagne. One after another. At least a couple of hundred Lisa Bates clones. It wasn't my subconscious mind tormenting me, it was just another sanity-challenging facet of the Nippon experience.

I excused my way through the crowd, looking for the one face without Japanese features. I finally found her sat behind a small table on the far side of the room, signing autograph cards of herself as a cut-out paper doll in white underwear with attachable team kit or cocktail dress options.

'Lisa, there you are. My God, this is ...'

'Insane, I know, but they're so dedicated.' She stood up and threw her hands in the air. 'I have the best fan club!'

There was a pause while the translator did her job, then a response of ear-splitting shrieks, squeals and high-speed claps.

I didn't have much time. 'Listen, if you're busy we could meet up later?'

'It's OK, Kate. I heard you've been doing the rounds.' She kept signing at speed and passing on each card with a smile to an excitable lookalike. 'Harry has a girl shortlisted for the job, but I don't think he's confirmed anything yet.'

'Really? Oh, thank God. If you can just check …' I could hear myself gushing, as relief flooded in.

She stopped signing and looked up: it wasn't a positive look; I was making her uncomfortable. 'I don't know and the thing is, even if he hasn't taken on this girl, I'm not sure if he's still interested.'

'Oh, but at the German GP, you said ...'

'That was before …' She busied herself with more signing. 'I think he just suspects you've been a little too brainwashed by Vincent, if you know what I mean.' She finished up with a nervous laugh. A couple of the fans took this as a cue to laugh along too.

'Oh, right, I see.' Even though they apparently didn't speak English, the fans in front of the table were now looking at me with excited faces, waiting for my reply. I forced a confident smile. 'Well, thanks anyway. I'll leave you to it then. You've got my number in any case. Bye.' And again to the beaming fans: 'Bye.'

'Bye, Kate Errison!' They chanted, clapped and bowed. I made my way out as quickly as I could before my smile evaporated.

Qualifying for the Japanese Grand Prix: end of Q2 Saturday, 2.40 p.m.

Enrico shoved his helmet at his physio with such force that the guy slumped back into the flimsy garage wall. It was harder to stomp out of the Suzuka garage because, like most things in Japan, it was a much smaller version of the usual garage. With both cars inside, there was barely enough space for the mechanics to move around each other, let alone factor in work benches, rear jacks, tyre guns and engine stations. But with innate Calabrian talent, Enrico forged his way out, leaving everything and everyone scattering in his wake.

I stepped gingerly over the post-Costa-quake debris, catching sight of a set of Dupont Lamborghini overalls disappearing out towards the hospitality area. From two sides of the paddock, Enrico's left and right, journalists, TV presenters, cameramen and soundmen advanced, running towards their prey. Head down, Enrico upped his pace. He had to cross the paddock thoroughfare to reach the safety of his room.

'Enrico, you must be disappointed with eleventh place. Are your championship chances over?' shouted a brave but desperate Dutch reporter, with microphone extended, aware that her high-heeled totter wasn't a match for the Costa march.

Mid-stride, he changed trajectory, swinging round at the journalist, red face contorted.

'SUCK MY ...'

I leapt into a pre-emptive strike, one hand lunging for the door handle to his room, the other braced for a shoulder shove.

Locked on target, door frame bypassed, bodies collided in awkward recovery. Incredulous look, Italian expletive, hasty apology. Situation averted.

'Marcel, seventh place. How did it go?' I lifted my dicta-phone tentatively, as he whipped off his balaclava. Instinc-tively his free hand shot up to fluff up the hair that was pasted to his head with sweat.

'Not bad, considering Enrico got the only front wing package.'

I was squeezed out of a circle formed by Vincent, Gideon and Marcel's engineer, who stared mutely at the driver's hand, raised flat to shoulder height, re-enacting car behaviour.

Dupont Lamborghini F1 Team

PRESS RELEASE

Japanese Grand Prix
Suzuka Circuit
Saturday

Qualifying

Qualifying for the Japanese Grand Prix in Suzuka did not reflect the true performance potential of the Dupont Lamborghini cars. Marcel and Enrico will start the race tomorrow from the fourth and sixth rows of the grid respectively.

Marcel Müller – 7th

'I think seventh was the best I could have hoped for today. I love this track, it's tough and allows no errors. On my final timed lap everything came together and the car felt good, so I expected to finish higher, but everyone just had more speed than us.'

Enrico Costa – 11th

'In Q2 I wasn't able to get a decent flying lap in as there were so many yellow flags. The car had felt good so 11th is not indicative of our potential. Hopefully with a good strategy I can have a decent race.'

Vincent Dupont, Team Principal

'Our only objective is to score the maximum points available in the race tomorrow. From these grid positions it will not be easy, but the team and drivers are highly motivated.'

Media contact

Kate Ellison – Kateellison@dupontf1.com

www.dupontf1.com

I walked down the paddock towards the media centre with the pile of freshly photocopied and still-warm press releases held against my chest.

'Are you Kate?' said an unfamiliar face, dressed too dapperly to be a regular F1 hack.

'Yes, how can I help?'

'I'm Patrick, the features editor of *Luxury* magazine.'

I rejigged the releases so I could shake his outstretched hand. 'Nice to meet you, I love the magazine.'

'I was wondering when I could sit down with Vincent today?'

'Today? Oh, I'm afraid it doesn't really work like that. If you could drop me an email with details of what you'd like to do,' – I reached in my pocket for a business card – 'I could try to schedule something in Vincent's diary. With only one race to go, I'm afraid there's not much time left before the end of the season.'

'But Vincent promised me an hour's interview ...'

'An hour!'

'... for a major feature called 'Vincent: The Man, The Brand'. It'll look at the professional and private aspects of his life, with a focus on the new Dupont brand. I need to get hold of one of the new watches too.'

Alarm bells were ringing inside my head. Vincent never set up his own interviews, and how did he know about the watch?

'All interviews usually go through the press office. When was it you spoke to Vincent?'

'Last week, when he visited the offices to introduce himself.'

'The offices?'

'Of *Luxury* magazine and TV. As the new owner, he wanted to meet his staff. I tell you, everyone was really excited that he seemed so hands-on and media-savvy. Sal was rarely in the office at all. I guess we'll be working together a lot more in the future.'

How fucking dare you, Vincent!

Vincent had taken control of Sal Ovitz's media empire. My boss, the moral crusader, had succeeded in ousting his depraved victim and had slipped into his still-warm, and no doubt knockdown-priced, loafers, securing a globally-respected personal publicity machine in the process.

I was marching back towards the team offices, press releases flapping against my chest. I turned to shout 'Four p.m.!' at the journalist, who stood looking confused in the middle of the paddock.

I was powered by a feeling so intense and all-encompassing, yet at the same time I felt calm and supremely focused. Gone was all the grey fog in my head, the questions over what was right, good, justified. I could see clearly again. I was capable of anything, and scared of nothing.

Vincent was always so many steps ahead of me. Was I furious because I was caught unawares, or because I had aided and abetted in the media manipulation required for him to pull off his dirty coup?

JB was chatting animatedly with Mike, recounting yet another grid-girl fantasy tale, when I stormed into the marketing office.

'Where's Vincent?'

'Dunno. What's up?' said Mike, no doubt trying to work out if there was any advantage to his taking an interest. 'You look like a woman possessed.'

'I need to find Vincent.'

'Of course you do.' They both shared a laugh.

'Forget it. Can you just put these on my desk for me.' I dumped the wad of press releases on top of Mike's mobile and marched off towards the garage.

Vincent was standing in the pit lane, watching the mechanics work on Enrico's car. I strode up and positioned myself in front of the car so he had no option to ignore me.

'I just met the journalist from *Luxury* magazine: it seems congratulations are in order – you're the new owner.'

Vincent's face relaxed in a self-satisfied smile; he looked like a schoolboy who had just conned his classmate out of a favourite toy, and was so pleased with his own cunning he couldn't help but parade his trophy for all to see. This was the first time I had seen a softening of his mask, the look that was too professional and focused to be trivialised by emotion. It proved that in spite of appearances, nothing had ever been for a higher purpose than pure greed. I was disgusted with myself for expecting better, for expecting someone extraordinary.

Just as quickly as it had disappeared, the mask and the attitude were back. 'What do you want, Keht?'

'I can't … This is not …'

Vincent shook his head in frustration and stepped forward, so I had to lunge to the side in order not to be walked over. As I steadied myself on the car's rear tyre I turned and shouted at his departing back,

'Wincent Ponieważ, you are a fake, and I resign!'

Vincent didn't flinch or turn, just strolled across the pit lane, took his seat on the pit wall and put on his headset.

I gripped the handset trying to will, through the force of my grasp alone, the recipient to pick up. I had called three times in succession. Each time it had rung to 'Message' I had hung up and called again.

'Ligas.'

'Tomasz, a-ha, there you are, it's me … Kate.'

'Yes. What's up?' His voice was a bit flat, but that was probably just the Polish thing; he always sounded pretty neutral. Anyway, I was excited enough for both of us.

'Well, I'm getting back to you about your texts.'

'Oh, right.'

'Let's do it!'

'What do you mean?'

'The article, I'm in, silly. I'll tell you everything I know. Anonymously though, I don't want to be named but, well, now that I've resigned it would only be detrimental anyway.'

'That's great. I didn't think you'd change your mind.' He almost sounded disappointed.

'You were right, people need to know the truth about him. I mean, people look up to him and he's just setting false ideals. People shouldn't want to be him, they should be disgusted by him.'

'That is what I was trying to tell you.'

'So when do you want to talk? I land in the UK on Monday morning and I've got something important to do at midday. But, well, I'm pretty much free all the rest of the time now.' I laughed.

'I'll come to your room later.'

'You're in Japan? What are you ...'

'After dinner; just got a few things to tie up first.'

Chubu Centrair International Airport (New Nagoya)
Sunday, 8 p.m.

I was wearing the team travel uniform. The team had paid for my flight, so I figured it was probably appropriate. I hadn't been able to decide if I still cared what was appropriate.

I sat upright on the bank of seats at Gate 43; the thin in-built navy leather cushions were no more comfortable than they appeared.

The screen above the gate read JAL 437 Paris CDG.

Since I'd started at Dupont Lamborghini, I'd never flown alone. Team-mates, colleagues and industry personnel were always on the flight. The journeys were annoyingly social. But this time it was just me. Kato had organised a post-race party at the Log Cabin, the infamous karaoke bar in the circuit hotel. Everyone was going.

I just needed to get out of Japan. Having waited a whole day in a ten-foot-square box of a hotel room, hearing the corridors outside abuzz with F1 in the morning and the roar of twenty engines accelerating away from the grid through my stamp-size window, and watching on the miniscule TV screen Santos's retirement with engine failure and Enrico's god-like charge through the field to second place, I was ready to get the hell out of Dodge. I wasn't having second thoughts, I was proud of myself for standing up to Vincent, but I was still scared of what might happen now. I hoped I wouldn't have to say goodbye to Formula One, but my options didn't look good, so if it had to be, it would be easier from a distance.

I was also proud of myself for not sleeping with Tomasz last night. I had had to make the point that my decision to collaborate was a considered, moral one, not a rash, emotional reaction. But it had taken some willpower to find reasons not to keep brushing up against him when he walked in fresh from the shower, hair all wet and tousled. With the rage subsided, I was feeling rather emotionally battered and was ripe for some ego massage, but Tomasz had been solemnly engrossed in scribbling notes on Victoria Bircher, Derek Capshaw, YouTube, Sal Ovitz, and *Luxury* magazine and TV. I hadn't left anything out.

'Are you sure you want to do this, Kate?' Tomasz had said when I'd finished my lengthy monologue and stubbed out my third cigarette.

'What are you talking about? You're the one who's been trying to convince me for weeks.'

'Yeah, but I like a fight. I'm not sure you do. Vincent is going to know it was you, even if I leave your name out of it. You know he's not going to just roll over and accept it. He's going to dedicate a lifetime to ruining your career.'

'If I don't make a stand, I'm no better than him,' I said, as defiantly as I could, to counter the seed of anxiety Tomasz had sown, and which I didn't immediately link to the subsequent night of fitful sleep.

My main priority now was to make things right with Danny and Em. Her wedding, the most important day of her life, and one I had pretty much been involved in planning for almost a quarter of a century, was in two weeks' time. That meant only a fortnight for Danny to recuperate, and ideally look presentable enough to not scare the guests. Fourteen days for me to win back their trust.

I knew it would take more than Janey's OTT hospital collection plan to do that, but I also knew Danny, and it was a bloody good first step. I was pretty sure that in the grand scheme of things, Em could probably overlook the carbon footprint.

I picked up my BlackBerry and checked the network signal; it was full. Since I had left the paddock my phone had barely rung. It was as if when I handed my pass back to an apologetic Janey my number had been simultaneously deleted from all the journalists' contact lists. I knew news travelled fast in the paddock, but hadn't really anticipated total radio silence.

I opened a text and addressed it to Danny and Em; he probably didn't have use of a mobile yet, but I sent it anyway.

Borat or Brüno?

As I pulled out my laptop I did another quick sweep of the departure lounge for a familiar face. I flipped open my laptop with my right hand, while instinctively reaching down with my left to feel for the Vuitton keepall. The keepall wasn't there: it was with its rightful owner, minus a midnight blue bespoke tailor-made suit and a white two-fold Egyptian cotton shirt that had found refuge in my carry-on bag.

Gordon Barry's 'Where Did All the Money Go?' article filled the screen. As expected it was incredibly specific, accurate and well-informed. I had read it twice since it came out this morning, the first time open-mouthed at the extent of Vincent's embezzlement. Now I no longer had to fear the implications: I found vindication in its honesty.

The small vibration that preceded the ringtone made my phone jiggle on the armrest. I pounced on it.

'This is Kate.'

'Hi, it's Em.'

'Oh, hey, so, Borat or Brüno?'

'What? I don't know, whatever. Listen, I just wanted to call cos I watched the race today and they said …'

I felt a release: I could finally talk to her about it without sounding selfish.

'… that the team had a big karaoke party planned tonight. Well, it's just, I wanted to check if you're still picking Danny up?' She sounded friendly, but the politeness showed there was still an underlying hostility. 'If not, I'll do it. It's just he seems to think you've got something special planned and I don't want him getting disappointed, not right now.'

'Em, I'll be there tomorrow at twelve, as I promised.' It was hard not to sound petulant. 'I've got something planned; no one will be disappointed.'

I knew there would be no car to pick me up, but I still slowed down to read the names on all the placards proffered by bored-looking drivers as I came out of the automatic doors. Fulham Broadway was the nearest Tube stop to the hospital; I needed a good hour to get there. I checked my watch: the timing was spot-on. I followed signs for the Underground. I had picked up a text from Janey saying she'd thrown in another security guard as a goodbye gift. I couldn't wait to see Danny's face – he'd get to be Justin Bieber for half a day.

Just as I stepped on to the long escalator down to Heathrow Tube my phone rang.

'Kate, there you are. I've been trying you for hours.'

'Lisa? Oh, hi. I just landed in the UK. Wait a second, I'm just ...' I tried to walk back up the down escalator, but with my suitcase and carry-on bag I just wasn't fast enough, and the other travellers weren't accommodating. Welcome back to London – overcrowded, single-minded, stressed. It was drawing me back, down to its signal-free underbelly.

'Well, if you intended to get Harry's attention with the resignation, it worked.'

'Oh, really? Well it wasn't quite a strategy but, well, great!' I was leaning back, trying to maintain signal contact for as long as possible.

'The thing is, the new press officer is due to start tomorrow, so she can shadow me at the last race. I told Harry that I think you'll do a better job as ...'

Here I lost her as I reached the bottom and had to drag and heave luggage around on to the up escalator, balancing handbag, coat and water bottle, my chin pinning a slipping mobile to my collar bone.

'... yearful of VD, ha!'

'What? Oh, I get it.' I laughed along belatedly.

'And he said, "At least you've finally grown some balls!" So that's great, isn't it?' She was talking fast, and seemed to be in a hurry.

'Yeah, it's fantastic.' I mimicked her excitement until I could fill in the blanks. 'Sorry, but just to recap, is Harry offering me a job?'

'Not yet, but he's agreed to see you. We got in just in time: it wouldn't have worked out if this meeting hadn't come up today.' She broke off to give some instructions on the other end, including some pretty impressive Japanese. 'He didn't want to mess the new girl around, but quite frankly I think he can't resist the chance to piss off Vincent.'

I so desperately wanted to be appreciated, to have some recognition for a season of endless slog, that I was only registering the parts I wanted to hear. Relief that I hadn't burnt all my F1 bridges, that I had left an impression on someone significant, was drowning out any rational thought process. I found myself quickly falling back into the mindset of the fanatic, the same one that had had me running naked on hot coals for Vincent. *Just do whatever it takes!*

'So anyway, you'd better get a move on. Midday in the Dorchester Bar. He has this major meeting at twelve forty-five and needs you long gone before then.'

Walking back into almost the exact same situation I had just left was not the solution.

'… if you hop in a cab you can still make it on time.'

If I had learned anything it was that Vincent Dupont was what happened when you had nothing else in life that mattered to you.

'Kate? Are you still there?'

And I did.

'You know what, Lisa, I'm going to have to pass.'

'You're going to what?'

'I have a clash.' I got back on the down escalator.

'This is it, Kate: there's no second chance. The new press officer will start tomorrow, then.'

'Yes, I know. So be it. I'm really grateful for all you've done, but this meeting I have is just non-negotiable.' And I was back in the mobile dead zone.

His doctor told Danny that the hospital buzzed with conjecture and gossip for a full twenty-four hours after his departure. The switchboard had lit up with calls from the tabloids using various guises to try and get information about the 'superstar overdose', which became the general consensus. The fact that no name was forthcoming only made them more persistent and creative. Internet gossip sites fuelled the rumours for a further week with thinly veiled references to Lady Gaga, Zac Efron, Liam Gallagher and Wayne Rooney, until the story finally and grudgingly joined the ranks of great celeb mysteries, somewhere (we decided to believe) between the biological parentage of Michael Jackson's kids and whether OJ really did it.

CHAPTER 17

St. John the Baptist Church
Eastnor Village, Herefordshire
Sunday, 3.30 p.m.

The *Morning has Broken* refrain was laboriously wrested from the church organ by an elderly woman with a grey bun and a huge fox-fur stole.

On an elbow jab from Danny I switched into mouthing the high part, rejoining the congregation for the last line.

Everyone settled back down on to the pews as Em and Freddie prepared to take their vows. I knew that was the next step because I had memorised the order of service, as well as having overseen the printing of the service cards, gold-embossed on ivory hammer-finish card.

In the last two weeks I had become the maid of honour *extraordinaire*. After googling my duties, I set to carrying out every task that remained with a fervour that occasionally veered towards mania. Em had forgiven my moral off-roading, of course because she saw the good in everyone, but I wanted to prove I had learnt my lesson.

Not that there could be any lingering doubts about my rectitude once the Vincent exposé was published. I clung to that positive to drown out the cold-light-of-day worry that I had gone too far in co-operating with Tomasz, that resignation would have been enough, that a media betrayal would solve nothing and only annihilate future career potential, that my motivation had not been for the greater good but from self-disgust and a bruised ego.

I watched Em, eyes shining, her voice wobbling with excitement and nerves as she repeated her vows, those familiar words known by heart to all, and yet still incredibly powerful when spoken in front of a hundred and fifty guests in a nineteenth-century church. She had opted for her grandmother's antique-lace wedding dress and looked truly beautiful. And thanks to Danny, the bridesmaids wore elegant, long low-backed dresses in deep crimson silk, not a puff sleeve or bolero jacket in sight.

By the end of today a lot of things would be different. Em would be married, one team and driver would be crowned world champion, and Vincent would be exposed as a murderer. I was trying to keep my head on vows, hymns and poetic readings, but there was nothing like a wedding for raising questions about the future.

One minute I was clutching Em's lily bouquet, teasing the ribbon with fidgety fingers, the next I found my hand sliding pickpocket-style out of Danny's jacket, which contained my BlackBerry. I clicked 'Refresh' on the browser. Still nothing. I slipped it back in his pocket and received a sympathetic look in return.

'Hey Babe, are you snooping around?'

I jumped and turned, slamming the oversize door of the Red Hall in the process.

'Jesus, Danny, you frightened the life out of me.' I exhaled loudly as I regained my composure. 'Look in here, it's full of suits of armour, really spooky.'

'Any news on the article?' Danny kept his lips pretty much closed when he spoke; there hadn't been time to get the dental repair work done yet.

'No, I've checked the *Daily News* website about twenty times: it's just not there. I don't get it; if it was in the paper it'd definitely be online. It's a huge story. I called Tomasz … you know, the journalist, before the reception … there was a strange ringtone, then the line cut out.'

'I'm sure they'll just print it another time, then; maybe they want to see who wins today.'

I shrugged. He could be right.

'So what were you looking for? The loos are back there.'

'Well, I was trying to escape my table partner. You and Em are so transparent.'

'Come on, Jasper's all right-looking, and Em said he's very smart. You looked like you were getting on famously.'

'Because this past year I got good at faking it! Honestly, if I have to listen to another *crazy* financial anecdote, I swear to God, I'm going to be donning one of those suits of armour myself. And since when do I have to make do with "all right-looking"?' I opened a door on a library with floor-to-ceiling bookshelves.

'You've been a single workaholic for over a year. You've got to get back out there. Although you might want to tone down the whole power-crazed career-bitch thing, I think it scares them off.'

I mimed a cuff around the ear. 'Doesn't scare them all away …'

'You sly dog, Ms Ellison, stop marching so fast and give me details.'

'No can do, amigo, but for future reference arrogant bankers are not my type. Especially ones who say "Successful bankers have balls, not boobs".' I crossed the hall on my toes, so as not to slip on the polished parquet, to a set of double doors, opening them on to another TV-less reception room. Danny followed, limping carefully.

'Did he mention about the job?'

'As the bank's PR manager? Yes, he did. You two really have thought of everything, haven't you?' I checked my watch.

'We're worried about you.'

'Thanks, but don't be. Tomorrow I'll type up my CV and get out job-hunting. I promise. But I can't do financial PR. It's a whole other world from what I've been doing. I know whatever job I take now will be a terrible comedown, but finance really isn't me. And not because I don't have balls! I must have earned a couple of weeks as a job snob, surely.'

'OK, OK, I'll leave you alone. And tomorrow we'll do our CVs together. With the glowing references from our previous employers, we'll be snapped up. You'll see.'

I started up a wide staircase flanked by huge hanging tapestries, lifting the front hemline of my dress. Danny took one step at a time.

'How about we finally launch your site?'

Danny pulled on my arm, forcing me to stop and turn. 'It's not going to happen, Kate.'

'But why? You know everything about fashion, and you're a great stylist.'

'I agree, but I'm just not driven like you. I don't want to be my own boss, go it alone, have all the responsibility. I'd kill to work as a fashion stylist, but I want to know I'll get a definite pay cheque at the end of each month. I don't need to be a leader.'

We continued up the stairs.

'Now, pity the poor invalid, and tell me what you're really looking for, and why you keep checking your watch?'

I shot him a guilty glance.

'You were looking for a TV, weren't you?'

'All right, all right.' I raised my hands in surrender. 'You caught me. But I have to know who won.'

'Come on then, let's go, but only because I love a good nose around a castle, and Great-aunt Libby is getting wandering hands.'

We took a left at the stag's head at the top of the stairs.

Danny and I squatted on a pile of empty water-bottle crates, staring at the tiny portable TV screen that was balanced on a trestle table with the chef, sous-chef and someone called a 'commis', which Danny assured me wasn't an indication of his political leanings. I had helped myself to a tumbler of Merlot. Danny was, more sensibly, sticking to the Highland Spring.

One camera focused in on the row of Dupont Lamborghini faces in profile as they hung over the pit wall staring to the right. I picked out Rob, Dave, Anton, Mike, Celine, Tuffy, Janey and Gareth among the cluster of faces. My ex-team mates.

I took a big swig of Merlot.

The feed cut to another camera watching the empty start/finish straight. Then a split second later the silver and aqua nose of the Dupont Lamborghini number five car driven by Enrico Costa appeared, hazy at first, then in full focus. It flew past the furiously-waved chequered flag and swerved in towards the Dupont Lamborghini pit wall where bodies hung out at varying degrees of perilousness, limbs waving in salute to their driver. The new world champion.

A close-up of the cockpit showed Enrico punching the air furiously in front of his visor.

A cut to the pit wall. Vincent leaned over the back of his stool looking up to the heavens, arms spread Saviour-like.

'God is probably the only person Vincent Dupont considers his equal!' I barked at the TV, waving my hand in an angry gesture inherited from Enrico.

The chefs shot me an awkward look, which I ignored.

'Seriously, what are the fucking chances of that? Both frigging championships, drivers' and constructors'.'

The other viewers shuffled wearily back to their work stations, sharing quiet comments.

The Dupont Lamborghini pit wall was a seething mass of hugging, semi-naked torsos as team shirts were hastily replaced with the aqua winners' shirts. *My* winners' shirts.

The camera was moving now, following Vincent's back as he marched through the swarming pit-lane crowds towards the podium, arms held aloft, hands balled into fists, repeating the double air-punch at intervals. Congratulatory arms shot out from the crowd for high-fives and shoulder slaps. Vincent ploughed on undeterred.

The crowd at parc fermé, the area under the podium where the victor would imminently park, was solid, and there the Red Sea no longer parted for Moses with such ease. Vincent was forced to drop his victor's stance and push and squeeze his way through the human wall as far as the barrier, the four-and-a-half-foot-high fence that kept the seething masses from being run over. The cameraman did a noble job to follow in his wake and stay upright. Vincent could have passed through a side door to access the stairs to the podium, but he would have missed out on the ultimate photo: the victory hug with Enrico when he got out of the car. That was the shot the photographers wanted: the raw emotion of a driver high on adrenaline and the buzz of victory, before it was muted by composure. It would be the shot most in demand by the global media. Vincent was not missing getting in on that shot. So he had to vault the barrier. No mean feat for an unsporty fifty-year-old in a cramped space, and with a camera trained on his back.

He elbowed a bunch of Martini Magna mechanics to create some room, then swung his left leg up, falling just short of the top of the barrier. Flustered, he slipped his right foot into a narrow slot between two vertical bars. From the heightened position, he swung his left leg again. Vincent's sporting endeavour, as well as being beamed into billions of homes worldwide, was also picked up on the giant screen facing the stands, so the excited Brazilian fans began to whoop their support and the parc fermé crowd, who were also following his progress live, switched their focus from the incoming car to this bewildering spectacle. His left foot hooked itself successfully over the barrier, to a roar from the stands. He stood immobile in this spreadeagled position, as the camera zoomed in on his right Oxford brogue wedged in the vertical slot. Two Martini Magna mechanics stepped into the breach, one crouching and tugging at the Oxford brogue, the other latching on to Vincent's calf. Two more unnecessarily supported his raised leg, creating a picture of a comedic human tug-of-war. Finally the foot was released and the mechanics finished the job by rather enthusiastically throwing the supporting leg over the barrier. Vincent landed from his undignified cartwheel to huge applause and cheers, with a smile so tight it could have been lockjaw.

Danny looked at me with a cheeky grin and we clinked glasses.

Schadenfreude was sweet. This mini-example of cosmic justice would be stored for ever in my mind's iPod to be replayed at will, whenever a pick-me-up was required.

Except, of course, that in the grand scheme of things Vincent had triumphed totally. Somehow he had pulled off the incredible, by winning both the drivers' and the constructors' world championship titles. In fact, everything he had put his mind to this year had come off: the Kato deal, the renewal of Enrico's contract, the successful launch of Dupont the brand, inheriting Sal Ovitz's publicity machine, beating Harry Bircher at every step. Had he somehow managed to kill the exposé before it was printed, too?

Responding to a sudden craving for sugar, I reached over to grab two petit-fours off a tray placed temptingly close to the TV, rearranging the remaining ones to disguise my theft.

'We should get back to the reception before anyone notices,' I said, mouth full of mini-profiterole. I had to distance myself from all the Brazilian celebrations.

The podium music died down and I reached for the knob to switch off the TV. The screen filled with a close-up of my champagne-drenched, yet perfectly coiffed, ex-boss, raising his hands in a one-question-at-a-time-guys pose. With Enrico in the FIA press conference, he had the paddock media all to himself. Just how he liked it.

My right hand hovered on the on/off button, while with my left I popped a strawberry tartlet into my mouth. As Vincent began to relate how emotional he felt (*yeah, right!*) and what a special moment this was for him, the camera drew back to a wider angle, showing the throng of people behind him: print journalists catching his quote on their dictaphones, photographers and cameramen jostling for space.

'Ooh, who's your hot colleague?' Danny said, slapping his hand on my thigh. 'You kept quiet about him.'

Danny was referring to the man in the Dupont Lamborghini aqua winner's shirt directly behind Vincent, standing to attention as Vincent's media guardian. In the press officer's position ... my position ... was ... Tomasz.

Everything seemed to move in slow motion. I was transfixed by his officious face hovering just too close to Vincent's shoulder, ensuring there was no doubt, either to F1 media or public, that he was the man.

I couldn't move. The noise of blood pounding in my ears was deafening.

'Hey, Kate. Are you ok? You look really weird.'

How?

My brain careered at high speed through paddock meetings, the drunken and subsequent sober shag, the Monza Pizzeria revelation, the text messages, the surprise Japan appearance, my confession. Images and words flashed up, fragmented and obscure.

'Kate?' Danny stood in front of the TV screen. I waved him angrily to the side.

But he hated Vincent, didn't he? What about the exposé? He was so serious about his job. How could he work for Vincent when he knew so much about him?

And then I got it. He could work for him exactly because he knew so much about him. He had taken his knowledge to the highest bidder.

'Kaaa-aate!' Danny growled with frustration as his head swivelled between me and the TV screen like a Wimbledon spectator during a high-speed volley. 'Oh, oh, oh, wait a minute. Cute guy, you looking gutted. It was him! Wasn't it? He's the secret shag!'

Did he play me? Was I part of his scheme? Was I just a pawn in his power-grab, too?

'Oh, shit!' Danny finally picked up on the vibe. 'He's got your job, right? Oh, God, major betrayal. Arsehole!' He put his good arm around my shoulder.

There were so many questions racing through my head, I didn't know what to feel. Angry? Upset? Betrayed? I was thrown because I really hadn't seen it coming, but I didn't want my job back. I resigned because I couldn't have worked for Vincent any more. If Tomasz could work for him knowing what he knew, then he was welcome to the job.

I searched for the negative, the betrayal in not running the exposé, but I only seemed better off. It was unlikely to have changed anything because the murder would have been impossible to prove now, so many years later, and Vincent would have found a way to either kill the story or spin it to his advantage. High-level politicking was where he excelled: it necessitated his kind of cunning, dedication and funding. And as Tomasz had pointed out in Japan, Vincent would have ensured I was blacklisted everywhere from Martini Magna to McDonalds.

I helped myself to a packet of Embassy No. 1s on a window sill by the fire exit, lighting one off a gas ring as Danny looked on, surprised.

There was, of course, the neon-light flashing question of whether I had been seduced into co-operation. As tempting as it was as a means of exculpation, while Tomasz had indeed floated the question, I was pretty sure it was me, on both occasions, who had enthusiastically closed the deal.

I took another swig of Merlot.

And yet I was still twitchy with rage. If I had to identify the root of the aggression pumping through my system, it was a big fat frustration at myself for being a passenger in my life these last nine months; for thinking that everyone involved in this industry I worshipped was by association somehow blessed; for just assuming that if I followed instructions and worked like a serf I would succeed. Janey was right, where the bloody hell was *my* agenda?

The Chinese Bedroom, Eastnor Castle
Monday, 10.20 a.m.

A shaft of brilliant light burned through my eyelids. I recoiled away from it and a solid weight in my head thudded on the wall of my skull. The tell-tale sign of an industrial hangover.

'Wakey, wakey, Kate.' Danny was so chirpy in the mornings now he was teetotal. 'Em's on her way in. We're having a sneaky last breakfast, just the three of us, before she abandons us for her honeymoon and married life.'

It hadn't really sunk in that we wouldn't all live together again, just the three of us in the flat in Shepherd's Bush. Freddie was moving in, of course, and while Em had been sweet about there being no rush to find somewhere else, that just wasn't true. It was time for Danny and I to pull ourselves together, grow up and fly the nest.

There was a knock on the door and Em flew in, in a white fluffy robe, followed by a suited waiter pushing a delicious-smelling silver trolley. I dragged myself up to sitting, pulling a pillow behind my back as Em leaped up beside me. The antique four-poster bed creaked under the force of her enthusiasm.

'Wait!' I realised, horrified, that in my drunken stupor I'd left the bedspread on top of the duvet, the impression of my sleeping face was still visible in the satiny cover. I retreated to the top corner of the mattress, pulling myself on to my knees and lifting a corner between the tips of my fingers; I swept it off in one swift motion and with minimal contact. 'Do you know they once found eighty-seven different types of sperm, vomit and phlegm on a single bedspread in a five-star hotel.'

My friends replied with amused smirks.

'Repeat after me,' Em chanted. 'I am Kate Ellison, not Vincent Dupont. OCD is not for me.'

It was all about cutting the cord.

'OCD is not for me!' I grabbed a big wadge of bedspread from the floor and pulled it cautiously up to my chin. I double-checked my friends' faces, they nodded with silent reassurance; I took a deep breath and plunged my face into the polyester, to a burst of applause.

'Right, it's scrambled eggs on toast all round, with fresh orange juice and strong coffee!' Danny announced as he waved away the waiter. 'For this special last breakfast I shall serve my favourite girls.'

With Em to my right and Danny to my left, between forkfuls of egg, we dissected Em's big day. There was lots to cover: her dress (beautiful), the hymns (I did warn them), Freddie (incredibly handsome but very clumsy with the ring), Uncle Walter (no one fooled by the hairpiece), her dad's speech (a real tear-jerker), cousin Beth (had really paid attention at the pole dancing class) and me (who obviously hadn't).

A muffled Nokia ringtone interrupted our chatter. Em and Danny tapped at their pockets, Em pulled out her silent phone, and Danny got up to retrieve his from the desk.

The ringing continued.

'It must be yours, Kate,' Danny said, holding up his phone as proof.

'It's not, mine only rings with cheesy songs. Now, if it were 'The Birdie Song' or 'Bob the Builder' …'

Em stood up and started pulling my clothes, and a couple of towels, off an armchair.

'Kate,' – she held aloft the offending, and still ringing, handset – 'it's *your* phone.'

I took it, swallowing the reminder that I no longer worked for Dupont Lamborghini.

'Hello.'

'Hey there, Kate, it's Helen Miller here. Long time no speak. How are you?'

'Great, Helen!' I did my best to sound convincing.

'Good, good. Listen, I'm flat-out so I'll get to the point. Can I interest you in working for me?'

I mumbled something excitedly unintelligible.

'You probably heard I started Sport Image Management. It's a step forward from a classic PR agency. We work with top sports people, offering a full package of media co-ordination, sponsorship, image management, right through to styling, to make them more presentable and marketable to attract the big campaigns. We have a football and tennis department so far, and now we're ready for F1.'

'That sounds amazing – I always knew you'd go on to something great.'

'So come and head up the F1 arm?'

I felt the rising tide of excitement. I had heard 'F1', 'head of department', and 'Helen as my boss'. A squealy *Yes* was bursting to get out, not helped by Danny and Em's wide-eyed stares.

'Wait.' I had found my sparring partner. 'I have to be able to properly manage the client's media and PR programme. I don't mean in title only, and in reality end up as just a security buffer and suitcase carrier.'

'The difference with an agency is that the client pays for our service: it isn't forced on them. So they've acknowledged that they want our guidance by coming here in the first place.'

'I'll work race weekends but not all weekends. I'm not on twenty-four-hour call. I have a life outside F1.'

'Kate, you're talking to the woman who was single until she was forty-five. I get it! Plus, we're London-based, so you get to move back home.'

'I will not work for Vincent Dupont.' I got a thumbs-up from Danny.

'OK.'

'OK?'

'Yes, Kate, OK. And I'm offering a thirty-per-cent bump on your salary.'

'So do you have an F1 client yet?'

'Of course, and they requested you.'

'They did?' The squeal escaped. 'Who?'

'The world champion himself, Enrico Costa.'

There was a voice-activated cold shower.

'Oh no!' It came out in a wail. 'And I said I couldn't work for Vincent!'

'Number one, Enrico is a pain in the arse but he's not stupid: he's realised he needs to approach things better, which is why he's sought the agency's help. You can't do better than come back with the world's number one driver, and improving his image is a nice challenge, don't you think? And Vincent won't be a problem, trust me. Check the web tomorrow.' Helen seemed to be marching somewhere, and was slightly out of breath. 'Now I have to go as the stylist just quit, and I've got to find a replacement before a shoot with Nadal in five days' time.'

I looked at Danny, who was holding up a scribbled note saying *Celebrate?*

'Helen, I have the perfect candidate.'

14A Waverley Road, Oxford
Monday, 10 a.m.

I surfed the key F1 websites in the UK, France and Italy as I blew on a steaming mug of Tetley. There were hundreds of motorsport sites, but only very few were connected enough to have an industry exclusive. The country of origin of the news was likely to get the story first, but as I had no idea what the news was, I kept circling the sites.

Danny flitted around making my flat more 'homely'. I only had two weeks to go on the lease, but he rightly claimed that it was 'depressing and unliveable'. He'd already achieved quite some transformation with some throws, a couple of framed arty prints, and a small cardboard garden bonfire.

I clicked on my Hotmail inbox. An unread message from Gordon Barry greeted me with the subject: *Enjoy!*

Hi Kate

See attached. This story will be up on www.telegraph.co.uk shortly and there'll be a fuller story in tomorrow's paper.

Thought you'd also be interested to know Vincent's memoirs, humbly entitled 'Vincent: One Man, One Brand' are due out at Christmas, apparently ghost-written by one Tomasz Ligas. Also my spies tell me Adriana has left Enrico for Shinsei Kato, no less, and she is the new global face of SK Technologies.

Take care,

Gordon

Of course, Gordon had the exclusive. I clicked on the attachment.

Magna Buys Lamborghini and Control of Dupont Lamborghini F1

Gordon Barry, Motor Racing Correspondent

Magna International Inc. will announce tomorrow the acquisition of Automobili Lamborghini S.p.A. This latest purchase is part of a major strategy by the Ontario, Canada-based automobile parts manufacturer to become a global car maker.

In addition, Magna's Sport Division has completed a 15% share swap with Dupont Lamborghini shareholder Shinsei Kato, thus bringing Magna's stake in the newly crowned World Champion Constructor to a controlling 55%.

Magna's Sporting Director, Harry Bircher, sought to clarify future plans. "This is a very exciting development for Magna. This deal underlines our commitment to competing at the highest level in Formula One. We will, however, have to evaluate whether running two teams in the F1 Championship is a viable option. Whatever the outcome, Magna will honour Lamborghini's 5-year race drive contract with Enrico Costa. We are also delighted to welcome the unparalleled technical team of Gideon Black and Etienne Clément into the Magna family. Their reputation and success rate precede them."

Secrecy surrounding the acquisition appears to have been extreme. A senior source at Dupont Lamborghini revealed the team management were only informed via telephone at lunchtime today.

It would appear to be the end of Dupont Lamborghini F1 as we know it and the question remains of the future of incumbent Team Principal, Vincent Dupont. Harry Bircher would not be drawn on whether there was a role for Vincent Dupont within Magna, and Mr Dupont was unavailable for comment.

Notting Hill Gate, London W11
Monday, 8.20 a.m.

It was one of those beautiful cold crisp mornings where London was at its bright autumnal best. Danny and I walked side by side, our pace just faster than comfortable, Starbucks cups in one hand, grinning inanely.

Danny had sailed through the interview: he and Helen had immediately hit it off. We had even wangled the first visit on a new two-bed flat in Chiswick at the end of the day.

Danny linked his free arm through mine as we turned into Kensington Park Road.

Three weeks had passed since the Japanese Grand Prix. I'd taken a good pummelling in the ring this season, but I was back on my feet and ready for round two. I wasn't kidding myself. Vincent had had his team swiped from under his nose, which was sweetly satisfying, but he wasn't finished. He was still very rich (in spite of the hundred million dollars that was swallowed by his debts), very determined and very vengeful. Dupont would become a mega brand, there was no doubt. Vincent would always succeed because he would fight longer and harder than anyone else: that was all he lived for. I was pretty sure he'd return to F1, Darwinian style, stronger and even more formidable. In the meantime, there were plenty of others queuing up to take his place. But it didn't matter because I'd realised that wasn't the point. I was in control of what I was prepared to do. I didn't have to be like him, but I did have to look out for myself, have my own agenda, if I wanted to get on.

We stopped just before the entrance to the modern glass and red-brick building. Printed across the double doors in a black hi-tech font was 'Sport Image Management'.

Danny stacked my empty coffee cup in his, chucking them both in a nearby litter bin.

'So.' He took a deep breath and squeezed my arm. 'Do you have any advice for me on my first day?'

'Yes!' I grinned back. 'Don't be a fan.'

Thank yous

For reading (& being kind): Stephanie, Sally, Ben, Matt, Jonny

For being a sounding board (not that there was much choice in a studio office): Sandra

For endless positivity: Juliet

For the experience: Fiona, Marye, David, Sophy & Thommo

For making boredom an unimaginable concept: Felix, Charlie & Oscar

For everything: Alex

THE AUTHOR

Julia Wurz ran the Press Office for the Benetton Formula 1 Team, that became Renault F1. Dedication above and beyond the call of duty led her to marry her colleague, the Austrian race driver Alex Wurz, and to make the tough decision to move from the Cotswolds to Monaco. There she runs a communications agency while running behind her three boys.
Twitter: @juliawurz

www.dupontf1.com

www.superegof1.com

Printed in Great Britain
by Amazon.co.uk, Ltd.,
Marston Gate.